Irrelevant Experience:
The Secret Diary of an
Assistant Psychologist

Spatch Logan

Dedicated to Bitsy

"*Every philosophy is the philosophy of some stage of life.*"

Nietzsche

ACKNOWLEDGMENTS

Although this is a fictional piece of work, the novel draws from many of the stories I have experienced or heard. I must thank the many assistants, trainees, support workers, qualified psychologists, nurses and students who inspired the events herein. Don't worry, everything has been anonymised and fictionalised to protect the guilty.

A big thank you to the ClinPsy crew Miriam, Ruthie, BlueCat, Astra, Gilly, Ell, Campion, Borrowed Cone, Pink, Eponymous, Schizometric, Jessibelle, ElizabethB, Peach, Sarahg, FuzzyDuck, Russ, DrDot, Lakeland and all the rest of you reprobates. May you keep guiding the unwary, clueless and confused through the dark waters of applications.

Big thanks to Ili, Nancy, Abraham, Adam, Vanessa, Michael M, Paddy and Shane, Clare, Gerard, and several others who have requested to remain anonymous from my psychology and university related travels.

I am indebted to Linda and Ade for their input and suggestions on the early drafts.

Huge gratitude to RyoSeven for the awesome book cover. (Less gratitude for the unceasing rudeness however.)

Thanks to Christy for editing and commentary duties.
Mum, Dad and Bitsy, for everything.

I would also like to thank RLJ, with whom I co-produced the blog **"Confessions of a Reserve List Jockey"** from 2008-2009, which forms the inspiration for much of the novel.

CLEARING HOUSE FOR POSTGRADUATE COURSES IN CLINICAL PSYCHOLOGY

APPLICATION FORM FOR ENTRY

Personal statement: Background Information

Question 9: Reflection. What would you hope to gain training in clinical psychology? (750 _character_ limit)

I would hope that gaining a place on a clinical psychology training course would enable me to be a reflective scientific practitioner that uses a person centred approach. No, wait. Or is it a reflective practitioner using a scientific approach? Or should that be a person centred scientist. I should probably be mentioning something about being "holistic" here too. True, I don't even know what the word holistic means, but I am _so_ holistic if that is what you are looking for. Or not holistic at all, if it means something bad like I enjoy knocking elderly ladies into swimming pools (I am very much against that particular practice by the way. Old ladies, in my opinion, deserve to be dry.) In essence, whatever sounds impressive and buzzwordy, I am that woman.

Did I mention I really, really, really like research. Especially all those complicated, tedious statistical equations, writing huge essays and lengthy reading lists that taper off into the distance. I would hope to gain lots of that.

Okay. Straight up. I really want to get a place on a clinical psychology training course because I want to be a clinical psychologist. In fact I did a degree in psychology because I thought I would learn what makes people tick and be able to use that to help people with mental health problems. Imagine my annoyance to find that you have to go off and get experience and then do a 3 year Doctorate in Clinical Psychology course

1

before you get to do anything that interesting. I was even more annoyed to find out that practically everyone graduating with a psychology degree appears to want to do this as well. My annoyance turned to dismay when I discovered the level of competition I would have to face to get onto a training course. Which is why I presumably have to fill in this form for the second time, despite the fact that you chose to disregard my last application in what I may say was a fairly cavalier fashion. But don't worry I won't hold that against you. (If you pick me.)

So, as stated in your requirements section, I went out there and did several fairly low paying and often no paying jobs. All to get that important "relevant experience" that you seem so keen about. What I would hope to gain from training is some kind of validation that the last three years since I graduated was not in vain, and that I have not made a seriously questionable life decision that may amount to nothing. That and a sense that my life is moving forward in some way. While I realise that it may not be directly answering your question, I think my ever-despairing parents and long suffering friends would hope to gain some sense of this too.

Cool. That is definitely under 750 words.

OCTOBER

Monday 1 October

When I was a little girl, I wanted to be (in chronological order): a fireman, a ballerina, a school teacher and then a marine biologist. However, when I was a slightly bigger girl (and by that I mean older, not fat), I got stuck on the idea that I wanted to become a clinical psychologist. In retrospect I sometimes think I should have stuck to my first choice.

That little girl did not know where she would be living when she was older. Possibly she thought she would live in a cottage by a stream, or if she drank too much orange squash and became overexcited, maybe a full size replica of the My Little Pony Dream Castle. Instead, she now lives in a shared, grotty Victorian terraced house somewhere in the teeming sprawl of South London. Nevertheless, the little girl probably would have liked the idea of living with her best friend, Sarah (who also wants to be a clinical psychologist) and Sarah's friend Scarlett (who definitely doesn't).

Yet this is where I find myself at the start of my 25th year. It's my birthday today and my ever doting grandmother decided that it was about time I started to keep a diary. Actually, my grandmother has had the same idea since I was about 10, in her mind imagining me as a modern day pre-teen Samuel Pepys commenting thoughtfully on the world around her. Sadly, Grandma's little booklets have been resolutely left more or less empty, a testament to her touching naivety. "Went to school. Had potatoes", reads the single entry for the whole of 1993, suggesting I was never going to win the Nobel Prize for Literature.

However, where years of not-so-subtle nagging by Grandma have failed, a single meeting with my fellow graduates and assistant psychologists last week succeeded. The buzzword everyone talked about was "Reflective Journal", a place where I could write deep, deep thoughts about important things and learn all about myself. I was told that this would make me wise, but more importantly an attractive candidate for clinical training courses. Plus, everyone else said that they were doing one. I didn't want to feel left behind, so Grandma's latest birthday gift arrived through the letter box and avoided the fate of its predecessors. Instead of being thrown to the back of my desk drawer, I am going to write in it. That way maybe I can figure out what it is I am doing and where I may be going. Or win that Nobel Prize. Whatever is easiest.

Tuesday 2 October

It rains today like it is going out of fashion. For the duration of the half hour walk from my house to the bus stop. Past the dodgy takeaway that always stinks of stale oil, which we suspect is responsible for most of the missing dogs in the area. Past the gormless youths that stand around in their school uniforms talking about shooting gangsters in *Grand Theft Auto*. As the rain really starts to hammer down, the bus arrives, only for the sadistic driver to splash through the considerable puddle that has collected by the side of the stop. I arrive at work, sodden and miserable to find my supervisor had left me a pile of documents to photocopy and instructions to take minutes at the afternoon managers' meeting.

I work as an assistant psychologist. A much coveted and competed for entry level position in the world of psychology. Or so I tell myself. They tell you that the first step on the ladder is always hard. What they don't tell you is that the ladder is still in the garden shed, festooned with splinters and that there are hundreds of creepy crawlies all trying to clamber up it along with you.

I work under my supervisor, Nancy, who is a proper clinical psychologist. She does all the things that people think of when they hear the phrase "clinical psychologist". She sees patients for therapy, conducts tests of intelligence and cognitive ability and works with the doctors, nurses and other healthcare professionals to provide some idea about how a patient may be psychologically functioning.

Not that I get to do any of this interesting stuff myself. I don't have the training for starters. As an assistant psychologist, I "assist" with her duties by doing whatever it is she does not have time for. A lot of this is keeping records, data entry, photocopying, phone calls and admin. Don't get me wrong, I do get to work face-to-face with patients, but often at a lower level providing information, giving out questionnaires about symptoms and checking in with people to see how they are doing when asked. But there is a lot of admin.

I share a small cramped office that used to be a cupboard. I share it with Olga, whose job I was once told but instantly forgot. I think her title includes the words "data management" and "governance" (is that even a real word?). To be fair, she probably doesn't know my job title either. In the Cupboard, like personal space and dignity, titles don't matter. What does matter though is that she has the worst body odour this side of the Danube, and on humid days like today I should be issued with a gas mask. Olga likes to think she outranks me. A thought I fail to share with her.

As I come in she says, "You look very wet. You look very bad. You are late", in that blunt Eastern European way that I have come to know and love so much. She points to my medium length black ponytail that is dripping water, as if to prove her point. I smile and thank her for her well timed and thoughtful observation, before heading out to the photocopier room.

It may be uncool to admit, but I actually quite like the photocopier. I can load up whatever I have to, switch off my mind, and daydream about better things. The rhythmic whirr of the copier is soothing, like the tide and I can transport myself beyond the beige painted walls and the ever present smell of Nescafe. I imagine myself photocopying my own book for one of my future patients. Or perhaps I am preparing notes for my own TV programme about helping disadvantaged children. With special needs. Who all happen to be orphans.

I am leaning on the photocopier, having churned out my 60th document, when Hunky Nick turns up. He is part of a health research team and I definitely know his title, mainly because he is the most attractive male in a three-mile radius. Nick is a Research Officer, but outrageously isn't required to wear an Army/Navy/Chippendale style uniform or anything. I think he is part Greek or something, and he looks like the dictionary entry for "Tall, dark and handsome". Finely chiselled features, dark brown eyes with thick lashes and olive-skinned he belongs on the cover of a romance novel, rather than amidst boxes of A4 paper and printer cartridges.

Rumour has it that he has a girlfriend. Lucky cow.

Cheekily he asks if he could cut in front of me as he only has a two page spreadsheet to print. I let him interrupt my 30 page document, acting as if it's no big deal, despite knowing it's going to be a pain to re-arrange. I know this is incredibly two-faced of me because, if Olga or anyone else asked the same, I would tell them to come back later. However, the "fairness" part of my brain must have been occupied, along with the part that would consider staring at him as he leant over as rude and unladylike.

The afternoon managers' meeting is the usual snooze-fest. I start my minute taking as diligently as possible, but when they start arguing about the budget being three decimal places out, my carefully recorded minutes degenerate into a doodle of plant leaves, rain drops, and ever increasing squiggles. The doodle reaches dimensions that can no longer be hidden, and gets me a glare from one of the managers. I blush with shame, immediately sit up, and pretend to pay attention for a good ten minutes before I go back to doodling. At the end of the meeting I type up my notes and email them to everyone. Where they will no doubt sit in an in-tray and be forgotten about, as this is how the NHS works.

It rains all the way home too. As I get in, Scarlett is in the living room watching telly still wearing her pyjamas despite it being well past 6 pm. Is she ill? Is she working a night shift? Bollocks is she. What we are witnessing is her in her professional uniform. Her job? To sit and smoke Marlboro Lights in prodigious quantities whilst watching ITV2. She grunts as I come in barely looking up, and grunts again when I ask where Sarah is. I ask her what she has been doing, and she grunts and nods her straggly mop of crimson dyed hair at *J Lo's Dancelife*. I decline to ask her anything else. There is only so much grunting I can take and I no doubt will hear her grunting much louder through the walls later on when one of her several wastrel paramours come around and they retire to her bedroom. Instead I go and sit in my room, eating a Morrison's pasta meal for one, poring over my laptop and watching YouTube. It's only when I realise it's nearly 1am, and way past my normal bedtime, that I realise it has finally stopped raining.

Wednesday 3 October

Due to her strange working hours, I will often be coming in from work as Sarah is getting ready to leave for a late shift at the nursing home she works at. Today is one of those days and I watch Sarah carry out the little routine she always does before she leaves for work. This is as follows:

1) Brewing a massive mug of peppermint tea.

2) Rigorously combing through her frizzy mousy brown hair and plaiting it into a bun. That way her hair can't be grabbed,

pulled, or fall into anyone's dinner (or anything foul if she is on toilet duty).

3) Washing her face, applying a brief hint of makeup and fishing her clothes out from her overstuffed wardrobe.

4) All the while the movie *Pretty Woman* will be playing in the background. She doesn't even watch the film anymore, just the presence of Julia Roberts portraying Hollywood's happiest prostitute is enough to act as a calming mental security blanket. I have now seen this film so many times I can recite the script from memory, and find myself lip-synching along to Roxette's "It Must Have Been Love" like a musical version of Pavlov's dog.

As well as the nursing home Sarah works across two other jobs, each with its own irregular timings, which means she comes and goes at fairly odd hours. Her shifts as a nursing assistant give her some hands-on clinical experience with the elderly. A few days a month she volunteers at the local mental health unit, which is a little bit more relevant to mental health and clinical psychology. The rest of the time she is often press ganged by her father to help with his cash-and-carry business (totally unrelated career wise, but she feels guilty he is struggling and he slips her a few quid to help her pay the rent in return). Like many of our generation, Sarah has a portfolio career. Portfolio in this case meaning overworked, underappreciated and chronically tired like everyone else, only she gets to do it in several different locations.

She wasn't always like this; I met Sarah on my second day at university when we were both young, carefree and gifted with endless leisure study time. My first day at university had mainly consisted of:

1) Trying to get Mum and Dad off campus as quickly as possible after unloading the car. Ideally before anyone else saw them, lest my fellow students thought I was deeply, deeply uncool.

2) Trying very hard not to cry when Mum and Dad left me all by myself in my new little room not knowing anyone.

3) Putting up posters to express my quirky sense of character and uniqueness. Shame I picked Leonardo in *Titanic* and an old black and white print of a man kissing a woman in Paris under a lamppost. As did every second girl on my corridor.

4) Asking and answering the same three questions with everyone on my corridor:

"Where are you from?"

"What are you studying?"

"What A-levels grades did you get?"

In the end I realised I should have sellotaped a piece of A4 to my front reading **"North Yorkshire", "Psychology", "Two Bs and a C (but I was sick on the day of the final exam and that should have been an A)"**.

However, at our introductory lecture, I sat next to a petite ruddy-cheeked girl, who was so unassuming she nearly disappeared into the background. She said so little, I initially thought she was deaf, or possibly still learning English. Thankfully, she didn't find the experience of being talked at by me that bad, because she tagged along with me for coffee after the lecture.

We became practically inseparable from that point onwards. Although always on the shy and quiet side, Sarah really came out of her shell in the following term, and quickly settled into her role as my partner in crime. The Sundance Kid to my Butch Cassidy. The Paul McCartney to my John Lennon. The Debbie McGee to my Paul Daniels.

In class, I developed a reputation for being opinionated and vocal, with Sarah being my softly spoken counterpart. Our physical appearance also seemed to emphasise this difference as

I am quite tall and on the statuesque side (again, *not* a euphemism for fat). The contrast eventually got us labelled as "Big Gob" and "Little Gob" by the class clown, a label that stuck with us for three years. (He currently sells double glazing from a stall in the Elephant and Castle Shopping Centre. I feel this is adequate karma.)

So Sarah and I spent three years struggling to write essays, drinking cheap wine and taking turns at making wake-up calls for early lectures. In our final year, she somehow got together with her boyfriend, Tom. I am not sure when exactly, but in the sliver of time she didn't spend with me she had tracked down the only human being on campus more quiet than her. Scarlett and I eventually nicknamed him "Boring Tom", mainly because he was studying accountancy, but also because he was painfully difficult to engage in conversation when we first met him.

Sarah and I came to the conclusion that the world of clinical psychology needed us when a visiting clinical psychologist gave us a talk in an abnormal psychology module. He clearly loved his job, was full of amusing anecdotes, and made the subject come alive. Little did we realise that everyone else in the room, and the country (and maybe the world) felt similarly.

Thursday 4 October

Mum decides to make her weekly phone call in the middle of EastEnders, so I am unceremoniously ushered out of the living room lest my call spoil any impeding adultery, murder, or the Queen Vic being burnt down.

"Darling, I don't understand why you seem to be earning so little and still living in that hovel?"
"Everyone my age lives like this, Mum."
"You are not taking crack are you, love?"
"No!"
"I was reading in the paper about crack dens," I hardly need to add my mother takes the *Daily Mail*. "I hear it's very popular

with people your age. It would explain the state of your room when we last visited."

"I am not on crack. My room is my business. As is my job, which was difficult for me to get by the way. Besides, it's not about the money, I need the experience."

"But you have a degree. You should be going for a proper job."

"Everyone has a degree nowadays. And no one has a proper job anymore."

"I told you that you should have studied something sensible, dear."

This, and other popular hits of the mid 2000s such as "Why do you have to move to London?" "Laundry time (featuring Clean Underwear)" and the "Are you getting enough Vitamin C? -Extended Remix", continue to pop up frequently on heavy rotation. Nothing I can say will stop her.

It wasn't always like this. For a while I was the pride and joy of the family as the first to enter higher education. On the day I found I had got a place at university Mum and Dad mortifyingly spent the whole day calling friends and family with the news of their "little scholar". I don't think a conversation was had by either of them that didn't mention that I was off to university that summer. Things had come to a head when I found out they had tried to arrange a story in the local village gazette to come around. Thankfully the gazette had more sense and didn't go for it. Probably because I wasn't perky, blonde, a triplet, or 14 years old with 26 A*s.

Now they tend to go quiet when their friends ask how I am doing. It doesn't help they don't really understand psychology (either the academic subject or the noun) or the fact that nowadays university is the start of a long chain of things. In their minds being a graduate equates to waltzing from the graduation ceremony straight into a corner office at a major multinational. It's less a case of international travel and more a case of, "David went to Cambridge and got a First. Now he stacks shelves at

Tesco for £6.19 an hour."

Mum is having none of it. She thinks that I am doing this out of sheer perverseness, or that I am deliberately choosing not to take a swanky job just to annoy her. Dad has a slightly different problem that involves spectacularly overestimating my abilities. Classics include, "You were good at drawing at Primary School. Why don't you become an architect?" or "They are advertising for the CEO of Barclay's. Have you thought about applying?" I love him to bits, but he is not so hot on minor details.

Nope. I deal with this the only way I know how, which is mumbling "uh huh" as she drones on, whilst I try to watch Ian Beale shouting at someone through the crack in the living room door. This always seems to work.

Friday 5 October

I am not ashamed to say I live for the weekend. Despite this fact, I would definitely regard Friday as a close second. I have the Cupboard all to myself (Olga doesn't work on Fridays), and my supervisor is usually away. Generally the pace of the workflow stalls at the end of the week. All I have to do is show my face in the morning, sometimes attend a 45 minute meeting and the rest of the day is usually mine. All mine! Let joy commence unbound.

This means the copies of *Heat*, *OK*, *Bella* and *HELLO* that collect in the waiting room are all read cover to cover. Facebook is scrutinised, uploaded pictures are judged, and Wikipedia tabs multiply like horny rabbits. The internet is surfed and surfed. Accumulated free minutes on my mobile are lavishly spent on a multitude of pointless calls. These cover a diverse range of topics from "What are you having for lunch, Mum?" to "Hey, you may not remember me, but I just got your number off Facebook". Being lowest in the food chain, and having no one really care how effectively your time is utilised, definitely has its perks.

Sometimes my mischievous side comes out to play. Investigating drawers is a favourite pastime, although it can often be dangerous and borderline unethical. For instance, I was innocently looking around in Olga's desk drawer (for a stapler, honest) and I found a bottle of something that smelt so pungent I don't know if it was a type of poison, cooking ingredient or a contraceptive. Another hoot is calling up Sarah and pretending to be the credit card company. She has fallen for this twice already (I feel my faux Glaswegian accent should be nominated for a BAFTA). The last time she didn't cotton on until I threatened that we would start repossessing her family members, starting with her youngest sister.

Obviously I don't actually tell anyone that I could be working more on Fridays. As soon as someone comes in, I am just like everyone else. I bring up an impressive looking spread sheet and pretend to be snowed under. I did feel guilty about this at first, but soon picked up that everyone else does it. Now I am untroubled by it and instead feel slightly ripped off if I actually do have to do some work on a Friday.

Saturday 6 October

So far I have managed to keep my reflective diary for 5 days. I was quite impressed I had been able to stick it this long. However, on reading what I have written, I am dismayed by how humdrum and boring my life is. All I seem to do is moan about work and the people that I know, which I am not really sure is the point of reflection. Or perhaps it is. Perhaps reflection is just a psychological way to describe "moaning".

Perhaps I am doing something wrong here. Perhaps I am doing everything wrong. I have to admit I do get this feeling a lot. That some magical national-lottery-style hand is going to descend from the sky and scold me for getting everything hopelessly incorrect, before going on to administer a spanking (which would at least make for a pretty interesting local evening news bulletin).

This would also explain the nagging feeling that everyone else seems to be doing better than me. As a moderate (i.e. heavy) user of Facebook, Twitter and various other internet time sinks, I can't help but see everyone else going on about how great life is and getting on with the important business of having fun and doing interesting things. Childhood friends regularly update that they have found the love of their life (often for the third or fourth time), are trekking in Patagonia, starting their own jewellery-making business, designing houses, and spotting Ryan Gosling at Sainsbury's.

Though obviously not all at the same time.

The worst thing is that no one tells you where or if you are going wrong. There is no Mr Foster from GCSE history screaming **"NO! The Russian October revolution was not 1912 it was 1917!"** at you. Not that this specific fact would be helpful right now (or ever, come to think of it), but it would be great if there was someone out there who would just helpfully tell me what to do and how to do things properly. It would be even more helpful if that person didn't have a tendency to scream if you made a simple date based error. Or blatantly stare at the boobs of the girls sitting in the front row.

Hmm. I think I am starting to get the hang of this reflection lark.

Sunday 7 October

I waste an enjoyable morning singing into my hairbrush while listening to the radio. Nonetheless, all good things must come to an end and I decide to buckle down to handwrite a reply to a letter mailed to me a few weeks ago. Not a Facebook wallpost or an email. An actual hand written letter that was put into an envelope with a stamp and posted. I can't remember the last time I received one of these. The letter in question is from Maddie, an old friend I grew up with. Writing to her takes me back to a more innocent time, where I cringe at how clueless I was. So, in addition to writing back to Maddie (and getting wicked hand cramp for my trouble), I also idly imagine what I would write to my younger self.

Dear 6th Form Me.

Hi, it's me, a 7-years older you. I know what you are going to say. You are stressed and snowed under with all that A-level studying, and there are mocks around the corner. You probably feel you don't have time to be reading letters from your future self. Just do yourself a favour and take a second to read this. Besides, we both know that you are really just up in your room reading "Harry Potter and the Prisoner of Azkaban" *while pretending to revise. My advice to you is as follows:*

1) *Do not take up Natasha Renwick's kind offer for a make-over before the school dance. You will end up looking like you belong in the chorus line for Starlight Express.*
2) *Turn down that fourth rum and coke at your eighteenth birthday party. Or if you can't do that note where the nearest plastic bag is at all times. You may want to wear a scent that complements the odour of vomit.*
3) *You were right all along. No one pays attention to the Duke of Edinburgh Award or whether or not you did General Studies. Feel free to skive both or treat them with the contempt they duly deserve.*
4) *Get rid of* **that** *jacket because, it makes everyone else think you are a lesbian. This is not a homophobic slur. It's the main reason no boy will kiss you until you leave school (but several girls will try).*
5) *That idea about giving yourself an achingly cool nickname when you start at university. Forget it. You will be given a nickname in due course and spend the next few years trying to live it down.*

So we come to the main reason for me writing to you. My ulterior motive. I would be really, really, really grateful if you could shift your expectations slightly downwards, just a tad. Thanks. That idea that you will be earning loads the instant you graduate is just that – an idea. A heartbreakingly cruel idea at that. I would also like you to not have "ideas" about owning your own sports car or making plans about where to put the grand piano. Much obliged.

As well as saving time, save as much money as you can. Come to think of it, you really don't need any of the stuff you are spending it on now. While I won't scare you with phrases like "debt" or "overdraft", you really need to think twice about your current spending habits. For example, in a month's time you will come across a yellow hat, you think will make you look debonair and mysterious. Don't. No one wears hats, especially yellow ones and it will spend more time perched on the bedpost than on your head. Also those CDs will be lost, and you will be downloading all your music in the future onto an iPod (don't ask). Trust me, Mum isn't right about much, but she is bang on about you spending too much on stuff you really don't need.

I beg you, don't waste your time contemplating any of the following: interior furnishings, exotic travel plans, the Conservative Party, owning an Aga, making friends with anyone called Maxwell, a career writing poetry, or needlessly expensive coffee makers for your spacious kitchen. It is unlikely that any of the above will, may or could happen.

Other than that, all is good. Mum and Dad are fine and just as troublesome. Monty the goldfish sadly dies in two years' time, but you will get over that quickly. Grandma sends her love and has started Yoga.

Lots of love

Your future self

PS: 06, 19, 22, 23, 28, 29. Bonus ball 18.

Monday 8 October

I may have been exaggerating that I just photocopy and run errands for my supervisor. There is more to my job than I let on. For instance, I signpost. No, not some strange religious practice, nor does it involve creating or putting up signage (which would be fun though). In theory, signposting is telling people about the many options out there in the community that may help them such as telephone help-lines, support groups, and charities. In practice it feels like I am giving a consolation speech for people that weren't deemed severe enough to get someone qualified to help them. A sort of runner's up badge in the sports day of healthcare.

To assist me with this, I have a big file of relevant material painstakingly gathered by the efforts of long departed assistant psychologists. Some of these go back to 1992 and you can tell. Some of the leaflets feature people with "Rachel" haircuts or who are wearing shell suits. Despite my best efforts, I have accidentally given out numbers for long defunct helplines or services that shut down when Tony Blair was in Downing Street.

While many are happy, signposting doesn't always go down well. I can get incredulous looks when people unburden their life story to me and their efforts earn them a dog eared leaflet. Usually I will actually go through the leaflet with them, and do my best to convince them I am not telling them to go away and bother someone else.

I get lots of people suffering from anxiety or depression, but today I was met by a dishevelled bald man who reeked of Lynx. He came in hurriedly, grabbed the chair in front of him and sat down. Unbidden, he proceeded to angrily inform me that he had contracted a very popular sexually transmitted infection. After a good 20 minute discussion of the "stupid little slapper" who had passed it onto him, his burning piss and anchovy smell, he concluded his sorry tale with, "...and what do you *intend* to do about it?" As if he was somehow blaming me as a representative of my gender for putting him in this situation. I was sorely tempted to reply "Well, I *intend* to not sleep with you for starters". Instead, what I did do was blush, scrabble around the leaflet folder for a few minutes and refer him onto the sexual health nurse. It's amazing how some of us earn our money.

Tuesday 9 October

I am awoken at an ungodly hour by my mobile buzzing. It interrupts a rather interesting dream where I am trying to explain to an elderly lady why I don't really want to join the bell ringers of St Paul's Cathedral, but I am flattered that she is offering. As my phone is in the pocket of my trousers, which are somewhere strewn around the floor of my darkened room, I stumble about the murky dimness of my untidy bedroom floor trying to find the damn thing (not helped by the fact that I haven't had a chance to put on my specs yet). Just as it is about to ring off I locate it and answer.

I wish I hadn't bothered.

A nasal sounding man, with a thick Indian accent whose name is obviously not "Kevin", badly mispronounces my name. When I reply it is indeed I, he goes on to tell me that he has some great news about several exciting offers as I start to make my way downstairs for breakfast, clutching my mobile in one hand whilst trying to tie up my dressing gown with the other. According to him I only need to answer a few security questions and we can proceed. He asks for my date of birth and to confirm my address. Starving and still semi-asleep, I am about to mindlessly hand over the information.

It then occurs to me to ask, "What if I don't?"

This makes him shirty and he whines he cannot proceed with the telephone call if I don't cooperate. I tell him that's totally fine with me. He gets really condescending, asking me if I want to save money in the most patronising way imaginable. He repeatedly asks "Will you not cooperate?", but the way he says it is more like an instruction rather than a question. I am just pouring myself a bowl of cereal and am about to hang up, when Scarlett gestures with a single chipped black nail-polished finger, to give her the phone. Against my better judgement I hand it to her.

"Yeah, about those security questions?" she says with a syrupy sweet voice, "I will be delighted to answer them, but first I would like to ask you some security questions of my own. What was your name again?" She goes quiet as she listens to the reply. "Okay Kevin, could I have your number and call you back at say, around midnight tonight?" Kevin sounds confused and takes a second to answer. "Oh, you are going to be off-shift? Can I have your home number and call you there then? Right, you don't want to be contacted at home. THEN WHY THE FUCK DO YOU THINK I DO?"

She presses the disconnect button and tosses the phone back over to me. "Now that is how you deal with tossers like that."

This is fairly typical for Scarlett, the mistress of high etiquette. I would not regard her as a friend exactly, more like a minor ailment I have learned to put up with. Like car sickness. I like to think that we have come to some kind of mutual arrangement; she is allowed to think I am an overachieving prissy little madam, and in turn I am allowed think she is the sort of stereotype people think of when they hear the phrase 'art student'.

The only reason I am living with her in the first place is because she and Sarah have known each other since they were in nappies (and the minor fact that she was living here first). Initially, it was quite amusing to have this weird Doc Marten shod, heavy mascaraed goblin hanging around the living room. In those early days both of us were on our best behaviour to please Sarah. Six months later, her noisiness, inability to clean up after herself, and her very liberal open-door policy on overnight visitors have made me prematurely middle-aged. I have started noticing I quickly turn into my mother, coming up with such gems as:

"She treats this place like a hotel."

"Would it kill her to do the washing up?" and most horrifying of all,

"Does she have some kind of illness that stops her turning off the light when she leaves the room?"

Sarah is always trying to tell me to go easier on her, and pleads for both of us to be more accommodating to the other. Then again she spends a lot of her time at Boring Tom's flat so she doesn't get the full picture/noise/annoyance. She doesn't get the joy of finding toenail clippings embedded in the sofa, or discovering we have run out of toilet paper because Scarlett has used it all to remove her makeup. However, in dealing with tossers her advice can be extremely useful.

Wednesday 10 October

It is a training day at work.

Translation: It is a day when someone hired from the outside comes in to tell us all about hand hygiene and how to move boxes around without putting your back out so you won't sue your employer. The National Health Service loves putting on lengthy, in-depth seminars about all the policies and procedures they have, and telling you about which folders you can find them in. I have now come to understand that this is the primary aim of the NHS (if you don't count its habit of re-organising itself every few months).

I can't begin to count how many times I have been given fire training, but the only time I have ever been faced with a real fire (Youth hostelling at Kettlewell with the Brownies. Toaster left on too long), I ran out of the room like a coward and cried in front of Akela. I suspect I would behave the same today. What I know I certainly would not do is run to reception pull the dusty, heavy file of policies down from the highest shelf and read through it while the place burned around me.

We get this all morning, and it continues after lunch. I find myself sitting in the second from last row gazing out the window. The heat of the room, the monotonous drone of the man's voice, and the effort of digesting a large tuna sandwich results in me gradually falling asleep. This is a fatal error, as the fire warden suddenly directs a question at me. I jerk awake and flounder, desperately trying to remember what I was supposed to be listening to. Thankfully, Hunky Nick comes to my rescue. Sitting behind me, he leans over and whispers, "It's the cream foam one."

I tentatively repeat his answer loudly to the room, but it comes out as more of a question than an answer. Happily, this seems to pacify the speaker and he next picks on one of the receptionists who has started to read her *Cosmo* secretly under her bag. I smile my thanks to Nick and we start whispering to each other sarcastically about how lame everything is, like naughty school kids.

"Hey, remember that time when we were doing life support, and the woman brought the resuscitation doll to practice on?" he says in a low voice, tantalisingly close to my ear. An image of the woman bending over to give the doll mouth-to-mouth, only to spit out all the coagulated saliva that had collected in the doll's mouth from the last time it was used, flashes across my mind. I laugh out loud, which makes everyone turn to look at me, and earns me a stern glare from the fire warden.

Thursday 11 October

I normally meet Nancy on alternate weeks for supervision. Supervision involves her asking me to do things, expecting me to get them done, and then asking me to think about how I did it (the reflective bit). Generally, I am happy to do this, as it is all good experience and I find the discussions interesting. However, I am in awe of Nancy as she seems to know everything, and am often afraid I look stupid in front of her. Nancy is also possibly the most stylish person in human existence, with her sleek elfin looks, well-tailored suits that are perfectly accessorised, and intelligent green eyes that seem to know what I am thinking before even I do.

She listens to what I have been doing, nods that it sounds fine, and tells me to get the data I am collecting sorted and analysed for a report. I diligently take notes, doing my best to convince both her and myself that everything is in order. She then mentions she has some plans to run a therapeutic group for people with anxiety, and asks me if I am happy to be involved with it. I agree to this. It's always useful to watch her work, and although I will have to make phone calls and organise the venue, it's nothing I can't handle.

Nancy has been working for the service for about four years and hired me last November, when her last assistant managed to get a place on clinical training. Her bosses know she is damn good at her job and she has attained a senior position despite being in her mid-thirties. Her main role is dealing with complex cases and conducting specialist assessments, but she is also involved in research, teaching and other management duties. As a result she is phenomenally busy. I often get emails sent at 2am with instructions for the next day. Despite having a few control freak tendencies, she is generally even tempered, even willing to overlook some of my more regrettable comments.

I am grateful that she is not like some of the supervisors I have heard rumours about on the grapevine. One supervisor made her poor assistant go and fetch her dry cleaning and her kids from nursery. Another wouldn't even let her assistant send an email without making her retype it multiple times before it met with her approval. By the end of it she wasn't able to sign a Christmas card without having a minor panic attack. Nope, I am more than happy with my supervisory relationship. I only need to make certain she thinks that too, as she will be writing my future reference.

Friday 12 October

My usual quiet Friday morning is interrupted by Justine knocking on the Cupboard door. She ducks her lanky frame through the low doorway, nearly knocks over the spider plant behind the door, and asks if I have finished writing my clinical application form yet. My mocking hollow laugh should indicate that I haven't, but I find myself having to explain my laughter, and being explicit that I am no further on in filling in my form properly, or anything to do with life in general.

Mental note to self: Justine does not do cynicism.

I first met Justine at a party on a grim autumn afternoon the year I graduated. In the way these things tend to go, I had gone to accompany a friend who fancied a guy, who might have been there but wasn't. It was the sort of situation I am forever finding myself in. It was obvious to everyone who was at the party that it was fairly pitiful. The few that were still staying were doing so out of an obligation not to destroy the hosts' feelings. I was about to make an early exit when a person I vaguely knew pulled me into the path of a clashingly dressed girl with a wonkily cut fringe.

"Oh, you must meet Justine" she wittered on, "She studied psychology too just like you. You probably have a lot in common". Yes. Because I am automatically going to be bestest of friends with the thousands of other people up and down the country who happened to have made the same degree choice as me.

Justine turned out to be a fellow traveller on the clinical trail. At first, she gave me the impression she was living the dream. Justine had graduated the year before, (I later found out she got a 2:2; a degree classification famously known for making life difficult). She was raving about this dream job she had just got doing "anti-smoking work", which on further investigation was actually a fairly exploitative minimum wage gig where she had to hand out leaflets to passers-by for six months. Dressed as a giant stubbed-out cigarette.

At this point I should have realised that her grip on reality may be a little shaky. She told me she was dating a guy who sounded like Mr Darcy. I later found out that he basically came around whenever he wanted to, shagged her, ate her food, made her feel like dirt, before disappearing for long periods with his "band". (I mean band in the loosest sense of the word. I have heard more pleasant sounds coming from an industrial assembly line). He then had the audacity to dump her for being too tall.

If I was writing Justine's primary school report, I would describe her as "tries very hard and plays well with others". However, despite lacking any bad intentions, or ego of any kind, she has an uncanny ability to rub people up the wrong way. There is something near child-like about her cluelessness. For example, one time when she was looking for work she spammed the ENTIRE university email address book with requests about "wanting to help mentals". All this got her was irate emails back from everyone for her hideously misjudged language, (including the classics department, who thought she was making defamatory implications regarding their staff).

She has submitted a form for clinical training every year since she graduated, but has never received a single interview. The same form. Every year. To the same four courses. Unchanged. You would have thought they would have called her out of sheer curiosity by now. Nonetheless, she maintains the indefatigable optimism of a teenage boy hoping Britney Spears will be moving into the vacant house next door. She regularly applies for every job with the word "Psychology" in the title. Sure, her chances of nailing that "Chief Psychology Advisor to the Government" post may be slim, but no-one can fault her on effort.

Saturday 13 October

I have procrastinated writing my application form for clinical training long enough. Today is the day I am going to make a start. It has now been out for a month and I have only just managed to summon up the courage to download the necessary documents. I reckon my dedicated avoidance of it is why I have been able to keep my reflective diary going for so long. I am literally writing anything else to avoid filling out the form.

The application cycle starts in September, when the form is officially made available, and we have to finally submit them around late November. We normally hear back in February and interviews are held between then and June. But everything starts with the form. Always. Last year was my first time in the scrum and I downloaded the form the second it was released. I then immediately got scared for the following reasons:

1) There are punishing word counts. You have to cram your aspirations and personality into snappy, easy to read sound bites that are going to appeal to someone you don't know, whilst standing out from billions of others who are trying equally hard to be snappy and appealing.

2) You can't sound like a conceited bighead, but you can't

assume that quiet understatement is going to win the day. You can't just list your jobs, they want you to *reflect*. From the Latin *reflectere,* meaning "to spill one's guts out in a clever sounding way".

3) You can't really ask anyone else for examples or inspiration. I once made this error, and the sharp intake of breath told me I had committed a hideous social faux pas, like wearing a clown costume to a funeral, or asking someone how often their parents have sex. Conversely, you can't really ask your peers to look at your form either, in case they nick your best bits.

I remain scared. On some days I get inspired to write a sentence, then go back, think it's absolutely terrible and delete it. Then write it again. Then save the form to my hard drive and make myself forget about it, while worrying about it in the back of my mind. Asking Sarah about how hers is going is always a mistake. As she is hyper-organised I just know she will be far ahead of me.

Applicants are limited in applying to four programmes each year, but last year I got nowhere. So I told myself it was a practice run and it didn't really count. This year is going to be different. Eventually, I manage to pluck up my courage, take a quick look, get spooked, and immediately close the document. Then I go on YouTube and watch videos until my mind is taken off the whole unpleasant business. Besides its still October and it's not due in until the end of November. That is *ages* away. Why am I even worrying about this yet?

Sunday 14 October

Dad has discovered Facebook. Crap.

This may not seem like a big deal, but he is using it in ways it really wasn't designed for. I only have myself to blame as I stupidly accepted his friend request. I rationalised at the time that I would give him limited exposure to some parts of my profile and allow him the same degree of access that I let my younger cousins have (i.e. nothing that could be conceivably used against me at a future date). All he would see is a few innocuous details that he already knows.

What I didn't take into consideration was how he would take to it. Now my Facebook wall is plastered with inane comments about the weather being nice, and do I want to look at a photo of Mum near some furniture. He then befriended several people from my friends list and went on a massive "LIKE!" binge. The unprecedented amount of "liking" would give a casual observer the idea that Dad must have some kind of head injury.

Things Dad LIKE!s includes (but are not limited to): gardening, Toploader, an out of focus picture of Barclays Bank, a comment on the weather I made last spring, Halfords, the *Daily Express*, Wales (the entire country), Richard Dawkins, a photo of Scarlett at Glastonbury, and quantum physics. He must have thought he was under instruction to list everything in the universe he has the slightest modicum of goodwill towards.

He has befriended Sarah and by teatime I get a comment about "Ooh I didn't know your dad was into quantum physics!" My dad couldn't spell quantum physics, let alone know anything about it. It's just so embarrassing. He will insist on making a total fool of himself at the slightest opportunity. Like that time he told the assembled company at my sixteenth birthday he was really into Sisqo. The humiliation of watching a balding, cardigan wearing man singing along to *The Thong Song*, his middle age spread bouncing up and down to the music, will never be forgotten. I nearly died of shame. I would like to explain this away as some kind of mid-life crisis, but honestly he has been like this as long as I have known him. I am just going to have to pretend it's someone who has the same name. Who just coincidentally happens to have a similar-looking wife.

Monday 15 October

Today they came.

I could hear the war cries in the distance, followed by the fleeing columns of refugees and orphaned children. Then came the relentless, thudding war drums of the IAPT horde. IAPT stands for "Improving Access to Psychological Therapies"; a fairly recent mental health programme that trains up graduates (Psychological Wellbeing Practitioners, or PWPs) to work at a basic level with patients. However, one could be forgiven for thinking IAPT actually stands for "Inevitably Always Pretty and Thin" or "I Am Perpetually Tired" if you were to go by the workforce composition and what they are always telling you.

There are three things you need to know about IAPTers.

1) They are always overworked and tired. Massive amounts of work. Like a particularly unethical Chinese sweat shop if reports are to be believed.

2) They <u>love</u> their acronyms and will use them at any opportunity. IAPT, PWP, CBT, PHQ, GAD. I am starting to think it's some kind of sexual fetish.

3) They travel in packs and there are loads of them. Swarms of them. Like Oompa Loompas in *Charlie and the Chocolate Factory*.

Unfortunately, our building has the only meeting room big enough for all of them to have their quarterly team meeting, so they turn up here occasionally like Vikings on a raiding party. As many of the PWPs want to eventually pursue clinical psychology training (of course), they will never fail to take the opportunity to tell you all about their amazing work, and show off how much relevant experience they are gathering.

The horde then descends onto the staff room eating all the good biscuits (including the Viennese chocolate ones that I had been *really* looking forward to). They ransack the resource cupboard for stationery and pillage the resource stash I so carefully put together. Olga and I desperately hole up in the Cupboard and pretend we are dead. She has learned the lesson of direct engagement from last time. One of them asked her for her help on some statistics, which she was assured "would only take a minute". It created enough work for her to last two days.

The leader of the IAPT horde is this pale, painfully skinny, blonde girl whom I have nicknamed Spiny. She speaks in an annoying posh voice and laughs like a cat being pulled through a hot exhaust pipe. I particularly dislike her because she shamelessly monopolises Hunky Nick on her frequent visits, and refuses to listen to anyone else talk. When she speaks I can hear her voice from three rooms away. Most unforgivable is her saccharine smile and fakest of fake greetings whenever she sees me. I have come to dread her high pitched squeal of "HI-YA!", whenever our paths cross which means I have to spend the next ten minutes pretending I am happy to see her. Or that I give a shit about what her supervisor is letting her do now, which if she is to be believed, is running the entire National Health Service.

Unforgivably, the IAPT horde smashes the ceramic teapot, push the broken pieces under the fridge and deny all knowledge when asked about it. Instead of being collectively fired on the spot and taken out to the back of the building to be thrown under a bus, the service manager gets *me* to clean it all up. Several of them loudly discuss their application forms, which I pretend I don't hear. They flood out promptly at 4pm, leaving behind broken teapots, empty biscuit tins and high blood pressure in their wake.

Tuesday 16 October

I turn up to work a bit earlier than usual this morning, and find there is a naked man standing in the lobby. The rest of the lobby is empty, and he stands there in the centre, motionless as a statue. The first thought that hits me is that I am still asleep and this is a strange dream. The next is that he is some kind of predatory rape fiend on the loose. Of course it is too early for anyone else to be around to fetch help.

However, I manage to compose myself and think for a second. He doesn't look frightening or aggressive. On the contrary he looks tragic and out of place. His sagging pot belly, greying chest hair and hangdog look of sadness swiftly moves my fear to pity. Still, staying close to the door, I cautiously greet him, as if what he is doing is the most normal thing in the world. He turns around and casually wishes me good morning before turning his back on me and looking out of the window. Feeling a bit bolder, I ask him if he is waiting for someone or if I can help him. He starts to reply but quickly becomes confused, his words flowing rapidly but making no sense. He asks for his Dandy, and I wonder if this is a person, a comic book or simply just one of those things that people say if they are suffering from a psychotic illness. Instead, I ask if he is feeling cold and whether I can fetch him a towel. He replies that he is, and I nip off to fetch one from the staff toilet.

As I bring the towel back, Eva the receptionist comes in. She says "Good Morning", clocks our visitor, and then screams. This makes the man panic and he starts to become agitated. I have no idea how, but I find myself taking control of the situation. I calmly explain our visitor looks like he may be lost, and would she mind calling the mental health unit to ask if they are missing someone. As she goes off to make the call, I ask the man if he wouldn't mind waiting in a side room as he may find it warmer. This is a particularly good move as the arthritis care group are due to turn up in a few minutes and it may have been a bit awkward. I suppose I could have explained it away by saying it was a performance art piece, but I don't think their tastes are quite that avant-garde.

Thankfully one of the psychiatric nurses comes over shortly and bundles him away under a large coat. Eva coos about how well I handled it. As she does, I realise how much I have come to learn from my experiences. Helping the man get home is rewarding for me, and I no longer fear people with mental illness like I used to. This is an achievement coming from a background where people think it's something contagious like the flu.

Wednesday 17 October

This is the first proper assistant psychologist gig I have managed to score and I take considerable pride in this. Yet the gap between being incredibly-grateful-you-won't-regret-this to taking it for granted has been dismayingly short. My latest episode of ingratitude sprang up in the middle of this afternoon when Olga kept doing her best to annoy me by brewing the most noxious smelling herbal tea/organic juice drink/eye-of-newt witch's potion, and stinking out the Cupboard. It had gotten to the point where the lady in the office next door knocked and asked if "something had died in there and started to rot". It's at times like this I find it helpful to mentally revisit the dead ends, near-misses and crash-and-burns that got me to the place where I am today. Doing so helps me keep my cool, and avoid a manslaughter charge.

It took about three years after graduating to score this gig. Like most, I spent the first few months after graduating wondering what the hell it was I was supposed to be doing and frantically looking for relevant work experience. My blood, sweat and tears (more truthfully edit, copy and pasting) were met with complete and deafening silence. I may as well have been radioing messages into space for all the good it did. On rare occasions I did receive an automated response telling me I had been unsuccessful. I particularly remember one hastily dispatched response that read:

"Dear NAME OF APPLICANT. Your application for JOB REFERENCE NUMBER HERE was unsuccessful. Please contact [HR DEPARTMENT] if you have further questions."

CC'ed to everyone rejected, so I could helpfully find out who else felt like a failure that morning.

However, when the stars aligned and the gods smiled, I would receive a letter inviting me to an interview. There were quite a few of these opportunities I managed to mess up with my own characteristic style and panache before I started getting anywhere.

Job Interviews I Have Messed Up. #1

The first interview I got was for a research assistant post at a cutting edge research institute. Even now I have no idea what I wrote or said to get as far as the short list, because I had only graduated a few weeks previously and had done no real preparation for it. I also turned up without bringing my interview letter, knowing the name of the person I was seeing, or the name of the department hiring, so there were a good few minutes of me waiting in the lobby while the receptionist scurried about. Due to a recent recruitment drive, many of the departments were interviewing. So before I even got started we had to establish that I wasn't here to interview for a lab biologist, project manager role or the Consultant Neurosurgeon job (although the salary for it would have been perfectly acceptable).

I was eventually ushered into a narrow office, filled with filing cabinets and computer equipment and too many chairs for such an enclosed space. The two men interviewing me were dressed formally with shirts and ties, which made me feel a bit out of place in my jeans and Guns N' Roses T-shirt. However, they did their best to be friendly and smiled as they flicked through their notes.

"I would like to begin with the basics," said the older one sitting back and grabbing his coffee cup, "So this project is going to look at people who suffer from bipolar disorder. What do you know about that condition?"

"Well it's an illness," I tentatively started, completely out of my depth "It's a... mental illness."

"Yes. Yes it is," he nodded encouragingly.

"Um, I think Russell Crowe had it in a film?" I said leaving a lengthy pause after my answer. The interview had started somewhere near rock bottom, but by the second question I had started drilling.

The younger, more nervous interviewer piped up, "The post requires a lot of organisation, data management and liaison work. Do you have any experience of this?" He looked at me hesitantly, unsure of what to expect.

"Oh yes". I eagerly replied. "I have experience of that when I did a third year project. It took me three weeks and needed a lot of organisation. It was really intense. I did sort of leave things to the last minute." I laughed as if I had cracked a hilarious joke.

The older interviewer frowned, pulled up his sleeves, rubbed his eyes and sighed. "Well, as our team website outlines, this is a six year study being carried out at multiple research sites across the UK. It has a budget of £1.3 million. It will need coordinating with about twelve different clinicians and researchers. Do you think that may be a bit *intense* for you?"

In hindsight, I should have brought the interview to a close there and then, thanked them for their time and left with what little dignity remained. Instead, I thought at this point it would be a brilliant idea to impress them with a question of my own.

"So, how much would the position pay?" I butted in, trying to be hard-nosed and business like.

"Um... it would be on an RA point 6 which would be between £21,000 and £24,000. As stated in the job description," said the older one, clearly taken aback by my impertinence.

"Yes. So would I be starting on £24,000 then?" I was going to be rich!

There was a pause and the younger one looked at his colleague before saying, "The...candidate that was successful... would be able to discuss this on appointment, but it would be based on experience and other factors".

"Also would this be my office?" I asked glancing around looking distinctly unimpressed.

"No. This is *my* office," said the older one, his facade of professionalism now cracking. "The RA post would be mobile. It would be across many sites. As stated in the website and job description." By now they had stood up and were practically bundling me out of the door. "We have other candidates to view, but we will be in touch."

I realised things may not have gone as smoothly as I imagined when I received a rejection message via text before I even left the building. What is worse, much to my eternal shame, is I remember complaining to Sarah afterwards that I thought I had done well and how surprised I was to be turned down.

Thursday 18 October

Olga and my supervisor are away at a conference in Preston. As I am uninterrupted, I manage to steam ahead with my workload and quickly find myself at a loose end. After the usual rounds on Facebook and Twitter, I find myself dragged into a lengthy thread on ClinPsy about appropriate font size to use on the form. I panic, as this is something I hadn't even considered. Who would have thought that font size would be something you would be judged on? I briefly imagine 'the Gods' reading my form, and casting it down from Mount Olympus because I dared to use Verdana.

ClinPsy has a way of doing that to me.

Ostensibly, ClinPsy is an online forum for aspirants on the clinical psychology path, where people solicit advice or provide it. In reality it combines the two wildly divergent pulls of wanting to see how everyone else is doing and at the same time wishing you hadn't. No matter how much you try to stop yourself, you inevitably dwell on how you stack up against your peers. I know you have to take a lot of it with a pinch of salt. Sucker that I am, I read way too much into everything.

There is a crew of regulars who seem to have been around there forever. They range from all knowing authority figures, helpful and calming types to a couple of blokes that talk about the most abstract theoretical subjects, that I imagine as the two cantankerous old men who heckle from the balcony in *The Muppets*. The regulars are especially fond of telling people to use the 'search' function, which is the forum's equivalent of the Lord's Prayer. Apart from the hard-core regulars, most of us hide in the shadows, only piping up if we have any breaking news to share.

I am a complete addict.

I have been on the website six times today and it's only 11:30 in the morning. I just can't help myself. I know that I already know half the stuff that's posted on it. Yet I am still compelled to read every new post and waste hours surfing through it. At least I am open to my addiction. Sarah swears point blank that she doesn't read it yet always seems to be shutting down the front page as I walk into her room. Sarah is always remarkably well informed about what is going on in the forum, much like those people who swear blind they don't watch reality TV, but can list every single testicle-eating celebrity to ever go into the jungle. I suspect she is not the only one...

Friday 19 October

I am merrily working away when Hunky Nick appears at the Cupboard door. He is going out for coffee and asks if I want to join him for a quick break. Despite the fact that I have a deadline and should be getting on with writing a report, I find myself readily agreeing that a break is what is needed. After all, Nancy is always telling me about the importance of maintaining a good work-life balance.

So I find myself sitting at the little coffee shop on the corner, staring through the huge glass window watching the busy traffic outside. The coffee shop is one of those indie places that has spent a lot of money to look as shabby as possible. I sink into a distressed leather couch as he goes to the counter to fetch me a latte. Apart from our brief conversations in the photocopying room and chats in the corridor, it's the first time I have actually been out alone with him. It almost feels like a date. True, it would be the world's tamest, most innocuous and deniable if-anyone-from-work-happens-to-pass-by sort of date, but beggars can't be choosers.

As we sip our coffees I start to tell him what I am doing, and how I am brilliantly avoiding writing my report. He tells me not to worry as he is doing an even better job of putting off working on a huge data project. Apparently, he spent last week running around town trying to collect urine samples from pregnant women.

"It was like taking part in a bizarre Japanese game show," he says, shuddering at the memory.

I laugh, trying not to mentally visualise the image. I rifle through my store of amusing anecdotes, but can't find anything amusing, interesting, or sanitised enough to tell him. Although I resolved not to, I end up telling him about my application form. To my surprise he seems to know all about it.

"The only thing more competitive than that racket is going into research," he says with a weary laugh. Nick seems a pilgrim on another equally competitive journey, getting a job as an academic. He makes me look lazy, managing to cram in a master's degree and blagging his way into working on several research projects.

Despite all this, he is on a series of short-term contracts that only get renewed if they get enough funding. I find myself getting alarmed at the prospect that he may be whisked away without warning, because some pen pusher takes a dislike to his project and opts to pull the plug. I have to remind myself that my own job is on equally shaky ground.

"Don't worry about it," he says "all the best people live life on the margins. It's the price you pay for living on your own terms. Artists, musicians, philosophers all have to live on a day to day basis. You know, like Holly Golightly in *Breakfast at*

Tiffany's". I tell him I loved the film and he does that annoying thing where people tell you the book is so much better and tells me I simply **have** to read it. I am not the biggest reader and always feel slightly embarrassed to admit the last thing I read was written by a celebrity that regularly appears in the pages of *Heat* magazine.

The hour passes all too quickly, and as we walk back he says he enjoyed it and we must do it again. This little innocuous comment basically means that's it for the rest of the day. My productivity on my form drops from "minimal" to "none" as I spend the rest of the afternoon wondering how much time has to elapse before it is dignified to suggest we go out for coffee again.

Saturday 20 October

Ouch.
When I woke up this morning I found I had not only spectacularly failed to remember much of what happened yesterday evening, but had also lost the power of speech. However, from the trail of destruction and my keenly honed forensic detection skills, I think I must have been on a bit of a high last night when I got back from work. I vaguely remember thinking Scarlett's idea to go on "a proper Friday night out" was an excellent one at the time. I also remember dragging Sarah and Justine out to some godforsaken nightclub called "The Blender". Aptly named, because that is exactly what my head feels like this morning.

Sadly, my alcohol tolerance and powers of recovery have started dropping as I get older. At seventeen, I could spend an entire Friday evening drinking cheap cider in a bus shelter with Maddie, and still manage to turn up to my Saturday job the following morning. Granted, it was sorting letters at the village post office, not Heathrow air traffic control, but sorting letters still required some degree of motor control. If I were there this morning I would have not been capable of reading the address, and would have probably vomited on some kid's birthday card by now.

I take the decision not to get out of bed, and instead snuggle into the duvet with my laptop to watch DVDs. I come across the remains of a stash of Milky Bars that I had forgotten I had put in my bedside cabinet. I figure this could easily be both breakfast and lunch, and if I can manage to persuade Sarah to bring me some food I could even arrange to have my dinner here. Ooh. I could even phone for a pizza which means, in theory, I may only have to get out of bed for work on Monday.

Annoyingly, Mum puts a dampener on my plans for extreme laziness. She calls in the mid-afternoon to tell me that her and Dad are coming down to London to see some musical and would like to meet for dinner afterwards. Even from the other side of the country she still has the ability to mess up my plans without even trying.

Sunday 21 October

They say you are always a child in the eyes of your parents. That was definitely the case last night, when Mum and Dad arrived earlier than promised and saw the state of my room. It didn't help that Scarlett failed to stall them by asking them to sit in the living room, or offer them distracting cups of tea, like any rational human being. Instead, the cow cheerfully greeted them with, "Hi! She is still in bed. She's been lying there all day. Go straight up." Cue much humiliation and explaining, as they found me hung-over, amidst the mess of my bedroom.

Dinner was at the local Chinese restaurant, and was tense, featuring the following topics:

1) "You know the Johnsons' daughter has managed to get a job running the UN." (Good for Mrs Johnson, her daughter, and the UN.)
2) "Have you ever considered taking up a hobby like..." (Insert spectacularly unappealing activity like taxidermy, marathon running, morris dancing, etc.)

3) "Any boys we should know about?" (I pointed out that I was spending Saturday night with my parents in a mid-range Chinese restaurant. Surely this was the answer to their question.)
4) The state of my room.

I am sure they enjoyed their dinner watching their daughter regress to a sulky 16 year old. Usually (1) and (3) are the preserve of Mum's line of questioning while Dad definitely seems partial to (2). Question (4) is variable.

Last time we met it was, "Why does that girl [Scarlett] want to put all that metal jewellery on her lovely face? I don't understand why these young girls do it." I tried to explain that eyebrow rings and more than one piercing per ear is fairly normal nowadays, but this fell on deaf ears. Instead, they went onto an in-depth analysis around their views on tattoos. According to Mum and Dad they are acceptable on sailors and prostitutes, but nobody else.

Don't misunderstand me. I love my parents to bits but they have a special ability to wind me up. I think they dimly understand that things are harder for young people now than in their own time, but still really don't get it. For instance, Mum's inspiring message of the evening is, "Yes, life is tough, but that doesn't mean you need to start shopping at Iceland. Sainsbury's do a very reasonable line in 'basics' nowadays." Clearly, it seems in their eyes my life, just like my room, is a simple case of getting my act together and deciding to pull my socks up. I console myself that at least I am getting a free meal out of this.

Monday 22 October

As part of my Efficiency and Organisation Drive and desire to put a stop to my procrastination, I put together a professional looking to-do list of everything I need to get done. It reads as follows:

1) Make sure all signposting appointments are clearly marked in diary and follow-up letters are done that day.
2) All requested reports will be written and submitted 48 hours before deadlines.
3) Stocks of clinical forms, questionnaires and scales must be checked on a weekly basis.
4) My application form will be completed by mid-November.
5) I will read at least one scientific article or journal paper every day.

...and it goes on and on to point 15.

When I read back over the list, it almost feels sarcastic. There is no way I am going to be able to do everything. I share my list with Olga, hoping for a little encouragement or praise about my efficiency. She rather unhelpfully points out that in the time it has taken me to compile my to-do list I could have crossed off at least four of the stated activities. I shouldn't have bothered. Stupid Olga always misses the point of these things. To prove that my scheduling is not in vain, I doggedly stick to my new plan and get through a serious amount of work. I only stop to read Facebook at lunchtime (and a little ClinPsy, but I justify it to myself as equal to reading a scientific journal). She fails to notice any of this, but I have the smug sense of satisfaction at proving her wrong.

I get home and realise that in order to achieve point (4) on the list I will need to do some work on my form this evening. I find Sarah at the kitchen table already writing hers. It's a bit awkward. Almost instinctively, she wraps a protective arm around her form, as if we are in primary school and I am out to copy her spelling test. This is very unlike how Sarah normally behaves, and I truly hate it.

Sarah and I have opposite problems in essence. Whereas I don't know where to start, Sarah doesn't know where to end. She complains her current draft is at about 8,000 words, which is more an encyclopaedia than a personal statement. To get that kind of volume she must have crammed in her entire life since she was six. She has repeatedly tried to cut it down, but every revision has resulted in it expanding even more.

Thankfully the tension is broken by Boring Tom bringing around some much needed groceries. Deciding to put off point (4) for another day, the three of us put dinner together. Tom isn't bad as a cook (well for an accountant anyway), apart from the unfortunate habit of putting too much salt in everything.

Scarlett only comes downstairs to join us when the possibility of her helping out has long passed. God knows what she has been doing in her room, but judging by her smell it has involved chain smoking huge quantities of Marlboro Lights. I'm annoyed, as this violates our tenancy agreement, but she never listens no matter how much I point this out. As she sits down and grabs a plateful of spaghetti, she points her fork at Sarah and me.

"There will be no talk about sodding application forms. The first to mention anything to do with it will get dismissed from the table!" she declares, and gets stuck into her food before the rest of us have a chance to serve ourselves. Evidently artistes do not require table manners.

As the rest of us start eating, Sarah reminds me that the monthly assistant group is on Friday. I thank her for letting me know, as this had completely slipped my mind. Scarlett takes objection to the way the conversation is going and, with her mouth still full, refers to her earlier threat.

"I don't see why either of you go, all you do is complain about it," adds Boring Tom. "Are you sure you both really want to go?"

Sarah and I dismiss them both as having no understanding of the Assistant Psychology scene, and that they couldn't possibly understand. Besides, what if we missed something really important? Sarah markedly changes the subject to which of us has not yet paid the rent. Scarlett, (for it is she) gets defensive and shifts the subject to who has left the towels hanging off the shower rail, causing them to smell funny. That would be me. So, I change the subject to how much toilet paper gets used. Which would be Sarah, and round and round it goes. Sadly, this is all too often how dinner ends up at our house.

Tuesday 23 October

I turn up to work today and guess who is occupying my desk like a workplace Goldilocks?

"HI-YA!"

Bloody Spiny. All of her stuff is sprawled out across my desk, she has moved my in-tray, and messed up my highly complicated system of notes, files and memos. I have only been at work for thirty seconds, and she has already managed to annoy me. This has got to be her personal best.

I return her phony smile through gritted teeth as she tells me she has a "super important meeting" with Nancy. Olga is hunched over her desk trying not to listen, but I can tell from the way her leg has suddenly started jiggling that she is getting seriously annoyed.

I try to make out that it is no big deal and that she is welcome to come in and take over my desk at any time. She takes my offer at face value, and makes no effort to bunch up or leave. With nowhere else to go, the three of us sit there firmly pushed into each other's personal space like we are having to work crammed into an elevator.

As I start trying to figure out how my various notes and files have been reshuffled, Spiny asks me how my form is going. Actually, she doesn't care. She will pretend to listen for a minute, before launching into her real agenda; boasting about how *her* form is progressing.

"Do you think I should talk about my 1st Class honours degree first, or should I write about how I am writing this article that will probably be published in *The Lancet*?" I swallow my irritation and tell her something vaguely constructive, and she replies, "I am SO glad I'm able to ask you about these things, it's always really helpful," in a way that implies neither.

My heart rate starts to climb.

She then rabbits on about how hard it is to choose a colour for her car. Her father is buying her a brand new Vauxhall Corsa, but it's proving impossible to decide between Passion Scarlet and Midnight Magenta.

"I find mentioning I have a car is such a plus at interviews, because so many posts need you to travel, you know?" she says. I have to physically hold myself back from pushing her into the corridor and slamming the Cupboard door behind her, but fate intervenes. Nancy knocks on the door and Spiny leaps to her feet.

"SEE-YA! Don't forget the meeting on Friday!" she says as she leaves the Cupboard door open.

I can't wait.

Wednesday 24 October

Mum phones me up asking me what I want for Christmas. I remind her it's only October, but she insists that I tell her now so she has enough time to make sure she gets everything. What do I really want? A room without a huge damp patch on the ceiling? The people I live with not to use the last of the milk without replacing it? Some stability and prospects for a happy future? Instead, I decide to ask for a new coat and she seems happy with this. Mercifully, she doesn't bring up the state of my room, imagined drug use, or whether or not I have a proper job yet, but does ask me when I will be coming home for Christmas. I feel this is a constructive telephone call.

"Could you NOT make personal phone calls in work time," Olga says, the second I hang up. "Some of us have work to do."

I defend myself saying that I had only been on the phone for two minutes, max. I also point out that she makes dozens of personal calls at work. Olga gets grumpy, and whines about her project and how the rest of the team were so incompetent they couldn't find their arse in the dark without a map, torch and a GPS guidance system. She works long hours and is constantly clearing up everyone else's mess, so she figures she is entitled to make a few phone calls.

"You need to remember who your seniors are," she says, with a self-satisfied look as if this automatically wins her the argument.

"Yeah. Not you," I reply, under my breath. I mean, if she really was so *senior*, she wouldn't be sharing this crappy little bolthole with the assistant, would she?

Thursday 25 October

Last night I had the most fevered and vivid anxiety dreams. I dreamt about my last boss, Dr Mildew, a crusty old bloke who fancied himself as psychology's answer to Richard Dawkins. He was making me stand in front of a lecture hall, telling me that I was unscientific, undisciplined, and I need to get my act together for my form, or I would be an embarrassment to the whole country. I woke up screaming, "I'll write it soon, I promise!"

My last job was as a research assistant on a large clinical trial project. It was pure research and had little clinical work, but it was another step on the ladder. Dr Mildew (he insisted we use his title and *never* his first name) was a big shot researcher, who seemed to view supervision as a tedious obligation at best, and at worst an opportunity for him to drone on about his opinions. This wouldn't be so bad if he'd just restricted them to what he was good at - his research - but he would often use the sessions to spout off about his alarmingly right wing views on immigration and "communist influences".

Even worse was his habit of saying whatever I had written or produced for him required "slight alterations". More often than not these "slight alterations" were massive changes or total rewrites that meant I almost had to start from scratch. On reading the redrafted version, he would stroke his bushy moustache and make a load of pedantic suggestions that I had written in the first version. Since then I have developed a phobic dread of the words "slight alteration", even to the point where I have to breathe into a paper bag when I overhear the phrase being used at the dry cleaners.

Conversations with him also seemed to necessitate comments about how little I seemed to know and frustrated sighs if I asked for details about some obscure theory. No matter how much I tried to prepare, I would always leave the room feeling slightly humiliated and just a bit stupid. I spent the first six months of that job about to burst into tears until another researcher on the team, Brenda, took pity and informed me that:

1) He was like that to everyone.

2) I should always keep all prior drafts and when he asked for "slight alterations" I should just change a few words on the original version and send him that. That worked 99% of the time.

3) If I just dropped into conversation I was reading one of his papers, he would leave me alone.

To my amazement, these all worked. Things became gradually better after that and were pretty good around the time my current job was advertised. Sadly this seems to be the Assistant Psychologist's code; as soon as you start to get good at one job, they make you leave and find another.

Friday 26 October

It's 6:30pm. I am tired and cranky after spending the day cooped up in the Cupboard. I should be on my way home by now, looking forward to putting my feet up and watching the telly. Instead, I gamely make my way towards the monthly

Assistants' Group. Justine has also overheard us talking about it beforehand, and she seizes the opportunity to meet kindred spirits.

Despite the name of the group these meetings are frequented by support workers and psychology graduates, as well as Assistant Psychologists, all looking for advice and guidance on the clinical psychology path. It's a group of about a dozen or so of us. It's not officially organised or anything, but these groups are found all over the country. They spontaneously seem to spring up like magic.

However, I am willing to bet a substantial amount of money that most are not like our group.

Spiny is the (self-appointed) chair of our group, and she is usually accompanied by two of her favoured courtiers, Meryl and Cheryl. They both work in Spiny's IAPT service, laugh at her jokes, gasp in astonishment at her pedestrian observations, and generally kiss her arse. Although slightly taller and more statuesque than Spiny, they are also both blonde, and are wearing matching dark skirts and light blue blouses. Flanking her, they almost look like her bodyguards.

The other regulars include Melissa (who used to work in publishing and is distinctive as she is a bit older and the only non-white person in the group); Jane and Patty (veteran assistant psychologists about my age who are a bit of a laugh); and the group's only man who wears nerd-chic thick glasses and sports a trendy haircut. I can never remember his name despite him telling it to me it at least a dozen times. The group is now missing a few regulars who got onto training in the last application cycle. They will be airbrushed out of history, never to be mentioned again.

Spiny welcomes us all and hands out photocopies of an agenda. We have a speaker visiting, some local psychologist. She looks like Kate Bush might look if she had slept rough for a few nights at Paddington Station. She works with the elderly and launches into a well-meaning but way too technical lecture about assessing dementia and differential diagnosis. I give up when she starts talking about "dendrite decay" and the "composition of amyloid plaques in the neo-cortex". All I can hear is the speaker's voice, and the sound of Spiny's biro scratching on paper as she hastily scribbles every word.

Then we have a brief Question and Answer session. It's basically an excuse for Spiny to be smarmy and ask lots of questions that allow her to show off. When Sarah asks about what we can do to support carers of people with dementia, Spiny decides we have kept our guest speaker for too long and it's time for her to leave.

We then gossip about how hard it is to write our application forms, rumours we've overheard and stuff we've read on ClinPsy. I quite enjoy talking to the others. Jane in particular is very supportive to everyone, and Sarah comes up with some really useful suggestions about how Patty can get help with her dyslexia. The guy-whose-name-I-can-never-remember is a bit weary of it all, and sits at the back. Even so, Jane does her best to keep him involved in the conversation.

Spiny, encouraged by Meryl and Cheryl, is very forthright about her opinions, and some of the newbies mistake her outspokenness for knowledge. Justine in particular seems awestruck, and starts asking Spiny a whole barrage of rapid fire questions. Most of which would take about 30 seconds on Google to find out. Spiny, smiling like a python about to swallow a mouse, mockingly answers her questions, yet still lulls Justine into thinking they are now best pals. She laps up her adulation and leaves promising to add Justine on Facebook and "sort her out with her application". Not leaving an opportunity to stick the knife in, Spiny turns to me after Justine leaves and says,

"Interesting... friend you bought with you. I can see how you get on. You two are *so* alike."

Saturday 27 October

Sarah is staying the weekend at Boring Tom's flat, so I am left watching breakfast telly with Scarlett. Both of us are in our pyjamas and dressing gowns munching on my Coco Pops, idly wondering if we should switch over to the cartoons or if we are too old for that now. Suddenly, Serena Lawson, a girl who was at secondary school with me, pops up on the screen and starts talking to the host. To see her out of school uniform and on the telly is as surreal as suddenly seeing your grandma playing drums at a Rolling Stones gig.

Serena is part of a serious feature on plastic surgery and glamour modelling. Either that or it is a way for producers to legitimately put boobs on telly before the 9pm watershed. I am surprised, as Serena used to be quiet at school and certainly not known for courting attention or controversy. She was first soprano in the choir, wore Clark's shoes, and I think her dad was a bank manager. Practically the dictionary definition of the word "sensible".

Clearly something has happened in the intervening years to make her throw off the shackles of normality, dispense with her Marks and Spencer grey pullover, and plunge headfirst into the pages of *Big Jugs Monthly*. In the interest of debate and balance, they put her up against someone from some radical feminist organisation, and let the two at each other.

I tell Scarlett that I used to know Serena, and wonder why she would have gone on TV to make a fool of herself. I also wonder why she decided to hose herself down with enough fake tan to look like an extra from *The Only Way is Essex*.

"I thought you psychology types were supposed to be accepting and tolerant?" is Scarlett's response. "Can't she choose how she lives her own life, without you having to pass judgement? What does it even matter to you, anyway?"

Before I can think of an answer, she presses the remote and

turns straight over to the cartoons. She gets drawn into a cartoon of a cat trying to hit a mouse with a broom, as they run around an ironing board. She always does this when she feels the conversation is finished, and it's only when I have got back to my room that I am able to think of a good reply to her question.

Sunday 28 October

I am trying to get some tickets for a festival online. The only problem is that everyone else seems to have the same idea, and not for the first time I find myself in a situation with no guarantees, where I have to compete against thousands of faceless others. However, after a few times trying to log into the website, I get through, and before I know it I am entering my credit card details. If only everything in life could be this simple. I feel ecstatic and hurry downstairs to share the news.

"Jesus. It's just a few tickets for a poxy festival," says Scarlett, not even bothering to look up from the magazine she is reading. "Besides, if you really wanted tickets I could have got them easily. I know a guy, who knew a guy who was once a roadie for one of the support bands."

I am not taking this lying down and point out that if it would have been so easy for her why didn't she volunteer to use her tenuous contacts when we talked about it last night. I also point out that showing a little gratitude wouldn't kill her. I storm out of the house in a huff.

I soon regret this, because I haven't brought a coat with me. Still, I have no intention of slinking home to get one, and risk looking like an idiot in front of Scarlett. So I shiver as I walk towards the park. I can't believe how quickly I have gone from feeling great to feeling pissed off.

As I am stewing over this, I get a text that completely takes my mind off such trivial matters. Hunky Nick has just messaged me the following:

Hi. hope ur hvng a gr8 sund. r u up 4 coffee after
work 2moro? Nick

Not exactly an Elizabethan love sonnet that I can keep in the
attic to share with my future grandchildren. Nonetheless, I get
butterflies in my stomach after I read it. My little strop forgotten,
I quickly hurry back to the house and plan my reply.

When I get home I find Scarlett in the front room painting
her finger nails. She studiously avoids eye contact, but eventually
croaks out an apology that is at least sixty per cent sincere. I
accept and quickly fill her in on current events. Scarlett is
emphatic in her advice. She insists an hour is an appropriate
amount of time to wait before replying. I mull over whether I
should use text speak or write proper words.

"It's not a marriage proposal. Just text YES and press send,"
she mutters. This is the problem with people whose idea of
foreplay is a shared cigarette in a car park. They have no sense of
romance.

Monday 29 October

Well I knew it was too good to last. I find myself waiting for
Nick at the coffee shop. When he doesn't turn up at 5pm, I
excuse him that he may be a bit late getting away from the office.
I give it another ten minutes, thinking that it could take a while
to walk the three hundred yards from work. After all, he could
have sustained a sports injury on the weekend and will come
painfully limping through the door at any second.

When he still isn't there at twenty past, I start to check my
texts and voicemail at two minute intervals. At half-past, I find
myself getting more than slightly wound up. Part of me thinks
this is totally unacceptable and indicates a lack of respect. The
more accepting, pragmatic part of me suggests that I cut him
some slack. A less rational voice starts contemplating that it's
some horrible office prank and that everyone from work is

watching me on a CCTV monitor and laughing. Because they all obviously have nothing better to do after work.

It's at ten past six that the door opens and a familiar male figure comes in the door. Unfortunately, it's not Nick, it's Dudley. Oh God no.

Back in my first job when I was a support worker at a day unit, Dudley, was one of the people who I was tasked to look after. Initially, Dudley seemed a quiet, slightly awkward, dishevelled man, in his mid-thirties. He had a habit of silently looming by the vending machines and hovering by the nurses' station. I felt a bit sorry for him, and figured he probably had been dealt a bad hand in life. Taking pity, I tried my best to always be pleasant to him.

The only problem was that Dudley got a little "attached" to me. I should have noticed that the duty nurse always assigned one of the older ladies, or a male member of staff, to be his main worker, but I didn't register this at the time. However, I certainly did start thinking about this when he started following me down the road when I had finished my shifts.

Initially, I naively thought it was just coincidence. However, something told me this wasn't quite right, when he started openly commenting on what I was wearing, what I was doing, and his opinion about both. Once, he had spotted me in ASDA buying a sandwich, and approached me the following lunchtime while I was trying to put out the cutlery.

"You wen' bought a Sanwich yesterday. ASDA."
"Um, Yes. Dudley, I did." I replied distractedly, trying to remember where I left the spoons on the last shift.
"What'd you buy?" he asked insistently.
"Uh, I can't remember. Tuna Mayo I think," I looked up at him. His faced had darkened.
"I don't like that," he said, "Ham. That's what I like," his tone suggesting that all right minded people would think the same.
"That's great Dudley. I am sorry but I really have to finish this. I will talk to you later." I replied distractedly. That was

when he tried to kiss me.

The support worker with me on shift was a temp and told me to laugh it off clearly thinking it was either funny or harmless. Me, less so. Shortly afterwards, Dudley started leaving little gifts. 99p pot plants. Ham fucking sandwiches. He would ask other staff members when I was on duty, and do his best to sit next to me at mealtimes.

I wasn't sure what to do. Was this part of the work I had to suck up and get on with? Was I being weak by complaining? Maybe there was an entirely innocent explanation, or that I was noticing him more because I was feeling a bit freaked out. It was only when he started telling me about where I lived and which bus I took home, that I got scared. I broke down into tears in the staff room, and had to be taken to the manager's office. To her credit, the manager took the matter seriously. She made rota changes and made sure that someone had a gentle but firm word with Dudley. Fortunately, it worked.

In my career to date, I have met dozens of people with mental health problems, and have never had any major problems (in fact I find "normal" people far scarier). It's so bloody typical I happened to have my single scary incident when I was at my most inexperienced.

Even so, seeing Dudley now made me panic slightly. Having no desire to chat about the good old days, I wait until he is talking to the cashier, bolt out of my chair, grab my bag, and make a dash for the exit. As I briskly walk past the large coffee shop windows, I can't help but check my mobile. Still no message from Nick. A bitter voice in my head mockingly suggests that at least Dudley would have been attentive if I had arranged to have coffee with him.

I get back to the house and we pore over the implications of Nick's no-show. Sarah and Scarlett read through the original message trying to analyse it for nuance or hidden meaning, as if there is a secret message hidden in the text. Between the three of us we have probably watched every episode of CSI, but despite our detective skills even we can't draw much from 52 badly misspelt characters.

He had better have a good explanation for this.

Tuesday 30 October

No sign of Nick at work this morning. Perhaps he is ill? Maybe he has emigrated to South America to avoid my wrathful vengeance? Instead of dwelling on being stood up, I throw myself into my work.

One of the things on my super organised to-do list is the choice about which four courses I want to apply to for clinical training. Courses around London are an obvious choice, but these always have the most applicants and seem to keep pushing the bar higher and higher. They also have larger class sizes, and I would prefer somewhere a bit smaller. Oh, and somewhere that doesn't overload you. One of the Assistant Group members who got on a course up North last year starts every single Facebook post with the phrase "SO busy..." I very much want to avoid her fate.

I spend an ungodly amount of time combing through various university websites, but eventually I decide on my four choices. My first choice is my nearest course. I won't have to move, and already quite like my life around here. The second is a high profile well known university that seems a long shot, but you never know. Choice three and four sound good from their description, are close enough, and seem places where I feel I could fit in. I hope.

I briefly consider applying to the university where I did my undergraduate degree. I quickly dismiss the idea. Been there, done that. While it may be nostalgic, I don't feel the need to re-live the past that badly. I am also mindful of this one guy who stayed on straight from undergrad to do a Ph.D. There was something faintly tragic and ridiculous about watching him pretend to be a fresher again. If you popped in for a drink at the student union, he could be counted on to be dancing along to the Macarena on any given night. Badly. To this day he remains my mental yardstick for being the world's saddest man, and I have no desire to be his female equivalent.

Wednesday 31 October

At about 2pm, just as I am settling down to write up a few letters, Nick appears at the Cupboard door apologising about the other night. Some family crisis came up and he had to rush off just before our rendezvous. In his haste he left his mobile in his office, and has only just got back and picked it up and read my texts. He seems genuinely regretful and sincere, but it's quite hard to delve any further because Olga is sitting right next to me. Like a spinsterish maiden aunt chaperone, Olga doesn't even bother to pretend to ignore us and stares blatantly while Nick and I try to hold our conversation.

My cynical side points out that it sounds like bullshit. In the modern era, no-one can go for more than 24 hours without their phone for starters. I drop it though, and make out that it was no big deal.

"It was just a quick coffee to catch up about the way the research is going, no biggie," I say as much to Olga as to Nick, to keep her from jumping to any conclusions.

To make it up to me he suggests we catch up today after work, if I am free. I perk up and readily agree, but Olga (who the invite clearly isn't extended to) interrupts, and lets us know that she is free to join us. She mentions she has been trying to catch up with Nick as well, and it may be good for her to update both of us regarding the clinical trial data.

Oh joy of joys.

Ignoring the crestfallen look on my face, Nick casually shrugs and replies, "Why not?" The three of us agree to meet at the coffee shop after work. I do my best to swallow down my intense irritation as Nick leaves the Cupboard. Could my luck get any worse?

It can, and it does.

Emboldened by my sudden interest in her project, Olga spends the rest of the afternoon going into painful detail about trial data. Oblivious to my silence, and complete lack of responding apart from the occasional "uh huh", I hear far more about cortisol levels in women than I could ever hope to hear in a lifetime. I have to suffer three long hours of this for the simple crime of wanting to have a cup of coffee with a cute guy from work. The punishment hardly fits the crime.

We head out at 5pm and it strikes me that this is also the first occasion that I have gone anywhere with Olga outside work. I rapidly realise that this is for a very good reason, and resolve to never do so again in the future. While Nick and I grab our lattes and sit down, Olga is openly disdainful of the coffee shop's soft furnishings, and brusquely interrogates the barista about how, in precise detail, he makes his coffee. She takes her cup back twice because there is either too much foam on it, or the strength of the coffee is not to her liking.

She then sits down and dominates the discussion, relegating myself and Nick to the role of audience. We just sit there and sporadically make noises that allow her to continue her uninterrupted monologue. Nick glances at me, yawns and looks at his watch. After 20 painful minutes of this, I find my tolerance has evaporated. I can no longer keep up the facade of being even slightly interested, so I give my apologies and leave.

I walk back to the bus stop dazed, wondering what has just happened.

NOVEMBER

Thursday 1 November

I have been sent on an errand by my supervisor that takes up most of the day. As it turns out my supervisor has been asked to perform a specialist assessment but the various tests, scales and clinical records that are needed aren't kept in one location. That would be too straightforward. As the all-round Girl Friday here, I have to trek around South London to find them all.

After frantic emailing and phoning around, lots of dead ends and wrong numbers, I get a rough idea of where I can get a hold of all the bits and pieces. I plan my route and make sure to leave a good two hour window for traffic and any unexpected delays. With all of this accomplished, I feel justifiably proud I am on top of things.

However, fate decides to crank up the difficulty level, and floods my inbox with requests from some of the nurses and medics that need immediate action, and ideally would have been done yesterday. Of course, most of this is due to their incompetence but it results in additional needless work being dumped squarely on my shoulders.

Not that I can complain or tell them off, of course. I don't have enough ranking for that. I realise that as the lowest member of the food chain crap rolls downhill, but not for the first time I start to wonder where does the line between "useful experience" end and "unnecessary indignity" begin.

Olga is less than sympathetic saying that I need to snap out of my "attitude" and "entitlement" and instead be grateful I have a job in the first place. She goes on to add that if I didn't want to do it plenty would. Her overall stance is that this sort of thing happens to her, so it can jolly well happen to me, and I should suck it up. I'm not so sure. We wouldn't apply that logic to child abuse or polio.

After I get home, I vent my anger to Sarah while we eat dinner. She listens for a bit but then she starts to outdo my complaints with her own horror stories at the nursing home. I find it is often like this. No one seems to want to listen, or if they do it quickly becomes a competition about who is the most hard-done by. All of working life can't be like this, can it?

Friday 2 November

Justine comes around in the afternoon to get some advice on her application form. She is currently working as a receptionist at the doctor's surgery a few streets away, so she drops around whenever she gets a chance.

Justine is optimistic it will be fifth time lucky for her. However, she has decided to make changes to her personal statement this time, and wants advice. Unfortunately for her she has possibly picked the worst person on earth to ask for this, unless she wants advice about how to avoid writing it.

Justine pleads for me to look at her form, and against my better judgement I agree to have a look. I can tell in 30 seconds it doesn't look good. She has cut-and-pasted a list of things she did last year, most of it irrelevant (she mentions she likes puppies). Experiences are sprinkled in random order. Some sentences make no logical sense.

I want to be critical, but all I can see in her eyes is a plea for some kind word or assurance. I just don't have the heart to tear it apart.

"Maybe you could start with why you want to work in this area?" I suggest.

"Because it sounds cool," she pauses for a second before finally adding "and I really want to do it."

"Justine," I sigh, "That is not going to be enough. They are not going to interview you if you just write that. It's not like writing to Santa."

"Can't you just help me write it? You always know what to say," she asks in the tone of a 10-year-old hoping to defer bedtime with a baby sitter.

"No, I can barely write my own. This isn't a primary school spelling test where you can just copy my answers and no one will ever know."

"Do you think Sarah will know the answers?"

I emphasise that Sarah is unlikely to be any more help than I am. She wonders if she could ask Spiny. Justine is now her friend on Facebook, and she is privy to a never ending stream of updates and musings, that she now tries to fill me in on. I stress that under no circumstances should she ask Spiny for input. I can only imagine the horror that she would unleash on poor Justine's form.

I manage to fob her off with the suggestion she find someone more senior at work who knows her in a professional capacity that can help her reflect on how best to package herself. She thinks this is a great idea. Eager and freshly inspired, she happily rushes off to do this. Now all I need to do is find someone who will motivate me like that.

Saturday 3 November

An alumni newsletter plopped through the letterbox this morning. How the hell have they tracked me down? I must have moved about four times since I graduated and have never informed them of any forwarding address. I could move to the moon, but they would still be able to hunt me down. Sarah has noticed this too and suspects, as with the student loans company, that the alumni office have well placed informants in the CIA and British Intelligence. This is the only possible explanation.

I normally put items like the alumni magazine, along with any of the accompanying material hawking university themed hoodies and such, straight into the recycling bin (ditto letters from the Student Loans Company). However, today I decide to flick through it, my choice heavily influenced by the fact that I have run out of material to read on the toilet.

The brochure is strange, and unlike any memory I have of the place. Everyone is smiling, photogenic and unnervingly multicultural. The cliques of beautiful youths have wandered in from a soft drink commercial, and look as if they are in their mid to late 20s and have never suffered from acne or poor dress sense. The campus seemed unnaturally sunny and people are practically wearing beachwear. This is so far removed from reality I consider calling trading standards.

I remember things quite differently. Most of the men were at the end of their teens and had either terrible taste in facial hair or a penchant for wearing *Red Dwarf* T-shirts. The girls were usually bundled up in Parkas to keep away the hideous cold and constant rain. It was more *Blade Runner* than *Baywatch*. I don't think I ever saw a six-pack during the entire three years, yet according to the brochure, washboard abs seem to be an entrance requirement along with your A-levels.

Also, I notice the photographer took great pains to frame the shots in a way that excluded the rust and water damage of the buildings. There is no sign of the porta-cabins and dodgy 60's breeze block buildings where I spent most of the time studying. The staff featured are clearly from the younger and more attractive end of the faculty. Even the Vice Chancellor has not escaped this youthification. His photo is noticeably airbrushed and he is wearing a toupee that looks like a small animal is delicately balancing on his head.

I am uncertain what to make of the psychology alumni page. Everyone is either married, living abroad, working in human resources, or in I.T. and "loving it". I am not sure if this is a good or bad thing. It's definitely better than hearing my subject is associated with crack addiction or future homelessness (that distinction would go to Sociology).

Most galling was the four page insert that begged us to give a donation. The suggested amounts ranged from £1,000 to £10,000, which are just laughable. I can barely afford to top up my mobile phone credit, so the idea of throwing vast sums of money at a place I no longer go to is absurd. Besides I already have had the experience of paying them while I was there and still am, via my student loan repayments. Being an undergraduate was not so gratifying an experience that I want to continue paying for it for the rest of my life.

That is not to say my view of the brochure is wholly negative. Once again we are out of bog roll and I am happy to feed back to the Alumni team that their newsletter has remarkably absorbent properties, considering it is printed on glossy paper.

Sunday 4 November

After spending a pleasant afternoon strolling around the nooks and crannies of Hyde Park, I come home to something that resembles a break-in, or the aftermath of a small earthquake. Dishes are strewn across the kitchen, furniture is upturned. There is clothing strewn across the living room with a trail of underwear going up the stairs. The fridge door swings forlornly open with an impressive array of cream, fruit and various other sticky food substances smeared across the lino. I then realise that burglaries and hurricanes aren't normally accompanied by the soundtrack of very enthusiastic and loud copulating.

Scarlett. *Quelle surprise.*

If she is on a one woman crusade to shag half the men in Britain, then all power to her. Whatever makes her happy. But does she have to do it where I live? In such a flagrant way? And does it really warrant military grade collateral damage? I know people in developing countries have it tougher, but they probably don't have to put up with the imprint of Scarlett's arse in a puddle of Elmlea double cream when they get home.

There was a time I really used to love living with other people. At university, living with other people my own age was like a never ending party. After I graduated, it became a preferred choice because everywhere was expensive and I didn't want to be completely on my own. Now it has become something I just cannot wait to see the back of. It's undignified to be nearly 25 and still living like I was at 18. If things don't change, I am going to be living like this when I am 35. It is at this precise moment I realise my dearest wish is not to come to the end my natural life in a rented house share.

Monday 5 November

We are now into November and I still haven't decided on whom to ask for a reference. I need two, one that will speak about my clinical work and another that will attest to my academic ability and reassure the course that I am not a complete fool. Ideally for both to be taken seriously, they would need to bear witness to my overall wonderfulness, whilst having some idea about the requirements and stresses of clinical training. Glowing tributes from Dad are not going to cut it.

I hate asking people for references. It just can't be normal to approach people you know and ask "Would you mind telling a complete stranger about how great I am?" In any sane or rational world surely this sort of activity would be restricted to the fantasies of a narcissist.

It makes sense to choose Nancy as my clinical referee. She knows the rigours of clinical training, having been through it herself, and has supervised me for the last few months, so knows what I can do. I also trust her enough not to write nasty things about me, or make remarks that will lead to her judgement, taste, or sanity being questioned. Sadly, this cannot be taken for granted. I heard a rumour once of a referee writing two sides about how great *they* were, followed by a one-line aside about the person they were writing the reference for. I can't imagine Nancy doing that. Well at least I hope she wouldn't.

That leaves my choice of academic referee. This is a little bit trickier. Technically my most "academic" situation was when I was an undergraduate, but I am sure that none of my lecturers remember me. Why would they? There were 200 or so in my year alone and they spent most of their time trying their best to avoid us. I know that a fellow undergraduate, Suzy, sought a reference from our Director of Studies, for a highly sought after graduate scheme. She showed me the reference, which read as follows:

Suzy attended the undergraduate course in Marketing [C453]. She had an attendance rate of 93%. She had module marks of 62, 57, 61 and 66. She completed a dissertation as part of an optional module. She was pleasant.

Suzy observed that the Director of Studies could have fit this onto the title line of an email and sent the rest of it blank.

The other academic choice would be my last boss, Dr Mildew. However, I am loath to send him anything as he would no doubt have some "slight alteration" for my form, and mention something pedantic like I brought him filter coffee instead of decaf. If I left it with him I wouldn't put it past him to make me out as someone who could not be trusted to go to the toilet unaided, and enjoyed hitting orphans in her spare time.

I decide to opt for Brenda, the senior researcher from that lab. I know she has some balance to her outlook, we got on quite well, and she liked me enough to organise my leaving do. I dig around, find her number, and check it's okay with her. She assures me it's fine and that she will get straight on it. We catch up on recent gossip, and it looks like little has changed since I left. Dr Mildew continues to use his PhD students as clay pigeon targets for a form of stress relief. He continues to march up and down the corridor screaming at random people. Looks like I made the right decision in my choice of referee, (and leaving that job when I did come to think about it).

Tuesday 6 November

I am in a forest. I am wearing a red cagoule, a crash helmet, and am hanging off the side of a cliff on a rope. It's foggy and I can't really see above or below me. I hear vague voices in the distance telling me to hurry up. Strange metaphorical dream? Nope. It's the annual team-building away day.

Away days can be great. What is not to like? A chance to get out of the office and spend some time bonding with your colleagues. Maybe get an inspirational talk to rally the troops. Although this is not always the case. I heard of one away day where the speaker was one of the rejects from *Dragon's Den* who came along, spat out some business management jargon and then jeered at everyone for being "failures for working in the public sector". But that's a rarity. More often, they usually involve some hearty outdoor activity like team sports, orienteering or, case in point, rock climbing.

So I woke at some ungodly hour this morning to cram into a minibus for a trip to the middle of nowhere. Along with my workmates I was handed outdoor gear, maps and instructed how to get from point A to point B. While I admire their faith in our abilities, whoever organised this hadn't really thought it through. Two of the doctors are significantly overweight. Half of our secretaries are approaching retirement. Most of us are strangers to regular physical activity. All of us would prefer to be safely tucked in bed at this hour.

Nick may be the exception. His rugged build and impressive ability to make red nylon look quite sexy are at odds with the rest of us. The instructor points out a rope that has been bolted into the summit and gets Nick to demonstrate how easy it is to climb sheer vertical granite surfaces. Then, convinced that the rest of us know what we are doing, he clambers back in the minibus, tells us he will meet us at Point B, and drives off. What he can't know is that Nick has been rock climbing since he was a teenager.

We stand there looking bewildered at each other. Half us of expect the minibus to come back any second, when the instructor realises that we have been signed up for the wrong activity. Surely our away day should involve warm shelter, flip charts, and plenty of coffee and biscuits? Nancy gamely tries to scale the wall, hurts her hand and says, "You can all climb up that if you want to, I am going to phone a taxi to drive us there". Practically the whole group agrees with her. In agreement and team freshly built, they sit down and the smokers all light up in unison. Olga and a couple of the nurses wander off trying to get a mobile signal.

Nick is the sole person that is still at the base of the rock. "I reckon it wouldn't be too difficult," he says stroking his stubble, and then looks at me, "I might give it a shot. Do you fancy it?" My instinct is to stay with the team, partly to demonstrate unity, but mainly because I am tired and can't think of anything worse than throwing myself up a cliff. However, something in Nick's voice persuades me, and I agree to go along with him. Briefly we check-in with the others to let them know what we are planning before setting off.

I go first, and Nick attaches a karabiner to my harness and loops me onto one of the ropes. "Just a safety precaution" he says, "We have to keep you safe". Roped in, I start to scramble up the rock face. Initially, it's easy, but when I get 20 feet off the ground I start to think otherwise. "I can't do it." I say getting scared, and start to climb down. Only I find I don't know how to get back. I tightly screw up my eyes and pretend that none of this is happening. "Yeah, you can!" encourages Nick. He quickly gets to my level. "Look, all you have to do is grab that bit and you will be fine. Trust me." He places his hand over mine (which makes me instantly feel breathless) and puts it on a large rocky outcrop. I find that I can now leverage my weight and move my feet. I feel exhilarated and feel a rush of gratitude for being rescued. We slowly make our way up the rock face.

At some point it starts drizzling and gets foggy. I can't see Nick and I slip, I panic as I plummet downwards. My only thought is, "At least I don't have to do that bloody form now," but the rope goes taut and I halt, gently swinging. Nick starts pulling the rope upwards and my hands find rock. I start to climb again and I can hear his voice in the distance tell me it's not far. I believe him. A few concerted moves forward and I find myself at the top. Alone.

I untangle myself from the ropes and wait as Nick comes up after me. He grins as he pulls himself over the edge. "See, you can do anything if you set your mind to it." We look down to where the rest of the team is, but it's too foggy. "Come on, I think we have to go this way."

Nick's map reading skills are far better than mine, and he quickly susses out the direction we need to go. It looks like it shouldn't take too long, and we chat as we walk. The fog surrounds us so it feels like we are walking across a blank page. He starts talking about rock climbing and how he loves it because it pushes him and he feels unrestricted.

The ground gets boggy. My foot sinks into the mud, making me stumble. Nick quickly grabs me and stops me from falling. As he holds me, I get the feeling he is about to kiss me, but we suddenly find ourselves in the headlights of the minibus. "Ah, you made it," says the instructor congratulating us, "Well done on making it this far." He opens the door and I can see the rest of the team crammed in the back. As we get in the instructor tells us that the fog is too heavy to continue, after returning to pick the rest of the team up, they came searching for us.

I am not complaining. There are worse ways to spend a work day.

Wednesday 7 November

Nancy bumps into me as I arrive at work. "How is that audit going?" she asks casually. I assure her it's going fine and tell her that I am on top of it. "That's great because I want a draft copy by next Monday." My intestines turn to ice. I might have stretched the truth to Nancy a little. I meant I am on top of it in that it is on my to-do list as part of my Efficiency and Organisation Drive.

I felt the fact I hadn't actually started it was immaterial. It was there at the back of my mind, and surely it's the thought that counts? I am "on top of it" in a way though. I have collected all the information. All that remains is the slight matter of scoring it up, entering it into the database, processing it and analysing the statistics (sadly, the hard part). Then I have to write up the actual report.

A clinical audit is the opposite of all the interesting stuff I thought psychologists did when I was an undergraduate. There is no direct work with people. It's hard-core number crunching where you evaluate how a service "performs". The plain truth of the matter is that audits suck. We need to do them, but no one wants to volunteer. The consultant psychologists hand them over to the newly qualifieds, who hand them to the trainees, who in turn palm them off to us, the assistants. We only do them because we have no one else to hand them onto.

So, headphones in and playlist set, I slowly start going through the snowdrifts of paper that I was supposed to have processed several months ago. I also have to drag out and fire up the ancient steam-powered desktop computer where the database is stored. I hate this thing. It sounds like a jet engine taking off when it starts up, and will creak to a halt at the slightest pretext, ruining an entire afternoon's work.

I am not sure what these numbers mean to anyone. None of us ever use them, I think they go in a mysterious mail slot marked "management" where they are forgotten about forever. Every once in a while we get some meaningless circular, saying we worked at 76% efficiency in the last financial quarter, but without knowing any context this is meaningless. We were 76% efficient compared to what? What would 100% look like? What would 10% look like? Who even cares?

Me. I care, because as it approaches 5pm, I am not even at the point of properly getting started. I call home and tell my housemates not to expect me back until late. It's going to be a long night.

Thursday 8 November

It's the second day in a row where I have had to stay on until after 8pm. Reams of paper, multiple spread-sheets and hundreds of fiddly bits of paper have multiplied and even managed to force Olga to find somewhere else to work. She grudgingly grabbed her stuff and moved out to work in the staff room. My newly gained privacy is little consolation.

In the last 24 hours I have entertained the thought several times that I could just get up, walk out the door, and never return. Quietly slipping away has never been so attractive. I am on my fifth or sixth coffee of the day, and I am starting to develop a nervous twitch. Everyone else has left ages ago. Even the cleaners have done their rounds, and looked pityingly at me as they left. I have had to sweet talk the security guard into letting me set the alarm when I leave.

To rub it in, I get a text from Sarah asking me if I am up for going for drinks on the South Bank tonight with Scarlett and Boring Tom. I send a reply saying I would love to go and that I would prefer anything to entering file #3256 into my ever creakingly unstable spread sheet. I have mentally worked out that I can't leave until I get to #4500 and that is going to take at least another two hours.

The computer's hard drive grinds worryingly as the database AutoSaves. The idea that everyone else is out having fun, while I am stuck here makes my task even harder. My life wasn't supposed to be like this. I was convinced that being a grown-up was all about staying out until late, drinking red wine in a chic flat overlooking the Thames. Instead, I am sitting drinking instant coffee by myself in a cupboard next to the bins. It just seems spectacularly unfair in comparison.

Friday 9 November

I may as well not have bothered going home last night. My job was not helped by much of the data being missing, or badly organised by one of the other teams. Some of it doesn't even make sense. I read one report where someone's symptoms had kept escalating over the last four months, despite the records indicating the person had died in 1997. It must be a particularly skilled clinician who can assess people in the afterlife, or someone isn't doing their job properly. Someone who is no doubt paid more than I am, despite me having to fix their mess.

By 8pm the end is in sight. Everything is entered and it's time for the statistical analysis. Ordinarily this shouldn't be too difficult, but my lack of sleep and complete hatred for the task I am doing makes it a dozen times harder than it should be. I also fret that I am probably going to get it wrong and make hideous errors, but I steel myself and get on with it. Balancing the bulky statistics manual on my knee, I slot the variables into the statistics package and run the program. The computer whines and judders, but ultimately spits out the data that I need. I figure out what I need to write and get down to it. The cleaners and security guard, by now used to my nocturnal work pattern, wave cheerfully as they wish me a good weekend.

It will be. As soon as I finish this sodding report. I am going to do everything I can to ensure that after I lock up tonight, it will be the best weekend mankind has ever witnessed. It's the least I deserve after the last three days of hell.

Saturday 10 November

The universe thinks differently.

I awake to find myself run down and feverish. This is what comes from working too hard, and I will make sure that I think twice before I ever decide to do that again. I feel like I am slowly and painfully dying. I am not a happy bunny. I feel so bad, I mentally compose my will. I leave my laptop and books to Sarah, and my student loan debts to Mum. Scarlett gets nothing, as the loud braying laugh from her latest overnight guest kept me up until God knows when. What is worse, the damp patch in my ceiling has formed a proper crack that leaks water from some mysterious source, and the intermittent drips do little to raise my mood. I am abandoned by my housemates who clearly have better and more interesting things to be doing. Thankfully, a snivelling self-pitying Facebook update brings Justine rushing over with a flask of chicken soup to keep me company.

She perches on the side of my bed, as there is nowhere else in my room to sit that isn't covered in clothing, discarded magazines, or bits and pieces of application form. She seems happy to see me and starts talking as I greedily gulp down the only food I have had since breakfast yesterday.

"I bet you must be glad it's Saturday," she says. "I read on Facebook you have been snowed under at work. It must have been busy. You only updated your status once."

"Mmm, this is good," I say, handing her back the empty bowl for more. She dutifully pours in more soup, handing it back to me in a wary manner, as if she is worried that I will bite her hand off if she is not careful.

Justine remarks it is funny that Spiny has been ill too. According to Justine, Spiny has been on Twitter keeping everyone briefed about the colour of her phlegm (yellow-green, according to the last tweet). This image puts me off my soup, and I let the last dregs on my spoon fall back into the bowl. I get the impression that not a single thought or opinion passes through Spiny's head without being captured somewhere for posterity. I mentally congratulate myself for ignoring her repeated friend requests.

"She has finished her form, and sent off for her references."

"Good for her."

"She also put up pics of her new car, and her last trip to the beach. Cor, have you seen her boyfriend. Total hottie," she fans herself for dramatic effect. "It's purple. The car that is." I honestly can't bring myself to care about what inbred chinless-wonder Spiny has managed to sink her claws into, but hearing about it is making me tetchy.

"Justine, I forbid you to mention anything about that woman, her car, her holiday, or her perfect boyfriend, ever again in my presence." I say, putting my bowl down by the side of my bed. I need all my strength to recover, not getting worked up about that witch.

Agitated, I try to sit up straight in my bed and struggle to do so. Justine notices and plumps up my pillows, which I find incredibly comforting, and I feel a bit bad about snapping at her. Changing the subject, I ask her how her job is going. Justine starts talking enthusiastically about all the clinical experience she is receiving.

"I thought you were the receptionist there?" I say surprised

"Yeah, but I get to read all the clinical notes and medical records on my coffee breaks," she replies, obliviously.

I start to choke and cough. I tell Justine that she can't do that, and she needs to stop it at once. I explain that people's medical notes aren't there for her education, and emphasise the issue of confidentiality and having respect for people's privacy. Justine seems clueless and says no one ever told her this before. I get her to promise she will stop doing it from now on. She agrees and kindly tidies up some of my room before leaving me to have a lengthy recuperative nap. A nap that is improved by a dream of me running Spiny over with her new purple car.

Sunday 11 November

I am feeling a bit better, which means I will have to go to work tomorrow. Typical. However, Scarlett is less sympathetic and rolls her eyes at me before snorting, "Bloody hell! Give her some real work to do and the girl nearly dies."

This is ironic as Scarlett has never known a day of real work in her life. Her most concerted effort in the last month was when she spent an hour piecing together cigarette papers, before rolling a spliff the size of a marrow. However, when it comes to earning actual money, I have no idea where she gets her money from (I think drug-dealing or prostitution are the most likely sources, but Sarah tells me "not to be silly"). This is a particular sore point at the moment as the rent is due. Everyone is aware that a certain someone hasn't put her share into the joint account this month. Scarlett keeps assuring us that someone owes her a couple of hundred quid and she will get it soon.

"Soon" is not good enough I remind her. "Soon" is not going to satisfy the landlord. "Soon" is not going to prevent us from becoming homeless. Sarah pleads with her, telling her that we have to pay it soon and to borrow the money from her father if necessary. This makes Scarlett get stroppy and she tells us where we can stick our rent money and stomps off up the stairs. Left alone in the living room, Sarah and I then make small talk about our forms, and spend forty minutes discussing the acceptable use of abbreviations.

I have to move out of here before the last of my sanity disappears.

Monday 12 November

On the bus to work I imagine how I am going to stride into my supervisor's office and lay the report on her desk, to impressed looks of gratitude and gasps of amazement. My imagination wanders and I start to imagine how the report may revolutionise healthcare, or even save the NHS. I am mentally preparing my address to the World Health Organisation as I get off the bus.

I triumphantly walk into Nancy's office and announce the report is completed. She barely looks up as she takes the smartly bound folder from me and casually tosses it into her in-tray. She then starts telling me something about the group she is planning. I am not listening to her. All I can see is the report just lying there. I want to pick it up and thrust it at her, demanding she read it right this instant, ideally praising me while she does so. With considerable effort, I manage not to do this.

Instead, I walk out the door sulking about the lack of gratitude. I console myself that for all she knows, I did this months ago. To be fair, I did say I was on top of it, and she probably thinks all I did was press PRINT on Friday afternoon. I mentally resolve to keep cool and move on.

My resolve lasts an hour. I can't help sending Nancy emails that subtly drop in references to my report. (*"Did the audit report print out properly? Just checking"*, *"Did I give you my request for annual leave? I think I gave it to you when I gave you the report"*, *"Can I go with you for a joint visit next Thursday? As the report is done, I think I am free"*.) Embarrassingly, she sends a terse email back saying: yes, she still has the report; no, she hasn't yet read it; but she'll let me know if there are any problems when she does.

Despite this little hiccup, the rest of the day just seems easier. Better still, without the report hanging over me, the evening is full of possibilities. Cinema, art gallery or bowling (I haven't gone bowling since I was 12 but I could in theory). Then I remember that Sarah is on a late shift at the nursing home, and

Scarlett is out at a gig tonight and Justine is already going out this evening. With no one to share my freedom with, my elation slowly starts to drop. I am grumpily making myself a packet soup in the staff room, when Nick comes in. He thanks me for the report and I perk up, grateful that someone has finally noticed my efforts.

"It's great," he says, "But as you were the only one that handed it in on time, and none of the other teams have done it yet, we have had to extend the deadline for another two weeks..." The rest of his sentence is drowned out by my sobbing.

Nick, sensing he has said the wrong thing, sits me down, and asks me what is wrong. I tell him about the late nights I spent working on the report, that I was unwell over the weekend, and that I have an entire evening devoid of company ahead of me. I don't mean to say any of this, but it all comes spilling out. Nick puts his hand on my shoulder and tells me not to worry.

This is how I find myself sitting opposite him in an Italian restaurant after work, grabbing a bite to eat before catching a movie. "Was supposed to catch up with some mates," he says squinting at his phone, "but they have each other to talk to. I get a sense you may appreciate the company more."

I agree completely.

We end up at a bar after the movie (which was about as good as one can expect from a film that only constitutes of people jumping from buildings and things blowing up every 30 seconds) and the evening is certainly improved by Olga not being around. As we sit and chat, I am not sure if he is flirting, or if I am reading too much into the situation. He tells me about his plans and how he intends to take the next year off and maybe travel across South America.

"And will your girlfriend be going with you?" I ask, trying to fish about for some clarity regarding his relationship status. Infuriatingly, the waiter brings the bill at that moment, so the question is never answered. Hope can be the cruellest thing in the world, but it doesn't stop me daydreaming on the bus home about trekking through the Andes with Nick before I officially start my clinical training. In fact I am so deep in reverie, with a happy smile on my face, that I just miss my bus stop and end up having to do an undignified jump off at the traffic lights.

Tuesday 13 November

The Assistant Group this evening is completely dominated with how everyone is progressing with their form. No guest speaker is required. Spiny kicks everything off by announcing that she has already completed hers and submitted it. Apparently when she handed her form to her supervisor to sign off, she was told, "Definite interview."

You can almost taste the tension in the room.

After she finally shuts up, the rest of us mortals start tentatively discussing how we are doing. Without anyone giving too much away, there is a common consensus that you have to come across as having some sort of outside life, and not be a total nerd. At the same time you don't want to come across as if you may pose a problem because of all your various interests and demands. Or be seen as a weirdo because you are the custodian of Europe's largest collection of toilet paper cardboard tubes.

This leads on to a conversation about where to apply. Spiny is clear about this. She launches into a tirade about how there are only four courses worth applying to in the whole country and the rest are beneath consideration. By now even Meryl and Cheryl are looking at her funny. Spiny realises she's gone too far, and backtracks saying, "Of course, everyone else will have different needs."

However, she succeeds in panicking the group. The discussion descended into full scale speculation and rumour swapping as follows:

- Were courses with written tests easier to get into than

courses that do interviews alone? What about group tests?

- Did course A have 'better' placements than course B?
- Was it good or bad if service users and former patients were on the panel?
- What 'counted' as a disability?
- Did Course X prefer research assistants whilst Course Y values clinical? (Or is it the other way around?)
- Was it easier or harder for you if you were a bloke?
- Do they set your form on fire if you went to a former polytechnic?
- My cousin's previous dog's owner's ex-boyfriend went to this one course, and apparently the tutors all made the trainees stand in a row and cane their buttocks if they were late for lectures. Do they still do that?

I may have daydreamt the last one, but I have to actively keep myself from getting drawn into it. Bloke-whose-name-I-can't-remember makes the point of how the whole thing is a lottery and completely unfair. This strikes me as odd, because a proper lottery would ensure total fairness, as everyone would have an identical chance of being drawn out of the hat (even if they submitted a form with only their name and address). However, before I can point this out, everyone starts talking about font size.

As everyone else is talking I start to feel so far behind everyone else that I will never catch up. I fear I am going to need a time machine to get back on track.

Wednesday 14 November

We are in the living room arguing about what to watch on TV this evening. I favour a gritty police drama, ideally with a corpse being subject to some kind of farfetched scientific procedure. Scarlett would rather watch attention seeking members of the general public blessed with little talent or intelligence, cooped up in a prefabricated house. This starts off small, but quickly escalates and ends with an undignified grappling for the remote control. Eventually things hit a climax when Scarlett takes the incredibly childish step of standing in front of the screen, hands on her hips, so neither of us can watch what we want.

I turn to Sarah to back me up but find she is no longer there in the big armchair. I start walking to the kitchen to look for her, which makes Scarlett think she has won. She punches the air exclaiming "Yes!", flicks over the channel and dives onto the sofa. The living room is filled with the sound of half a dozen idiots howling "drink, drink, drink" on the TV.

I find Sarah in the kitchen staring at the sink. I go over to her and ask her what is wrong. "Nothing," she says, "I am just tired of you two fighting." She starts talking about how work today was a total nightmare from the second she started her shift to the moment she left the unit (two hours late, none of it paid). The patients were restless and demanding. Her boss was being vile. Her favourite co-worker quit because of a disagreement and no one is replacing her so everyone left on the roster will have more to do.

"Today they said they would start timing our toilet breaks," she moans. "I don't think my pelvic floor can take it."

I explain that all jobs are rubbish at times, but she ought to stay while she looks for something else. As soon as she gets something better she can leave. Just stick it out a little longer. She sighs and nods. However, as I walk away, I end up wondering if I am telling her this for her own sake, or for mine.

Thursday 15 November

I am wondering why I haven't heard from Nick for ages, when a frantic phone call at lunchtime breaks my reverie. At first all I can hear are heaving sobs. Justine. It sounds like she is in trouble, but I can't make out what she is saying. Eventually, she agrees to meet up with me and I catch up with her at the coffee shop. I don't even have time to order a drink before the whole sorry mess comes tumbling out. It turns out that Justine has just been fired from her job.

"I was only giving them advice about what I thought they should do." she yelps, blowing her nose on a tissue.

Yes, Justine has been giving people attending the surgery medical advice on a range of different conditions. A one-woman NHS direct. People would call in to make appointments, and Justine would shoot from the hip. From colic to impetigo, nothing at all was beyond her competency to diagnose or dispense advice about.

What I find even more disturbing is the fact that the patients just accepted it. Some were even happy about it. It was only when the service manager noticed that appointment bookings were down that she was rumbled. People were getting their consultations on the spot, so didn't bother to stay and see the doctor. It's only sheer luck that Justine didn't end up harming anyone.

Justine is not even aware that what she was doing was wrong. She justifies her actions as her trying to be nice, and that she got lots of compliments about how helpful she was. I explain that while that nice Dr Chakraborty may look like a chubby, ageing Omar Sharif, he also has attended medical school, and has decades of clinical experience. Justine still feels it is incredibly unfair, and perhaps she should take them to an employment tribunal. I tell her she is incredibly lucky she is not about to feature on *Crimewatch*.

Her mind then flits to how she needs a new job, and how her dad will go ballistic when he finds out. I try my best to calm her down, and suggest she goes to the Job Centre, or starts looking on various websites. This cheers her up, and she immediately gets over-optimistic about the possibility she may not even need a new job if she gets onto clinical training this year. It's at times like this I have trouble deciding whether she is just extremely childlike or simply dense. It could be both I suppose.

Friday 16 November

Work is impossible today. Every time I try to settle down and get anything done, I get a worried call from Justine. It feels like I literally have to hold her hand with everything. For example, I have to tell her that searching for work on the internet requires a bit more than typing "JOB" into Google and hoping for the best. What isn't helping is her dad continually having a go at her. I have to remind her that she isn't a failure because she hasn't managed to land a job in less than 48 hours, regardless of what he says.

My phone rings. Again. It must be my eighth or ninth call today. My reserves of tolerance are badly depleted, so I answer it with an exasperated, "What? What is it?! What more could I possibly do for you? Perhaps I can tell you how to use the toilet properly. Would you like me to do that?"

Unfortunately it is Nancy on the other end. An alarmed Nancy.

"Um, I am really sorry if this is a bad time", she says warily, "I just wanted you to know that I took your audit report home and read it last night. It was very good and you clearly put in a lot of work. I thought you wanted feedback as quickly as possible, but if this is a bad time..."

"No! Wait! That wasn't meant for you," I cringe. "Not the report I mean. That was meant for you. Obviously. I mean what I said when I picked up the phone. The toilet thing. Not that I normally talk to other people like that when they call me. It's just that my friend was fired for giving unqualified medical advice." Aware that I am probably making a bad situation worse now, I decide to shut up.

She pauses before replying, "I know you did quite a lot of late nights last week and I want you to promise me that you will try and get some rest this weekend. Take care of yourself, and I will catch up with you first thing on Monday." Great. I have now given the person who is responsible for my reference the impression that I have completely lost it. This is not the best start to the weekend.

Saturday 17 November

Eager to move on from the mistakes of the week, I wake up and start writing my form with renewed determination. To my surprise it is going well. I am writing quite a bit and all the boxes are slowly getting filled in. I am tempted to announce to the house, "Look at me! I am writing the most incredible form ever". In fact I am working so hard, my keyboard makes enough noise to wake Scarlett. She thumps on the wall yelling, "It's 11am. Some of us are trying to sleep". Feeling virtuous, I also go for a run, do a load of grocery shopping, and call my parents.

My buzz lasts until Sarah reminds me it's Boring Tom's birthday, and they have invited a few friends from his accountancy firm for dinner tonight. She mentioned this ages ago, but it just bounced off me at the time. I complain (quite reasonably) that surely Boring Tom should have his boring birthday with his own boring friends over at his own boring flat. Sadly, this isn't an option, as his landlord has arranged for some major building work this weekend.

"Don't worry," she says brightly. "You are invited to join us."
Hmm. Not too thrilled because a) I don't want to meet Boring Tom's boring friends, b) I had plans to work on my application form this evening, and c) being invited to your own house is hard to get excited about. I ask Scarlett how she feels, thinking I can stir up some opposition from her. No chance of this, she feels that it will be fine as long as there is plenty of booze. Outnumbered, I give in. I tell Sarah that I will come along, but warn her that I may disappear off early to my room. All of this is fine by her.

To be honest, it's not much of a party. Well not the sort of party that I am used to. There isn't any loud music, and people aren't dancing by moving spasmodically against each other. Instead, it's all very mature. About twelve of us squeeze around our hastily extended kitchen table, while Sarah serves coq au vin (not bad at all, but I note it is made with *my* garlic cloves I bought this morning). One of the blokes does that thing where he swishes the wine around his mouth before drinking it, announcing it "a wonderful year". Someone talks about changes to pension contributions and new tax formulas. The couple sitting next to me complete each other's sentences. Sarah winks at me from across the table, and subtly mimes sticking her fingers down her throat.

I look across at Scarlett to see if she is as bored as I am. I secretly hope she is planning on doing something dramatic, like farting loudly or announcing she is going to worship Satan (or possibly both). No such luck. She is shamelessly flirting with the two men she is sitting between. She is already on her fourth or fifth glass of wine, and is doing a good job drinking them both under the table. Sarah and Boring Tom try their best to keep me included in the conversation, but I am rapidly losing interest. After dessert is cleared away, I make my excuses and head upstairs.

Things are coming along quite nicely when I hear a discreet knock on my door. I look up as the door opens, and see the portly and slightly tipsy figure of George, the wine enthusiast at dinner.

"Just thought I'd see where you've got to," he says, unsteady on his feet. He carries a full glass of red wine in one hand, and is carrying the rest of the bottle in the other. "C'mon, have a little drink."

"Sorry, I have got a bit of work to do." I take my glasses off and press save on my computer.

"Making you work at home? On a Saturday night? And I thought we finance bods had it tough. Your boss must be a complete arsehole," he says, leaning against the doorframe.

"My boss is lovely, and no one is making me do anything. I just need to..."

George meanders over to my desk, and pushes his wineglass towards me. "Go on. It's a great vintage. Full-bodied and a little cheeky. A bit like you," he leers.

Unfortunately, his judgement is a bit off and the red wine sloshes over the rim of the wineglass. My anger spikes, as the wine splashes onto my notes, my computer, and over me. I pull the wineglass from his hand and yell at him to get out, searching desperately around the room for something to mop up this drunken fool's mess. As I go to grab the tissue box on the shelf, he lunges and tries to kiss me. He pulls me closer and I can smell the alcohol on his breath. His mouth inclines frighteningly towards mine.

Something snaps. I swiftly put the straight edge of my hand against his nose and move it backwards. His head recoils and he stumbles backwards. It's an unthinking reflex action, a legacy from Mum's paranoia and her enrolling me in self-defence classes as soon as I hit puberty. George yelps in pain, his grip loosening. The bottle of wine is now on the floor and its contents are draining away onto my carpet. I quickly break free and squirm away from him.

"You bitch!" he yells, as he staggers back to his feet. I am terrified. Self-defence is one thing, but George is twice the size of me. He rushes at me, and pins me up against the wall in a chokehold. All I can see is his red, angry, spittle flecked face getting closer and closer.

"I'll show you," he says ominously.

Only he doesn't. His expression changes to one of surprise as his head is wrenched back by Sarah. Tom (in a way that is not boring at all) helps her grapple with George, and together they get him in a headlock. Tom is a writhing blur of straw blonde hair and blue pullover, but Sarah is practiced and deliberate in her movements.

"You bastard," Sarah screams, as she expertly puts the flailing George into a restraint. "If you have hurt her, I will kill you."

Leaning on the wall and gasping for air, two thoughts cross my mind. The first is that Sarah can be loud when she wants to be. Second, is that her ward based control and restraint skills are frighteningly good. She belongs in *The Matrix*. Scarlett has come up the stairs by now to investigate, and helps Tom and Sarah bundle George back down the stairs and out through the front door.

The party is over. Scarlett and Sarah console me in my room. I am still quite shaken, but am starting to come down from the adrenaline rush. Sarah apologises, feeling guilty for allowing George into the house. I tell her she couldn't have predicted that kind of thing, and thank her for the rescue.

"And thank Tom too. I am sorry his party was ruined." I genuinely mean it.

It's quite enough excitement for me for one night, but clearly not enough for Scarlett who is making karate gestures and begging Sarah to show her some of those "psychology kung-fu moves".

Sunday 18 November

Sarah and I spend the morning clearing up the mess from yesterday, both from the dinner party and the spilt wine on my bedroom carpet. We spend ages scouring my carpet before admitting defeat. It's going to have to come out of our rental deposit.

When I eventually get around to re-reading what I wrote yesterday my heart sinks. What was written in the heat of enthusiasm now looks like utter crap. Clichés and nonsense. It could have been written by a monkey banging a keyboard against its forehead.

No one in their right mind would read this and think, "She is the one!" I come across as either a narcissist or as desperate. My personal statement is also way too long. What on earth possessed me to think it was a great idea to include my childhood thoughts about my grandma? Or made me think that my teenage experience as a waitress at the local Harvester was worth reflecting on? Why have I given a strong implication that my hobbies include *skydiving*? I have never skydived. I have no intention to. In fact I can think of nothing worse than an activity where you play "chicken" with the ground.

They are going to take one look at this and throw it in the bin. What makes it worse is that I really thought at the time I was coming up with pure gold. I try to go easy on myself and tell myself that being attacked by a stranger in my own bedroom is a pretty good excuse to have an off day, but I did write most of this before George had even arrived.

I hit delete and painfully start again from scratch.

Monday 19 November

"You need to calm down," Nancy says as we start supervision. "If you are like this now, God knows what you are going to be like by interview time."

She has a point. I recount the various events of last week. Although she is clear that supervision is not the same as therapy, going through everything in a systematic fashion has the effect of kicking my arse out of the cloud of self-pity. It's been a hard week but I (and my friends) have pulled through it.

The final point on our supervision agenda is my application form. I shamefacedly hand over my draft, and can barely look at her as she starts reading through it. I expect her to start laughing but she looks thoughtful. As she reads, I look out of her window and watch a small girl chase a plastic bag around a garden. The bag does not want to be caught and is whipped around in the wind. It's a strangely fitting metaphor, but my thoughts are interrupted by Nancy's voice.

"You have made a good start," she finally says. "Try not to be defensive or explain too much. Stick to the facts. Remember, it's not about listing what you have done, but more about what you have learned from the experiences."

"Okay."

She looks at it again and frowns. "Yeah," she muses, "there is something else. You don't really get your personality across in this."

"What if they don't like my personality?" I say, mindful that at times even I can't stand it.

"Then you are doing yourself a favour," she replies, "Trust me, you do not want to spend three of the most intense years of your life stuck with people that are not on your wavelength. Better they reject you for being you, rather than you having to pretend to be something that you are not."

I'm not entirely convinced about this. Right now, I would pretend to be Ultara the She-Demon from Mars if it would get me a place. However, I am pleasantly surprised that Nancy hasn't just crumpled up the form into a ball and thrown it in the waste paper basket. She tells me that she is more than happy to be my reference and wishes me luck with it.

As I get up to leave, she mentions the anxiety management group again and that she wants me to be more involved. As I have helped her run groups like this in the past, I say I will be more than happy to do whatever she suggests.

"Great," she smiles "It's probably going to be in the New Year, but I'll let you know more when I set the dates. Have a good week and I hope it's more pleasant than the last."

It had better be.

Tuesday 20 November

At breakfast, Sarah tells me she has seen an Assistant Psychologist job advertised online, and she is keen to apply for it. She hands over her laptop and I start scrolling through it. Certainly looks like a good fit. The job is local, and the more I read the job description, the more familiar it sounds. A horrible memory starts to surface. I realise they are re-advertising a post that I was rejected from last year.

Job Interviews I Have Messed Up. #2

This interview was one that I should have been a dead cert for. It was for a post in the same area where I was working as a research assistant, only with a clinical focus. Better still was the fact that I had prior contact with the team through various meetings. I also knew one of the people on the team quite well, a friendly psychiatrist called Ken. By the time I pressed SEND on the application, I felt I was practically an internal candidate for the job.

Aware of where I had gone wrong last time, I prepared obsessively. I made sure I knew everything the team was doing. I read their research papers and triple checked their website. I was ready for anything.

Unfortunately my previous familiarity worked against me because I got a little bit too sure of myself. So, when the panel introduced themselves, I greeted them as if they were old pals.

"Hey, great to see you all. What is Good ol' Ken up to these days?" was my opening line.

During the rest of the interview, I spent most of the time namedropping the nurses or letting them know I knew the heating in their portacabin was playing up. I spent far less time talking about the job I was being interviewed for.

My over egging didn't end there. They asked a very reasonable question about what support I might need to help me develop into the role. Instead of seeing this as a valuable opportunity to think about my strengths and weaknesses, like any normal person might, I opted to hammer down their throat the message that I really didn't need their thoughtful offer of guidance. I intended to hit the ground running. It was imperative they recognised *that I already knew everything.*

Except I didn't. Different team, different service and different job. In their feedback, they explained they needed someone who was willing to learn and open to developing new skills. If that meant they had to pick someone who didn't know the intricacies of their faulty heating system, then so be it.

They let me know that they would be offering the job to a fresh graduate. The graduate in question did a great job, and a few months later, used the experience to get onto a graduate medicine course. Hence the re-advertising. Sarah looks at it again and comments that if I didn't have a job already that this would be perfect for me. I quickly change the subject and pretend I am late for work.

Wednesday 21 November

The ever-efficient Brenda has written up her reference for me and forwarded a copy. It's pretty good and she has been far more positive than I expected. I can barely recognise the "efficient, capable and industrious" person she has described. I am not complaining, as I am more than happy to take my luck where I can find it.

Helpfully, she has even dropped in lots of details about when I went above and beyond the call of duty that I had forgotten all about. Some late nights, long distance data collection, and even the way I helped this foreign-exchange scientist one time. I had wiped most of this from my memory, and now wonder what else I have done that I should have remembered. Beaming proudly, I show it to Olga who raises a disbelieving eyebrow and asks, "Are you sure she hasn't got you mixed up with someone else?"

Thankfully Nancy doesn't share Olga's lack of confidence. This afternoon she sends me out to help with a case she is working on. A gentleman called Alan, with severe agoraphobia, that hasn't left the house for the last eight months. My job is to help Alan get more used to being outside. Although he has been meeting Nancy for weekly therapy sessions at his house, I am tasked with gradually getting him further beyond his front door. This is more like it. It is so much more rewarding to directly help people. It certainly beats the admin type duties I get stuck with in the Cupboard.

That is until I get to the house and it is pouring down with rain. Alan views me suspiciously through the letter box as I explain why I have been sent. He opens up the door and stares outside.

"I am not going out in that," he says looking doubtfully at the downpour.

"Look, you won't even have to get out of your slippers," I plead, trying to coax him at least onto the front door step. After an hour of negotiation and him gradually watching me as I get more and more drenched, he eventually agrees to step out for a second. Alan's motivation seems to be the prospect of getting rid of me rather than working to overcome his phobia.

"Yay!" I squeal unprofessionally, as he crosses the threshold. He peers out from under the awning, looks around, and goes back inside. He concedes it was not as bad as he thought it would be. I look pleased, but this is the moment the guttering above me decides to give way and I am soaked in stagnant rainwater. At least I amuse him enough to overcome his suspicions to agree to see me tomorrow.

Thursday 22 November

I spend the morning trying to catch up on my to-do list before heading out to my afternoon visit. Using the directions and prompts from Nancy, I get Alan onto the garden path, before he is beset by a barrage of negative thoughts. I reinforce that nothing went wrong, and while I could see that it was scary, remind him that he could do it. He seems dubious, but is impressed he got as far as he did today.

As I recount this story after work to Sarah, she starts smiling. I ask her what she finds so funny, and she points out the irony that all this is coming from someone who is a mistress of avoidance and not believing in herself. I tell her this is *so* not the case, and she points out examples of my cynicism and failure to act on opportunities.

"Take your thing with Nick," she says.

"In what possible way could that remind you of a man who can't get past his garden gate?"

"Well, you're avoiding calling him, so you haven't spoken to him for days. You complain about it, rather than *do* anything about it."

Without a credible counter-argument, I sit on the sofa sulking and guilt-trip her into making dinner. As she disappears off to the kitchen, I am determined to prove her wrong. I grab my phone and call Nick. I am free tomorrow night, and I scan the local newspaper for ideas about what we could do. As I am deciding between the cinema and the late night opening at the Natural History Museum, the phone is answered.

"Hello?" It's a woman's voice.

My mind goes blank. I panic, and hang up. Then I go wailing to Sarah.

Friday 23 November

"Did you try to call me last night?" asks Nick passing me in the corridor, as I am on my way out to visit Alan (Operation Garden Shed starts today).

"Um, not sure. I can't remember," I reply, not wanting to have this conversation in the middle of the corridor. Unfortunately, my response has the completely opposite effect.

"You are not sure whether or not you used your phone to call me less than twelve hours ago? Should we be checking you for early onset dementia?" he says, with mock concern. Feeling slightly stupid, I try to give the impression that my social whirlwind of a life leaves me little time to pay attention to every minor phone call I may, or may not, have made.

"Things have generally been quite busy," I say breezily, patting my bag. "In fact I am off now, to see someone. A gentleman actually."

Nick looks at me sceptically. "A gentleman?"

"Yes. Alan. We are going out somewhere." I neglect to add that a) Alan is a patient, and b) "somewhere" is nowhere more than 50 meters from Alan's front door.

"Oh, okay," he shrugs, "I was going to ask what you were up to later on. I haven't been around because my sister has been staying with me since getting out of hospital. She has needed a lot of support, but she is back with my parents now. I was free so thought we could hang out after work, but it sounds like you already have plans. Perhaps another time?"

Of course. Self-sabotage. Even the fact that I get Alan to the far end of the garden does little to improve my mood. When I get home, Sarah has to physically stop herself from saying, "I told you so." Instead, she shakes her head with weary disappointment.

Scarlett prefers to stir. Eavesdropping, she jumps in with, "You know just because his sister is staying with him, doesn't mean that it was her that picked up the phone. You could have been right in the first place. It could be a girlfriend. Or even a wife."

"Nick and I aren't engaged or anything," I say, refusing to give her any satisfaction. "I don't really care if it is his sister, girlfriend, wife, or any other of the 3 billion possible women on this planet who may have answered his phone."

"If that really is the case, why are you getting so touchy about it?"

"I can't have this conversation right now. I am busy and have stuff to do," I say stomping off up the stairs. This is technically true. I have been too busy being annoyed at myself to even check Facebook this evening.

Saturday 24 November

I oversleep, badly, which means I am horribly late to meet Mum. Not that she gave any warning, just a call last night announcing she will be coming to London today. Plus an instruction to meet her at Peter Jones in Sloane Square at noon for lunch. I rush around trying to find my keys, apply a spot of foundation (I am not big on makeup), and grab something to tie my hair back, so I can look halfway presentable. As I am hunting around the living room, a perky Sarah comes up to me asking, "Guess what?"

"Unless you have found my Oyster card, I don't really have the time to care right now," I say not in the mood to play games.

"Fine," she says, "I was just going to tell you that I have submitted my application form online. I am free to join you for lunch if you want."

I freeze. I know I should say something along the lines of "Congratulations" or "Well done", instead I blurt out, "But... but...how?"

"Well, you see I went onto this magic place called the internet, uploaded it on the website and pressed 'submit'." She hands me my Oyster card, which she has fished out from the jacket I normally wear to work.

"Are you sure?" I say, slightly alarmed.

"Yes. Pretty sure. The deadline is next Friday, and I thought it was probably a good idea to get it out of the way, so I can relax this weekend."

I feel a surge of panic. I feel horribly, horribly behind. I am reminded of all the times at university when Sarah diligently did all her coursework long before the deadline, while I struggled to pull an all-nighter while hoping the computer room printer wasn't out of order. I hated it then. I hate it even more now. Without any grace or consideration, I start muttering about how the whole world is against me.

"Wait. Are you annoyed at me?" she asks, any remaining perkiness draining quickly from her voice. "You had the same deadline as me. You even had help from your supervisor. Yet the world is against *you*. Are you mad? As for me coming with you for lunch, you can shove it up your bum and eat it by yourself."

Scarlett chooses that moment to wander in. "Sounds unhygienic," she yawns.

Sarah points at me. "Little Miss Centre-of-the-Universe here has managed to take the only thing I have been proud of all week, and turn it into something about her."

Scarlett mulls this over and shrugs, "Yeah, so what's new?"

This is *so* unfair. I do NOT turn everything into all about me. In fact, Sarah should look at Mum, who starts gabbling the moment I enter the top floor café, about how dreadful the traffic was and how busy she has been. She has to buy a hat for some wedding and the "ghastly shop assistant didn't know a fascinator from a fedora". She continues, unstoppable, as we finally find seats.

"Don't ask me how my last fortnight has been," I say, gazing out over the city skyline. "It couldn't possibly be as harrowing as your experience with the pay and display." Sarcasm flies straight over her head, and my eyes glaze over as she starts explaining why traffic wardens should learn their place.

I tune out and slowly start to play with my piece of cake as she continues to gossip. I know I need to apologise to Sarah. I didn't mean to take away from her achievement. I just panicked, that's all. I resolve to be less self-centred in the future, if for no other reason than to avoid turning into my mother.

Sunday 25 November

"I am sorry. I was out of order yesterday. What I should have said was 'well done'," I tell Sarah, as I stand in her bedroom doorway. I hold out a pack of her favourite biscuits that I tracked down in Selfridge's Food Hall yesterday.

"Thanks. I have a double shift today," she explains, stashing the packet away in her bag. "These will help keep me going." She gives me a quick hug and asks what I am planning on doing with my Sunday afternoon. I tell her that I am going walking on Hampstead Heath to get my head straight.

"Good," she remarks. "You probably need it."

As I walk around in the chilly winter afternoon, I realise that it has been a while since I have spent any significant time in a place that is not work, home, or that sells coffee. I am not sure how my world has become so narrowed. I am not this kind of person. I used to have several hobbies. I used to play tennis, and was no stranger to regular physical activity. I used to volunteer for things (real volunteering, not CV stuffing).

However, since I have left university these activities have gradually been replaced. Either everything is psychology experience related, or I come home so knackered all I am good for is vegetating in front of the TV. It takes all my energy just to get up the next morning to do it all over again. I pray that it is not going to be like this forever.

As I pass a few dog walkers, and head off deeper into the trees, I start to think about how there is a near constant bass line in the back of my mind wondering what will happen if none of my plans work out and I never get anywhere? Not just about the course, or even a career, but life in general. What if all the hard work and struggle is for nothing? For the last few years everything has been clearly marked and the decisions to make seemed obvious. School, university, work. Now, I feel like I am drifting in an infinite sea.

I sit down on a park bench and try my best to snap out of my self-pity. This isn't the real me, it's just the pressure. By next Friday things will be far clearer and settled. Surely, anyone would buckle under the task of having to justify their entire existence on a single piece of paper. I remind myself that in a few weeks it will be Christmas and I will be relaxing with my family. In a few months, I will know more about what I need to do next. In a few years, I will be sorted, and all of this will be a nostalgic memory I can tell to my kids.

I just have to stay calm.

Monday 26 November

How am I supposed to remain calm when the world has people like Spiny in it? This is the only thought that occupies my mind as I hear the familiar screech of "HI-YA!"

I am in the photocopier room and the machine chooses the moment of her arrival to start scrunching up the copies I have spent all morning sorting. It appears that Spiny has a similar effect on technology to that which she has on me. No doubt if she visited a farm, the crops would wither as she walked past. I wrench open the photocopier panel and fish around in the mechanical innards of the machine.

"What brings you here?" I ask, more out of courtesy than really wanting to know.

"Oh, just dropping off some data for the clinical studies team," she says looking at the photocopier with distaste. "I would offer to help you with that, but I have just had my nails done". She waves her French manicured fingertips at me by way of explanation. How does she manage to hold a pen or type on a keyboard with those?

"Don't worry, I think I have got this," I reply. I am wrong; I feel my hand get covered in something wet and sticky that may be many things, but definitely isn't the jammed bit of paper I am looking for.

"I also wanted to catch up with Nancy about something. Then I am meeting Nick for lunch..." she says glancing at her nails.

My hand involuntarily clenches. Something hard and metallic cuts sharply across my index finger. Damn. I pull out my bleeding and ink splattered hand. There is a thin laceration right across the finger, and I apologise as I hurry off to the ladies' loo. Not one for respecting personal space, Spiny follows me in. She stands near the hand-drier, babbling on as I gingerly wash my hand.

"Ooh, before I forget, how is your form coming along? The deadline is this Friday," she says, with far too much enthusiasm.

"Fine," I say trying to scrub away the stubborn black splodges. "Nancy has had a quick look through it and I just need to..." She interrupts my sentence.

"Nancy has had a look at mine, and says it's really good. I also had two other psychologists go through it. Really good feedback from everyone. It's been such fun to write it, hasn't it?" The acoustics of the toilet make her voice sound even more shrill than usual.

I can't bring myself to answer this. Instead, I dig around my handbag looking for a sticking plaster. Spiny doesn't even wait for a reply, and whizzes off for her meeting.

Later I am brooding in the Cupboard as I eat my lunch. I can hear her talking in the corridor to Nick. My mood is not helped by the salt from my crisps stinging my cut finger. Her high pitched voice reverberates down the corridor, and is contrasted by Nick's soft low murmur. Why do I let her get to me like this?

"You know she applied for your job you know? Before it was your job." says Olga wincing in the direction of Spiny's voice.

"No, I didn't know" I say, turning around. I shouldn't be that surprised. There are usually hundreds of applicants each time a post is advertised.

"She used to be friends with Rebecca, the girl who was doing your job beforehand. Then they had this big falling out when..." Olga's big reveal is cut short when the phone rings and she spends the next twenty minutes reciting random numbers down the receiver. Nonetheless, I am comforted to know my predecessor also left the Cupboard validating my opinion of Spiny. It's good to know I am not alone.

Tuesday 27 November

After considerable effort, planning and courage, Alan is able to make it down to the shops today. This is a huge achievement for him. I reinforce how well he has done, and help him go through the worksheets my supervisor has given him to plan for his next activity. He thanks me for taking the time to go through all of this with him. I tell him it is no trouble and agree to see him the day after, but encourage him to try again on his own tomorrow. He has started to trust me, and promises that he will. Justine also calls when I get back to the Cupboard, and tells me she may have a job lined up in the next few weeks. It's just as well, as she is getting frantic and has run out of money.

"Congratulations! What kind of job is it?"

"Oh, I am sort of an assistant," she replies.

"I am impressed. Is it anyone who works locally?" I am familiar with most of the local psychologists, and start thinking it could be fun to have someone I know around.

She thinks for a second. "I can't really talk much about it now. I will find out more when I start," she says.

This is some much needed good news for her, and I only pray she doesn't mess this one up. Sarah takes a slightly different view when I tell her afterwards.

"How come I didn't see it advertised?" she moans. "I have alerts set up on all of the websites, and I have been applying for anything that comes up within a 20 mile radius."

"I don't know. Maybe she heard about it some other way. Or a friend hooked her up?"

Sarah mutters she wishes she had friends who could hook her up. Scarlett, who has been dozing on the couch, manages to catch the last part of our conversation. Offended, she drowsily shoots back, "Unfair. I offer to hook you up with weed all the time."

Wednesday 28 November

"You know you are not paid to come in here and write your form?" Olga helpfully reminds me this morning. I am tempted to reply, "And you are not paid to be such an annoying sour-faced interfering old boot, so that's both of us misusing

95

company time."

I don't say this. Instead, I make a show of putting up an intimidating looking spreadsheet file, but secretly get back to re-drafting my form in the minimised window. I try adding the things Nancy suggested, but realise that this is near impossible. What does "more reflective" look like? How am I supposed to get my personality on a form that is supposed to be focussed on work? Do I write **I have experience of writing up assessment reports as well as being partial to Coco Pops? Though not when I put on too much milk and they get soggy, although I have since used this as an important learning experience and it is a good example of how I handle unexpected setbacks.** They really should teach you this at school rather than telling you the date of the Battle of Bosworth Field (which was 1485), or the relative atomic mass of Helium (which is 4).

Faced with the grim task of having to wade through it all, I do what I always do in this situation and distract myself by starting an argument with Olga. This works a treat. My form doesn't come on any further, and I do it so well, I am nearly late for my afternoon appointment with Alan (Post box at end of street).

Thursday 29 November

It's finished! It's finished! My form looks perfect. I have managed to successfully blend the various elements together to really show how my skills and outlook make me a brilliant candidate. The words effortlessly glide from my fingertips, and I know that the selectors will have to sit up and pay attention to my sparkling prose. The whole thing just hangs together beautifully. It feels just right.

Then I wake up.

My bedroom is freezing and the pile of paper lies accusingly on my desk. Aw hell. I can't do this. I don't want to do this. I mentally will it to be over. How can I be writing so much and expressing so little? The more I write, the more I have to cut down, so I'm spending more time hitting the delete key than save. I have started obsessing over whether I should remove commas, or even the dashes in compound words. I notice I use certain words too much. I notice I use "the" too much. I change all the bits where it reads "I feel" to "I think" as it makes me look more cerebral, then I change them all back because it makes me look too heartless.

How has anyone ever successfully written such an application? After going through all of this, I should be offered not just an interview, but a training place, and my first choice of the next three jobs after I qualify. Around midnight my head is pounding so much I have to admit defeat. I save my draft where it is and vow to wake up early to finish it.

Friday 30 November

6:00. I have been semi-awake for the last two hours with a churning gut and vivid anxiety dreams. The only thought that is occupying my head is that the form has to be submitted today at 1pm at the latest, and it's still not done. I can't face getting out of bed let alone look at that infernal document of Satan's.

7:00. I am eating breakfast and enviously looking at Sarah who has the smug, well-rested, fresh faced look of someone who hasn't left things to the last minute. This feels spectacularly unfair.

8:00. This is the earliest I have ever been to work. I look at the various drafts, re-drafts, supplementary notes, and sheets of feedback. I don't actually like any of them. Assembling various pieces from across 6 different drafts into one single coherent form is going to be like stitching Frankenstein's monster together. Only uglier.

8:15. Should my first world be "I". Does that sound too self-centred? Maybe "One feels..." Nope, note to self: I am not The Queen. Perhaps I should start with something dramatic and eye catching? Perhaps "OH MY GOD! LOOK BEHIND YOU, THE ROOM IS ON FIRE!" Maybe not the best idea.

8:45. Several deep breaths and have just started **Version_7_final_draft.doc**

9:00. Should I put more emphasis on my current job or the one that sounds more impressive? Or what about the stuff about my earlier influences? Surely that is more important.

9:10. I definitely should mention the disabled.

9:45. Read online advice about not stigmatising certain groups or objectifying their condition.
9:46. Removing stuff about "the disabled".

10:00. Should I use the reflections paragraph from Version 3 or Version 4?

10:10. It is definitely Version 4. It's far more real, and reflects on my motivations for this career.

10:30. No, that makes me sound too Emo. Version 3 it is.

10:50. I am not going to get this done on time.

11:00. Olga really, really needs to shut her stupid face. Does she suffer from some pathological condition that means she cannot stay silent? I am trying to put together the life experience section and keep typing the words she is yapping at me. I have just typed

...and an important formative experience was the time that the hairdresser decided that I may be better off with a side parting.

11:10. I have told Olga off. Maybe in overly strong terms, but she is finally silent.

11:12. I have wasted valuable time reassuring the admin lady next door that everything is okay.

11:40. Done! My form looks okay. Now I have to submit it online.

11:50. Why is the site so slow? Why does everyone else have to leave things till the last minute?

11:51. **404 Error message**. Please kill me now.

12:00. Aaaaaaggghhh I can't log on. NOOOOOOOOOO

12:15. I am on. The form isn't uploading properly.

12:30. IhatemylifeIhatemylifeIhatemylifeIhatemylife

12:56. Uploaded. Submit goddamn it. Submit. Why does the internet hate me?

12:59. It's in. OH YES! I CAME, I SAW, I CONQUERED. TRULY THEY SHALL IMORTALISE TODAY IN LEGEND AND SONG!

13:00. What have I just done?

13:05. Spotted typo. Just a minor thing. Probably no one will notice it.

13:14. Another misplaced comma. Oh hell.

13:20. Have to physically stop myself from looking at the submitted form.

14:00. Have apologised and managed to stop Olga crying.

18:00. Just got at home and receive this email notice:

We are currently experiencing technical difficulties. Due to the high volume of applications, and issues with our servers, we have reports that many applicants are unable to submit their documents online. Therefore we are extending the deadline until Monday.

Rage to Sarah that this is completely unfair and that people should be more organised, and I am now at a disadvantage as I could have really done with extra time to check my application. Or give me extra points for getting through before the "real" deadline.

Sarah stares me with chilling contempt. I decide to shut up.

DECEMBER

Saturday 1 December

I haven't slept this well since I was a child. There could have been a rock concert in the front garden and I wouldn't have noticed. I wake up hungry, but am still a bit groggy. I grab my mobile and phone Sarah to bring me a cup of tea and a couple of slices of toast.

"I am not your maid. Bring it yourself. I can't believe you are using your mobile to call me in the next room," she says, irritated. "You know, I would love to spend the day in bed, but some of us are already late for work."

I groan and tell her that it's an emergency, but she hangs up on me. I swing my hand over to grab my laptop. I will get up in a second I tell myself, just after a little computer aided assistance to wake me up. I hear the door slam as Sarah rushes off to work.

After ninety minutes of watching YouTube videos of cats falling off roofs, Americans getting hurt in a variety of interesting ways and three reviews of long forgotten 90's cartoons, I realise this is not helping me get out of bed. What finally gets me up are the raised voices from downstairs.

"Your grandmother didn't leave you that money to fritter it away like this," says an unfamiliar posh male voice.

"You can go and fuck yourself!" shrieks Scarlett.

"I would be grateful if you could be slightly more civil when you address me," replies the man.

I slowly plod downstairs. Scarlett immediately stops arguing as I come in the living room.

"Ah, yeah. Sorry we woke you." she says looking awkward, "Uh, this is my dad". I turn around to say "pleased to meet you", and stop in my tracks.

Scarlett's dad is a vicar. Dog collar and everything. This explains *so* much.

I manage to shake off my initial shock and introduce myself, but am not really sure what to say. I wonder if I should address him as Your Holiness or if that is just reserved for the Pope. Hell, I can never remember this sort of thing.

"Oh, lovely to meet you. It's always nice to meet Faith's friends," he says sweetly. I think he is using some quaint religious turn-of-phrase, but realise he is addressing Scarlett. "Faith, would your friend like to join us?"

"No, we don't have time now for all that," says Scarlett hurriedly. "We're just heading out, and she takes too long in the shower." Scarlett grabs her dad's arm, and ushers him into the hallway.

"Nice to meet you, your worship," I say, not really thinking about the words coming out of my mouth. Well, isn't that a turn up for the books? I watch them go down the path, open the gate and get into her dad's Vauxhall Astra. Scarlett/Faith angrily gesticulates at him as they drive off.

I fix myself some breakfast, have a shower, and then get around to doing some long neglected laundry. I have avoided most of my chores for ages. I am in the middle of tidying the bathroom, when I hear a noise from downstairs.

"Sarah is that you?" I ask.

"Nope, it's me," answers Scarlett. "Sarah has a double shift today and is on nights." I come out to the kitchen, trying my hardest not to grin.

"Hello, Faith!" I mock.

"Don't start. I am not in the mood, and if you ever call me Faith again, I will break your legs," she says menacingly.

I can't stop myself, I am on a roll. "I never knew your daddy was a vicar, Faith," I tease. "Could have been worse I suppose. He could have called you "Chastity". Wow. It must have been just like *Footloose* growing up with you two in the house."

"You can fuck right off," she says eyes narrowing as she fetches a stashed bottle of Vodka from the shelf, "I got enough of that shit at school, I don't need any from you." She liberally splashes a shot into a wine glass (the only clean glasses we have left in the house), and downs it in one.

"I never took you for the religious type," I press on. "How did you survive all those sermons and moralising".

"Oh, I don't know. I manage to survive fairly well living with you." She pours herself another shot.

Humph. Not being able to think of a decent comeback I ask, "What was he was doing over here this morning?"

"Being an arse," Scarlett looks morosely into the wineglass, contemplating another shot. "He came around to tell me that he can't take me out for my birthday."

"When is that then?" I ask trying to remember.

"Today."

"Oh, happy birthday." I say lamely.

"Don't bother. No one else did."

I try to remember what Scarlett normally does for her birthday. I always assumed she went out with her friends in bands, or whatever other people that she prefers to party/take illicit substances/sleep with. Looks like I am mistaken.

"Normally it's just my family and Sarah," she explains. "But she is working her double shift tonight, and Dad is going away with Adam."

"Adam? Adam who?" I say, wondering if she has mentioned a brother before.

"His boyfriend" she says.

"Fuck me! A *gay* vicar." I blurt out.

I really have to stop doing this. Scarlett slams her glass down, sticks two fingers up at me, and walks off.

"No, wait. Scarlett," I say, rushing after her. "I didn't mean to say that. It's just the shock. Listen, I know it's not the same as your family and Sarah, but I am free. I mean, I can do something with you. If you want to."

She stops and thinks about it.

Sunday 2 December

Its 4am. I have no idea where I am. Somewhere north of the river I think. My ears are still ringing because we were standing way too close to the amp at the gig we have just come out of. My breath condenses in the freezing December night. I have no idea how much Scarlett and I have drunk, but it's a lot. I wouldn't even be standing if I hadn't just fortuitously vomited most of it up, along with the best part of a kebab. I missed the nearby bin I was aiming for. A stray dog has come over to the steaming puddle, and takes a few licks. It looks up at me disapprovingly and trots off. The dog is right. I am a disgrace.

"Come on, Miss Bossypants," Scarlett giggles, as she takes my arm and drags me into the middle of the road. "Let's have a little sit down," she suggests as she slides onto the asphalt.

"Probably best not here." I say, pulling her back towards the pavement.

"Spoilsport," she slurs. She reluctantly sits on the kerb. "So tell me about this Nick bloke? Are you shagging him or what?"

"No."

"You should. You could do with it." she says, laughing at her own witlessness. "Or at least ask him out." I try to pull her to her feet to stop us both freezing to death. "Wait! I have an idea," she says getting steadily to her feet and regaining her balance.

The wall is high, but we somehow manage to scale it. Our Doc Martens are surprisingly good at getting purchase on exposed brickwork. We creep across the lawn and hide behind a shrub. A large three-storey Victorian house stands before us. It's mainly dark, but a few lights are on in the higher windows.

"I feel ridiculous," I whisper. "Why are we doing this again?"

"Because it's hilarious. And it's better than listening to you go on about your application form," replies Scarlett. I am about to tell her that is all done now, but she puts her hand over my mouth. "Shh! Wait. Look over there."

We catch a brief glimpse of a figure quickly walking past a set of bay windows. We try to creep along by the wall and follow it. The figure turns up a corridor. Scarlett taps on the window nearest us. We duck and cling to the wall and can see the person's reflection in the darkened window. An obscured outline looks out, before turning and heading up the corridor.

Scarlett has scrambled up some stone steps, and glances

through the glass panel of a fire escape. She grabs a handful of gravel and throws it against the glass panels of the door. The figure spins around and walks purposefully towards us. I am bricking it, and hold my breath as I try to back myself further into the shadows. The door opens up. "Hello?" a female voice speaks out into the silence. Scarlett gets up to move, but a security light comes on.

We are blinded and exposed.

"You nearly gave me a heart attack. Have you two not got anything better to do?" says Sarah shaking her head. We sheepishly smile and she lets us in through the fire escape. She guides us down a maze of corridors until we come to the nurse's locker room. She tells us to wait there until her handover in about an hour.

"You have to be quiet. If Debbie finds out, I am going to be fired," she whispers.

Waiting for her, we manage to smuggle some breakfast off a food cart Scarlett spotted near the door. We hungrily cram fistfuls of toast into our mouths, not even bothering to chew.

"That was so much fun," I say, as I warm myself on the radiator. "Did you see her face?"

Scarlett nods, butter and jam smeared on the side of her mouth. "Wicked," she grins, "Best birthday ever."

Monday 3 December

Like the ending of a crappy horror film, just when I thought the whole application form thing was over, I realise how mistaken I am. Nancy emails me, asking when the deadline for her reference is. I panic as I assume it was yesterday.

A quick call to the central clearing house informs me that my fretting is unnecessary. She still has until next Friday to send things off. I quickly email Nancy the date, who assures me she will get straight on it, and have it back to me soon.

On a much happier note, Nick emails me, suggesting we meet for lunch on Friday. Aware I acted like a bit of an idiot last time, I write back immediately, accepting his invite. I deserve some fun for once. Who knows, maybe I will take Scarlett's advice, and ask him out. (No, not *that* bit of her advice. Well, not yet at least.)

Tuesday 4 December

"Straight on it" must mean something slightly different in Nancy's world, because when I ask her about it this afternoon, she still hasn't written it. I feel tense and on edge. The final deadline is next week and I really don't want to be going up against everyone with a blank reference. I also know for a fact that she is going away for the weekend, so she has to get a move on.

Olga is ignoring me. She says that she isn't paid enough to put up with this. She rounds on me when I try to tell her about the whole reference thing. She says that the last two weeks has been like working in a tiger's cage. I have no idea what she is talking about, and tell her she is overreacting.

"Bloody assistants!" she mutters, before cursing in her mother tongue.

She is such a drama queen.

Wednesday 5 December

We are holding the Assistant Group meeting early this month, because most of us are going to be away over Christmas. As usual we pile into the long-forgotten corner of the local mental health unit after work, and try to arrange the seating to accommodate everyone. The squeeze is because of the larger than usual number of new faces -probably new graduates- so half of us end up sitting in each other's laps. Not what you want to be doing at 6:00 pm on a freezing winter's evening; everyone is wearing their heaviest winter coats.

Sarah and I sit towards the front, along with the regulars. The new folk all hang around in a bunch, shyly talking to each other as more people arrive. Spiny, of course, takes her self-appointed role as mistress of events, her blond shoulder-length hair swishes about as she gestures animatedly at the newcomers.

I predict she will be three-quarters of the way through her CV by now.

Sarah has started talking to one of the newbies, Megan. She seems a fairly affable girl (and I do mean *girl*; I look like a withered old crone in comparison) who has been working as a support worker in one of the learning disability units. She just started two months ago after graduating, and is still getting her head around everything. Sarah explains what to expect and points out some of the more familiar faces. Megan looks on with wide eyed admiration.

"Relax," I want to say "By the time you have been to a couple of these, you will be itching to go home at 6:30, just like the rest of us." I don't. Far be it for me to burst her bubble.

Spiny officially welcomes everyone and starts the meeting. Sarah suggests we get the newcomers to introduce themselves, and we go around. There are a few men, but it's mainly women in the new crowd. One or two have jobs as care assistants or voluntary posts, but most have just started looking after the long care-free summer after graduating. The Unholy Trinity do a good job at patronising them. Cheryl in particular when she talks about how, if they follow their advice, they too one day will be able to reach the heady heights of the £18k salary of an Assistant Psychologist.

The graduates react in horror.

We don't have a speaker, so after going through the minutes, and talking about what is happening in the local area, we get onto discussing how much of a nightmare filling in the form was. Guy-whose-name-I-can-never-remember complains about the form system crashing, and how he nearly threw his monitor out of the window trying to get it uploaded. Others sympathise. Not Spiny, who delights in telling us she had hers couriered up by Federal Express at great expense.

"Is she always like this?" asks Megan, looking worried.

"No," I reply, not taking my eyes off Spiny, "She's not normally this nice. She's usually unbearable."

Thursday 6 December

What the hell is taking Nancy so long? Can't the dozy bint just get her act together and put a few words on a blank piece of paper? I mean how hard can it be? Has she forgotten how to read and write despite holding a doctorate? Obviously, I don't say any of this to her face, but do send out a few more gentle reminders asking if there is "anything I can do to help".

Mum calls me asking when I am coming up for Christmas, and for how long I will be staying. They have plans for my room. I feel oddly hurt and offended by this and tell her I hadn't decided, but had hoped my arrival would be met with happiness rather than be seen as an obstacle to plan around.

"Stop making such a fuss," Mum says. She then goes on to make her own fuss about people coming over for Christmas, do I want a pair of gloves (no), an Xmas stocking (yes, of course) and will I be there for New Year's (still not sure). I tell her I will be coming up on the twentieth of December, which is when my annual leave starts. She makes an impatient sigh and tries to guilt trip me into coming sooner. Not a chance. She will have me cleaning the cupboard under the stairs, and running errands in town if I stay too long.

Friday 7 December

Nick comes around for our lunch date just before noon. He is cheerful, and just listening to him raises my spirits. He asks me if anything interesting has been happening, since I have reclaimed my life from the dreaded application form.

I fill him in about Scarlett's dad, our nocturnal visit to Sarah, and the meeting on Wednesday. I continue for a good twenty minutes about Spiny being on top form at the last Assistant Group. Aware of how she is around him, I warn him to stay away from her, for his own sake.

Nick looks bemused. "Well, I will try to keep that in mind, but it may be a bit hard. She is my girlfriend after all."

My insides turn into icy water. Spiny is the rumoured mysterious girlfriend? Is he fucking kidding me? Out of three billion women, he picks the worst specimen of womanhood imaginable? I struggle to think of what to say next.

A thought hits me. "Wait. You have sat with me for half an hour, while I have been openly bitching about your girlfriend? Not to mention what I have been saying over the last three months? And you didn't think to tell me?"

Nick shrugs. "You seemed to be having such a good time ranting. I didn't want to stop your fun. I thought you already knew. I mean, isn't that why you kept bringing her up in conversation?"

"In an entirely negative way. Of course I didn't know!" I feel like a total idiot.

"I thought it was all part of your refreshing honesty. You know, the way you go on about your dingbat doctor's receptionist friend, and your weirdo housemates."

I realise I may have been just a tad critical in our previous conversations, but at least I don't casually conceal the fact that I am dating someone who belongs on *Made in Chelsea*. It makes for an awkward lunch.

"Oh, I see," says Sarah, when I get home and spill the news. "No wonder she wants to show you up half the time. She is seriously threatened by your interest in her boyfriend." Scarlett is even more straightforward. According to her, I should make an all-out effort to bang Nick immediately, ideally on National Health Service premises, preferably in the patients' waiting room. She frames this as a win-win situation as I would both be accomplishing a personal goal, and smiting a much-hated foe at the same time.

"Stop telling me to have sex with everyone," I answer back. Their comments aren't helping. I am still annoyed, and feel betrayed. I don't know what to think any more.

Saturday 8 December

I wake up in a foul mood. It's not lifted by everyone on Facebook talking about raucous Christmas parties, writing updates about spending Christmas Eve in the Maldives, or uploading photos of couples smooching under the mistletoe. I irritably snap shut the cover of my laptop, convinced that the entire internet is a conspiracy to rub in my face the fact that the entire world is happily paired up apart from me.

Sarah comes into the kitchen to make some tea and asks me what is wrong now. I tell her that I am just annoyed that everyone seems to have someone; Mum has Dad; she has Tom; and Scarlett has half of East London. Even Olga with her uni-brow and B.O. has Rasputin (obviously that is not his name, but that is exactly who he looks like); while the only viable hope I have had in God knows how long is literally sleeping with the enemy.

"Do you think your naturally cheery disposition, and laid-back attitude may be getting in the way?" asks Scarlett, getting her own back at me. I protest, but she stops me. "Look, you are blowing this all out of proportion. You work with women. All your friends are female. It's natural that the first bloke, in fact the only bloke that comes along, makes you swoon like he is Johnny Depp. You know what you need?"

No go on. Let's have it. What do I need? A fairy godmother? A make-over? A video montage, set to 80s music, of me learning how to dance? I am just dying to find out Scarlett's answer.

Sunday 9 December.

I am never going to listen to Scarlett again as long as I live.

"Trust me, you will like him. He is into the sort of stuff you are," she says, scrolling through her extensive list of telephone numbers as she tries to set me up on a date with her friend, Theroux. This is how I find myself sitting in an All Bar One looking for someone who "looks arty". How I even agreed to leave the house to meet someone with such a vague description is beyond me. She may as well have said that he looks "like a Londoner".

I am reliably informed that Theroux has admired me since a party at our house last August. I do my best to keep an open mind, and try not to linger too much on the fact that he completely failed to register on my radar. I scan the room, glumly noting that practically everyone in the bar could be described as "arty".

I am bored waiting. I have read the food menu for the fifth or sixth time. I am reduced to playing the game of, "How bad would it be if I was made to eat my absolute worst menu choice?" (Pretty bad as it turns out. They have liver and onions on here.) I suddenly get a tap on my shoulder and turn to meet...someone who I would have bet money on that I have never seen before in my life.

"Hey. It's *so* good to see you again," he says. I say hello and smile, pretending that I remember him.

112

Theroux (christened Raymond), sits down and disapprovingly looks around the bar. "I just can't stand chain places," he sneers. "They are just so inauthentic. Full of hipsters being ironic."

Not really sure how to answer that, I just keep flashing my pretend smile and hope to God there is nothing stuck in my teeth. I soon find out not knowing how to answer anything is not going to be an issue. Theroux is happy to monopolise the evening talking about his favourite subject. Himself. At great length. His work (he describes himself as a kind of poet/songwriter. The kind that sponges off his mother); his taste in music (something that is frighteningly obscure yet trendy); his favourite films (*Fellini's 8 1/2*, which I have never seen nor really want to truth be told); his day (you-would-not-believe-it); his views on politics (almost dictated by *The Guardian*). Plus many, many, many more interesting, essential Theroux-facts™ that the world is dying to know. Perhaps there will be a quiz afterwards, where I can win a prize for remembering Theroux-related information.

In addition to "Hello", I think I have said ten words throughout the entire evening. I know six of them were, "Just nipping off to the ladies". Not that Theroux seems to care. He is so self-absorbed, he doesn't notice me sinking into a pit of hopelessness. After a while I just tune out and start day dreaming.

We call for the bill. He motions that he will pay but I insist on splitting the bill with him. I really want to be under as little obligation to this man as possible. He grumbles, but what can he do? Wrestle the waiter to the floor and thrust the whole amount, plus tip, into his card machine? He suggests we go for a drink afterwards, but by now my brain is full to capacity with Theroux-related trivia, so I make an excuse about work the next morning. Managing to narrowly avoid a kiss, and end with a handshake, I skilfully extract myself. This is the only good thing that happens all evening.

"What the hell did you mean that I am into the same stuff he is?" I ask Scarlett, as I crash onto the sofa.

"Well, you both do talk about yourself a lot. I thought you might get on."

I tell her about the absolute wreck that my evening turned out to be, and she bursts out laughing. I am not sure if this was a deliberate wind-up, or if she was genuinely trying to help.

Monday 10 December

Nancy is not best pleased with my numerous reminders. She summons me to the office first thing. With icy detachment, she explains that she has to manage half a dozen people, treat an individual caseload of twenty patients, and has just had to contend with a death in the family. She is sorry that she is a "bit preoccupied", but my reference was slightly lower on her to-do list than arranging her mother's funeral.

Perhaps I have been a little pushy.

With a face like thunder, she hands over my reference and asks me if I care to comment on anything I disagree with. I quickly read it over. I am truly grateful to note that she hasn't painted me as an ungrateful, insensitive drama queen who has no appreciation of the concept of patience. On the contrary, she has been quite balanced. I may have once felt offended by the comment about my "awareness of the priorities of others", but considering the circumstances, I feel it's entirely justified.

I go back to the Cupboard feeling wretched. Nancy has done nothing but help me. The least I could have done is cut her some slack with this. Its only now I realise how pushed to the edge I am. I have to relax over Christmas and try not to let things get out of perspective.

Tuesday 11 December

"Have you been avoiding me?" asks Nick, as he busts me trying to dodge out as he enters the photocopier room. Despite my blatant near U-turn on spotting him, I try to imply he is imagining things.

"Oh, that's good. We can have lunch together," he says.

Checkmate. As we sit in the staff room I start to tell him I am worried I may have messed things up with Nancy. He listens to what I have to say and thinks for a second.
"Sounds like you need to apologise to Nancy. She has been through a lot". I agree with him and after discussing how I could make amends, we decide that I could get her a potted plant for her desk and some cake. It may not make up for my recent behaviour, but at least it's a start.

He also says that I should be kind to myself, and points out that the application process is not over yet. I wonder how he is so knowledgeable about it, but then realise he has probably had to put up with the whole thing with Spiny.

"Try to put it out of your mind. At least until February when the letters come back with whether or not you get an interview. Don't worry about it until you have to." he says, looking concerned. I nod, and ask him how his own plans are going.

Nick is seriously rethinking his own future. He complains that the trouble with ambition is that the advertisement is a lot better than the ride. He talks about his friends who have burnt themselves out working 70 hour weeks in labs. The best days of their lives spent hunched over agar plates and test tubes. He is keen to have something more positive to look back on his deathbed than a handful of publications that no one is ever going to read. I am taken aback by how strongly he feels about it. He notices my shock and softens his tone.

"Ah, don't listen to me. Do what you feel is right for you, but keep an open mind. Whatever happens, in February, whenever, don't change too much. You don't need to. You are great as you are."

I am moved by this, and I tell him that I am sorry that I've avoided him. I explain that it got a bit weird because of the whole Spiny thing.

"Hey. We're not Siamese twins." he says. "Just because her and I are dating doesn't mean we don't see things differently. If you don't like her. I can live with that. If I am honest, I'm not even sure I do at times."

Ooh, do I detect possible trouble in paradise? I decide not to push it, or get my hopes up. I'm just glad we are on speaking terms again.

Wednesday 12 December

I leave a potted plant and a small chocolate gateau on Nancy's desk before she arrives this morning. It seems the right thing to do. I then tackle the mountain of paperwork that has built up. I need to finish everything before the holidays if I am to avoid getting into serious trouble. I estimate I have about a week to cram in several weeks' worth of work. However, after the pace of last month, it will be straightforward by comparison.

I also get a postcard from the clearing house on my doormat when I get in from work. It tells me that both my references have arrived, and all the documents are in correct order. I feel distinctly under impressed by its puny size. I expected something far grander, like a trumpeter arriving on an elephant or something.

I get a Facebook message from Theroux suggesting we meet up. I decline his request and send him a message back suggesting how about we don't. I have no intention of having an encore of Sunday night. This leads to an argument with Scarlett when I get home for being too picky and not giving people a chance. I calmly tell her that if Theroux was to become the last living man on earth, I would rather date a random monkey.

She mulls it over in her head for a second. "That is assuming the monkey would want to date you."

Thursday 13 December

I am diligently working away at the stack of paperwork, when a sharp knock at the door breaks my concentration. Olga opens it and welcomes in an unfamiliar woman.

Olga completely neglects to introduce me to her, but after spending a good five minutes catching up, the woman introduces herself.

"I'm Hazel. So, are you the new Rebecca?" she says, offering out her hand. I shake it and introduce myself, trying my best not to be miffed that I am not the 'new' anybody, but am instead the 'old' me.

It turns out that Hazel used to be a former Cupboard-mate of Olga's, but is now an administrator in public health. She was on Olga's research team while she was here, but left the year before I arrived. From their conversation, I work out that there used to be three people squeezed in here, Olga, Hazel, and the aforementioned assistant, Rebecca. I can't imagine how that would have worked out. Perhaps they worked standing up? Or sitting on each other?

Hazel wistfully looks around the greying walls, the peeling paint and the light dusting of cobwebs in the corners. She says it hasn't changed a bit. She then talks about how she and Olga spent many a happy hour squeezed in here drinking endless cups of herbal tea. The way she goes on about it you would think she was describing a previous summer in Ibiza.

Hazel tells us about her swanky new job, mentioning she even has her own office now and a higher salary. A tad insensitive I feel, but Olga doesn't seem to mind. They talk about some former manager that used to cause them much misery. Hazel inquires if Nick is still up to his old tricks, which prompts Olga to groan, and imply little has changed. Intrigued, I listen closer for what "old tricks" these may be, but Hazel goes on to talk about something else.

Sweeping her gaze around the Cupboard, she remarks how the place used to be so much tidier when Rebecca was here. This opens some floodgate and prompts a lengthy tribute to St. Rebecca, our Blessed Lady of the Cupboard.

I haven't heard much about Rebecca before. However, Olga and Hazel soon fix this. They can barely count the ways in which Rebecca was amazing. She was *so* efficient and organised. She always had a smile on her face and a song in her heart. She could soothe the stroppiest patient, tame the haughtiest receptionist, and produce huge data reports in a single bound. Not only was she a certified genius, she was beautiful and really ought to have belonged in a shampoo advert. Everyone loved her, and she was especially kind to small animals and orphans. She got on training first time round with four offers at the most over-subscribed courses.

"It's not quite the same," Olga wistfully sighs, with the same look in her eye that some people get when they talk about Princess Diana.

I look around. My desk is messy; I haven't indexed my flip charts or alphabetised my marker pens. I am never impeccably styled and don't bring in homemade brownies that I happen to have made in my spare time. I am not destined to ascend to heaven with only a slight detour for clinical training. I decide at this point to take an extremely strong dislike to Hazel, and an even stronger dislike to sodding Rebecca.

Not able to take much more of this, I leave them to it. Outside, I see Nancy coming down the corridor. I tell her that Hazel is visiting and she says she will pop around to say hello later. I walk with her to the copier room, casually mentioning that they were talking about Rebecca.

"She was alright I suppose. The assistants we pick are all pretty good," she says, loading up her print job. The machine jams instantly. "What the hell is wrong with this machine?" She squints at the copier display and randomly jabs at various buttons. I swiftly unclog the jam and press RESET for her. She smiles gratefully.

"I will tell you what. She isn't half as handy to have around as you are." This makes me happy for the rest of my day.

Friday 14 December

Tonight is the office Christmas party. Although Nancy doesn't come (her mother's funeral is tomorrow), everyone else is attending. The admin staff, receptionists, medics, nurses, the entire research team, Olga, and Nick (not Spiny and the IAPT horde. We would need to book Wembley stadium if we were to invite them, and they would still probably manage to trash the place).

In high spirits we make our way along to the Italian restaurant we booked. It's tucked off the high street, but it's only when we get to the door that my instincts tell me something is wrong. It's too quiet. I realise the reason why, as a wall of hot air hits me as I go through the door. The restaurant has the temperature of an oven, despite it being near arctic outside. This means we have the option of roasting near the kitchen, or having regular blasts of wind freeze us every time the door opens.

The waitress seems to have no idea about how many people have booked, or what we pre-ordered. None of us can remember either, because we ordered it in mid-September. Judging by the taste of my dinner, they had started cooking it around the time we placed our order. Leathery meat and vegetables with any remnants of taste long gone. It makes hospital food seem like gourmet cooking by comparison. Only Olga seems happy with her food, suggesting there are at least some advantages to growing up in a former Soviet republic.

Nick makes exaggerated disgusted faces from across the table, which makes me laugh and spill spaghetti bolognaise into my lap.

Afterwards, we escape to a bar around the corner. We all drink heavily as if to wash away the taste of dinner. The atmosphere starts to lift, and I slowly start to relax. As more red wine flows, one of the nurses gets up to dance. Dr Anafu, who must be in his late 60s and could be Bill Cosby's slightly chubbier twin, gets up and starts to dance like he is starring in *Saturday Night Fever*. Well I think that's what he is trying to do; he could easily be having some kind of epileptic fit. The admin team starts singing karaoke to *Can't Fight the Moonlight* and getting the words all wrong. It doesn't matter; I am too busy having a good time.

I start talking (okay, gossiping) with Eva the receptionist, who I've never had a chance to properly chat with before. We work out that not only did we go to the same university (she was two years below me), but we know some of the same people. After a few more drinks, the subject invariably comes around to men.

As we are both single, we commiserate with each other on the lack of eligible menfolk. In the way these things happen, we get into a game of "Shag/Marry/Avoid". Eva gives considerable thought about the names I propose,

"I would shag Mick Jagger, marry Elton John and avoid Cliff Richards," she finally decides. "Okay, your turn. Oh, I have a good one. Men in this room."

"Easy, I would shag and marry Nick and avoid pretty much everyone else." I say, just a bit too loudly.

Nick, of course, picks that moment to magically appear at our side. He asks what we are talking about. Eva bursts into laughter, while I stand up and get flustered. As I do so, I manage to spill my wine down the front of my beige dress, nicely offsetting the spaghetti stains from dinner with matching streaks of Merlot. Unsure of what to do, I rush off blushing furiously, providing the talking point of the evening, and possibly the New Year.

I don't know if Nick heard or not. Please, please God make him not have heard. Also, God, if you are reading this please clean the stain off the front of the dress while you are at it. It's my favourite dress, and it currently looks like I have been moonlighting at the local abattoir. Much obliged. Amen.

Saturday 15 December

Sarah and I have gathered up the courage to brave Oxford Street this morning for Christmas shopping. Both of us have just been paid and we feel we ought to get gifts before our money runs out. After making our way through several shops, Sarah decides she wants to check out Selfridges. Though I am a bit tired, I am more than happy to go along with this. Mainly out of loyalty but also because it has a café which does great cakes.

The place is absolutely crammed. Little kids are getting under my feet. Bored-looking blokes, who would rather be at the football, are being dragged around by their wives. All kinds of people in cheap suits are trying to offer samples, special offers, or demonstrate trendy coffee makers. Seeing a massive crowd ahead of us surging, I pull Sarah into a lift and we make our way upwards. We arrive at the next floor but it's equally busy, so we make a break for the café to try our luck there.

Our heart sinks as we notice a huge crowd milling around the entrance. On closer examination the crowd is not for the café at all, but a hastily-erected Santa's grotto. There has been some space cleared, with fake plastic snow covering a few artificial trees. A painted cardboard reindeer slightly wilts under the hot strip lights. In the centre, surrounded by a whole pile of sparkly wrapped presents sits Father Christmas himself, red-suit, white beard, and complete with a squirming child on his lap. The kid pulls determinedly at the fake beard, which is obviously testing Santa's patience.

The children are kept in check by a couple of green suited elves who try their best to maintain some semblance of order. We try to edge our way around the chest-high mob, but from the corner of my eye I notice one of the elves is hiding behind the cardboard reindeer. Hiding quite badly. I move my head, trying to get a better view. Under the green nylon tights, fake ears, sparkles, and white greasepaint I can just about make out a familiar face.

"Is that...Justine?" I ask Sarah, pointing at the figure. "I know she said she was an assistant, but I think this might be stretching it."

"Oh, my God, it is!" she confirms. We stand there, staring at each other over the sea of small children. Not sure what the correct thing to do in this kind of situation, I awkwardly start to wave at her. Sarah grabs my hand and pulls it down. Justine realising that the game is up, stands up from behind the reindeer and walks towards us.

"I don't suppose you are here to see Santa?" she says, looking uncomfortable. Santa (aka Dave from home electricals) is good enough to let Justine take a break, and the three of us sit down with our coffees.

"You know I think you actually look quite good," comments Sarah. "Not many can pull off green nylon tights. Especially not with a hat that has bells on it."

Justine is not sure if Sarah is taking the piss or not, and explains that she needs the money. I try to make her feel better by assuring her that something better will come along, and that I have had to do my fair share of humiliating jobs. I desperately try to rack my brains thinking of one as humiliating as this, but I am sure that I have.

Justine talks about how she got into so much trouble with her dad when she lost her job at the surgery. He went ballistic about how much of a disappointment she was to him, and how she could never do anything right. This is consistent with all previous accounts of Justine's dad, who sounds like quite a piece of work. Despite this, Justine has done everything she can to make him happy, and win his approval. She tells us that he threatened to kick her out of the house if she wasn't earning.

She says being an elf is not as bad as it looks, and the people are really nice. I am glad, not only because I want things to be smooth for Justine, but also because it fits with my childhood ideals of how Santa should treat his workforce. The only problem is that Santa hires on a seasonal basis, and Justine will probably have to hang up her stockings for good on Christmas Eve.

I am horrified at the idea of Justine being turfed out of her home, and offer to put her up at our place if her dad throws her out. My heart melts as Justine breaks into a smile, but before we can talk more she says she has to get back to work. "Better go and feed the reindeer," she says full of cheer, hat bells ringing as she goes back to the grotto.

Sunday 16 December

"You said what!" yells Scarlett, after I tell her who we may have as a possible future housemate. The idea of Justine moving in has gone down like a bucket of cold sick. "No! No way! I forbid it," she says stamping her foot on the floor. I think Scarlett has been watching too many costume dramas, and now thinks of herself as a stern disciplinarian father telling his daughter she can't go to the dance.

"I'm not living with three people who are applying for that bloody course. This place is crazy enough as it is." She has a point. Besides there aren't enough bedrooms and there is only one bathroom. It's pretty cramped with just us. I am starting to regret my burst of seasonal goodwill.

I manage to calm her down by saying it's probably not going to happen. Sarah agrees with this, and reckons that Justine's dad wouldn't kick her out, if for no other reason than he would have no one else to take his aggression out on. An uneasy silence passes for a few moments as we think about this. Then we spend the rest of the day guiltily avoiding eye contact.

Monday 17 December

Work is practically deserted this morning as everyone who has any sense (as well as Olga) is already on holiday. I find several Christmas cards and a small wrapped bundle, on the top of my in-tray. The cards are from Nancy, Olga and several of the others wishing me merry Xmas. I feel a bit guilty, as I have not sent any, but quickly reassure myself that everyone sending them was old (like over thirty), and people from my generation do emails instead.

I unwrap the bundle and find it's a slim paperback copy of *Breakfast at Tiffany's* by Truman Capote. On the front page, scrawled in black biro it reads;

After our conversation, I thought it was about high time you experienced the real version. Sorry I didn't get to say goodbye the other night, but will see you next year.

Have a great Christmas and New Year.

Love
Nick

I feel a flutter of butterflies in my stomach. Not only has he left me something sweet and thoughtful, but he must have either come in late after the party, or possibly the weekend to drop it off.

The silence of the Cupboard, and the fact that my mind is prematurely in holiday mode, means I end up spending half the afternoon reading the book with my feet propped up on Olga's desk. I manage to get quarter of the way through it, and find I am getting drawn into it. I start to wonder if his choice of gift was a message of some kind. Maybe it's his way of telling me that I am his Holly Golightly? Maybe he will end up leaving his stuffy, clearly unsuitable partner to end up kissing me in the rain.

My thoughts are quickly drawn from New York streets and lavish parties by the sound of the burglar alarm being set. I hastily sprint out of the cupboard, yelling not to lock me in. Too late. The doors are locked and I know I will unleash hell if I trip the alarm's sensors. As I exit the building arse-first through the ground floor toilet window, I can't help thinking that this is not the sort of thing Audrey Hepburn would do.

Tuesday 18 December

I meet with Nancy for the last time before she leaves for Christmas. I am pleased to tell her that I have finished everything she has asked me to do for her. She seems impressed, and is especially grateful for the home visits I did with Alan.

"He can get to the clinic himself now. He sends his thanks by the way," she says, which makes me smile. She also thanks me for my gift and says how much she really appreciates it. I apologise to her and tell her that I had no idea that her mother had died, and that I completely let the angst get on top of me.

"I know it is tough, but you can't let your anxiety get the better of you. This process is hard enough, without making additional problems for yourself," she says.

"I think I am on top of it now, the worst bit is over," I say.

"Afraid not, just wait until the interview letters get sent out" she says. "Trust me, whatever happens in the New Year, always remember you can't let the outcome define how you see yourself as a person. Clinical training is a good option, but it is just that. One option out of many things you would be good at. Put it out of your mind over Christmas and try to relax."

I am a bit irritated at this. It is easy to say "relax" if you are in her position. Nancy has already got to where I want to be, so it's easy for her to say that. Her life is sorted. However, I do realise she means well so I thank her, and resolve not to be such a pain to her when I get back.

Wednesday 19 December

After a hard day of Facebooking and web surfing (I literally had nothing to do at work after 11 am), I come home and get ready to go out with Scarlett and Sarah. This is not to be. Sarah is yet again screwed over at work with her shifts, so she is not going anywhere tonight. She has also found out that she is down to work sporadically over the Christmas period, which will wreck her holiday plans. However, she works out she could still spend a bit of time with her family as well as going to see Tom's parents. Scarlett is clear about her plans. She intends to stay at the house over Christmas and the New Year, intending to have some "real fun" once we are gone. From the tone of her voice, I am doubtful there will be a house to return to.

Scarlett and I meet Justine at the bar as arranged. Justine somehow manages to get my back up within five minutes of greeting us, by telling me all about how Spiny has put up photos of her and Nick decorating their Christmas tree. I manage to change the subject back to how things are going for her.

She tells us all the latest news from Lapland, and Scarlett cheekily poses double entendres like, "What are you expecting down your chimney?" or "So what does Santa's bulging sack feel like?" All of which fly straight over Justine's head.

Scarlett spots a few of her friends at the bar and goes over to them. As she does, an unwelcome figure spots me. Wearing a vintage retro T-shirt and a trilby hat, Theroux sniffily comes over to the table, clearly intent on giving me a piece of his mind.

"Just who the hell do you think you are?" he says, glaring at me and looking particularly sour.

Justine, completely oblivious to who Theroux is, assumes the question is addressed at her. Mistaking Theroux as someone adopting an anger-focussed approach to chatting up girls, Justine starts talking about herself and explaining that while she works in retail at the moment she is looking for other opportunities. As she talks at him about her hobbies and star sign, I try my best not to laugh. Theroux, not quite sure how to react to this, petulantly walks off.

"He seems nice," Justine says, as he disappears into the crowd.

"He's not. He is a tosser," says Scarlett passing him on her way back to the table "He has been posting nasty updates all week about how 'all bitches are the same' and how 'stupid we all are'. I thought he was a harmless poseur, but it turns out he truly is an arsehole." Fairly certain that many of those comments were aimed at me, I am glad I wasn't aware of them before. Justine gets us another round of drinks, and I find the remnants of any tension start to drain away. I kick back, savouring the feeling that my holiday has finally started.

Thursday 20 December

The train journey back home is uneventful, apart from the snow that starts to settle across the landscape. As I approach my stop I find myself getting excited about returning home. My real home, not the temporary stop-over in the Victorian hovel where I normally reside, but a magical place where there is always enough hot water, food doesn't go missing from the fridge and arguments don't erupt over a 42p toilet roll. It's not just about the creature comforts of home, attractive as they undoubtedly are. As much as Mum and Dad do my head in, I do miss them.

The village where my parents live is sleepy enough not to warrant a proper train station. It has a tiny platform with a small brick shelter and a square of concrete next to it that functions as a car park. Even from about a mile away I can spot Dad's

Peugeot, as it is the only car there. He spots the train and waves, which would have mortified me when I was a teenager, but now see as quite sweet. I used to consider this place so boring when I was younger, but after the insanity of the last few months I can't think of anywhere else I would rather be.

During the first days whenever I return home, I am welcomed like the prodigal daughter. Everyone is excited to see me, and interested in what I have been up to. My room, which is exactly how I left it, like a little shrine to my wonderfulness (although those music posters really have to come down. It's just undignified at my age). My bed is made with crisp bed linen, and a freshly laundered fluffy towel has been laid carefully next to my dressing gown. There is a small stack of letters waiting for me on my little wooden writing desk. Mum tells me she is cooking treacle sponge which makes my stomach growl.

I know well enough that this is good for about 3-4 days, and after that it's diminishing returns. By day five, I will be ordered to fetch handbags or "just pop up to the local shop to fetch teabags". There is no broadband internet connection either, they probably should get some kind of award for being the only people in Britain still on a dial up modem. My father is fairly okay with the internet, but for my mother the internet functions as a mechanism to deliver pornography to small children and a way for scam artists to get her bank details. I fear I am going to have internet withdrawal symptoms.

Friday 21 December

Mum wakes me up from a rather strange dream where I am drowning in my duvet. "Maddie called and asked if you were back yet." she shouts up the stairs. This is just as well, as I was running out of breath and would have hated to die in my childhood single bed surrounded by stickers of plastic green ponies.

I have known Maddie since we were both four. Our first meeting involved her stealing a toy plastic tractor I was playing with at nursery, and me pulling her long brown pigtails in exchange. Thankfully, our friendship has come on since then. I call her back, and agree to meet her after lunch.

I walk to her house on autopilot. I must have made this walk thousands of times on our way to school together. Her mum, Carol, greets me at the door warmly. I wish her merry Christmas and apologise for being terrible at staying in touch. She ushers me to the kitchen and offers me a cuppa, which I eagerly accept.

"Hello stranger," says Maddie as she comes through from her bedroom. She looks tanned and relaxed from her travelling. I comment on this and she excitedly starts talking about her adventures teaching English in South East Asia. I glance at the mirror and see my unkempt dark hair and pale corpse-like reflection, bitterly bemoaning the fact that the London drizzle has done little for my own complexion. She asks what I have been up to while she has been away.

"Well, to be honest I have spent the last two months filling in an application form," I say, unenthusiastically. Carol, bringing over the tea, tells me that my mum has been keeping her updated.

"I hear you have to do some other course as well. Goodness me, haven't you studied enough already?" she says with a look of disbelief on her face. I try to fill her in on the finer points of clinical psychology training, but she just waves her hand, "Oh, I am sure you will be fine. You were always so good at school. You won't have any problems." The cruel tyranny of other people's expectations. I can now add Carol to the ever-lengthening list of people who have an image of me I have to live up to.

Embarrassed, Maddie arranges a quick exit, and we tramp off through the snowy streets. We spend the morning visiting some old haunts and catching up. The village seems smaller than I remember it, and we walk around in the crisp December afternoon gossiping about who is doing what and where. Maddie is back with her on/off boyfriend Matt. They had a break when she went away travelling, but absence made the heart grow fonder and they have got back together. I have known Matt since primary school, and although I have seen him often in the intervening years, I can't get beyond the image of him as a little boy running around the playground pretending to be Batman.

She asks me if there are any blokes on the horizon for me. I tell her about the whole Nick/Christmas Party/Spiny situation. Maddie just bursts out laughing and tells me not to worry. She tells me several stories about her travelling that are far worse. This is why I love Maddie; no matter how much of a fool I think I have made of myself, she can probably find a way to top it.

After lunch, we spend the afternoon going for a long walk before heading back home. Maddie points out all of the places where she has worked since we left school. She must have worked in pretty much every shop and office in a two-mile radius, and even just walking around, random people greet her on sight. I feel an acute sense of sadness as it dawns on me that my daily commute is longer than that, and no one knows me outside my front door.

Now she is back, Maddie is again looking for work. I can't help notice that despite having no money and living with her mum she seems far happier than I have been in the last few months.

"I am not a big career girl like you," she says, "but I am sure something will come up."

Part of me wants to scream "But what about gaps on your CV? What will employers think?" but a larger part of me just admires the way she's so relaxed about everything. Marks at school, choir practice, A-levels, her decision not to go to university. I know Maddie would never agonise over a job application, dwell on past failures, or spend hours wondering if she should do a part time course in German to make herself more marketable. If you asked her to work for free, she would tell you what pier to jump off. Maybe I need to start thinking similarly.

Saturday 22 December

I spend the day helping Mum do the groceries, among a panicking crowd of last minute Christmas shoppers in town. While the village is quiet, the town, which is only a five mile drive away, is heaving with people. Shopping amidst this is far from fun, and it's not helped by Mum keeping up an unending commentary about what needs buying, the new range of hosiery at Marks and Spencer, and minor misadventures my father has got into.

After I get back, I meet Maddie and head down to the village pub, the Fox and Hounds. There is a fair crowd, and most were at my school. It's funny, because back in the day if a person was in the year above or below you, it made a huge difference. Now no one cares, and everyone in a ten year age bracket hangs out with each other, often in the same pub as their parents.

We sit at a large table, and I spot some people I went to school with, including Matt. Clad in his black Metallica T-shirt, he comes over to greet us and gives Maddie a quick peck on the cheek. I can't help but notice, with slight envy, that they have the easy familiarity of a couple who have been together for ages.

Matt asks me how things in London are going, and if I have bumped into the Queen yet. (Yes, I tell him. In Waitrose. At the fish counter). He then asks me if I can read criminal's minds because I am "a psychologist and everything". I sarcastically reply that as I am merely an Assistant Psychologist, I am only qualified to read the minds of assistant criminals. Not used to irony, my joke goes unrecognised. He then spends the rest of the evening asking if I could do "some of that Derren Brown stuff" on him. Before I can hypnotise him into not asking me stupid questions, I get interrupted by someone who greets me enthusiastically with a thump on the back.

I recognise him as Aled, who I vaguely remember being in the year above us at school. He pulls a chair over and joins us. He tells me how great it is to see me again. I do my best to try and dredge up any memories of him. I dimly recall that his Dad ran off with his secretary in the mid-1990s, but that is probably not the best thing to be asking about right now.

I tell him what I have been up to since leaving school. Encouraged when I mention I am single, he immediately asks me what I am doing tomorrow night. Nothing, I truthfully reply. It's Christmas Eve, and Mum and Dad are going to be at the Martinson's Christmas party which I don't really want to go to. (They are all in the Rotary club, and will talk about patio extensions all night). He asks if I would want to meet him for dinner. Flattered and with nothing better to do, I agree. His face lights up as I scribble down my number on the back of a beermat. He promises to call me to arrange a time. Wow, I've only been back home three days, and men are already throwing themselves at me. This is awesome.

Sunday 23 December

Aled calls me to let me know he will pick me up at 7:30 pm. I am getting quite excited about my date this evening. However, things don't get off to a great start. Aled's arrival is promptly answered by my mother, who announces "I think it's an estate agent for you."

Aled's shiny polyester suit and gelled spiky hair have not done him any favours. He greets me with a kiss that is a bit too overfamiliar considering my parents are standing directly behind me. I introduce everyone. He responds by saying "Wicked!" to everything, which makes my mother wince. I try hard to overlook superficial appearances and any awkwardness, as these are practically inevitable in this kind of situation. It's only when he leads me to his gently rusting Ford Focus with his opening line, "We can go to Pizza Hut because I have vouchers", that I realise that I am in for a long evening.

Pizza Hut. The stuff that dreams are made of.

We drive into town, Aled hammering the accelerator all the way, as if he is competing in a Formula 1 Grand Prix. After a fairly awkward half-hour (no starter, no dessert, and a table just a little too close to the gent's), where we exhaust the tenuous mutual friends we share, the conversation dries up. I gamely try to talk about films I have seen recently, but he clearly isn't interested. Instead, he takes this as a cue to tell me all about his aspirations to become a professional gambler. He goes on at great length about how he has been getting into high stakes poker games down at the Fox and Hounds, and his sure fire system for winning big money on the fruit machine. He brags about being on first name terms with the staff at the village betting shop. "I am kind of a big deal there," he says with considerable pride. All I can I say is that Las Vegas had better watch out.

My mind rewinds back to this one time I watched Nancy assess someone with a severe gambling addiction. I wonder if he too once outlined his grand plan for poker domination over a medium deep pan meat feast. However, until his "big score" comes through, he is getting by on what he gets from the dole and can cadge from his mother. Classy. Adding to the debonair playboy image, he eats noisily with his mouth open and at one point calls the waitress a "dyke" because she took too long to bring his garlic bread.

Clearly, my prince has come.

After dinner, Aled suggests we go back his place to "chat" and show me around "his pad". I turn him down, as (a) I want to go home, (b) I know that chatting is the last thing on his mind, and (c) he's already let on that he lives in his mum's spare room and that any grand tour could easily be conducted via a single photograph. I try to make an excuse that I need to get home because I have important work to do/cancer to cure/Meltar the Vampire King to defeat, but he is stubbornly insistent. Stalker-insistent. Dead-girl-in-car-boot insistent. I compromise and suggest a local pub, secretly texting dad under the table to pick me up from there as soon as humanly possible. Why does this sort of thing always happen to me?

We get to a bar at the edge of town. If I was being charitable I would call the place a shithole. He orders double rum and cokes and plonks three of them on my table in front of me. "Rohypnol would be cheaper," I murmur.

As I slowly sip from one of the glasses, he complains about how most of the girls we went to school with are stuck up (translation: middle-class), nerds (translation: educated) and/or frigid (translation: failed to put out at the drop of a hat). Magnanimously, he says he won't hold my education against me, which is nice of him and shows an admirably progressive attitude. Halfway through his angry monologue, Dad arrives. I don't think I have ever been so happy to see him before in my life. I ignore Aled's frantic waving and hissing that he can drop me off later, and wave at Dad. As he comes over, I thank Aled for the evening. He asks to see me again, but I firmly explain that I am busy over Christmas, and probably for the rest of my life.

Monday 24 December

I now have 7 voicemail messages from Aled on my phone. All unanswered. Maddie thinks that number will hit at least 15 before he gets the message.

Tuesday 25 December

It's Christmas day, and in the morning Dad and I go and pick up Gran from her bungalow as Mum prepares Christmas Dinner. Gran talks non-stop on the drive home, asking me way too many intrusive questions. She asks me if I have been keeping my diary, and it's not even a lie this time when I tell her that I have been.

When we get home Gran drinks a frightening amount of tea and sherry, although sadly not at the same time. We all sit around talking and playing Monopoly and I notice my phone buzzing. Nick has texted me:

Merry Xmas. Hope U got the book.

After scrutinising message for far too long, I leave a respectable amount of time before texting back:

Loved it. Merry Xmas! x

I have second thoughts and regret putting the X there, and wondering if this potentially classifies me as a wanton, home-wrecking harlot. Thankfully Dad calls me over as it is my turn, which stops all this nonsense in its tracks as I have to decide whether or not to buy Mayfair. It's surprisingly effective, and I should market this as some kind of romantic over-thinking prevention technique.

I eat too much, drink too much, and watch too much telly. I open my presents and realise that Santa has nowadays gotten lazy and leaves gift vouchers and iTunes credit instead of putting real effort into things. However, I am grateful to get a nice winter coat from my parents, a small jewellery box from Sarah and a box of chocolates from Justine. Maddie and her mum drop by in the mid afternoon and we watch a Bond film. We get into an argument about whether this is the one with Jaws or not. (It's not, sadly.)

Maddie and I spend the rest of the evening picking at left overs and talking about what we hope will happen in the New Year. I can't be bothered to think too hard about this at the moment, so wish for a robot that makes my bed. Maddie tells me how much she misses my silliness, and asks if I am ever going to come back.

"You know, properly."

"Probably not," I say, feeling sad.

"Yeah, I didn't think so," she says, draining the last drops from a bottle of sherry. "Don't get me wrong, I loved being away, but the whole time I couldn't wait to get back here. But it's different for you. You always wanted to get out. Even when we were kids, I remember you talking about living in a big city."

I am not sure what to say. My initial reaction is that she is drunk and talking crap. Add to that, she is the one who has been travelling, and I have been stuck in the Cupboard for the last few months. However, I must admit that I don't really want to move back here permanently. For all the stress of London, there is more for me there. Still, it's good to remember I achieved at least one of my childhood goals.

Wednesday 26 December

Boxing Day is when the rest of the extended family comes to the house to make their yearly visit. This would be lovely, but for the presence of my odious Uncle Richard, the pride of middlebrow England. For whom the world ends at the white cliffs of Dover. Whose favourite stock response for most situations is either, "She was asking for it" or, "We should send in the tanks".

Unsurprisingly, Uncle Richard has never been shy at voicing his hearty scepticism at my going to university and seeking an education. "Bloody students. Bone idle more like." was his response when he heard the news. "Psychology! Mickey Mouse course. Sitting around a room talking about your feelings and they give you a degree for it nowadays."

It's always a barrel of laughs when Uncle Richard comes to visit.

Despite having little esteem for formal education, Uncle Richard never gets tired of telling us he graduated from the University of Life. Being disadvantaged by having attended a real university, I find myself taking a dim view of the "Life Uni". Their entry requirements seem low, and its graduates tend to be twats. I dread to think what their alumni reunion would look like. Their educational standards also leave much to be desired. Uncle Richard is proud of only ever having read one book in his life, and I would not be surprised if it had cardboard pop-up bits in it.

Of course, Richard dominated the conversation over lunch. My contribution to the lunchtime conversation was limited to:

"I am afraid I will have to disagree with you Uncle R, as I do believe there is such a thing as mental illness. I think it warrants more than pulling their socks up, because all that will do is make their legs a little bit warmer... Yes, I had heard that your daughter Holly had married very well and already has a second kiddie on the way. I understood the first time you mentioned it... Nope, still no boyfriend... Yes, you are quite right that it is funny- hilarious even- that I worked so hard for my A-level grades and yet still don't own my own house."

I can see Dad having to physically restrain himself every time Richard opens his mouth, and Holly's mortified expression suggests she wants the floor to swallow her up. The ever oblivious Richard moves his *Terminator*-like gaze onto the Asian family who have moved in across the street. He gets a good ten minutes into it, when Gran pipes up from the end of the table, "Richard, shut up and stop being such a prat. Be quiet and eat your dinner."

Owned! By your pensioner mum no less.

Chastened, Richard quietens down and starts eating as polite conversations resumes. Did I mention that I love my Gran?

Thursday 27 December

Mum is really getting on my tits now. The festive cheer and any novelty of being home have now completely worn off, and I am back into 16-year-old mode once again. Gran has now returned home, so I am spending most of my time holed up in my room, listening to CDs on my ancient hi-fi, being surly to my parents or getting exasperated if they ask me to do anything.

137

As a form of distraction, I help Dad clear the driveway of snow. This completely knackers me out and my muscles start to ache. It's nice just being with Dad, despite his naff jokes, or when he compares notes on 50 Cent. He also mentions he was getting worried, as I was so wound up the last few times I saw him. I hadn't really stopped to think about how my parents had viewed the whole situation with getting onto training, but it seems they had noticed. I brush it off, and assure him that everything is fine now.

Friday 28 December

I am out running errands in the village, when Sarah calls me on my mobile. She fills me in on how her Christmas has been going. From the sounds of things, she has been rushed off her feet. She has either been helping her dad chase payments or doing extra shifts at the nursing home. It sounds like she is absolutely worn out and I feel quite guilty about having such a relaxing time with my parents (which I don't complain about, because that will only raise her blood pressure).

She also mentions she has been short listed for the Assistant's job she applied for. I congratulate her on her good news. She also reports that Scarlett has managed to stay out of trouble so far, but there are still a few days to go before we get back, so anything could happen. If I don't think too hard about it, perhaps the damage won't be too bad.

Saturday 29 December

My mother 'strongly encourages' me to tidy up the spare room. I meet her request with a death stare and a huge overdramatic sigh. To be fair I have been using the room like a self-storage facility since I left home. I was under the impression that there was a tacit understanding with parents that you brought home the stuff you accumulated throughout the year in the holidays and then promptly forget all about it when you move somewhere else. Part of their sacred duty was to preserve all of my belongings like curators at a museum, until the magical day I need all my artefacts again. However, Mum thinks differently. She decided that today was a good time for me to bite the bullet and start clearing out what stays (very little) and what goes (most of it).

Going through it is an exercise in nostalgia. Look, there is that Health and Safety module I did for some long forgotten job. Can I bring myself to throw away that Health Psychology text book that I never even opened but which cost a bomb? I know I can't be arsed to put it on eBay. Do I really need those cinema tickets for *American Pie 3: American Wedding*? (The fact I felt it was important enough to see in the cinema is disturbing, but not as disturbing as the fact that I felt the need to keep the tickets as a reminder of the occasion.)

This room is a cross between a time-machine and a dustbin. Why did I decide to store all of this crap? I realise I may even need a skip to get rid of it. I am sorely tempted to pile it back into the cupboards and leave it for another time, but get the sense that Mum is not going to let that be an option.

It gets too much for me. In a haze, I start junking things without compassion or mercy. Slowly, the room starts to emerge as somewhere liveable. So much so that Dad has a quick look around, before deciding he now wants to turn it into a home gym. I have a vision of him slumped over an exercise bike after a heart attack, brought on by a too-tight towelling headband. Perhaps I should have left things the way they were.

Sunday 30 December

Although I tried as hard as I could to get out of it, I am reluctantly dragged along to my Auntie Rachel's post-Christmas/pre-New Year party. To be honest, I hadn't been paying attention on Boxing Day, when she ambushed me with an invite. She had got me to agree to come when my mind was being distracted by Gran falling asleep a little too close to the fire. Everyone else my age has managed to get out of coming, so

I'm the only person under the age of forty in the room. My presence here officially marks me as the world's saddest woman.

Many of the people here have known my parents since 1732. I am repeatedly told that they remember me since I was "this" high. Everyone asks me, "So, have you got a boyfriend yet?" which gets less amusing the more people ask it. However, when my aunt's friend Lionel, who is so deep in the closet he has his own holiday home in Narnia, asks me this question, I reply, "Nope, have you?"

I get told off for being impertinent.

I spend the rest of the evening hiding out in an upstairs bedroom texting anyone and everyone I can think of. As I do so, my copy of *Breakfast at Tiffany's* slides out of my handbag. I pick it up and continue reading it, managing to get to the end before my mother bursts into the room exclaiming, "There you are! We were supposed to go home an hour ago."

As I am led through the house like a naughty schoolgirl, my only thought is that I need to get back to London as quickly as possible.

Monday 31 December

As always, the New Year's Eve party is held at the Fox and Hounds. I am press-ganged earlier in the day to help get the place ready, and we have done it up well. Everyone from the village comes, which means I am parentally chaperoned in effect, but so is everyone else and they don't seem to mind. Maddie, Matt, and a whole group have colonised a large table at the far end of the bar. Aled is notably absent. I am reliably informed he is spending New Year's Eve on an internet poker room, which makes me simultaneously thankful, yet sorry for him. We listen to cheesy music, talk crap and reminisce about old times.

As I stand at the bar ordering my round, I look around at everyone laughing and drinking. I wonder what would happen if

I had never left. Maybe I would have ended up like Maddie, Carol or my parents? While that doesn't seem bad, I somehow doubt I would have been happy. I have only been here a few days and can feel myself getting claustrophobic already.

Yet, I feel I would quite like the security and belonging they seem to have and I miss the certainties that came with living here. Maybe it's the drink or the crowds of people but I am overcome by a sharp pang of loss. It dawns on me at that moment that this will be my last New Year's Eve here for a long time.

As the clock ticks down to midnight, I find myself dancing with my Dad. I stop worrying about whether this is uncool or not, and just enjoy it.

JANUARY

Tuesday 1 January

I get home in the early hours of the morning, slightly concerned that Mum and Dad had the stamina to stay out longer than me. Too tired and hung-over to do anything significant when I wake up, I opt to lie in bed and compile a list of New Year's resolutions. I manage to come up with the following:

1) Stop procrastinating and be more organised.
2) Keep going with my reflective diary.
3) Get on a clinical training course.
4) Try to be more chilled and relaxed in general.
5) Go to the gym 3 times a week.
6) Stop spending too much time on Facebook, internet forums, and other time sinks.

Even in my current state I realise these are either lame, out of my control, or most likely to be broken before February. Possibly even by next Monday.

In the afternoon, I am bullied out of bed by my mum who wants me to help with the hoovering. As I am reluctantly dragging the vacuum cleaner up the stairs, she stops me to make a fuss about me not eating properly. She spends the afternoon cooking and putting things into Tupperware containers for me to take back to London.

She then tries to casually drop in the idea that I may want to spend another week here, and we can paint the living room together. Thrilling as the proposition is, I firmly turn it down. By next week, the only thing we will be painting the walls with will be each other's blood.

Wednesday 2 January

The train journey back is not enjoyable. I can't get a seat for half the journey, and when I do, I have to listen to a small child tell his mother in exhausting, meticulous detail the plot of the latest episode of *Power Rangers*. As he yells this at considerable volume, I am certain everyone in the carriage is now aware of the subtle, but important, differences in abilities between the red and green ranger. I now feel my life is richer because of this knowledge.

I get back home laden with all the stuff mum has given me to carry back. Sarah is away, but Scarlett is in. She seems pleased to see me when I arrive, so I am suspicious she has trashed the house. Although I make a thorough inspection, even going to the lengths of checking my sock drawer for any irregularities, I find nothing out of place. She looks mildly offended when I congratulate her for keeping the house in proper order.

"I was going to give you your Christmas present, but if you are going to be like that..." she says, waving a wide brimmed hat at me. I greedily thrust my hand out and apologise. "Long story how I got that, but I figure it suits you more than it suits me," she says, handing it over to me. Looking in the mirror I think it looks good, and I thank her for it.

Feeling guilty I hadn't thought to buy anything for Scarlett, I hand over a large cake tin that contains Mum's Victoria sponge. Scarlett hungrily tucks into it, in a manner that suggests she hasn't eaten for days.

Cake crumbs dotting her lips, Scarlett starts telling me about her Yuletide adventures. From what she says, there is not a bar in London she didn't frequent or party she didn't attend. She also tells me about Sarah's increasingly demanding boss and the nightmare she has faced at work in the last few weeks. "It's been non-stop for her. I think her dad may be having problems with his business," she says, looking worried. Thankfully she was able to get away in the end with Tom, and will be back on Friday.

It's good to be back in my own place, despite the horrible sinking feeling about having to go back to work tomorrow. I manage to stave it off by catching up on my Facebook and internet addiction. After two weeks away from it, I feel like I am going to need more time off to catch up on what I have missed.

It seems an inordinate number of people have either got together/broken up/got together with someone else over New Year's, or have taken incriminating photographs of them doing things they shouldn't have been doing. My first thought is that, "EVERYONE ELSE HAS BEEN HAVING WAY MORE FUN THAN ME". Previously happy with my holiday, I now feel mildly deprived that I haven't been skiing, or hanging off the back of a yacht in Malta like the rest of the world seems to have been. Then I realise I have broken New Year's resolutions (4) and (6) without even trying.

Thursday 3 January

First day back at work and it's surprisingly painless. With no pressing deadlines, impending work, and half the people still on leave, the most challenging part of the day is waking up on time. Happily, I don't need to worry until February about hearing if I have got any interviews for training. The few people that are here are relaxed after their holiday. Right now, it feels like a magic pause button has been pressed on the soundtrack of ambient stress. I don't think I have ever felt so good about coming back from holiday before.

I dig my way through the avalanche of work emails that have accumulated while I have been away. Most are circulars and auto-responses about people being on holiday; the pattern seems to be delete, delete, forward, delete, delete, reply. After answering the few legitimate emails, I find myself quickly finishing everything that needs doing.

I go looking for Nick but find out he is still away. I have mixed feelings about this. On one hand, I want to thank him for the book, but at the same time I am slightly terrified he overheard what I said about him at the party. I can always deny everything. Maybe if I leave it long enough, I can pretend he had said it about me, and that his mind is subconsciously re-imagining things. That could work quite well.

Sarah got back today, and she announces her arrival by crashing face first onto the sofa. Scarlett and I stare at her unmoving form.

"Is she dead?" Scarlett asks, prodding at her gingerly with a rolled up copy of *Heat* magazine.

A groan, muffled by the sofa cushion, emanates from Sarah.

"Not quite," I say, going off to make some tea to revive her. Sarah slowly starts to come around, and tell us about how this has been the worst Christmas ever. In addition to her boss's attempts to break her, and her father's escalating desperation about his business, she has had to put up with several days of Tom's parents heavily implying that "he could still do better" with his choice of girlfriend. Sarah is now of the firm opinion that Christmas ought to be banned for the foreseeable future. After one like that, I don't blame her.

Friday 4 January

Work remains graveyard quiet. The most exciting thing that happens is a circular pinging into my inbox telling me the Assistant Group is scheduled for next week. This indicates that

Spiny is back, and has avoided the freak turkey carving accident many of us had hoped for. Thankfully, Eva is also back at reception, and seeing as it is so quiet for both of us, we chat about our holidays to pass the time.

Unlike work, things on the home front kick off this evening. Tom is around and Sarah is slowly starting to return to her normal self. We are all in the living room, when a phone call interrupts our all-important TV watching. Justine on the other end is in tears. I haven't really heard from her while I was away, and now begin to understand why.

As Christmas is over, the services of Santa's elves are no longer required. Although the regular workers got to return to their normal duties, the temps like Justine were let go on Christmas Eve. As if unemployment was not enough of a gift, Justine's father decided to take the opportunity to spend the whole of the period re-emphasising how much of a useless/stupid/worthless daughter she was. Justine, dependent on him for food and accommodation was not in much of a position to fight back. She took as much of this as possible and promised to find work and earn enough to pay him back. (I struggle with the idea that I ever could pay Dad back for everything he has done, or that Dad would ever ask me to in the first place, but it appears Justine's father has no such difficulty.)

So while I was unwrapping presents and arguing about who got to be the little dog in Monopoly (me), Justine was manically searching for jobs. Unfortunately, the post-Xmas/New Year period isn't the best time to be job hunting, so she came up with nothing. Not being the most understanding of men, her father quickly made it clear that this is not good enough and has now kicked her out of the house. She says she didn't know who else to call, so is calling me from a nearby bus shelter. Unsure of what to say, I tell her I will call her back.

I turn the TV off, and explain to everyone that Justine has been kicked out and may be coming to stay for a bit. This does not go down well. Scarlett says that this will be happening over her dead body and that we aren't running a hotel for waifs and strays. Sarah groans and says she is tired enough as it is and doesn't need this right now. She also points out that there isn't anywhere near enough space, and the landlord will definitely kick us out if he hears about it.

Even I start to have doubts. Their objections are valid and I can all too easily imagine the nightmare having Justine around 24/7 could be. Weighing up the options, I finally come to a decision. "She is cold, tired, and has nowhere else to go. I am not about to start turning away people that need help. Especially a friend. She is staying with us."

Tom nods, saying it is the right thing to do. He offers to drive me to pick her up. Looking ashamed, Sarah and Scarlett bundle into the back and we set off slowly through the slushy roads. After driving for an hour and passing every possible bus shelter in east London (Justine directions are as shaky as her command of medical ethics), we eventually find her shivering, bundled up figure. "I knew you wouldn't let me down," she says as she loads her tiny suitcase into the boot, and crams into the back of the car.

I am glad we didn't.

Saturday 5 January

The house is bustling this morning. After spending the night on my bedroom floor, Justine has gone back to pick up a few things and try to appeal to her dad. Tom, Sarah and I are doing our best to get the place ready. Scarlett is busy making herself scarce on the off chance she may be called on to do some work. Justine returns carrying a few bags. Her father is still adamant that the house she grew up in is no longer her home.

"He didn't even ask where I stayed last night," she says despondently. "I think he really hates me."

I want to respond that she is wrong, but I can't. It would just be a platitude, and a cruel one at that. I try to distract her by taking her up to my room and clearing some space where she can keep stuff. I hastily try to pick up my stuff from the floor and push my mess into a heap, while Justine looks out the window.

"Is life always this hard for everyone?" she asks, watching Mrs Patel from next door dragging her shopping through the snow. I am not sure what to say to this. I try to think of examples of life being hard, but am aware for all my bad experiences I have never faced being disowned by my father.

"It's me isn't it?" she says with tears in her eyes, "I know that I am a joke and everyone looks down on me. I know people laugh at me behind my back when they think I am not looking. I know I am not as clever as you and Sarah, and don't always say the right things, but I try hard. Really hard. It never seems to matter though. To anyone."

I really want to make everything better for her, but am completely powerless to do so. Even if I was able to buy Justine a house and offer her a job that starts tomorrow, I can't change her father's mind. Or make her the person she desperately wants to be. Generally I am good with plans, and overcoming obstacles, but for the first time in my life I realise how far out of my depth I am, and how little control I really have.

Sunday 6 January

I spend the day helping Sarah prepare for her interview tomorrow. It's one of the few assistant posts she has ever been shortlisted for, and she had to fight hard to get the day off work. There is a lot is riding on this.

We start off by going online and noting down the various typical interview questions that are normally asked. This is a questionable decision, as each one I ask makes her more and more anxious.

Question: *How would you compare two clinical groups on four different variables?*

Sarah's answer: "With great difficulty."

Question: *Think of a time you handled a difficult situation and what you learnt?*

Sarah's Answer: Friday night, and never leave the metal fork in the bowl when you are microwaving dinner.

However, we slowly start unpicking the questions in turn. Sarah begins to relax and gather confidence. I notice she needs some refreshing on the basics, especially around psychological theory. Sarah feels her time away from studying, and doing more nursing than direct psychological work has made her rusty. I do my best to suggest the areas she can read up on and wish her good luck for tomorrow.

As we finish, Justine calls us down as she has made dinner as a way of saying thanks. Scarlett makes a cynical crack about not trusting Justine to boil an egg properly. She is soon eating her words, along with a third helping of lasagne. Justine turns out to be a dab hand in the kitchen and the food is delicious. She even made the dough for the garlic bread from scratch. Maybe her staying over won't be as bad as we imagined?

Monday 7 January

Job interviews that I have Sarah has messed up #3

To put not too fine a point on it, Sarah choked. Badly. She was the last to be interviewed, so saw the parade of candidates entering and leaving, which got her more and more worked up. She felt they were all more knowledgeable, more sure of themselves and better in every possible way. By the time she was called in, she could barely get out of the chair.

In the interview, all of her careful preparation and planning simply leapt out of her head, leaving her confused. Things she actually did know came out as if she was guessing. When asked about how her experiences would help her do the job, she ended up reading her work schedule out to them. Item by item. Her answers were one-word replies. Having surreptitiously timed the whole thing with her watch, she was all too aware that her interview was the shortest of all of them.

On her way home all of the correct answers came flooding back to her. She was kicking herself over it all evening. Frustrated that the main way of getting a job in the modern age is doing the very thing she finds hardest, she raged how she can never think straight when put on the spot, and was given no opportunity to get her personality across.

I tried to cheer her up, and tell her about all of the messed up interviews I have had, and that it happens to everyone. I feel she could learn from this, but it all feels too raw for her now to hear that.

Tuesday 8 January

Nancy is now back at work. I know this because I am slowly being loaded up with tasks like the donkey from Buckaroo. She is remarkably sprightly for someone that has had such a recent maternal bereavement, but I don't remark on this, instead asking her if she has had a good break.

Nancy spends most of our supervision outlining the plan for the new anxiety management group she has in mind. She wants to get started on it quickly. All great clinical experience she assures me, handing over a scarily large pile of reading, and a bulging folder complete with notes.

I also get an e-mail from Megan saying that she is looking forward to my presentation at the next Assistant's meeting on Thursday. I have a minor heart attack, when I realise I had been put down to present at the last meeting. Ignoring the anxiety management group reading for now, I immediately get started on researching something that hopefully won't bore everyone at the meeting to tears. I curse myself that I could have been doing this when I first got back and everything was quiet, sadly observing I have just blown New Year's resolution (1).

Wednesday 9 January

Sarah is grimly struggling on. What didn't help were the two rejection phone calls she received today. The first came from the chair of the interview panel confirming what she already knew, but thanking her for coming. Fifty minutes later she got a further call from HR, informing her of her rejection. Again.

"They hated me so much they felt they needed to tell it to me twice," she says, clearly quite hurt. Justine is able to calm her down, with her indefatigable optimism, which succeeds where my rationalising has failed. Misery clearly loves company and I start to see that Sarah has mentally drawn a line between the lucky "haves" like me, and the miserable downtrodden "have-nots" like her and Justine.

This is only one part of Justine's impact in the house. Although I have to put up with the minor inconvenience of her taking up my bedroom floor, the whole house is tidier, the food is better and we never run out of bleach or laundry detergent. Even Scarlett has forgotten any previous objections, now she has a daytime companion to compare notes with when watching *Bargain Hunt*.

True, Justine is still able to dazzle us with her complete lack of general knowledge. The highlight of yesterday was her saying that she thought that the whole country of Greece was fictional because she had heard people talk of Greek Myths. We don't care. We are happier living in Justine's cloud cuckoo-land than anything reality has to offer.

Thursday 10 January

It's the Assistant's Group meeting. I am feeling a bit under the weather and would normally have missed it to recover, but the fact that I am down to present today compels me to turn up. To make matters worse, someone has cranked the thermostat up to maximum and I slowly start to boil in my clothing. All the usual crowd are there, plus a few of the others who came last time. Megan takes pity on me and helps me set up the projector, while I get my PowerPoint slides ready. She is way too enthusiastic about all of this.

"Hi-Ya!" says Spiny, as she makes a big show of air kissing me. Cheryl isn't with her (still on holiday), and Meryl seems almost naked or half-formed without her. Spiny tells Sarah about what she and Nick got up to at Christmas. Her daddy paid for them both to go skiing in the Alps, mentioning it so casually it may as well have been an overnight stay at the Skegness Travelodge.

The meeting starts, but when it comes to my presentation Spiny refuses to sit down. So both of us stand there, equally spaced in front of the others, like we are about to perform a duet. I start to give my talk, which is about Obsessive-Compulsive Disorder, but Spiny insists on providing a running commentary after ever point I make. After a while she just repeats what I have just said, like some kind of surreal English-to-English translator. With her blonde hair and dark suit (Jigsaw) contrasting against my dark hair, white blouse and light skirt (H&M), I am aware we look like a photo negative of each other.

When she starts fielding questions about *my* bloody presentation I give up. I feel too unwell to fight it out, so just stand there partly blinded by the light of the projector, as Spiny's voice washes over me. As she comes to the end, Bloke-whose-name-I-can-never-remember asks a question. Spiny, not being able to answer, turns to me and asks, "What do you think?"

The whole room expectantly looks at me. I try my best to focus my mind and start with, "I think...I think..." The room never finds out what I think because I vomit copiously into the waste paper basket fortunately near my chair. The group sit and watch horrified, as the contents of my stomach noisily shoots out of my mouth. This serves as an effective full stop to the proceedings. The warm temperature of the room intensifies the rising smell of sick, encouraging everyone to grab their coats and evacuate the room as quickly as possible.

Friday 11 January

Feeling a bit better today I turn up at work, only to be inundated with emails from people checking to see I am alright. What is even more embarrassing is that many are from people who *weren't even at the meeting*. How quickly my chunderfest has become stuff of legend.

"I heard you were feeling poorly," says Nick, as he enters the cupboard looking concerned. I bet he did, and can imagine the theatrical re-enactment Spiny will have put on for his benefit. Regardless, he doesn't show any signs of disgust, nor does he bring up anything about any Christmas party comments either, so it looks like I am in the clear. I assure him that I am feeling much better, and thank him for his present. Keen to move the topic on from what happened yesterday, I ask him about his skiing holiday.

"Never did like skiing. The whole thing was a bit too much for me if I am being honest," he says looking slightly uncomfortable. However, he was able to get some high altitude rock climbing done, despite a foot stamping tantrum from Spiny. He talks animatedly about some of his climbs, and several of the near misses that sound like they could have been worryingly fatal.

He tells me he thought of me as he was climbing this one particular stretch. He whips out his digital camera, and there is a beautiful view of a mountain valley bathed in mist, which is very reminiscent of our away-day climb. I love it, and set it as my screensaver.

Saturday 12 January

A call pierces the silence of the morning. I am particularly annoyed as I am in the middle of a lie-in. I run downstairs to answer the landline. It's Justine's father demanding a word with his daughter.

It takes all of my strength not to tell him to go screw himself and hang up. Instead, I go up to my room and shake Justine awake. I hover awkwardly in the living room doorway, part of me wanting to give Justine her privacy, but also wanting to be around in case she needs support. In the end, I decide to leave her to it.

We are all sitting in the kitchen making breakfast when she comes off the phone. She tells us that her dad wants her back at home. I ask what has prompted this change of heart, and feel crushed when I find out that it's not the fact that he has missed his daughter, or realised the error of his ways. His main motivation is that he didn't have anyone to clean the house or do the cooking. Justine doesn't seem upset at his reasoning, and is all too happy to be allowed to return.

"No fucking way! She isn't going back to stay with him. I don't care what he wants," roars Scarlett.

"Wait, I think Justine has to make her own choice about this," I say, overlooking the irony of her equally strongly reaction when it was first suggested Justine come in the first place. I do my best to try and calm Scarlett down. If I don't, I wouldn't put it past her to put a brick through his window. Sarah asks Justine what we could do to best support her.

Justine decides to go back. Although her dad can be quite bad, she feels that she does wind him up and it is her own fault. She brushes off our disagreement on this, and thanks us for all of our help. However, she feels she couldn't stay on without paying rent, and we're currently risking our tenancy agreement. After many tearful hugs, we reluctantly help her get her things together.

"It was supposed to be apple crumble tonight. Then I was going to take her dancing," is all Scarlett can bring herself to say as we watch Justine disappear off up the path, laden down with her bags. I can't help but feel that this isn't going to end well.

Sunday 13 January

After the intensity of yesterday, the three of us decide to get out of the house, and head to our favourite café. It's Sunday so the place is busy, yet we manage to find a table. Scarlett is still upset about Justine leaving, and this has made her obnoxiously loud. Sitting down opposite her with my pasta salad, I tell her to keep it down as I don't want to be chucked out. Scarlett ignores me and continues to talk about what she would do to Justine's father if she got her hands on him.

As I think that things could not get any worse, a man with a scarf covering his face walks in and nudges the tray from our table as he goes past. One of our cups spills tea onto the table, and Scarlett tells the man angrily that he should be carrying a white stick if he is that blind. The man turns around and pulls his scarf down. It's Nick. I try to think how unlikely it is in one of the largest cities in the world to bump into a work colleague. I swear it's as if the entire world consists of ten people that I meet in heavy rotation.

"Hey. I am really sorry to have spilled your drinks. Here, let me get you all new ones," says Nick glancing at all of us and smiling as he recognises me. Scarlett goes from irate to dappy in the space of a heartbeat.

"Don't worry," I say mopping up the tea, trying at the same time to introduce him to Sarah and Scarlett, who I can tell are mentally sizing him up and gauging whether he lives up to their expectations.

"Nice to finally meet you both. I have heard a lot about you", says Nick.

"Don't believe her. She is a pathological liar," says Scarlett, her voice two octaves higher than normal, which suggests she likes him. This irritates me. Sarah, sensing this could become dangerous, asks him where Spiny is. According to Nick, she is spending the morning at her mother's house then going on to have her hair done. Nick has been exiled to dropping off dry cleaning and carrying out miscellaneous errands for her in the meantime. He had only just finished and felt he deserved a snack as a reward. I think he deserves one for being with Spiny, and probably something larger than just a panini.

We chat for a bit until he has to leave, Sarah and Scarlett giggling at some of his amusing anecdotes. As soon as he leaves, they round on me. "He SO fancies you," teases Scarlett. Sarah seems more restrained, but still suggests using her smartphone to look for photos of him online.

"Don't bother. He is not on Facebook," I point out. Scarlett then says she remembers Justine's Facebook password, from when she had borrowed Scarlett's laptop during her stay at the house.

"So?" I ask, not sure where this is going.

Sarah gets it before I do and explains. Justine is friends with Spiny, Spiny will probably have lots of photos and information about Nick. Therefore we do. I try to raise the ethical issues about using someone else's Facebook account like this, but my words fall on deaf ears because Scarlett has already taken the phone from Sarah and logged onto Justine's account.

"I will apologise to Justine later," she says, possibly even meaning it.

After scrolling through dozens of Spiny's inane status updates, and even more inane wall posts from Cheryl, she finds a few pictures of Nick. Jumping with glee she thrusts various images in my face, trying to get me to comment. I pretend to be above it all and do my best to show that I am not interested in her childish ways. That doesn't stop me sneakily looking for signs of any further evidence that he is stuck in a miserable relationship, or madly in love with the girl from work. (I am only human after all.)

Monday 14 January

Olga is back, and barely condescends to wish me "Happy New Year". Our warm reunion is interrupted by Mum calling and threatening to visit on the weekend. I try to put her off (gas leak, rat infestation, nuclear bomb), but she is undeterred. She and Dad are coming to see a musical and are hell-bent on subjecting me to dinner. They even invite Sarah and Scarlett too.

"I will ask them, but the chance of them spending their Saturday evening with a couple of near pensioners is slim," I say, trying to soften the rejection in advance.

Turns out I am completely wrong. My half-hearted relaying of Mum's offer is met with immediate acceptance. I can't believe it.
"We would love to see your parents," says Sarah, with suspicious enthusiasm. Scarlett joins in with saying she could do with a nice meal out.

I accuse them both of wanting to come along out of malice. I do not intend to sit and watch everyone list my foibles as they tuck into a chow mein. Both of them tell me I am being paranoid, but I just know they will spend the evening smirking at my Dad's lame efforts at being cool, and my Mum's taste in fashion. I am not looking forward to this at all.

Tuesday 15 January

Justine called last night to let us know how she was getting on. Although things were slightly better than when she was kicked out, her father was still complaining incessantly. She was trying her best but it was clear it was bringing her down. In a moment of weakness, and against my better judgement, I agreed that I would try to arrange for her to meet Nancy. That way she may get some encouragement, or even some news of jobs coming up.

No good deed goes unpunished.

Justine takes my offer at face value, turning up outside work promptly at 9 am. Slightly weirded-out, I push her into the Cupboard, where she spends the morning trying to "network" with Olga. After ten minutes of this, Olga barks that I had better take Justine elsewhere, or she will not be held responsible for what she does. Not thinking straight, I decide to walk Justine over to Nancy's office to arrange a casual introduction.

It goes a bit strangely:

Justine: "I heard you were a really, really, really good supervisor."
[Awkward long pause]
Nancy: "Um, that's nice to hear."
Justine: "I was thinking that I may be able to help you"
Nancy: "I see. How exactly?"
Justine: "I was thinking that I could come and work for you."
Nancy: "That's, that's a very... kind offer, but I am afraid that is not possible right now. We have enough staff, and I don't need another assistant."
Justine: "But I could do other things."
Nancy: "Such as?"
Justine: "Like psychotherapy?"
Nancy: **[looking surprised]** "You're a qualified psychotherapist?"
Justine: "No, but I was hoping you could teach me."
[Even longer pause. Nancy smiles in a really forced way and looks at her watch].
Nancy: "It's been nice talking to you but I have an appointment now."

Horrified, I yank her out into the corridor.

"Hmm, do you think she may take me on?" she asks, before the door even has a chance to shut.

"Have you lost your mind, or are you making me look like a complete fool on purpose?" I snap.

Justine is taken aback by this. She tells me she thought she was networking and this was all part of her grand plan to hustle relevant work. Having read about "perseverance" and "making connections" in one of my books, Justine thought that this was the best way to put it into action. I try to explain why putting a total stranger on the spot and demanding a job may not be the best way to get hired, but I have no idea if the message gets through to her.

How has this happened? My efforts to help Justine have backfired completely. In the end, I get Justine to leave by promising her I will get her some feedback if she just goes. It arrives sooner than I anticipate. Nancy comes to the Cupboard later, for a quiet word. Her feedback, is brief, to the point and extremely clear, "If you have any other friends, do me a favour and tell them not to approach me like that. This must never happen again."

Wednesday 16 January

I get an e-mail from HR informing me my contract of employment is coming to an end in late August. This shocks me, despite it being something I have been aware of for some time.

Like many assistants, my job is a fixed-term contract. My supervisor had initial funding for a year, but somehow extended it to over two years (which stretched to cover the job of her holiness Rebecca, and then myself). Permanent assistant posts are rare (because that would make things too easy), and my job was supposed to end ages ago, so there should be no real surprises. However, I have to admit, I have got cosy here.

In an ideal world, my job ending would not be a problem. I

would get on training this year and all would be bright and sparkly, with the end of my employment giving me a nice little break before term starts in September. However, if this doesn't happen I am going to be alongside Sarah and Justine in looking for a new job. Autumn still feels far away, I know it will creep up on me before I know it.

I delete the e-mail. If it isn't in my inbox, I don't have to worry about it.

Thursday 17 January

In supervision this morning, Nancy asks about how my preparation for the anxiety management group is coming along. I tell her it's going well. She then asks how many people have responded to the invitations I have sent out, and whether I feel okay running it myself this time. I open the long neglected folder and scrawled in her familiar scratchy handwriting on the top of the first page is:

"Thanks for agreeing to run the group on your own this time. I am sure you will be great..."

Shit.

I knew I should have read the folder sooner. All I can think about is the millions of difficult and/or embarrassing scenarios playing out in my mind. There I go getting everything wrong and the patients booing. Or how about my trousers falling down when I bend over. I am just not cut out for addressing groups of strangers. I am not even sure when I agreed to do this, but thinking back can vaguely remember losing my concentration some time before Christmas and nodding when I wasn't really listening. I have to stop doing that.

The first session is next Wednesday. So far, from my list of twelve patients, I have managed to get seven replies, and four say they can make it. This was perfectly fine when I had Nancy to hide behind, but alone it may as well be four thousand.

Friday 18 January

This morning, I half-heartedly chase the final few people remaining on the potential participant list. Three can't make it for various reasons, and I don't really make much of an effort to convince them otherwise. However, the other two are interested, so in under a week I am going to be in front of six people trying to convince them I know my stuff. I try to think back to when we last ran the group. All I can remember is Nancy doing most of the work, while I hung around offering people cups of tea, and writing things on a flip chart.

"I can't spend an hour a week just giving them tea. That doesn't count as acceptable evidence-based healthcare," I wail to Nick, as I pester him into an impromptu support meeting. Olga is no use in this regard; she is from the serves-you-right-for-not-taking-notes school of thought.

"Relax," he says, looking me straight in the eye. "I know you know more than you think. Stay calm, read the hand-outs and just pretend you are Nancy. You will be fine. I promise." I listen while he slowly convinces me that I am not a total idiot. Better still, he offers to come around my house and help rehearse the material on Sunday.

Perhaps this presenting lark may have some benefits?

Saturday 19 January

My prediction that dinner with the 'rents, Sarah, and Scarlett would be mildly awkward is a serious understatement. Particular highlights include the following:

1) Mum and Dad arrive early at this little Italian place they picked out near the theatre. Scarlett arrives around the time we have just finished our starters and dressed like she has come from auditioning for the *Rocky Horror Picture Show*. She also downs nearly an entire bottle of red wine on her own. Although my parents politely

overlook all of this, and do their best to be welcoming, this does not win Scarlett any brownie points with me. Sarah valiantly tries to make small talk, asking Mum how she found the show. Sadly, the tables are so close together, the couple sitting next to us (who also saw the musical) keep accidentally answering her questions.

2) Mum embarrasses me in front of my friends by talking at length about Gran's recent hernia operation, and getting everyone's name wrong. She addresses Scarlett as Sarah and Sarah as Scarlett. At one point she starts calling them both "Estelle", which gives me cause for concern that she is developing early onset dementia. I don't think I have even met an Estelle in my life, and certainly don't have one in my circle of friends. I have no idea where she has pulled that one from.

3) I get the feeling that Dad is distracted just a little too much by Scarlett this evening. He directs most of his attention at her throughout the meal (even asking her about the sodding Arctic Monkeys at one point). He laughs a bit too hard at her jokes, and his look lingers a tad too long when her boob nearly pops out of her top when she takes off her leather jacket. When mum spots this, her face is like thunder. That is one conversation in the car home that I will be glad to miss.

Sunday 20 January

Nick bails on our rehearsal session at the last minute which puts the final nail in the coffin of the weekend. The ever-faithful Sarah steps up to take his place and I practice my first session of anxiety management in the living room. After the events of yesterday, Scarlett, the Dad-magnet, is very much in my bad books. Fortunately, she has had the decency to remain in her bedroom. Partly out of shame, but also because she is nursing a colossal hangover. Which she more than deserves.

I set up the PowerPoint slides, and clutch my written notes in sweaty hands. Unsurprisingly, I mess up the first few times. I get my cues wrong. I stammer. I forget huge chunks of information. I give out the wrong information. Entire slides go missing. Half way through the presentation, my laptop glitches and iTunes starts up. *Welcome to the Jungle* by Guns N' Roses belts out at top volume through the speakers. Scarlett starts banging on the floor screaming at us to keep the volume down.

I feel like crying. I can't do this.

Sarah diplomatically says it was a brave try, and convinces me to go through it one more time. Second time around I get through it okay. I nail most of it, and remember the sequence of slides, what to say and when to click to the next slide. Sarah even asks some questions that I am able to scrape through. My confidence lifts ever so slightly, and I start to think that maybe I can pull this off. We both cheer loudly as I get to the end, which makes Scarlett scream down the stairs again for us to shut up.

Monday 21 January

I have now come to two firm conclusions:

1) The more I think about it the more I really don't want to run this group.

2) The concept of "gathering experience" is a brilliant con trick perpetrated by the old on the young.

The idea of paying your dues, and working your way up the ladder is just a way for people who are older than you to get you to do the stuff that they don't want to do, despite being paid more. The idea that "We had to put up with it, now you can," doesn't hold any water. They used to put up with putting gay men in prison, but thankfully we don't do that anymore. That is the whole idea of progress.

I share my views with Olga who has the nerve to point out a minor flaw in my argument. Nancy still runs groups and writes reports. Bah. You can prove anything with logic.

Olga also bets that Nancy would be happy to trade places with me, as she would probably welcome a chance to "...spend the day messing around on Facebook and complaining about life". This is total nonsense. (Nancy doesn't even have a Facebook profile.)

Besides, my life is way more insecure and uncertain than hers. Olga looks at me with a stare that could strip paint off the Cupboard walls, and tells me she has spent the last ten years, her youth, her eyesight and any potential chance for motherhood in a research career built on uncertainty. I try to defend myself and say that she made the choice for the career, and that no one forced her to do it. With a smug grin she says the same could be said for me running the anxiety management group.

I shut up.

Tuesday 22 January

I am doing last minute checks all morning. As I come back from scoping out the meeting room to make sure there is a working plug point, I bump into Spiny who has just come from Nancy's office.

"Ooh, very important project. Challenging, but someone has to do it," she says brandishing a folder that looks suspiciously like my report. I immediately guess she has been asked to do something similar for her service, and is using my report as a guide.

She follows me back to the Cupboard, and tells me she wants to talk about some *essential material* for the next Assistants' Group. It is nothing of the sort, only some inconsequential decision about the agenda. I observe she makes it a point to raise her voice by several decibels to make sure that Olga can

164

overhear us, in some desperate attempt to sound impressive. It's a wasted effort. I know for a fact that Olga couldn't give any less of a shit if she tried because:

1) She doesn't like Spiny.
2) She doesn't like me.
3) She wouldn't care if we spent the duration of our Assistants' Group jumping around on a bouncy castle.

I know I shouldn't, but I can't resist showing off to Spiny that I am going to be running the anxiety management group by myself tomorrow. Her face goes slightly green with envy as I tell her. I casually mention I am really looking forward to it.

As Spiny leaves in a sulk, Olga turns to me in astonishment. "Really looking forward to it?" she says, mimicking my voice.

I explain that it was a way of getting back at Spiny, and I am really still terrified. I explain the prestige in doing clinical work by oneself, and how it's all valuable stuff to talk about at interviews. She shrugs as if to say she will never understand the Assistant Psychologist mind-set, and has no intention of trying.

Wednesday 23 January

G-Day.

I feel slightly hypocritical running an anxiety management group, as I am probably the most anxious person in the room. Six people turn up, two men and four women, and I explain the group will run weekly for the next four Wednesdays. Then I turn to my first slide and start going through it. To my surprise, they all sit and listen politely. No one stands up and leaves, or asks to see a "proper doctor". The whole session passes quickly and is over before I know it.

As they leave I give them the hand-outs and thank them. They tell me it was helpful and that they will be back next week. As I pack everything away I feel oddly exhilarated. I rush off and tell Olga all about it. Then Eva at reception. Then Justine, who squeals "Congratulations!" down the phone. And so on with everyone until Scarlett, who snarkily points out it was just a small talk for 6 people, and it's not like I have solved global warming. That girl is such a killjoy.

Thursday 24 January

I find Nick in the staff room, and he is extremely apologetic about bailing out on me on Sunday. Last minute family issues cropped up and he had to deal with it. I tell him it's no problem and sympathise, before telling him stories about my own strange family.

He congratulates me on how well things went yesterday. He knew I would be okay and tells me that I should have more faith in myself. He gets me to admit I am less anxious about next week, and that nothing went wrong. As we talk, I keep hoping he will suggest going out again, and am slightly disappointed that he doesn't. Instead he tells me that Spiny wants to talk to me. I can't think of anything worse, and wonder the best course of action. Refuse to his face? Make an excuse? Pretend to be dead?

"If you don't want to, I can make up an excuse," says Nick spotting my hesitation.

"Thanks. It's just that..." I fail to come up with a plausible reason.

"Don't worry, it will be our little secret," he says. A phrase that I would normally associate with child molesters, but he makes it sound sexy. Like we are co-conspirators or accomplices against the evil forces of Spiny.

Friday 25 January

My plans for a celebratory Friday night out are brought down in flames as I get home to find Sarah and Scarlett both in bed, pallid and sweating (individual beds; they are ill, not shooting a porno). Apparently there is a bug that has been going around, which scares me. I can't afford to get ill right now, so I quarantine them in their rooms, and obsessively start using hand gel and wet wipes.

Inconsiderately, they couldn't be sick in a convenient way; their illness just has to involve smells, noises, and long periods in the toilet. We only have one loo in the house, and its current state is so bad I am thinking of using my pot plant as a substitute until things improve.

So far, I have made several trips to the pharmacist, fetched soup, refilled hot water bottles, brought tablets, and have had to answer the landline on numerous occasions. They have far busier social lives than me, and I quickly progress from: "Hello. Hi, how are you? No, I am afraid she is sick. Yes, it is terrible. Can I take a message?" to "What do you want? No. Sick. Whatever." I learn fast that I am better with mental health than physical health. I wouldn't last a week as a nurse.

Saturday 26 January

I go out for dinner tonight. It is almost a mini-alumni reunion, with a loose group of people (loose as in 'approximate', not 'slutty'), who were living in the same halls of residence in our final year. Every so often we meet up, because we all ended up gravitating to the big smoke once we left higher education.

We mainly stay in touch by emailing amusing photos of cats falling off things or videos of Americans setting things on fire, and occasionally use someone's birthday as an excuse to get drunk in each other's company. Sarah normally comes along, but as the tone of the group is cocktails and urban sophistication, she feels her explosive diarrhoea may get in the way.

There are about a dozen of us at a tapas place. It's the sort where molten cheese gets everywhere, and you end up inadvertently eating someone else's dinner. The sangria flows, the conversation is enjoyable, and I find myself having a good time. I am sitting next to Helen, a former history student, who I once shared a kitchen with and together, we repelled the Great Ant Invasion of '04. She has brought her new boyfriend Hugo, who is joining us for the first time.

Helen inquires about how Sarah is doing. I explain how she is ill but still plodding along at the nursing home. Helen looks sympathetic and says it is a pity she has not been able to find a proper job yet. I get a bit defensive about this. I tell her that while it may not be exactly what Sarah wants to do forever, she does work hard and gets paid for her efforts. Sounds like a proper job to me. Helen, realising her faux pas, apologises. At this point Hugo swoops into the conversation.

"It's not a *real* job though," he sneers.

"Well, it's not fictional. She's not saying she is Harry Potter's bank manager," I reply.

"No, but it's not what you would call *graduate* level though, is it?" He says this with a smug note of triumph, like he has automatically won the argument. Helen looks around uncomfortably and tries to change the subject. Hugo ignores her and goes in for the kill.

"After all, you don't need to go to university for three years to wipe some old granny's arse do you?" he laughs loudly to the rest of the table and takes a swig of Sangria. I fondly recall Helen's university boyfriend, a sensitive and thoughtful poet called Rob, and wonder how she ended up with this smug self-satisfied prick instead.

I defend Sarah's decision, and explain that I too have done similar work in the past. There is dignity in labour, and a social value to what we both do. I also ask how he would feel if one of those arses he spoke of so dismissively belonged to his grandmother. He snorts and rolls his eyes, attempting to dismiss my comments as beneath his dignity.

"So, what exactly do YOU do that is so great?" I ask.

"I work in tech sales," he mumbles vaguely.

"He means he sells vacuum cleaners door-to-door," clarifies Helen helpfully. Hugo wisely remains quiet for the rest of the evening. I hope for Helen's sake she still has Rob's phone number stashed somewhere.

Sunday 27 January

Checking Facebook and the online forums, I am rudely reminded that we will find out if we have interviews soon. The process is drawn out across the whole month of February and goes into March. It means days of holding my breath as the postman comes, and my heart stopping every time an unknown phone number pops up on my mobile.

One of the courses that Sarah has put herself down for has a screening test. These are a relatively recent invention where courses that don't want to shovel through piles of forms set a written task. The best performers get interviewed, and it's all transparent and above board. For the chosen ones at least; the unlucky majority curse about what a stupid method it is.

This starts to make me feel unnerved. Having just got over the trauma of sending off the application, it seems far too early to be subjecting us to further stress. I find out Mum, during our weekly phone call, agrees with me, but I decide not to take her up on her kind offer to write a letter to her MP, as they probably have bigger fish to fry.

Monday 28 January

Justine meets me after work, and we have dinner together. It looks like she has been a busy girl since I last saw her. Not only has she had to fend off her father, but now the Jobcentre are on her case about finding work.

It is not for the lack of her trying. I gather she has been cold-calling almost everyone connected to mental health or psychology in the phone book, pestering them for work. Everyone has been fair game, ranging from the CEO to the floor sweeper. I try to explain, diplomatically, that neither of those two would be in a position to do any hiring and firing.

Justine interrupts me, "But the job centre says I should look for work everywhere."

"They don't mean it *literally*." I tell her. "You aren't likely to find work under your bed, or at the bottom of the garden with the fairies."

On a happier note, Justine mentions she is now dating Dave. I rack my brains to work out who Dave is or where I may have met him.

"You know, Santa," she helpfully reminds me.

It takes a second for me to realise she is not talking about the mythical character, but the department store stand-in from her last job. I tell her that red certainly suits him, but he probably could do with a shave.

Ignoring my sarcasm, she goes on to say how Dave has been really nice, and judging by the dippy little smile she gets whenever she mentions his name, she is clearly into him. I know that Justine has notoriously bad taste in men, but *Santa*?

Tuesday 29 January

I am in the middle of signposting some poor teenage boy who is being bullied about how to reach Childline, when Mum calls. Usually, I would tell her I am busy, but she breathlessly informs me that there is a letter and it looks official. I quickly deal with the boy, sending him on his (not-so-merry) way, before I grab my mobile and hurriedly call her back.

My throat is dry and I am trembling. They can't be sending letters out already, can they? It's not supposed to start so soon. It feels unsporting, like they haven't offered me a last cigarette before putting the blindfold on. Why did they send it to my home address? Was I so stressed I put the wrong details on the form. My mind races in fifteen different directions as I try to make sense of it all. It also crosses my mind that maybe they are specially writing to me because my form was so bad that they decided to nominate me for a "Worst Applicant Award".

"Are you still there?" My mother's voice sounds tinny at the other end. "Shall I open it?"

"Yes. Wait. No, don't! I mean yes. Open it." I tell her. My brain has no control over what is coming out of my mouth.

She opens it. False alarm. She starts reading out a circular from the British Psychological Society flogging books that are either too expensive to buy or too obscure to bother reading.

"NO!" I yell at my mother down the phone. "I do not want to buy any sodding books and you can tell them that they can stick their newsletter up their..."

"Is everything alright?" asks Dr Anafu, who I haven't seen since his stint on the dance floor at the Christmas party.

I apologise for my loudness, promising I will keep the volume down. Mum is upset at my outburst and is worried she has done something wrong. I spend the next ten minutes calming her down and tell to shred the letter. I then instruct her NOT to shred any other letters that may come through, but instead to call me at once. But only if they look official. Mum sounds confused by all this and I can almost hear her mentally blaming my choice of degree for my mood swings, bizarre instructions, and impending nervous breakdown.

Wednesday 30 January

It's the second anxiety management group session, but sadly the bug that has knocked out Sarah and Scarlett has taken its toll on the group. Only three people turn up this morning, and I sadly observe that we could have held it in the Cupboard, and still had room for the coffee making equipment. However, the show must go on. I go through the twenty minute presentation, guiding them through some basic relaxation skills and elementary breathing exercises. Except for an unexpected asthma attack that nearly brings things to a halt, it goes smoothly.

So much so, I fail to realise that it has gone over time, and our little chat is broken up by a harsh rap at the door. Three irritated looking health visitors peer in at us, asking pointedly when we will be finished. I apologise profusely and take this as my cue to wrap up the session.

Afterwards, I report back to Nancy about how the group is going. She tells me it sounds like it is going well, and asks me how I would feel if there was someone else helping me run it. I joke that it would have bulked out the numbers today, but if she wanted to join me she would be welcome. She shakes her head and makes it clear that Spiny has been the one asking. She contacted Nancy a few days ago asking if she could co-facilitate the group with me.

"What do you think?" she says.

As I would quite like to keep my job, I don't tell her the first response that crosses my mind.

Thursday 31 January

"I can't believe she would do this to me!" I rant to Olga. "She doesn't care about anxiety management. She just wants to pad out her CV and take the credit like she does with everything

172

else." I had kept it all pent up until this morning, until she remarked I was quieter than usual. She probably regrets saying this, because I unload both barrels at her.

I half expect Olga to respond with something along the lines of keeping it in perspective, and that it's not so bad. She doesn't. Instead, she takes my baton and sprints off into the distance with it.

Olga's character assassination exceeds anything I am able to come up with. From bitter experience on the research side, she brings up how annoying Spiny has been with getting data to her and how she has a tendency to completely ignore any instruction unless it comes from Nancy or one of the other psychologists.

"Don't get me started about that whole Rebecca thing," she says, the venom visibly gathering on her tongue.

"Maybe I need to start thinking about how I can get out of this?" I say, not wanting to get her worked up any further.

In the end I decide that the best thing to do would be to go to Nancy's office and explain I have given her proposal considerable thought, but feel it would be a bad idea. The rest of the group would have to get to know a new person half way through, and I have built up a good rapport with the participants. In fact I plan every possible objection that Nancy may have; short of announcing that I hate Spiny's guts and the only time I would be happy to work with her would be to demonstrate an invasive, painful surgical procedure with her being the test subject.

Instead of saying, "Tough. Just do it," Nancy listens to my concerns, thinks it over for a second and says, "Fair enough. If it ain't broke don't fix it."

Almost instantly, I feel a huge weight evaporate from my shoulders and I can almost see the sun shining through the rain clouds. I should have said this yesterday.

FEBRUARY

Friday 1 February

I am having a very peaceful morning in the Cupboard. Everything is prepped, answered and dealt with. I treat myself to a cup of proper coffee while my email inbox slowly loads up. Not the usual instant rubbish that I normally use, but proper stuff from the coffee maker in the small kitchenette. Someone bought it in ages ago but it had long since run out of real coffee beans and filter papers. In a rare moment of good natured magnanimity, I brought some of both yesterday and graciously offer some to Eva and the admin ladies next door.

As I sit down and take a long sip from my freshly brewed cup, my inbox pings. It's from Spiny. I open it up and nearly spit my coffee across the monitor. Spiny is not happy at being side-lined after hearing from Nancy yesterday and tells me she has had "further consultation" with her own team. Using her position as "the senior member of the data management team" (a meaningless term if ever there was one), she says she needs to attend in order to oversee the evaluation of the group.

I dash off a reply explaining that while I am incredibly grateful for her offer of assistance, I am more than capable of evaluating the group myself. I let her know that I would happily forward on the information to her straight afterwards, and get back to the important business of my cup of lovingly prepared (but increasingly tepid) coffee.

Twenty minutes later the phone rings. It's Spiny's supervisor, Matilda who is the service's lead psychologist, who just happens to have strong links to the clinical psychology training course I would most like to get accepted onto. Having been made aware of the situation she thought she would "drop me a line" and find out what the problem is. With gradually dawning horror I realise what has happened. Spiny has basically gone running to mummy to tell her all about how horrible I have been, and how mean I am for not letting her play with my new dollies/patients.

I am stuck somewhere between fear, deference, and extreme annoyance. I "umm" and "ahh" to Matilda trying to give her the impression that this stupid, obvious manipulation is a stroke of genius. Somehow I am able to negotiate that Spiny would be best off coming to the final group rather than to both remaining sessions.

Matilda considers this for a second before proclaiming that this is an excellent plan. I feel acute joy at scoring brownie points with her as well as complete and utter dejection that I have had to play along with Spiny's half-baked machinations. I ring off only to find that my coffee has now long since gone cold. I tip the contents of the cup into the soil of the spider plant, my morning ruined.

Saturday 2 February

A letter from the landlord drops through the letterbox this morning complaining that there was a spot inspection during the week. The gist of it is that the house is not being maintained to the standard set out in the tenancy agreement. Apparently Scarlett's pit of a bedroom and Sarah's habit of keeping all her electrical appliances on a single extension socket has not gone unnoticed. I yell for the others to come down and tell them I told them this would happen. (I don't tell them the letter mentioned the red wine stain on my bedroom carpet. I feel justified in doing this, as it was not my fault). Both of them make excuses and promise that it won't happen again.

Muttering dark threats, I find myself sitting on Sarah's beanbag munching on Maltesers as she gets ready to go out to work. Scarlett sits near the bay window and absent mindedly watches Julia Roberts shopping on Rodeo Drive as the well-worn DVD plays. Sarah listens to me complain about how crappy my week has been, and how I don't need this now.

"I know," she says sympathetically as she pulls on a sock, noticing that there is a massive hole where her big toe sticks out. "Don't worry, I will square it with the Landlord," she assures me, as she pulls the offending sock off and thrusts it into the overflowing wastepaper bin near her bed.

Her kind offer bursts a levy somewhere and before I know it I am babbling on at her about Olga being unbearable, my contract ending, and Spiny paving the way for a dance floor directly above my grave. Even Nick being flaky on me gets a mention. Sarah hugs me, and tells me it will be okay. That I am doing really well and the stress will pass soon. She points out all the positive things that have happened at work and all the great experience I am getting.

Scarlett, silent until now, evidently feels left out. From the corner of the room, she suddenly pipes up, "If you think you have it bad. I will match your shit and raise you. I am pregnant."

We both freeze. The volume of the DVD suddenly becomes unbearably loud. The air rushes out of my lungs as I struggle to process this. This cannot be happening.

"What...why...where...when...who..." is all Sarah is able to come out with.

"How?" I ask, immediately regret saying this. Out of all the things I actually do want to know, the "how" part is fairly clear. I am not sure whether to laugh or cry.

"I can't believe it," says Sarah, sinking onto the bed in shock.

"Don't." Scarlett turns to us and cracks a grin, "I am just messing with you." Sarah gives out a loud long nervous laugh. I don't.

"You bitch! I can't believe you just did that to us." I say, losing my temper.

"Hey, you were both having such a good time with your pity party," replies Scarlett. "I just felt you needed some perspective. Whatever you are going through, I guarantee you, others have it a lot worse. Besides, I bet you have forgotten all about the landlord and your precious group being hi-jacked." And with that she just waltzes out of the door.

Sunday 3 February

I still haven't forgiven Scarlett for that stunt she pulled. "Annoyed" does not even begin to describe it. So I do what I always do when I am upset and call Dad. I whine down the line telling him how everything is going wrong and how everyone is against me.

"We had this conversation the night before your exams, and look what happened," he gently reminds me. He tells me not to worry and it will all be okay in the end, and no matter what happens he will be proud of me.

As a clever way of distraction, he starts telling me how Mum keeps going on at him to take up salsa dancing. I find this idea oddly comforting. The mental image of my poor father being ordered around the village hall by some swarthy Latino/Patrick Swayze dance instructor makes me smile, despite myself.

"Oh, and isn't it great news about Maddie?" he continues.

"What news?"

"Haven't you heard yet?" he says. "Maddie and Matt have just got engaged. Sorry, but I thought you already knew."

I get off the phone to Dad and log straight onto Facebook. Yes, the signs are all there. Photos of the engagement ring. Wall posts about honeymoon destinations. Lots of "LIKES" regarding meringue type dresses. I feel miffed. How the hell did I miss all of this? There would have been a time when Maddie wouldn't have bought a pencil case without consulting me first, and now I find out she is getting betrothed second hand from my Dad. I sadly think that out of sight clearly means out of mind. I am far away and we aren't twelve-year-olds any more. (To be fair, if I am being really honest, I can't even remember the last time I checked her Facebook status).

I quickly text a congratulatory message. She messages me back a few hours later saying that it was all a bit sudden. So sudden that they are planning things to go ahead in a few months. Wow. She asks if I want to be a bridesmaid. To my eternal shame, instead of saying "I would be honoured," like any normal human being would, I respond "Well, it depends on whether I get interviews and when they will be."

God! Is there no end to the ways this application stuff hasn't taken over my life?

Monday 4 February

I am in supervision when Nancy lets me know that she has been invited to talk at a big conference at the end of the month. In her usual resourceful way she has managed to wangle some money and asks if I want to go with her. I almost bite her hand off at the offer.

"I am SO up for this conference. I am your woman. Just call me Miss Conference," I tell her. It's only after I leave her office I realise how strange my response probably sounded.

Olga is equally surprised by my enthusiasm when I get back

to the Cupboard. She takes the opportunity to go into lengthy rant about why all conferences should be banned, the lack of decent food, the horrors of leaving Rasputin and her dog behind, as well as worrying about parking in an unfamiliar place. (Olga worries about parallel parking to such an extent I think it qualifies as its own diagnostic category of motoring-related anxiety disorder.)

I don't listen to her. I am too busy being excited. The sad truth is that I have never had a single perk in any of my jobs so far. The nearest I have ever got to having a freebie is when I was a support worker, and the nurse in charge told me to help myself to all the incontinence pads I wanted (an offer, I am glad to say, I never felt the need to take her up on). So it's quite a big thrill go somewhere, hobnob with the great and the good of the psychology world, and get paid to stay in a hotel. My university friends in corporate jobs or on graduate schemes all brag regularly on Facebook about jetting off to New York on business, or post pictures of themselves relaxing in hotel jacuzzis. Now, finally, it is my turn.

I can't wait.

Tuesday 5 February

The apocalypse has started. The end is nigh. Interview season is upon us.

People have started to post online asking about whether or not anyone has heard news about interviews. Equal numbers have replied telling everyone to chill the hell out (but on the off-chance if anyone has heard something, please do feel free to tell). The rumour mill is cranking up and there are all kinds of strops and discussions about which courses give feedback, or which ones unfairly discriminate if you are older/foreign/male/have mediocre A-levels.

By the time I finish reading, I am under the impression that the primary purpose of clinical psychology training courses is to devise new and improved ways of excluding people on the most arbitrary of grounds. The actual training aspect is only a minor afterthought. I am not the only one. Sarah sits with me as I comb through various threads, blogs, and tweets, lapping up every minor comment and opinion.

"I haven't got any experience of sign language. Do you think that will be held against me?" she asks nervously. I tell her that it's probably okay. Then we read something about people that had the misfortune not to attend a top ten university, which prompts further angst.

"It was higher in the league tables when we joined, but it then dropped in *The Sunday Times* ranking by the time we left. They can't hold that against us, can they? That's not our fault!" Sarah wails.

"Don't worry" I assure her, with more authority than I feel. "It's still okay in *The Guardian* ranking chart. I'm sure most of the admissions tutors are probably left-wing, and are more likely to read that." Almost the second I say it, I start to wonder how long it will be before this newly made-up course-related factoid starts appearing online.

Wednesday 6 February

After the poor attendance at the anxiety management group last time I am relieved to find that everyone turned up this week. On one hand, this is good, as it means people are getting something out of the group. On the other hand, it means I have a larger audience to witness my clumsiness this week.

I trip over the kettle lead. I manage to spill the small jug of milk of across the floor. I pour boiling water into the sugar bowl for no reason whatsoever. It takes me four attempts to get people's drinks order because I keep forgetting what people want. By the end, one of the ladies takes pity on me and expertly takes over beverage duties. This is just as well otherwise my anxiety management session would have consisted of either the group laughing at me, or waiting for a little car to pull up and a dancing bear to come out. (Note to self: Possibly suggest to Nancy as new form of therapy).

However, once we are under way things start going smoothly. We go through the various techniques and practice the skills from last time. I can see they are all slowly getting better at it, and they seem happy. As they leave, I inform the group that we will be having our final session next week and to expect Spiny to join us. Dismayingly, they don't immediately grab torches and pitchforks, and nod obligingly instead.

Thursday 7 February

Mail watching officially starts today.

The reason I know this is because Sarah bounds into my room at some godforsaken hour of the morning, leaps onto my bed screaming, "Oh my God! Oh my God!" She thrusts a piece of paper into my face. Groggily coming around to consciousness, I am not really sure what she is yelling about until I take the sheet off her. I see the university logo on the top of it and read the arrangement for the scheduled screening test. Nice for her, but it certainly doesn't warrant using my stomach as a trampoline.

"I can do this. This is it, my big break!" she beams, eagerly re-reading it again. The test is next Friday and fortunately it is close enough that she doesn't have stay in some hotel the night before. She merrily bounces off to tell Scarlett, before coming back to my room and trawling through my book case. When I ask her what she is doing, she says she has to start revising and I leave her hunting through my room looking for long forgotten textbooks.

"Has she suddenly gone bipolar?" a bleary-eyed Scarlett asks, peering out from behind her bedroom door. I shake my head and explain the invite. Scarlett notices my comparative lack of eagerness and I have to explain that it's something that almost everyone gets selected for, and the real part comes after the computer test.

"Don't burst her bubble," she whispers to me, as we watch various textbooks go flying past us. "She really needs all the positivity she can get at the moment." I tell her that Sarah is coping just fine, and if anyone needs help it's probably me. Seeing her invite has brought me out in cold sweat, and I feel nauseous at the prospect of opening my own letters any day now.

Friday 8 February
No mail

The phone on my desk rings. I pick it up. "Hey beautiful." It's Nick.

"Hi," I reply

"Oh, I am sorry, I thought I was talking to Olga," he says facetiously. "Oh, well I suppose you'll have to do. What are you doing?"

I glance around at the piles of paper, the internet browser open at Facebook, and the stack of trashy magazines by my chair. "Not much. Have to write up the notes from the anxiety management group."

"Bored of surfing the internet already?"

"Oi, shut it you. If you've just called up to mock me, I'm going to hang up."

"If you do that, you won't be able to hear my invite to lunch."

It's a sunny day, so we decide to sit near the canal and have sandwiches there. It feels like I haven't seen him in ages, and he says something about having to be out of the office a lot these last few weeks. He asks me what I have been up to and I update him. I gripe about waiting for interview letters, and my feckless housemates. Without even being conscious of it, I even drift into complaining about Spiny muscling into my final group session, until a voice booms in my head, **"Stop slagging off his girlfriend, you idiot!"** stopping me in my tracks. I look over at Nick, but he doesn't seem to be taking offence. On the contrary he starts laughing.

"Ah, so *that's* what she was so hung up about last Friday," he says, as if a mystery has finally been solved. "You were the one that messed up her big plans. You would not believe what she..." he shakes his head as if to avoid a very long story.

I am dying to find out what the view from the enemy camp was, but am sensitive enough not to push it. Instead, I change the subject and tell him how I am looking forward to going to the conference with Nancy.

"Cool. I am going to that as well. Didn't Nancy tell you?" he says.

"Nope. You forget how far out of the loop I am," I remind him. "I am looking forward to a bit of high-class living."

"Hot and cold running water. Your own trouser press. As much sparkling water as you can drink. It's just like Vegas."

"Very funny. I don't suppose you have any advice for a conference virgin?"

"Hmm, let's see." He thinks for a second, "Whatever you do, don't take a taxi because it's only a five minute walk. Never use the vending machines because they don't work. Oh, and above all else ask for a rear facing room, otherwise instead of the rolling hills, you will end up with a stunning view of the A543."

I carefully write all of this down, underlining "NO A543!!!" several times. This whole conference thing is going to be good.

Saturday 9 February
No mail.

Sarah is getting into some serious heavy duty revising. She isn't going out, she refuses all Tom's attempts at coming over, and has almost glued herself to her desk. This makes me feel uncomfortable. I feel guilty that I am not revising, even though I have nothing to actually revise for. Just glancing through Sarah's open doorway makes me feel unproductive and lazy.

This is nothing new. Unlike me, Sarah has always been one of those annoying types that does her homework on the first night it has been set. However, she has gone beyond her usual efforts and has gone into a Zen-like higher state. The only time I saw her today was when she came into my room, babbled something about "homogeneity of variance" and walked out again. She has stick labels, mind maps and clever mnemonic phrases Blu-tacked everywhere. Watching her work is like watching the world's most boring *Rocky*-style training montage.

I go downstairs and find Scarlett in the living room. "Can you tell me why I found a post-it note with 'stages of infant development' stuck to my bum?" she says accusingly.

"Don't blame me. Blame Sarah."
"That girl's getting more and more stressed." Scarlett sighs.
"And you know this because..?"
"Well, she is eating more. And all of it junk. I saw an empty packet of Pop Tarts in the bin, which means it's pretty bad now."
"I think you are over-reacting. It's just that some of us are more used to hard work than others." I reply, slightly smugly.

Scarlett rolls her eyes at me. She stomps off to make some coffee, muttering darkly that at the rate Sarah is going, there isn't

184

going to be much left in the confectionery aisle in Tesco's by the end of the week.

Sunday 10 February

Justine comes around to the house, sees Sarah at work, and immediately starts fretting about hearing back from her course choices. I tell her to relax and that Sarah is just going a bit over the top for her screening test.

This is the wrong thing to say. Justine sulks that she was rejected from that course because of her 2:2 degree class. She maintains it's monstrously unfair they turned her down, despite the course in question being clear about this requirement on their website. She feels that they should somehow make an exception for her, because she was trying really hard, and that is more important than how good she was at studying.

I am not sure about the logic of this, but I decide not to pursue it. We go to the kitchen to make tea and I ask her how things are going with Dave. Rather well as it turns out. The two have been spending quite a lot of time with each other, and he has been taking her out to all kind of lovely places. I keep waiting for any mention of dismissive comments/alcoholism/evidence of a wife, but hear nothing. She may have picked a winner this time. She says that Dave would really like to meet us and suggests that we all go out together for dinner. "Why not?" I reply, intrigued about this specimen of masculine perfection.

She is even thinking of moving in with him. It is on the tip of my tongue to tell her how she needs to be careful about choosing who she lives with, but a glimpse of an empty packet of chocolate digestives in the bin and Scarlett's ever increasing pile of washing up, suggests I may not be the best judge of this myself.

Monday 11 February
Mail!

Sarah has a special sixth sense about application letters and hands me a rather formal-looking stiff envelope. "It's thin," she notices sombrely. Thin is definitely bad. Thick letters are bountiful happy things bursting with success, maps, itineraries and interview schedules. Thin letters emerge from the Devil's anus - brief and pointed with snippy little comments about it being all so tough this year and "all the best for the future". Thin letters include bills, increases in rent, and speeding fines. We do not like thin letters in this house and know from bitter experience nothing good comes from them. I hold my breath as I hastily tear open the envelope. A slight flicker of optimism sparks in the back of my head. I mean it could be positive, I think to myself. It may only be a reminder for a smear test.

It's not. Sarah's uncanny ability is spot on. Cold, brutal rejection. Ouch. I dimly hear my old primary school teacher telling me that it's not the winning; it's the taking part that counts. My old primary school teacher always was full of crap.

I don't even need to fully read the dreadful little message.

"Dear Applicant. Thank you for your application for the clinical psychology course at the University of.... Unfortunately, we are unable to offer you a place at interview this year...Record number of applicants....high standard of competition..."

I feel someone has smashed a chair over my back. Rejection never gets easier.

Gutted. It was my first choice place, and I really thought I may have stood a chance with this one. It turns out I am not even worthy of consideration at all. I have a little mini rage attack and angrily scrunch it into a ball, jamming it as deep as I can into the overflowing bin. Scarlett looks on in alarm. I snatch my bag and stuff it with my things, getting ready to leave for work. Sarah tries to say something sympathetic but I am not in any place to hear it.

I brood about it on the journey in. All that study, all that sacrifice for this. An anonymous mass produced page of A4 telling me that everything I have built up is for nothing. They didn't even put my name on it. I try to keep the tears from welling up as the bus glides to a halt.

The thoughts come thick and fast. Why? What else do I need to do? How the hell can anyone stand a chance? What is the point of this? Would it be too much to at least have provided some feedback? They get darker as I approach the building. What if I never make it? Have I wasted all my time, effort, money on what is only a pipe dream? What are my parents going to think? I picture my father's face, always so proud of me, and imagine telling him that it's all been for nothing. Nancy is going to think I am an idiot. What else am I going to do? Am I going to be like this at fifty when everyone else has a steady job, kids, and a proper home?

Then there is a thin, reedy voice in the back of my head that starts up. Maybe you aren't as good as you think you are? You aren't clever or good enough to do this. Unbidden, a hated memory of a crusty old social psychology lecturer swims into view, "Clinical Psychology? Too competitive. I wouldn't even bother. You'll never make it".

As soon as I sit down Olga looks concerned and says, "You look constipated. Here. I have dried prunes in my bag for you." I am not in the mood for this and plug my earphones in. Over the next hour I studiedly ignore the various calls and texts flashing up on my phone.

Instead I torture myself by going online to Facebook and the forums to see how everyone else did. This is the only thing that seems to help. I read about the vast swathes of people that are also in the same boat as me. There is comfort in shared misery. Clearly a single rejection on the doormat is an individual tragedy, but a huge faceless crowd of people also talking about the same thing makes me realise I am in the overwhelming majority.

187

By lunchtime, I manage to gain more perspective and hurriedly contact everyone and apologise where I need to. Throwing myself into work helps. I even end up taking Olga up on her kind offer and spend the afternoon munching dried fruit. To my surprise, this helps my mood considerably. Afterwards, I suspect she has soaked them in Prozac.

One down, three to go.

Tuesday 12 February
No mail.

However, Sarah got an identical rejection letter from the same course that rejected me yesterday. All things considered, she takes it better than I did; shrugging that if they didn't pick me they probably wouldn't have picked her. We then spend an inordinate amount of time discussing why two identical letters sent to the same address arrived on different days. Conspiracy theories abound. Perhaps my rejection was more of a rejection, and that they wanted to make it known to me sooner that I was out of the game. Sarah feels the opposite that her later arrival somehow emphasises her second-class status. We debate how they may have some kind of clandestine sorting order, or if the delay conveys a secret message of encouragement.

"Stop. You are both starting to scare me," says an unnerved Scarlett. "Being with you two is like living in some weird cult. It's not the sodding *DaVinci Code*, its Royal Mail being crap as usual". Making it a point to ignore her, we start carefully checking letter dates and postmarks (mine being covered in potato peel and pasta sauce from being fished out of the bin). We both agree that you can never be too careful about these things.

Wednesday 13 February
No mail.

The day of the last group session has rolled around. Just as I finish doing all the hard work setting up the room and struggling to move the heavy chairs, Spiny waltzes in.

"HI-YA! You didn't forget I was coming, did you?" she asks with a smile faker than her nail extensions. She is carrying a pile of paper and is decked out in a Harvey Nicks power suit looking like she has just been kicked off *The Apprentice*.

"How could I?" I reply truthfully.

As she creates a nest of forms and clipboards, I attempt to set some ground rules, knowing too well what she is capable of. I explain that I have a programme already worked out that has my supervisor's approval. Her job is to focus on the group evaluation and leave the content and teaching to me.

Spiny immediately starts to talk over me, telling me how much she has read about anxiety management and nearly boring me into a coma about how she is such an expert at doing groups. Fortunately the arrival of the members shuts her up and we get started. I take great delight in delegating coffee making duties to her, barely concealing my glee as the packet of instant coffee explodes as she tries to open it.

In theory, the session should have been a gentle ending and recap of the key points. In practice it quickly becomes a bitter power struggle. After my introduction and letting the group know about Spiny and her evaluation, I start with my first slide. Which she hijacks. I move on and she undermines the next ("Actually a paper has just come out saying that doesn't really work as you put it"). When she is not publically implying that I am an idiot she takes a good ten minutes giving her opinion.

I try my best to keep my cool but I lose it. Unable to block it out, I find myself snapping at her or trying to score petty points. Embarrassingly, at one point we race to grab the hand-outs so we can give them out before the other can. I manage to stop myself in time before it gets any worse and surrender. She dominates the last ten minutes.

Needless to say, I am a little apprehensive as the hour finishes, and Spiny picks up her "evaluation forms" and starts handing them out. I thank everyone for their attendance over the last few weeks, tell them I am really glad to have worked with them and wish them well for the future. Some seem genuine in their appreciation and my spirits are slightly raised by one of the older ladies who is sweet enough to give me a little card to say thanks. This almost makes up for the disaster that the final session descended into.

Almost.

Thursday 14 February
No mail.

I meet Nancy for supervision this afternoon and we talk about the anxiety management group finishing. She has been going through the week by week data and says it apparently went quite well.

"One thing though. Why did you put together such a negative evaluation form at the end?" She shows me the questions and my heart sinks:

Question 1. What do you feel was wrong with the group?

Question 2. In what way could the facilitator have done a better job?

Question 3. What was missing from the material supplied?

...and so on.

Talk about loaded questions! It's a wonder I got any positive feedback at all. Nancy sighs and says that while Spiny has several good points to her, she needs to be less perfectionistic. Two things cross my mind. Firstly, I am curious about what good points about Spiny could Nancy possibly see. Secondly I would suggest that Spiny being a bitch of the highest order is more likely an explanation than perfectionism. It's a moot point, as the last data set is unusable, so according to every other measure the group is a success.

She then asks me if I had heard any news from courses. Hesitatingly I tell her about my rejection letter, almost afraid of her scornful reaction. To my surprise, she chuckles and tells me that she remembers getting rejected from the same place a long time ago. Really? I find it hard to believe that the near omniscient Nancy would have ever faced failure of any kind. Obviously not. She tells me how she used to plaster her wall with rejection letters from job applications. She had got halfway up her bedroom wall before she started getting anywhere.

"Happens to all of us. And it hurts. But don't let it take over your life. You are far more than your form." She thinks for a second before adding "Well at least try not to. Easier said than done. I know." I tell her I will resolve to try my best. She asks me if I am ready for the conference next week.

Um. Maybe not yet. (But I will be).

Friday 15 February
No mail.

It's the day of Sarah's screening test. Her insane level of work culminated last night in an all-nighter. I know this because I kept being woken up by frenzied bouts of scribbling and the rustling of crisp packets. At breakfast she seems fine. Eating her toast with one hand and holding some research paper in the other, she wishes me a good day at work. I wish her it back, and leave her to get on with it.

Most of the day is taken up preparing for the conference. Even though I am not presenting, there are laptops, projectors and poster boards to track down. Hand-outs have to be printed. Itineraries have to be checked and coordinated. By the time I have completed everything it's nearly 6 pm.

I hurry home, keen to find out how Sarah has fared. However, when I get home, there is no sign of her. In her place is a worried Tom, pacing around her bedroom. Sarah, who was due back hours ago, hasn't called or made any contact of any kind. I check my phone, and find a text. It simply states:

"Hate this. Call me".

That was eight hours ago. I am wracked with guilt, and hastily start to explain that I had to do quite a lot of work today as I am going away next week, but that doesn't mean I'm a crap friend. Tom tells me that he understands and I haven't done anything wrong. We try to think of where she could have got to. My mind has a field day imagining her being so pre occupied she walks under a bus, or something worse. Typical of Scarlett to be missing at a time like this. I try calling her to check, but the many calls I make to both of them go unanswered.

They both come rolling back shortly after midnight. They stumble through the front door arm-in-arm, tripping on the door frame and dropping to the ground in a heap. Tom and I both drag them up. "Are you alright?" he asks as he kneels by them. Sarah slowly moves her head up and looks at both of us. Her hair is messy and plastered to her face. "I love you," she slurs at him. Then she starts giggling.

I can smell the alcohol from where I am standing. I can't believe she was out getting drunk while we were sitting at home going frantic and wondering how long we should wait before contacting the police.

"I can't believe you did that! We were both going out of our mind..." I start, but I am met with gentle snoring from Sarah. Scarlett, in slightly better shape than her partner in crime, has started slowly crawling up the stairs.

"Whass the problem?" she asks. "Girl's had a hard day and wanted to kick back. Maybe you should have a drink yourself and calm down."

I'm so angry I don't know what to do, but Tom gives Sarah a fireman's lift upstairs and tucks her in bed, still half-dressed. He shuts the door and tells me we can talk to them in the morning.

Saturday 16 February
No mail.

At noon, I knock on the door of a very hung-over Sarah. She is lying there with her head under the covers, Tom having left long ago to get to work (the poor sod often works whole weekends). I perch on the side of her bed and place a cup of hot chocolate on her bedside table. She groans as she slowly comes around, and I ask her how yesterday went.

Sarah had turned up stupidly early and had to waste time walking around the university campus while the cleaners mopped the stairs and opened up the main building. She killed some more time when the student union café opened, drinking several free refills of black coffee while trying to cram last minute information into her head.

The test was held in the computer centre, and gathered outside was a sea of hundreds of applicants milling around. Sarah walked among them in a caffeine induced rush watching everyone else whizz by her, as she struggled to keep her anxiety from mounting.

Although the test was due to start at 10am, it was delayed by a good half an hour. Eventually she got in, found her allocated desk, and sat down. It was only when the invigilator told them to start, she realised just how unsound it was to drink all those refills. The caffeine rush left her unable to focus and her mind skittered over the questions in front of her. She became aware of her heart palpitating so loudly she was convinced it could be heard across the room. Even more disturbingly she now really, really needed the toilet.

She did what she could, but as she emerged from the hall in a daze, blinking into the morning sunshine, she was aware she had been left badly out of time, control and bladder space. After the longest (and most satisfying) toilet visit of her life, she sent me the text.

Then waited, and waited, getting more and more wound up as she saw batches of even more people coming and going into the hall for the second sitting of the test. After she could bear it no more she called up Scarlett, who nobly sacrificed her daytime TV plans and went out to meet her.

The rest is history. After hearing her story, I no longer feel angry at her. Just sad. Still, I know she has coped with worse in the past. After she gets over the initial slump (and the hangover) she will be fine. Even so, I don't have a go at her for making us worry last night. She has had a rough enough time as it is.

Sunday 17 February

There is a frightening amount to arrange at the house before I leave for the week. The bins need emptying. I need to get Sarah to agree to do the bins and recycling, and Scarlett has to be told that we are expecting someone to fix the leak in the lower bathroom on Tuesday. As I usually do everything around here, the other two look at me in horror when I try to get them to take on any additional responsibility.

With regard to "mail watch", Sarah agrees to open all my letters and is told to text me as soon as there is any news vaguely interview related. I spell it out to her that even brightly coloured junk mail should be drawn to my attention, if it has a postmark from the vicinity of one of the remaining courses. She humours me and swears on her father's life she will uphold her sacred duty.

I spend far too long to decide what to pack, and planning what to wear for each day. Uncharacteristically, I have taken the trouble to buy an evening dress (Zara, but it was in the sale. It would have to be on my salary) for the swanky gala dinner. I feel chuffed that I am able to pack it into my case without wrinkling it.

While I am packing, Scarlett, who used to work at the bar of the local Holiday Inn when she left school, sits on my bed and advises me how I can score free drinks at the hotel bar, make free telephone calls, and the secret to ordering room service and charging it to someone else's bill. Interesting to know, but I am unlikely to do any of it, as I have a tiny aversion to being sent to prison. Although it would give me much to reflect on, it would take quite a lot of effort to re-frame it as a positive in future interviews.

Monday 18 February

Wake up at 5 am feeling slightly unwell. Run into shower. No hot water. Forget shower, overdo the deodorant. Dress in the dark. Look in mirror and realise I look like I have dressed in the dark. Jump into taxi. Get to train station. Supervisor late due to inability to read train schedule despite having two doctorates. Supervisor arrives 4 minutes before the train leaves. Recover from minor heart attack. Spend long journey next to child picking nose and eating it. Feel queasy. Arrive at hotel for conference. Feel slightly disappointed hotel is more "Travelodge" than "Hilton". Supervisor disappears into lobby lumbering me with luggage. Wonder around conference suite aimlessly getting lost. Supervisor re-appears an hour later schmoozing with friend. Head up to main function room. Set up laptop for supervisor. Make sure supervisor knows which buttons to press. Make double sure supervisor knows which buttons to press. Sent to local shop to find drawing pins. Can't find drawing pins so buy Sellotape. Eat lunch on bus back to hotel. Get back to massive over crowded main function room. Supervisor lost. I am lost. Look for Nick. Can't find Nick. Find supervisor schmoozing with old friend. Help schmoozed old friend set up his presentation. Lend Sellotape. Lose Sellotape. Sit through first talk. First talk very boring. Eat lukewarm buffet snack food. Second talk equally boring. Mobile phone rings during boring second talk (thinks it's about interview letter but

195

only Mum). Whisper apologies to person whose talk I have disrupted. Attend inaugural drinks reception. Get chatting to the only other Assistant Psychologist at conference. Resolve to avoid only other Assistant Psychologist for rest of conference. Drink too much sparkling wine. Have conversation with man with strange beard. Hide under table to avoid bearded pervert. Get late night munchies and raid vending machine. Remember Nick's advice way too late. Ask for Coke. Get Vimto. Drink Vimto for first time since puberty. Go to bed.

Tuesday 19 February

Day two starts off with a bit of excitement. There is a three-person panel about treatment for severe psychiatric disorders and Nancy is on it. Almost immediately after the panel are introduced an audience member stands up and launches into a rabid attack claiming that some obscure form of unsubstantiated therapy is being systematically supressed by the "establishment". After fifteen minutes of unscientific raving, someone is level headed enough to fetch security and the woman is escorted off screaming. This does not do the lady, or her preferred form of therapy, any favours.

Nick finally arrives at lunchtime. He spots me before I see him and he waves across the crowded seminar room. We meet up at the buffet and grab a table near the window. We are soon joined by Lisa and Jeff, two researchers who he met at last year's conference. Nick greets them warmly, and introduces them to me as we budge up to let them sit at our table.

We are also joined by the only-other-assistant-in-the-village who I met yesterday, Martha, who cannot stop talking. I get the impression Martha thinks she will drop dead if ever a silence is unfilled. I am held trapped in the tractor beam of Martha's stream of consciousness, until Nick rescues me by telling me we should network.

He guides me around the hotel filling me in as we go about who works with who, who hates who, and who to meet or avoid. It's staggering to find out that famous researchers in the room, who I had read about as a student, have held grudges against each other since long before I was born.

It's Nick's talk immediately after lunch, so I go with Lisa and Jeff to lend him moral support. Not that he needs it. As soon as the presentation starts, he is electric. Exuding stage presence he holds the audience in his palm like a rock star. He has genuinely amusing jokes that make people laugh, beautiful images, and avoids the lame near-obligatory *Far Side* cartoon everyone else includes. For twenty minutes he makes some obscure aspect of chronic fatigue syndrome sound as interesting as flying a bi-plane through rings of fire. He has the whole room focussed on him in rapt attention. Myself included.

At the end people applaud loudly. Jeff and Lisa whoop "Encore". Afterwards, Nick is swamped by people wanting to talk to him. I try to make my way to see him, but am completely crowded out. I also can't help but observe that there are a disproportionate number of pretty young students, flipping their hair and giggling at his comments. I suppress pangs of possessiveness, and push myself to the front to congratulate him.

As Nick is called away to meet Adam, his project lead, Lisa and Jeff ask if I want to go to the next seminar with them. I politely decline in favour of taking advantage of the hotel swimming pool. Although it's cramped and funny shaped, it is empty. I spend two glorious hours splashing about, swimming lengths and diving off the sides. It is far better than any seminar.

As I get to my room, I can see Nick and Jeff coming down the corridor. They invite me down to get a drink and I tell them I will come down as soon as I clean the chlorine out of my hair. Sadly, the drink never happens. Almost as soon as I get out of the shower, Mum calls me on my mobile, and talks for nearly an hour about redecorating the spare room. She then demands I tell her about every aspect of the hotel, to the point where I am verbally describing the view out of my window ("It's dark. There is a parking lot. I think I can see a dog rooting through a big wheelie bin. There is a Ford driving up. No, wait. It's a Nissan."). So by the time I am done with her, I feel so tired I end up drifting off to sleep in front of the telly.

Wednesday 20 February

I oversleep badly and end up missing the enormous breakfast the hotel has laid on for us. Managing to get up, wash and dress in under fifteen minutes, I make it just as the first session of the morning gets started. If only my commute to work was this short every day.

In the break, I find Nick and Lisa sitting in the back row. Both are looking a little worse for wear. I find out I missed a great night, and that between the three of them, they managed to empty several quiz machines.

"Well, these two did," says Lisa, pointing to Nick and Jeff "Between them, there is almost nothing they don't know."

"We couldn't have done it without you Lisa", replies Nick gallantly. "Who would have known Oscar De La Renta was a fashion designer? I thought he was a character from *Sesame Street*".

"It's a pity you weren't there." says Nick looking at me. "We had such a good time."

I am annoyed that I missed all the fun. My only consolation is that I do look fresh and well rested. Especially compared to Jeff, who turns up a few minutes later looking like he slept in his clothes. As the second half of the morning gets underway, we have to break up into twos to do some workshop task and I end up being paired with him.

Neither of us is really sure what we are supposed to be discussing, so we end up chatting in general. As I talk to him, I find Jeff very sweet, good natured and very easy to talk to. A Canadian by birth, he has been slowly working towards his

Ph.D. He blames this for his jet black hair starting to grow prematurely grey and his expanding waistline. He says it's nice to finally meet Nick's girlfriend, but that I am very different to what he had imagined. I realise that he has mistaken me for Spiny and I quickly correct him. He sounds surprised, saying that we seem so comfortable and familiar together, that he was certain we were an item. I tell him how I have got to know Nick, giving him the details about our misadventures on our lazy Fridays.

I don't get to see Nancy all morning, but I have to stand in front of her poster, and answer questions about her project all afternoon. I have been briefed enough to know the basics. Answering questions initially starts off fun, but this soon wears off as I explain the damn thing again and again. One short, toffee-nosed lady quizzes me about the project's background. I answer the best I can but she is clearly not satisfied, asking me why I haven't quoted "the Richardson papers". Unable to answer this myself, I tell her if she gives me her name, I can get Nancy to respond to her directly. She looks awkward and in a quiet voice replies, "Uh, it's Sarah-Jane Richardson." She doesn't stick around too long after that.

Nick comes and gets me at the end of the session, and helps me take down the poster. The afternoon symposium is to be held in the "West Partington" suite, but we take a wrong turn and get lost in a maze of similar looking conference rooms. After finding the "Chelmsford" suite, the "Doncaster and Henley" room, and the rather pokey "Lord Dunley" annex, we give it up as a dead loss and sit out in the garden. Nick manages to find a bottle of wine left over from the lunch buffet and pours out two glasses. We sit on the garden wall, overlooking an ornamental fountain.

"Are you having a good time?" he asks.

"Yep. Even though you cruelly left me out of your fun last night," I say with mock hurt.

"We did that deliberately. We thought Martha would be far more fun to hang out with instead."

"That would explain why she hasn't been around all morning. She is probably trying to avoid you all," I tease back. "Funny though. I thought you would have taken one of your 'groupies' from your talk yesterday. You-know-who is going to be jealous."

He lets out a long whistle indicating that Spiny gets jealous about a lot of things. "She is upset she didn't get invited to come to the conference. I am glad the session wasn't webcast," he says as he drains his glass.

I pause for a second. "I know that she doesn't really think much of me either. How does she feel about us hanging out?"

"It's not a problem. Well not for me anyway. I have my friends and she has hers. I think it's entirely possible for two adults to be in a relationship yet live quite different lives don't you? It's not like I feel left out when she hits the bars with Meryl and Cheryl." He gets off the wall and stretches. "By the way, it's not quite right she doesn't think much of you. She may not like you, but that's because she thinks you have it all. You are clever, funny, very attractive and seem effortlessly successful at whatever you try. Sadly your confidence tends to bring out the worst in her."

I perk up as he says all this. "So, you think I am attractive?"

"No." he raises his finger as he clarifies. "She thinks you are. I happen to think you look like a hobgoblin with a ponytail."

Cheeky sod! I move to playfully hit him, but we are interrupted by a rather flustered Japanese lady, one of the organisers, who tells us as no one has been able to find the West Partington suite, the whole afternoon has been a disaster. We follow her back to the hotel.

Lisa, Jeff and Martha are sitting in the lobby. We sit with them and they describe how they got lost and nearly ended up walking onto the A543. As we talk, Jeff and Nick quickly disappear off somewhere. We aren't sure where, but suspect that the local pub quiz machines aren't safe. We decide to grab some food at the hotel restaurant.

As Lisa and I eat, Martha talks at us about her job and how she has been busy all morning. She starts talking about clinical applications and interviews, but before we can really get into it I am whisked away by Nancy to go over her lecture notes and slides for tomorrow.

I follow her to her hotel room, which is strewn with papers, books and notes. As soon as the door shuts she descends into panic. I don't know why, but she is convinced she is going to mess it up tomorrow.

"I knew I should never have accepted the invitation," she mutters.

I do what I can to calm her down and we spend the rest of the evening slowly going through the copious notes and slides she has prepared. I have never seen her so anxious before and she constantly writes and re-writes parts, reading them out to the mirror and then scrapping them for something else. Then she adds the bits back in.

Perhaps she is more similar to me than I thought.

It gets to midnight, and she is finally happy with her slides. She celebrates with a crafty cigarette, and puffs out the smoke through the hotel room window (as it is a non-smoking room). "I have been off these for nearly three months. I promised my girlfriend that I would give up," she explains. I nod; amazed that I have learned more about Nancy this evening than I have since I started working with her. She glances at her watch as she puts out the cigarette butt, hiding it in the bin.

"Oh, I didn't realise it was so late. I have kept you from going out and having fun tonight." she says.

"Don't worry about it. I probably owe you far more than an evening's work anyway," I say.

"Anyway, I hope you are enjoying the conference. It seems like you have made a few friends. Watch out for Nick though, I know you are friends, but he is a notorious charmer."

Slightly patronising, but I appreciate her intentions. I leave her to finish her notes, and head down to the hotel bar. I see a few familiar faces, but can't find my little crew of companions. I call it a night, annoyed that once again I have missed out on all the fun.

Thursday 21 February

It's the morning of Nancy's keynote speech. The main hall is filled with thousands of faces eagerly looking up at us. I get nervous just being on the stage while I set up the presentation. I wish her good luck as I step down.

Nancy shows no sign of nerves as her talk starts. She is slick, knowledgeable, and engaging. If I hadn't seen it for myself, I would never have been convinced that this woman was nervously tearing-up her notes at 10pm last night. The talk is very well received and prompts all kinds of discussions. She gets a glowing vote of thanks from the conference organiser and people queue up to talk to her afterwards, to discuss potential future collaborations.

Nancy is in way too much demand to hang out with me. I can't find Nick, Lisa, Jeff or even Martha. I end up spending the coffee break by myself, and after poring through the schedule, I decide to skip the dull looking afternoon sessions. Picking up a leaflet at the front desk I head out to visit the local museum that is holding an exhibition on Greek sculptures.

I am not the only one that doesn't rate the afternoon line-up. When I arrive I see lots of people I recognise from the conference already there.

Inside the main exhibit hall, I get talking to a small group of delegates. The four men are quite a bit older and look like the dictionary definition of "intellectual"; grey hair, thick glasses and full beards. One is a medic, two are research scientists and one is German (which isn't his job, but is the only thing I can gather about him). They are all very friendly and we walk through the exhibition having in-depth discussions about the various statues and sculptures. (I say we; it's mainly them, with me nodding and trying to keep up the best I can.)

We take advantage of several glasses of free wine that have been left over from another museum event, so by the time we get back to the hotel I am more than a little squiffy. This is when I find out Nancy has been looking for me for the last two hours.

Damn. The only two hours I have bunked off the whole week and I get busted for it. Typical.

I quickly search her out, anticipating a major bollocking. I consider my words very carefully, partly because I don't want to upset her, but mainly because I don't want her to realise how tipsy I am. I shouldn't have worried. All is forgiven when she finds out I have spent the afternoon with Professor Vogel (the German from the museum).

He is a leading authority in Nancy's field that she has been dying to meet for years. She practically twists my arm and frog marches me over to him for an introduction. I am happy to oblige her. The professor compliments her on the talk this morning. Nancy can't stop grinning as he suggests we join his group at their table for the Gala dinner this evening.

Leaving them to it, I head up to my room and spend a good hour getting ready. As I head to the arranged meeting point Lisa suggested. I realise the dress was a good choice as both Jeff and Nick eyes' practically pop out of their heads as I walk down the stairs. Lisa compliments me on the dress, while Martha looks on impressed.

This is extremely unusual for me as I normally struggle trying to look vaguely human on most days, but it's nice to know I scrub up well. The boys both look dashing in their suits and I can't help but notice that several of the girls make a beeline for Nick. He chats to them, as the rest of us head off to Professor Vogel's table. Nancy is already there with them, and there is enough room for all of us. Nick eventually takes the last chair next to me, and on my other side is Martha, who is really quite sweet when her stream of talk is broken up by her eating.

There is even more wine at dinner, and because our table is nearest to the kitchen, they end up giving us twice as much as everyone else. We decide not to make a fuss about this. The conversation flows as quickly as the wine. Professor Vogel compliments Nick on his (now legendary) talk, and Nick wins him over instantly by talking about Vogel's recent publication. Jeff launches into an amusing impersonation of one of the more boring speakers which makes the whole table laugh loudly in the middle of a speech commemorating someone's death.

Nick turns to me and says he hasn't seen me this happy in a long time. It's true. In this weird bubble of the unfamiliar I feel like a different person. With a start, I realise I have hardly thought about interviews, or anything negative at all, since I have arrived.

After dinner, we head towards the hotel bar. The professor buys us all a round of drinks. By this stage I have gone from a little tipsy to happily wasted and lose all track of the time. Our table is joined by other tables and we end up taking over most of the bar. At some point people start to drift off, and groups start to split off. At around 11pm, Nancy bids us all a good night. Martha left a while ago, while Jeff and Lisa have been edged away to another table. I am sat in one of the more shadowy recesses of the bar but am still next to Nick, who is whispering something amusing from a previous conversation at work. He makes a comment about Olga that makes me laugh and snort wine through my nose.

He takes my glass and helps me wipe up the mess with a cocktail napkin. As he is dabbing away the remnants of wine, he looks up.

"You have a habit of doing this. Didn't you spill something on yourself back at the Christmas party?"

"I refuse to confirm or deny anything." I say, grabbing another napkin.

"Oh, in that case, I wonder if the lady would care to confirm or deny something else from that evening?"

"I have nothing to do with Dr Anafu's ill-advised dancing." I slur. "I refuse to take responsibility for his actions."

"I had wondered about that. That is comforting to know. How about the rumour that you said something....interesting to Eva at the Christmas party?"

I blush when I realise what he is referring to.

"It's true isn't it?" he teases. As he hands me back my wine glass, our fingers briefly touch. I feel an electric current pass through my body. He smiles, takes another sip from his glass, and puts a hand on my knee. Just for the briefest of moments. A surge of desire wells up inside me, and I look him straight in the eyes.

Fifteen minutes later, we discreetly slip away. We kiss urgently, breathlessly, in the hotel elevator. I am not sure how exactly, but we end up in my room.

Oh my god.

Friday 22 February

So after all our adventures what have we learned about conferences?

1) It's not all five-star hotels and champagne. More scampi and chips with Vimto.

2) There is nothing more boring than listening to someone who is *so* into their research only they understand it.

3) [Age + power] / humility = lechery quotient.

4) A great way to make an enemy for life is to say something vaguely challenging about their research.

5) A solid grasp of clinical theory, research, and innovation get you only so far. You can get far, far further by gossiping in the bar.

And most importantly

6) It's probably not the best idea in the world to sleep with one of your co-delegates. Especially if you normally work with him. Even more so if he is already in a relationship with someone else (regardless of how unpleasant she is).

I wake up and find he has slipped out of the room at some point in the morning. Unsure of what to do, I text him a simple:

Where are U?

I don't get a reply. To be honest, I am not really sure I expected one. My head is reeling and it's not just the effects of the alcohol. Yes, I could chalk it up to being drunk, but deep down I knew what I was doing. In the harsh glare of the bathroom light, I feel horribly guilty. I can't help thinking it was a mistake. I shouldn't have done it.

Well, not like this.

As I pick up my rumpled dress from the floor, I keep thinking how tawdry and tacky this all is. Squalid. The feelings of shame rise as my train approaches Paddington and the real world of Sarah, the Cupboard, Assistant Groups, and Mum's wallpaper plans all come flooding back.

I do my best to push it to one side. I tell myself that I survived my first conference and Nancy is ecstatic. The only people more pleased than her are Sarah and Scarlett, as I empty my bag of the huge haul of conference related swag that I managed to bring back with me. They squeal as pens, magnifying glasses, key rings, sweets, silly fuzzy sticker things with drug company names on them, mouse mats, notepads and even a brilliant laser pointer (that Scarlett immediately grabs) tumble out of the bag.

I feel like Santa Claus, albeit a very slutty one.

Saturday 23 February

Justine comes over after breakfast and we all go out to Primrose Hill. She seems quite upbeat and is even able to get Scarlett out of bed long before she normally wakes up on a Saturday. As we sit on the grass and look out over the city, Sarah starts to tell me what happened in the Assistants' Group that I missed on Wednesday. Justine chips in when necessary. Sarah explains that everyone was on edge waiting for letters.

Spiny had one rejection so far, but made sure to let everyone know that the course in question was biased "against traditional applicants" favouring ethnic minorities, men and other "trendy" groups. This naturally upset bloke-whose-name-I-can-never-remember, who was so incensed he ended up quoting the statistics from his smart phone. Sarah was commiserated with her experience at the screening test, but was slightly comforted by the fact that several of the group also found it tough (the test being tricky, not about the-needing-to-pee problem).

Scarlett has by now started yawning loudly at "Assistant Talk", and decides to go on a little wander. Justine brings up how Spiny had told everyone about the anxiety management group "she had been running". She and Sarah had made sure that the record was set straight about my involvement. I think they were expecting gratitude for their loyalty, but I found myself snapping,

"Christ, must everything be about that witch? Is there nothing else left on this planet to talk about?" They are taken aback for a second. Even Scarlett hears my outburst, and heads back to investigate.

"I thought you would find it funny" says Justine looking worried.

"What has Miss Prissy got her knickers in a twist about now?" asks Scarlett, slightly breathless.

"Nothing. I am sorry. I overreacted. It's been a long week."

"Fine. Have we finished talking about work stuff now?" says Scarlett.

"Not yet," interrupts Sarah. "You never told us how the big conference went."

"Ooh, yes. Come on, spill the gossip. Did you see anyone famous?" says Justine rubbing her hands together.
"Well, it was okay, but nothing much really happened," I reply trying to look as indifferent as possible.

"Rubbish. I bet you had a great time. You never answered your phone, and hardly replied to texts," says Sarah winking at Justine.

Justine pleads that she has never been to a conference, and really wants to know what goes on. Guilt tripped I start to give a sanitised version of events, and talk about how Nancy's talk went down well. Thankfully this satisfies them, apart from,

208

Scarlett who whines like a small child that this counts as "work talk". I am all too happy to move the subject on. They don't need to know everything that happened.

Sunday 24 February

I am dreading going into work tomorrow. I just know Nick will be there, and that we are going to have to have what could be the most awkward conversation of my life so far. What the hell do I say to him? Do I pretend that nothing happened and it's business as usual? Do I be laid back about it and act like it was no big deal? Maybe I should tell him that it was a drunken mistake, and we ought to pretend the whole thing never happened?

Then I start to think if denial is what I really want. Maybe if I take a different approach it could be the trigger for him to break up with Spiny and get with someone more suitable (i.e. me)? That could happen, right? Do I become his mistress? What is the standard protocol for this kind of thing at work? How do the French do it? Why is it always the woman and never the man that looks bad in this situation?

Please God, don't let him have told Jeff and Lisa. What if he has told people at the office? What if the admin team find out and form an impromptu lynch mob complete with crudely painted signs reading 'HANG THE HOMEWRECKER'? Regardless, I don't think I can ever risk going past that corridor again. Unfortunately, this will now make getting to the Cupboard difficult. Then again, maybe if I use the toilet window as my main entrance from now on, I may be able to avoid everyone else for the rest of the time I work here.

Monday 25 February
Mail!

A reserve list place for an interview, where they will call me up if any of their preferred candidates turn their interviews down. In other words, limbo. I have mixed feelings about this. I would obviously have preferred to have a proper interview, rather than the mere possibility of one at the mercy of another candidate's decision. Still, it's better than the flat-out rejection I received a few weeks ago.

Interestingly, it is from a 'very prestigious university'. The one I didn't think I stood a cat-in-hell's chance of getting anywhere with, but applied to on a whim. It's the sort of place that mothers tend to brag about. Of course, I make the tactical error of letting her know and by lunchtime, I am getting calls, Facebook messages, and emails from everyone congratulating me.

It gets worse. Clearly, the message gets lost in translation somewhere in the interim between the morning and evening, because by the time I get home from work, my reserve list place for an interview has transmogrified to the status of undisputed fact that I will be starting my training there next week. "Will you be taking up punting?" I am asked by some long lost uncle who I haven't spoken to for five years, and thought had died long ago.

No pressure or anything.

Mum is clearly living in her own deluded little world. She must have finally snapped after having years of being starved for anything positive to report about her daughter's life. Presumably she is taking this morning's mail as a sign from the Gods that things are turning around, and she finally has something to be proud to share with the other mums. Minor issues around "proportion", "fact", or "reality" are not allowed to come into it.

I call her in fury, asking her what she has been telling everyone. Mum is deaf to hearing anything she doesn't want to hear. For her, my letter is not a tentative possibility, but just a mere formality. In her mind the interview is just a quick chat over cup of tea while I discuss start dates, acceptable salary, and what colour wallpaper my office needs. I sense she has already picked out a suitable hat for the graduation ceremony.

So, sadly, it is left to me to look the fool as I message everyone to explain the actual situation. I have never experienced such a humiliating climb down. I politely thank everyone for their good wishes, but explain it may be a bit premature to be soliciting local restaurant recommendations or advice about how to spend my weekends when I get there. The only saving grace of the day is that Nick was nowhere to be seen. There is only so much awkwardness I can cope with in a day.

Tuesday 26 February
No mail

I see Nick leaving the photocopier room as I turn the corner onto the main corridor, but I duck behind the large ficus plant. He doesn't see me. I am too busy dealing with maternally-inflicted damage control, but I know I can't avoid him forever. To start with there aren't enough plants in the building to hide behind. As he walks away, I realise I should really talk to him. Just not now.

Everything feels like a grinding chore at the moment. Even simple letters and telephone conversations that I could normally dash off in a few minutes feel like pushing a bus up a steep hill. I am not really concentrating on my work at all and Olga is getting annoyed at having to repeat requests.

"You should get a hearing aid now," is her supportive comment.

My mind keeps jumping around. I get the feeling that something is going to happen any second. I am going to get a call from Nick, a visit from a vengeance seeking Spiny, a letter about the reserve list moving up, or some disaster at home. At the same time, I feel none of these things are going to happen. The whole world feels like it has suddenly become unreal. I would just like to have one small area, any area, of my life where I have some control.

No mail.

Things are getting worse. My workday now consists of:

9am: Get to work.

9:05am: Make coffee

9:10 am: Superstitiously check ClinPsy to check if there is any news about interview letters or reserve list movement.

9:20 am: Hate self for wasting time and try to get started on work.

9:40 am: Find myself on Facebook. Try not to think about Nick.

10:30 am: Shut down Facebook. Berate self some more. Discipline self to do work.

10:30 am: Coffee break. (Check ClinPsy during break to monitor movement. Nothing has changed since this morning). Avoid kitchen in case I bump into Nick.

11:00 am: Force myself to start entering data into database.

11:20 am: Get bored. Stare out of window. Feel sad. Check phone.

11:25 am: Hear Nancy's distinctive footsteps and make a half-hearted attempt to look busy as she comes into the Cupboard.

11:40 am: Nancy leaves me with huge pile of photocopying. Find the soft hum of the copier soothing.

12:00 pm: Lunchtime. Complain to Olga about various things. Listen to Olga complain about various things.

12:20 pm: Awkwardly walk past Nick as he is talking to someone in the patient waiting room.

12:30 pm: Try not to cry.

12:45 pm: Compose self.

12:48 pm: Composure of self fails. Cry in toilets. Berate self for not being stronger.

1:00 pm: Try to bury myself in more work. Check phone.

1:10 pm: Respond to email asking why work carried out is full of errors. Apologise profusely and do it all again from the beginning.

2:00 pm: Get ready to send final versions to supervisor after triple checking everything. Notice more errors on every reading.

2:10 pm: Check phone.

2:40 pm: Check ClinPsy again.

3:00 pm: Check Facebook and phone.

4:00 pm: Check ClinPsy and Facebook together.

4:30 pm Check Twitter. Realise how desperate I have become to be doing this.

5:00 pm: Chalk up day as a total loss and go home.

Thursday 28 February
No mail.

Work is a near identical repetition of yesterday. Even Olga can't be bothered to speak to me and it feels like everyone else is avoiding me. Mum calls and asks what I have been doing. "Nothing. Pretty much nothing at all." It's not even an exaggeration.

There is some distraction this evening as I've agreed to meet up with Justine and Dave for dinner. I hardly recognise him without his white beard and red suit, as he has a crew cut and is wearing a Manchester United shirt. Dave seems really nice, though not as nice as Santa (which to be fair, is an unfair comparison). He is quite shy, but I can tell he is into Justine in a major way. He comes across as very reserved at first, but slowly warms up when we get talking.

Dave is a little older than us and works at the store during the day and goes to night school to get his electrician's certification. He is down-to-earth, personable and lacks any sort of pretension or attitude at all. He is the total opposite of Justine's regular type, who are often condescending, prejudiced, and exploitative. I think this one might be a keeper.

I can't bring myself to talk about what is happening in my life, so I keep the conversation focussed on them. Justine excitedly breaks the news about a job she has been offered. She explains she will be selling these "products" on the internet. There is no salary and she has to put up a £600 to buy her first inventory of stock, but she is convinced she will get all her money back and more. What could possibly go wrong?

Exasperated, I am about to point out it's an obvious scam and ask how can she be so foolish to fall for it. However, Dave steps in before I can say anything and gently mentions that it's good she has been offered something, but £600 is a lot of money. Maybe it would be good for her to keep an open mind, and do some more research about it. Justine happily agrees to this and avoids getting royally ripped off.

At least there are still some good men out there.

Friday 29 February

"What's wrong? You have been acting weird for days." Sarah confronts me after she gets back from work and finds out that I am already in bed. It's only 4pm and I have been sent home from work early for looking like crap.

"Is it the embarrassing stuff your mum is coming out with about your reserve letter?" she asks, before quickly dismissing it. "No, you've been like this since you got back from the conference."

I try to change the subject, but Sarah refuses to let it go. I do everything I can to deny, deflect, disregard, or derail. No good. It's clear that she isn't leaving my room until she finds out what is going on. Without any energy left to resist, the whole sorry story comes tumbling out.

"It's not half as sordid as it sounds." I talk fast as Sarah's eyebrows rise in disbelief. "It's not like I have killed anyone."

Sarah thinks it over for a second, before telling me that I may not have made the wisest decision, and it's going to be incredibly messy. Tell me something I don't know. I tell her that I feel guilty and awkward enough as it is. I am not proud of it, and have no plans to repeat the experience. Satisfied, she nods. The look on her face is that of a nursery teacher happy that lessons have been learnt. I plead with her to keep it a secret.

"Of course," she says. "What kind of best friend do you take me for?"

MARCH

Saturday 1 March

The kind that blabs everything to Scarlett less than 24 hours after I confided in her.

"I was thinking of going for a walk this afternoon. The weather looks lovely." I remark to Scarlett, as I gaze out of the living room window. It's bright, and for once the sunshine makes the normally grimy and cramped looking terrace of houses look almost Mediterranean.

"It certainly does. Not as lovely as getting drunk and shagging Nick though" she replies, a smirk plastered across her face.

Betrayed and grassed up, I go ballistic at Sarah. "I can't believe you told her! You may as well have announced it on Facebook."

"I didn't say anything! I swear." Sarah is wide-eyed and looks like she is about to cry.

"So, who did then?"

Scarlett grins. "Sarah didn't tell me anything. You just did."

As it turns out, Sarah had been walking around all morning with that naughty "I-have-a-secret" look on her face. Scarlett, doing her best Sherlock Holmes impersonation, put that together with my stroppy teenager act over the last few days. Her not-so-wild guess unfortunately happened to be correct. I resolve not to underestimate her intelligence in future.

"Very clever," I say, resigned to the fact that the whole household now knows. I do my best to ignore Sarah's look of outraged hurt. I can always apologise to her later. "Is it even worth me asking for you to be discreet about this, or drop the subject all together?"

She thinks about this as she chews her breakfast, no doubt weighing up the benefits of being sensitive and considerate against the pure joy of watching me squirm. "I'll think about it. *If* you tell me the whole story."

Reluctantly, and after agreeing it will buy her silence, I fill her in on all the gory details. Scarlett listens carefully, and asks if Spiny knows. I explain I am not sure if anyone other than the people in this room know at this stage, and of course, Nick. I again beg her to keep it to herself, saying I already feel terrible about the whole thing.

This riles her. "If you were a man, you would be high-fiving us and giving us a graphic description of what happened," she says, mounting her high horse. "Yet here you are sitting looking sorry for yourself. It was only some sex."

I tell her I am more concerned about being the subject of workplace gossip for the next two thousand years. Scarlett shrugs her shoulders, and says that I can't change the past, and should hold my head up high and move on. "Consider this part of that stuff you always go on about. You know. Valuable experience."

That's not exactly what I had in mind, and I have yet to deal with Sarah being hurt by my unfair accusation. I really have to clear my head, so I am going to need that walk after all.

Sunday 2 March

After having had some time to think things over, I realise three things:

1) Trying to get a job helping others with their mental health seems to be correlated with the degree my own suffers. There aren't enough words in the English language to express the irony of this.

2) Scarlett may have a point (although she didn't have to be so irritating about it). I haven't actually committed a crime. I am beating myself up way too much over this.

3) I think I still like Nick.

Clearly, judging by the events from the week before, he likes me. While I am quite upset about the way we got together, and with him still technically being with Spiny, I have to admit I don't really know much about their relationship. For all I know they could be blissfully in love with each other, or just about to end things. Perhaps, even without my intervention, he could have already been gearing up to break it off with Spiny (and let's face it, who could blame him?). I can't imagine his desire for freedom and adventure fit well with Spiny's grand plan for a perfect life. I can't imagine her in a sleeping bag, roughing it in the jungles of Borneo. I could just be speeding along something that was already happening.

Also, to be brutally honest, I am just a tiny bit sick of having to do everything perfectly. Being a good little assistant at work. Trying to do the best by my parents. Having to be a success. Where the hell do I fit into all of this? Don't I deserve just a little bit of happiness? Sarah has Tom. Maddie has Matt. Justine has Dave. Aren't I allowed to feel a bit lonely and want someone of my own?

Aren't we always being told that all relationships are compromises? Tom is not exactly Indiana Jones, and I know for a fact that Matt still finds farting loudly in front of his friends wildly amusing. While Nick and I may not have got together under the best of circumstances, that doesn't mean that we don't belong together. Am I really doing anything wrong?

Okay, that seems clearer in my head now. All I have to do now is put it in practice and find the courage to talk to him.

Monday 3 March
No mail.

I spend the whole journey to work summoning up the courage to do the mature thing and have it out with Nick. I talk to myself over and over again to the point where others on the bus avoid sitting next to me. Completely focussed and determined, I stride purposefully towards his office. I keep repeating to myself over and over: "We need to talk."

I should have guessed. When I get to the office, his desk is empty. I am told he is gone for most of the week, and no one seems sure when he will be back. 'Infuriating' isn't the word. I scan the rest of the office in an attempt to gauge whether the team "knows". It's too hard to tell. While no one openly laughs at me, I think I detect some avoided eye contact. Then again many of them are known to be socially awkward, and would do that anyway.

Why the hell does this have to be so hard? Couldn't they produce a handy memo stating that they know what is going on, and yes, they will all be talking about me as soon as I leave the office? Something along the lines of:

To: All clinical staff/ research team/ senior managers/ office staff/ Admin support/ reception/ Janitorial staff.

Cc: Assistant's Group, Spiny, Parents, ClinPsy, Twitter, Facebook

You may have heard certain rumours circulating about myself and a certain male colleague. I would like to take this opportunity to find out what you may, or may not, know. I would be grateful if you could fill in the following form and slip it back under the Cupboard door at your earliest convenience. It shouldn't take you more than five minutes and the results will be kept strictly confidential.

(Please circle ONE of the following)

No. I haven't heard any rumours.

<u>OR</u>

Yes. I heard rumours but they were nothing to do with you and Nick sleeping together at the conference.

<u>OR</u>

Yes. I heard rumours. They were to do with you and Nick sleeping together at the conference

<u>AND</u>

- I now think less of you. (If so: please rate how much on the following scale: A little/ moderately/ lost all respect I have ever had for you)

- I think it's a disgrace, you home wrecking hussy.

- No big deal. You are both adults. Besides, I heard his 'girlfriend' is a right dog anyway and probably had it coming.

- Nice one. If you hadn't I would have.

<u>AND</u>

I will/ will not be telling everyone in my vicinity (*delete as applicable*)

Thank you for your time.

Back in the Cupboard, I watch Olga like a hawk to see if she may have heard. After about 50 minutes of this, I realise my staring may not have been as discreet as I would like to have thought. She spins around on her chair and shrieks "WHAT!

WHAT ARE YOU LOOKING AT? HAVE I GROWN A SECOND NOSE? WHAT IS IT?" Thinking quickly I manage to come up with an impromptu save and say that I was wondering if she had done something to her hair, and that it looked good on her. Thankfully she had just visited the salon a few days ago, and starts telling me all about her new hairdo (which looks exactly the same as her old hairdo, but never mind).

Tuesday 4 March
Mail.

Not of the good kind. Another course rejection, leaving just one shot left. The infuriating thing was that I knew I shouldn't have applied there. I have only had one experience with this university and even now I shudder when I remember what happened.

Job interviews I have messed up #4

Quite early on, in that tricky time between graduating and getting my first real job, I saw the ad for a research assistant. From the description it sounded fantastic. Clinically focussed. Sexy area (forensic psychology). The commute would have been a dream. I made a phone call to ask about the post, and the woman on the other end of the line sounded warm and enthusiastic about me applying. It was print-circulated so I could take my time and not worry about HR closing applications before I had even had a chance to apply. So I planned and drafted and sought help to make this the application to end all applications. Lo and behold, my efforts were not wasted, as I was invited for interview.

The interview was held at a medium secure unit. I wasn't put off or intimidated by the security guards, cracked Perspex windows, or heavy-duty wire fencing around the site. In my no-nonsense suit I fancied myself as Dana Scully from the *X-Files* (only younger and less ginger) as I waited in the small lobby area. To complete the image, I was issued with an attack alarm and a visitors badge (no handgun, sadly), before being ushered along to where I was to have my interview.

The office was spacious, tastefully decorated, with a large desk dominating the centre of the room. Behind the desk, on a padded leather chair, sat my interviewer. He was stocky, in his fifties, and distractedly combed his fingers through his greying hair. I had read that my interviewer was kind of a big deal and I remembered his name from my undergraduate textbooks.

He was reading through a print-out of my application form, his face almost touching the desk as he scanned it. He didn't look up, so I just stood in the doorway feeling like an idiot. After an eternity, he glanced up and motioned to a small chair metal chair. No genial introduction, not even "Hello".

Just a small hand gesture as if I was a puppy.

I sat down and was about to say hello, when he put a finger in the air; an exclamation mark to indicate I was to remain silent. He continued to read my form, while his desk appeared to grow in size as my tiny seat felt even smaller and more metallic. Eventually he looked up as if to scan every inch of my face.

"Your university," his voice inflected upwards as if it was a question. "Middle ranked is it not? It's not exactly the best psychology course?"

Slightly put out, I shook my head and acknowledged it wasn't. This was hardly my fault. The place had existed for almost a century before I was born. I felt it unfair that such a broader institutional failing was being blamed on me.

"...And you haven't really had much experience," he continued. Again I nodded, starting to wonder if I could get through the interview by just nodding or shaking my head. "And you got a 2:1? Why was this?"

I replied that I didn't realise that it was a problem that needed apologising for. He gave nothing away as I murmured something about doing several extra-curricular activities.

If I was so rubbish, why did he invite me in the first place? Perhaps he got some kind of strange erotic satisfaction about pointing out other people's academic failings? For all I know he could spend his spare time paying prostitutes to lament that they had gone to former polytechnics. He sat back in his chair and sighed. There was a long uncomfortable pause.

"What do you understand about the term 'forensic'?" he asked finally. I started talking about my understanding of forensic hospital settings, that they were not jails and dealt with people in the crossover between health and the legal and judicial system. He stopped me.

"No. No. No. I meant the *word* itself. What does the word *'forensic'* actually mean?" he said, as if he was a schoolmaster addressing a particularly dim student.

At this stage I took off my glasses, looked him square in the eye and replied, "Well, the Oxford English Dictionary defines the word 'forensic' as relating to a court of law, or in the scientific frame of relating to or denoting the application of scientific methods and techniques to the investigation of crime. It was coined in the mid-17th century and derives from the Latin term *forensis* as pertaining to public or in open court".

Okay, I didn't say that. I just shrugged my shoulders and said "Uh. I think it means something to do with crime".

He shook his head in dismay, and asked me to talk about my experiences. I quickly launched into a brief recap of my interests and university-era activity, how I did support at Nightline, student union health promotional activities, and how I was involved at sixth form in doing volunteer work with underprivileged kids. The look of boredom on his face intensified as my words kept getting shorter and eventually petering out into silence. He muttered something under his breath that sounded like "complete waste of time" before he summarily dismissed me.

I wasn't offered the job. I wasn't even offered feedback. He probably had very important things to be doing, rather than feeding back to insignificant little people like me. Perhaps I could have been a bit more dynamic or thoughtful in some of my answers, but I know that these aren't the things I really should have done. What I really should have done was finish the interview after five minutes, called him a tosser, and left with what little self-esteem I had remaining. The satisfaction of this would have outweighed any amount of feedback.

Wednesday 5 March
Mail!

Not the kind I was expecting though.

I find a crumpled, handwritten letter in my mail slot at work. The handwriting looks familiar. It must have been put there late last night or very early this morning, as I checked it before I left work yesterday. I slowly fish out the scrap of paper and start reading.

Hi

It's been a few days since that night at the conference. You probably hate me now for leaving like I did and not getting back to you. I guess I deserve that.

The truth is I just can't stop thinking about you. I know we have always had something between us but last week something just clicked for me. You looked so beautiful at dinner and I just couldn't stop looking at you. I know it's stupid, but I even felt jealous when I noticed Jeff staring at you. That was when I felt I just had to do something. The only thing I can remember from the whole of last week is just how amazing you are.

I know it's all a mess but could we just talk? I am away now but will be around on Friday. I know you don't owe me anything, but please meet me at the coffee shop. I will be waiting there after five.

Yours

Nick

Thursday 6 March
No mail.

My already unproductive pace of work has not been helped by the letter. I am not even able to concentrate on surfing the internet and I can barely remember the last time I went on Facebook. Instead, I start a task, forget what I am doing halfway through, and start another. I spend way too much time staring out of the window and trying to settle on one of many rapidly shifting moods.

What do I do? I showed the letter to Sarah last night. She told me that I shouldn't meet him tomorrow. She felt that nothing good could happen, and the best thing I can do is to stay well away. Maybe she's right, but what if she's wrong? Maybe this could be something really good? Maybe it could explain things?

Too many maybes meant that I hardly got any sleep last night. This didn't do my already addled mind any favours when it came to work. I just wish I knew what I should do. Normally, I would discuss things with Dad, but that's not happening. There is no way I could even bring myself to telling him what happened. I would just die of shame. Looks like I have to handle this one by myself.

Friday 7 March
No mail. (Don't really care.)

Every five minutes I switch between definitely going and definitely not going. As the clock rolls around to five all debate stops. Almost on autopilot, I grab my things, leave Olga to lock

225

up, and head to the coffee shop. I would like to make an excuse; that I am possessed, but I am not. I really do need to talk to him. I am not sure what is going to happen, but not going isn't an option anymore.

He turns up about 15 minutes late. Typical.

We greet as if we're strangers. A brief twinge of awkwardness as he apologises for being stuck in traffic. I tell him it's fine. He lingers at the table instead of ordering, and asks me how I have been. I shrug as if I am not bothered, feeling that he ought to do most of the talking. To onlookers we look more like workplace acquaintances than lovers. God, I am thinking of myself as his "lover". How did this happen? Surely I should be middle-aged and stuck in a dying marriage before moving into this kind of territory.

Shut up. I have to stop overthinking this.

We make small talk. How has his week been, how has mine. He tells me how he has had to chase down something obscure, and how the traffic has been a nightmare. I am not really listening. It's all prologue we need to get through out of politeness. I bitterly reflect that I have seen this man's penis, yet he still feels the need to discuss the road works on the south-bound lane of the M25 before we can get down to talking about anything real.

Eventually, when I can take no more of it, I mention I got his note. The atmosphere changes instantly. He looks uncomfortable, searching for the words, before saying,

"What do you think?"
"I think that Sarah is right and that I shouldn't be here."
"Just as well for me that you never listen to anything Sarah has ever said."
"Now is not the time to be a smart-arse, Nick." I say, I can feel the anger rising in my voice.
"Look. I messed up." He holds his hands, palms up as if

surrendering. "I walked out on you. I didn't call you. I am really sorry. You don't know how sorry I am."

"Not as much as I am, Nick. Trust me."

"Hey, both of us felt something. I thought that this was what we both wanted." He says "we" but makes it sound like it means "you".

"Not like this. Not with *her* still in the picture. Not like how it went at the conference. You made me feel like a total fool." I shiver as I think back to *that* morning.

"I am sorry, I just panicked. I wasn't thinking straight. I just needed some time to figure things out."

I really don't want to be here. Or having this conversation. "I should go. I don't know why I..." I reach for my bag. His hand grabs mine. I feel a surge of something. I don't know what. Adrenaline. Fear. Longing.

"No stay. Just hear me out." I stop, and he lets go of my hand. "If I wasn't with...if I was single. Would things be different?"

"Possibly, but they aren't different. Are they?" I say

"Look, things are really complicated. I don't want to sound horrible, but we don't really want the same things. I mean, she spends so much time planning her career, her training, how things are going to be in the future. It's like I don't even exist."

I overlook the fact that I too have spent more than my fair share of time thinking about my career, and I empathise. Always having things happen to you rather than making a choice sounds very familiar. I feel a flicker of sympathy.

"While we were away things just seemed so different. Clearer. But it's only when I got back I realised how much I missed you," he cradles his coffee cup and looks out the window before glancing back. "You are important to me. I have something with you that I have never had with anyone else. I'm just sad it took me so long to realise that." He looks at me for a second trying to read my expression. "Okay, that was embarrassing. I'm going to shut up now."

I really don't know what to say. Or even think. Even so, I can't help myself smiling. "No. Don't be sorry. That was really... well it was sweet. It's been really good to talk to you, but I need to think about it. Look, I have to get going." I say, flustered and trying to buy myself some time.

He gets up with me and offers to walk me to the bus stop. I insist he doesn't need to, but he accompanies me anyway. As we walk out the door, I trip on the step. He immediately puts his arms out and catches me as I stumble. I feel his arms draw me up and find myself facing him. We kiss.

I don't stop him.

Saturday 8 March
Haven't bothered to check the mail.

I dream that a huge tree has toppled over in a storm and is crushing me underneath its trunk. I struggle and yell but no sound comes out. I can't breathe. Just as I feel the trunk slowly constricting my chest, I wake up. Still disoriented I feel the weight still spread over my chest. For a split second, I think that my dream was true and a tree had smashed through my bedroom wall during the night, and is now pinning me onto my cheap pine bedframe. It's only when I turn my head I see the weight is an arm. An arm that belongs to Nick.

Fuck. Not again.

There isn't much space in my single bed and his weight is distributed across most of my torso. It takes some effort for me to wriggle out from underneath him, but I manage to stumble naked into the cold morning. I search through my messy bedroom, looking for my dressing gown and the last remainders of my dignity.

Nick is gently snoring, his mouth open and his hair sticking up at odd angles. Despite this, he still looks cute. I can't say the same for myself. Catching my reflection in the mirror mounted on the door, I see my makeup smeared face. I look as if I have been auditioning for the role of The Joker from *Batman*. I find my dressing gown, find my slippers under the bed, and head downstairs. I am starving. We didn't even eat dinner last night.

Scarlett and Sarah are sitting in the living room watching children's TV. Scarlett is eating fistfuls of Coco Pops straight out of the box on the sofa, and has dropped little brown pieces of cereal all over the floor. I can't bring myself to complain.

"Hey!" says Sarah "Didn't see you come in last night."

Scarlett turns her head around "Didn't see you, but we heard you. God, you're loud!" She turns her attention back to the TV. I don't point out the hypocrisy. Instead, I tell her to shut up, grab the cereal box from her, and head towards the kitchen.

"So, who's the lucky fella then?" inquires Scarlett, following me to the kitchen. Sarah trails behind her with a hesitant, fearful expression, closing the door after her. I ignore them, and concentrate on putting the kettle on, and finding two relatively clean mugs. I spoon out instant coffee into each.

"Oh my god!" Scarlett squeals. "He is still upstairs, isn't he? Is it anyone we know?"

I don't need to answer that as Nick chooses that moment to slowly poke his head through the kitchen door. He is faced by the three of us looking straight back at him. We all stare at each other, the only sound we hear is the sound of children cheering from the TV in the living room.

Up until now the three most awkward moments in my life are as follows:

3) Wetting the bed at Brownie camp when I was eight years old and away from home for the first time.

2) Catching Dad sitting on the toilet after he forgot to lock the door. Then laughing and running away.

1) This.

Sarah breaks the silence with, "Hi Nick", her face betraying her worst fears are confirmed. For reasons I will never understand, even if I live to be a hundred, she decides to add, "Olga and the rest of the team not with you?"

What the hell! Scarlett emits a bark of laughter as Sarah cringes, realising what she has just said. Nick doing the only thing he can do in this situation, looks mortified. He motions he is going back upstairs and closes the kitchen door after him.

"I can't believe you just said that." I say. "Olga and the team! Did you think I had them all stashed up in my bedroom? Like we were holding some kind of team building away-day gangbang up there?"

Sarah apologises, saying she was nervous and it just slipped out. Exasperated, I leave them both in the kitchen and rush up the stairs. Nick is hurriedly getting ready to leave. It looks like he would rather be anywhere else in the world other than here.

"Walking out on me again?" I am only half joking.

"I was thinking that we could go out for breakfast, eh?" he says, pulling on his shoes.

"Sure, but technically it's lunch."

We are at the small greasy spoon café at the corner of the street. Nick is enthusiastically tucking into a fry up. I sit opposite him looking out the window. I am hesitant to start the conversation in case I hear something I don't want to. How did this happen? Again. We were supposed to "talk" last night. If I recall correctly we did practically everything but talk.

I am about to say something but he starts at the same time "I felt like just turning around and running out the front door when Sarah said that thing about Olga and the team. I didn't care that I was still undressed," he says grinning.

"I am glad you didn't." I say. "You would have given Mrs Patel a heart attack."

"We couldn't have that. But seriously, I am glad I stayed. I am not going to make the same mistake again." he says.

"So you don't think that last night counts as 'another mistake'?"

"Nope." He grabs my hand and I smile.

As he goes up to pay the bill, I notice his mobile beeps. A text. Without meaning to look (honest), I notice eight unanswered messages with Spiny's name on the display. He comes back and notices me looking at his phone. The unspoken question remains hanging in the air.

"Look, things have been rough between me and her for a while, so we agreed that we would call it a day. She's just finding it hard to accept. That's what I wanted to tell you last night. At the coffee shop, I mean."

I tell him I understand, knowing full well that Spiny is the last person on earth to take "no" for an answer. He has tried to be gentle in breaking it to her and, as their families know each other, it's been messy. I ask if Spiny knows about me being in the picture.

He shakes his head. "I've tried to keep you out of it. You don't need to be involved in all that."

He changes the subject. He tells me that he has kept the weekend free for me and that we should make the best of the day. I tell him I want to go to the zoo, so we make the journey north on the underground and spend the day like a normal couple. We lark about, have fun and he takes me to this lovely little bistro for dinner. Sadly, he is a bit short on cash, so I have to lend him some money. No matter, I am happy to take my luck where I can find it.

Sunday 9 March

Nick left around teatime. He managed well to withstand the not-so-subtle death stares of Sarah and the deliberate winding-up coming from Scarlett. (Most charming question of the weekend must have been "Is it bigger or smaller than a Sky Plus remote?"). Apart from that, the weekend was lovely, and it was great having Nick around. It's only after he leaves that reality starts to flood back. It's back to work tomorrow; do I tell people there about me and Nick?

It's not as if I haven't got other things to worry about. Next week is the final deadline for hearing back about course interviews, so Sarah will find out about her last two choices, and I will hear back from my remaining one. I will also find out if the reserve list interview at the 'very prestigious university' comes to anything. Probably not, but then again it is possible that I may have to unpack my interview suit at very short notice. I suddenly have a twinge of guilt that I haven't really done much in the way of preparation if anything does turn up.

After the events of the last few days the last thing I want to do is slog through *Advanced Statistics for the Behavioural Sciences*. Regardless of what I want, I knuckle down and make myself start reading. I do so reluctantly and half-heartedly, but it makes me feel better. At least this is something I have control over.

Monday 10 March
No mail.

A mid-morning phone call shatters any hope Mum may have had about weekend tours of ancient buildings. A very apologetic lady calls and tells me that the 'very prestigious university' has confirmed all of its slots. Game over, as far as they are concerned. I sigh and thank her before hanging up. Deep down I knew it was a long shot, despite what everyone else thought. The only consolation is that I didn't do a Sarah and nearly kill myself preparing for it.

Mum is less understanding. When I call and tell her the news, she is outraged. She feels that there has been a horrific miscarriage of justice.

"I am sure there has been some mistake. Here, let me call them!" she says, speaking the words that no mother should ever think of uttering. I can picture her in my mind the cordless receiver balanced in the crook of her neck, her pulling off her green gardening gloves, and aggressively unstringing her apron. I demand she does no such thing. I have no desire to ladle a good dollop of humiliation over the already painful sting of rejection.

She says that I should call them back and "try to negotiate". With what I ask? I haven't got anything to bargain with. She thinks for a second before proclaiming, "Well, it's sheer discrimination. Someone should tell the newspapers!"

Checking the mirror, I wonder on what criteria I could be possibly be discriminated against. "I don't think that is going to work, Mum. I am hardly Rosa Parks."

"That's exactly it!" she says with venom. "You are being discriminated against because you are *advantaged*."

This is a leap of logic too far for me. Very slowly and very clearly, I spell out to her that I will not be following her hair-brained scheme. I also spend a good forty minutes telling her that my non-materialising interview is not due to a conspiracy, nor is it a damning insult on her parenting skills. She needs to let this go. As I am telling her this it occurs to me that I should be the upset one being calmed here, not vice versa.

"I don't know what I will tell my friends," she huffily snorts. "I will simply have to tell them that you were offered a place, but decided you didn't want to go in the end". I tell her to do whatever makes her feel better, and hang up. I am still not sure what was worse; getting rejected in the first place, or having to deal with Mum afterwards.

I go to search out Nick and find him in the photocopier room. He kisses me as the door shuts. I hug him and explain how I have just wasted half the morning.

"There is something about middle-class mothers and universities," he says, shaking his head. "They go crazy. I know someone who dropped out of his GCSEs and ran off to start a band. His mum ended up Photoshopping him onto a graduation picture from the newspaper, just so she could have something to put on her mantelpiece."

I laugh and am about to ask him what he is up to tonight, but we hear footsteps outside the door. We spring apart, just before Nancy comes in. She nods at Nick, and hands me a large stack of paper that I need to copy, cross reference and file. "Ideally quite soon," she says indicating its time Nick left. He hurries away and leaves me to it. Great, even my supervisor seems to be getting in the way of my budding love life.

Tuesday 11 March
Mail. For Sarah.

Sarah's third rejection arrives. She guesses it is a "No" before it even hits the mat. Opening it to confirm what she already knows, she deals with it in the best possible way by setting it on fire with Scarlett's cigarette lighter. Just the course we have both applied to remains, who are notorious for notifying applicants as close to the deadline as possible.

"Maybe this rejection is a sign. It may mean that we end up on the same course," she daydreams as she gets herself ready for work. "We could live together still. It would be so cool to be back in lectures together like the old days," she says wistfully, gazing at Julia Roberts going shopping on Rodeo drive on the DVD player.

"Yeah, that would be something," I reply, but I'm not really holding out hope. We are both currently down three for three so far. If we end up moving in somewhere else, it will be because we have been evicted from this dump for not keeping it tidy. As we walk to the bus stop, tiredness washes over me. We have both come so far and nothing has panned out. I don't know if I can go through this grind again next year. I don't think she can either.

Sarah is clearly in a very different state of mind. She maintains that all of our efforts must come to something. "This is just the struggling bit before the happy ending," she keeps saying. "Our horrible landlord, my cow of a boss. We're going to look back on this in a few years and laugh. You'll see."

By the time we get to the bus stop, she has not only convinced herself that we both have interviews, but she has got to planning new wardrobes for our forthcoming lives as trainees. I just don't have it in me to crush her happy daydreams, so I just listen. By the time I get on the 73 and move upstairs she is quite excited. She waves chirpily as the bus pulls away.

I haven't heard from Nick for a while, so I text him asking if he wants to meet up for lunch. He texts back that something has come up. He is going to be rushed off his feet for a bit, but will get back to me when he is free.

I am feeling slightly put out, and am wondering what is the point of having a shiny new boyfriend if I have to eat lunch by myself, when I hear a shriek of rage. It's coming from the Cupboard. Olga. As I walk in I hear the tail end of a rant she is having down the phone.

"NO! YOU HAVE LET ME DOWN! I WILL NOT ACCEPT THIS! YOU ARE AN IMBECILE!" she screeches.

I am sorely tempted to turn 180 degrees, and walk as fast as I can in the opposite direction. I don't. I warily take my seat, and try to make myself as small as possible. She listens to the voice at the other end for a few seconds before slamming the receiver down on the cradle and throwing the phone across the room. As it is quite a small room, the phone bounces back, and almost hits me.

"Fucker!" she yells, then says something in her native language. I bring her herbal tea and try to bring her anger levels down. After some deep breathing, and a walk around the block, she is calm enough to tell me what has happened.

There is something seriously amiss with the project data. A lot of it is missing and, what's worse, it looks like some of it has been made up. Although I am not the most clued-up with this kind of thing, even I can tell that this is very serious.

For a horrible moment, I worry it's something I have done wrong and it's my fault. I quickly reassure myself that I haven't lost anything (it's late, not missing; big difference) and I know for a fact I haven't made anything up. Olga's call was to the project co-ordinator, whose job it is to specifically look out for this kind of thing, and has missed this entirely for the last eight months. The whole period where they were measuring the outcome of the project. Olga feels they have been either negligent or incapable; she is unsure which one. Either way it is bad news. The last four years of her professional life may have just disappeared down the toilet.

I am about to say I know just how she feels as I didn't get that reserve list interview on Monday, and will probably get another rejection tomorrow. I manage to stop myself. If ever there was a suitable time for me to be self-absorbed, this truly isn't it. Instead, I make a start at doing my best to help Olga get to the bottom of this.

Wednesday 12 March

Nancy pulls me into her office this morning. I have never seen her so tense, not even that time in the hotel room before her big speech. The loss of the clinical data is going to seriously set her back, as she is directly responsible for the grant money, and much of her clinical research is being built around it.

She explains that it also has implications for patients. "For all we know our treatment may be completely useless. Or even harmful. Without the data we just won't know if anything we have done is effective at all."

I tell her how sorry I am. I also mention that I worked late with Olga last night, trying to make sense of what had happened. Nancy thanks me, and says that she appreciates all I am doing. Despite watching her hard work (and possibly her career) circle down the drain, she takes the time to ask how things have been for me.

I explain how my reserve interview didn't come through on Monday, but that Mum was more disappointed than I was about it. I tell her that I am not holding out much hope for my final choice. Nancy is sympathetic and says she will try to find money to extend my contract if she can. Or she will give me a great reference, and try to help me find something else.

It's touching. While Sarah's manager, Debbie, routinely barks at her for taking too long on toilet breaks, mine takes the trouble to care about my career, even when her own is in jeopardy. It also makes it feel as though I am letting her down in some way, by not getting interviews.

"Just one last thing before you go. I know, it's probably none of my business, but I noticed that you got quite...uh...close to Nick at the conference, and that you spend time outside work with him." she says, as I am just about to reach the door.

"Yes..." I reply, wondering what the point to this is.

"It's not really my place to tell you how to spend your spare time, but things may be a bit complicated with him. You see the other assistant who..."

I feel a surge of irritation and interrupt her. "I appreciate you looking out for me, but I know all about it already. It's fine." I

237

don't really want to hear her dredge up the past about Nick and Spiny. I know she means well, but I am pretty sure she doesn't know about their break-up, or any of the events that have happened since.

"If you are sure," she says doubtfully, before dropping the matter.

Back at the Cupboard, Olga's mood is not getting any better. As I pass his office, I see that Nick is also being dragged into things. Looking through the glass panel on the door, I am shocked at how pale he looks as he talks and gesticulates to the rest of the team. I want to go and hug him, but I don't. That probably won't help him right now.

Thursday 13 March
No mail.

Waiting for the mail is becoming a chore. I can't bear to think of all time spent waiting for the postman. I complain at breakfast that they should have just announced it on the course website that they intend to keep us waiting for as long as possible. Scarlett points out that this is rich coming from the queen of leaving things until the last minute. Sarah agrees with me though. She intercepts the post so often she is now on first name terms with the postie.

After work, Justine comes around to the house. Along with Sarah, we eagerly chew over our application news. Scarlett leaves the room in disgust at the prospect of more Assistant talk, pausing only to scoff from the pan of brownies that Justine has brought.

For Justine, once again, it is a full house of rejections. Fifth time was no different from the previous four. However, unlike other times, she doesn't seem too upset. I would like to chalk this down to maturity, but I think this is more to do with her moving in with Dave last week. Not only has this got her out of the clutches of her horrid father, it has also bagged her some part-time work. Turns out that Dave's housemate needed someone to help out in his restaurant, and convinced Justine to step in.

"It's not psychology stuff," she says, slightly ashamedly, "I still want to do something with my degree, but I can still do this in the meantime, right?"

Sarah nods, and tells her that anything beats being dependent on her dad. She congratulates Justine, before getting off the sofa, grabbing her things and says good-bye as she heads off to work. Now alone, Justine looks at me as if she is waiting for my opinion.

"You don't need my permission to do anything," I say. "In fact, I think you are doing better than I am right now."

"What do you mean?" asks Justine.

"Well, let's see. Work is now incredibly scary because everyone is always shouting and on edge. I am getting rejections left, right and centre. I am probably going to be jobless in a few months, and I am really not going anywhere in my life..." I don't intend to say any of this, but it all just slips out, unbidden. Even more horrifying, I start to sob in front of Justine.

"Wow. I never realised how tough you were finding it," she says taking my hand. I attempt an answer, but can only snivel and watch in embarrassment as a long string of snot drips out of my nose. It land on her top. She notices, but doesn't seem to mind.

"I have just let everyone else down," I babble. "My life wasn't supposed to be like this."

"Hey, it's okay," she says soothingly, as she hugs me closer. "I just thought that you were always on top of everything."

"No, I am just as screwed up as everyone else," I wail.

"No. No. Come on. I will tell you what is screwed up," she

says, suddenly sounding very serious. "You know, at New Year's, when my dad kicked me out. I didn't tell you at the time, but I was heading to the bridge that evening..."

I stop crying at once. She leaves the rest of the sentence hanging, but the implication chills me.

"Things had gotten so bad over Christmas, what with me losing my job, and dad constantly having a go at me. I just didn't see the point of going on. Then you and Sarah saw me in that elf costume. It was just so..." she shudders as she pictures the memory. "After I got kicked out and I was about to...well, you know. At the last second I thought I would call you. Because you always know what to do. And you did."

I feel a flash of guilt over every negative or condescending thought I ever had of Justine. I am so, so glad we decided to help her out that night.

She pauses and thinks for a second. "Whatever happens in the next few weeks, good or bad, you will get through it. I promise. Your mum and dad will still be there for you. As will Sarah and Scarlett. And me."

Friday 14 March

Sarah wakes me at 7 am (and unfortunately Scarlett as well, who swears at us both before slinking back to bed). I remind Sarah that it's pointless. The mail turns up regular as clockwork. Why waste valuable sleeping time?

I am right. At 8am, the postie appears at the front gate. Mail.

He hands Sarah and I two identical letters. They look official, but Sarah's powers of prediction fail her for once. She can't tell what is inside. She tears hers open the second the door shuts behind us. The pieces of discarded envelope flutter onto the doormat as she hurriedly unfolds the single sheet of A4. Her excitement turns to anguish as she reads it.

240

"Thanks, but no thanks." Deflated, she slumps down onto the sofa. "Looks like we didn't make it. That's all four". She keeps scanning the brief letter for any hint of code, or secret message, suggesting there may be something she has overlooked.

"Fuck!" she says loudly.

"Fuck!" I echo, as I open mine.

Thank you for applying to our clinical psychology training programme. We are pleased to inform you that you have been selected for interview...

It doesn't register at first. I get suspicious that they have worded it in a way so that I am misinterpreting it. Nope. It seems like a legit, bona fide offer for an interview. I let out a scream of joy as it sinks in. This wakes Scarlett again. She screams down the stairs, "For Christ's sake, will you two shut up?"

"But you got the same size letter that I did!" says Sarah, clearly confused. She snatches the letter from me and checks it, before handing it back to me disbelievingly.

I continue to read out the rest of it. "The interviews are scheduled for the morning of April 25th. We will send you details and directions by email shortly." No wonder Sarah's psychic mail power got all confused.

I text Nick, who doesn't respond, then Mum and Dad, who immediately call back and start chattering excitedly as she asks me to read out exactly what the letter says. As I am doing this, Scarlett angrily storms into the living room, dressing gown whipping about her furiously.

"No one in this house has any consideration. Can you please keep the noise down!"

"Look, I got an interview" I say.

"Oh well done" she says, and then turns to Sarah. "Did you get one too?"

Sarah shakes her head slowly.

"Bollocks," Scarlett sighs, placing a hand on Sarah's shoulder.

I have no time to commiserate with Sarah, as I am already late for work. I fly up the stairs and hurriedly get myself ready, sprinting out the door only to stop and come back to carefully stash my precious piece of paper.

Olga is in the Cupboard early today due to the ongoing data crisis, with Nancy. After telling her the news, she seems quite happy for me. Well I think she is, as the actual words she uses are, "Well done. You must be happy to not feel such a reject". Nancy congratulates me in a slightly more normal manner.

Later that morning, I find Nick. He is by himself in the office and he smiles as I walk in. "Well done. You really deserve it. See I told you that you need to have more faith and confidence in yourself."

I start to talk about how best to prepare, but he cuts me off, "Sorry darling, but I am seriously behind. I need to get a move on with this," he says, pointing at all the emails on his computer screen. Noticing my look of hurt, he adds, "Hey, I promise we will celebrate this evening."

Nick is true to his word and we make up for it after work. After a movie, dinner, and celebratory drinks, it's after midnight before we both come back to the house. We are both cheering loudly as we walk through the gate, but we are met at the door by a distinctly unimpressed Scarlett. She eyes us up warily holding a kitchen knife, and waves it menacingly at us.

"I am going to bed now. If you make any sounds that are loud, interrupt, or in any way disturb my sleep, I will kill you. Then him. Then I will burn this house down. Then run off to Mexico. Is that clear?"

That girl is way too tense. She *really* needs to be more laid back about things.

Saturday 15 March

Lying in bed this morning, I suggest to Nick that we could do something on the long Easter Bank Holiday weekend. Perhaps go away somewhere. I plead to him that I really could do with a break. Mulling it over for a second, he agrees. He leaves, saying he will think about possible destinations, and get back to me.

My first mini-break. I feel quite the grown up.

Lying in the warm bit of the bed he has just left, I open my laptop. The promised email arrived in my email spam folder. Slightly annoyed, I open it. I read through the details about how to get there. They tell me that my interview is at 10 am and not to be late. That is not going to happen.

I then go onto the forums and Facebook to catch up with who else has got an interview. I track the various rumours going around and try to get as much information as possible to prepare. There is a mammoth list of interview questions on the forum which makes my blood run cold, but I pick up a few tips about what I could be reading and what to think about. A couple of people on Facebook I know that have applied are either commiserating their rejections or celebrating their success.

My online activities are interrupted by the phone ringing. I yell for someone else to get it, but no one else is home. I rush downstairs to pick it up, but they have hung up. I check my mobile and there seems to be no messages, so it's probably not for me. As I get back into bed (carrying half a jar of Nutella and a couple of digestive biscuits, which will serve as lunch) the phone rings again. I drag myself down the stairs and answer the phone with an annoyed groan.

"What?"

"Hi. It's Tom. Is Sarah with you?"

"No? I thought she was with you." I reply.

He has been trying to find her all morning as they were supposed to go out today. I tell him that I will make sure she calls him when she turns up. I am annoyed that he expects me to keep track of her whereabouts at all times. The house is empty all afternoon, but Sarah eventually comes back around teatime. As promised, I tell her that Tom called, but she doesn't seem bothered. I ask her where she has been, and she mutters something evasive under her breath. She looks very preoccupied and goes straight to her room.

Perhaps she is having an affair?

Sunday 16 March

Maddie calls me about the wedding plans. Clearly, she is attempting to juggle a dozen things at once in preparation for her wedding. After talking about table settings and seat covers, I am able to gather that they have set the date for late April. April 25th to be precise.

Of course it would be. The wedding of my oldest friend would just HAVE to coincide with my interview. It couldn't be any other date of the year, could it?

I let out a loud groan, wondering if life could be any more difficult. Maddie picks up something is wrong and asks what's wrong. I carefully explain that the interview (the one that she had earlier proclaimed to 'Like!' on Facebook) is on that day. She goes quiet.

"So, you are not going to come to my wedding then?" she says, eventually.

"I didn't say that. It's just that it's the interview day."

"Can't you just do it on another day?"

"It doesn't work like that."

Another pause.

"I can't believe you are even thinking about bailing out on me. On my wedding day."

"Hey! Don't blame me. I didn't arrange the times." For either, come to think about it.

"If you are going to be like that, you needn't bother coming at all."

"Fine."

She angrily hangs up. I stand there, wondering what the hell just happened. I mean she can't expect me to turn down the interview after everything I have worked for. I call up Dad, and complain down the phone at how unreasonable Maddie is being.

He is even-handed about it. "Maddie is probably just upset that's all. She wants you there, and it means a lot to her if her oldest friend doesn't come." A bit of a guilt trip, but he has a suggestion.

"Phone them up and see if you can alter it, or swap your slot with someone else. You may be able to do something. If not, we'll think of something. Don't worry." Phoning can't hurt, but I can't help wondering what he is going to pull out of his arse if they don't switch the dates. A helicopter? A time machine? Whatever it is, it had better be good.

Monday 17 March

I am on the phone first thing, trying to re-arrange the interview slot. What should be a simple process takes a frighteningly long time. The switchboard operator seems to have no idea which department to put me through to, so I end up going to:

-Academic Psychology ("We don't do DClinPsy interviews here, but please send us your UCAS form for undergraduate entry," Oh, piss off),

-Clinical Health Sciences (who mistake me for someone else with a similar sounding name, and start asking about whether or not I have marked the exam papers. They had better hope not)

-The School of Graduate Studies (receptionist appears to be having a nervous breakdown)

- The 'close but not quite', Department of Clinical Physiology. Fortunately, the person I speak to in clinical physiology is used to this mistake. She even has the correct number for Clinical Psychology Sellotaped to the side of their phone, so at long last I finally get through.

The administrator is a cheery lady with a strong northern accent. She pauses when I request to change the interview slot to another day, and tells me to wait while she goes to check. I am left on the line, while Olga glares at me. She whispers angrily that she needs to make some calls. I ignore her.

The admin lady comes back to the phone and says she isn't sure if she can do that now, but if someone else makes a similar request she could make the swap then. She promises that she will email me as soon as someone else asks for a swap. I thank her for being so accommodating, and trying to help. As soon as I hang up, Olga snatches the phone out of my hand to make her own call; giving me dirty looks all the while.

I Facebook message Maddie, writing that I am sorry I upset her. I explain that I am trying to sort something out. She writes back saying she is sorry that she snapped at me, and that she hopes it all gets sorted. She also asks me to come to her hen night in the middle of April. I agree, I can at least I make that, (if nothing else goes wrong).

Tuesday 18 March

As I arrive at work I am told by one of the secretaries to go straight to the meeting room. Intrigued, I enter the room and am met by Nancy, Nick's boss (Adam), and Pamela, the service manager. There is also an older man wearing a suit who looks a bit like a chubby version of George Clooney. I can't make his name out from looking at his NHS badge but can read the phrase "Clinical Director".

Wow. This is heavy. At first, I worry I am about to be fired. Then I reason it would be overkill to call this many people to fire someone on a temporary contract earning under £20,000 a year. If this was standard practice, they would probably have to summon the Prime Minister to fire anyone else here.

Nancy thanks me for coming in, and asks me to take a seat. The others at the table greet me, and Pamela starts asking about the clinical data going missing. She throws phrases around like "misconduct", "falsification" and "data fraud".

I am having some difficulty keeping up. It sounds like this isn't a simple mistake, but is something deliberately dodgy. They say that there may be confidential patient data left unsecure. The service could be sued. Several years' worth of work is trashed, and there may be very serious legal negligence issues, or potential court proceedings.

Oh my God. It's worse than getting fired. They're going to send me to jail.

Adam shuffles his notes, gets my name wrong, and asks me if I have observed anything untoward. The word "untoward" makes me think of a man in a cloak with a Jack-the-Ripper hat, slinking around the filing cabinets. I tell him I haven't noticed anything, and that I have just been doing the data entry as I was told. Now scared, and on the verge of tears, I am even prepared to admit to that time when I was seven and I shoplifted a Twix when Mum wasn't looking.

Pamela notices my concerned look, and tells me not to worry. On the contrary, my data is the only stuff that they are sure is legit. Probably because I was collecting and entering it independently from the rest of the team. The reason they are talking to me like this is because they know I am definitely *not* responsible.

I feel a weight rush from my shoulders and angels sing. I'm not in trouble.

Nancy then says that she knows I am friends with both Olga and Nick. Technically, I am "friends" with neither, but for very different reasons (I don't tell her this). She asks me if I think either, or possibly both, could be responsible. Not expecting this, I am stuck for what to tell her. It's like finding out your parents are Russian spies, or that your kindly primary school teacher sold guns on the black market. I tell them that nothing either has done suggests they have been dodgy. They all thank me for my time and tell me they will continue their investigation. I exit the meeting room, dizzy and confused.

Back in the Cupboard, Olga is sitting anxiously. "I suppose you have heard?"

"Don't worry. I told them I hadn't seen you do anything wrong."

"It's not me. It's someone in the office. Kevin, Estelle or Nick." she says. Feeling the tension rise, and the walls of the Cupboard feel like they are closing in, I make an excuse and leave to go to the staff room. On my way there, I see Nick coming out of the big meeting room. He looks shocked. He spots me, glances around, and takes my arm. He leads me to the stationery cupboard, and shuts the door behind us.

It's pitch black inside. "They are accusing me of all sorts of things," he says, his voice betraying his distress.

"I know. They talked to me. Don't worry I told them you were okay."
"It's all Olga's fault," he says, angrily. "You know how she can be."
I am not sure how to take this. "Please don't put me in the middle of this. But you do know I am there for you."

I sense him move in the dark, as he comes over towards me. His hands trace the contours of my face. "I know you are. The whole thing is a mess. I don't know what I would have done without you." He leans over and kisses me.

"Don't be silly. It will all get sorted out." I say, stroking the stubble on his cheek.

"I knew something was up, but I thought I was being paranoid. I would have mentioned it, but you were having all that stress with your course applications... "

"Hey, when we go away for the Bank Holiday, we will have some fun and forget all about it." I try to make the prospect of this sound as appealing as possible.

He pulls away from me. I can hear him shift uncomfortably.

"Yeah, about that. Um, I am really sorry. I don't feel like going away for the weekend. What with everything going on..." He says it awkwardly, almost as if he is unsure. "I know you were really looking forward to it. I will make it up to you, when this all blows over. I promise."

"That's okay," I say, trying my best to hide any disappointment in my voice. "We can do it some other time."

"What I would really like to do is go and visit my parents. I think it would help to just get away from everything for a bit. It's a pity I am still broke this month."
I offer to give him some money. He resists, saying it would be awkward, but I insist. Feeling around in my handbag, my fingers find an envelope. It's money I had taken out from the cash machine yesterday. I thrust it into his hands.

"There is over £200 in there. I took it out yesterday when I was thinking about our mini-break Here, take it. You need it more than I do."

He tries to refuse it, but again I insist. Eventually, he takes the money and kisses me again. "I am so lucky to have you. I will get it back to you soon. I swear."

"I know."

"Best we don't go out together. In case we are seen." he whispers, before slipping quietly out of the stationery cupboard.

I sit in the dark for a good ten minutes just to make sure.

Wednesday 19 March

Over breakfast I tell Sarah everything that has been happening at work. Instead of showing any sympathy or concern, Sarah rolls her eyes.

"Why does everything always have to be about you?" she snaps.

"Oh, I am sorry. I thought you might find it interesting I am potentially involved in a criminal investigation concerning my boyfriend. Do let me know if I am overlooking some breaking news in your life. Has there been a hostage taking at the nursing home? Or is Tom under suspicion of murder?"

She puts down her cereal bowl, and looks me straight in the eye. "You have no idea about anything going on around you? That other people have a life outside your precious little bubble?"

"I don't need to hear this." I get up and leave her to eat her cereal alone.

The atmosphere at work is just as horrid. It gets so bad, that I ask if I can work away from the office. Nancy thinks this is a good idea. So I end up doing my work in the coffee shop on the corner, and eat way too many muffins. I don't even get that much work done because I keep getting distracted/eavesdropping on the conversations around me.

Giving up for the day, I am packing my things when Nick texts asking me to meet him. He has chosen a bar strategically far away from work, and tells me I am to meet him at a secluded booth at the back. My love life has gone from slightly sordid to Cold War espionage. Still, many would see this as progress.

As I arrive, he doesn't even say hello. "It's a nightmare. Everyone's at each other's throats half the time. I have managed to get a few extra days off, so I am out of here tomorrow."

"When are you coming back?" I say, slightly surprised at how soon he is going.

"The week after. I wish you could come with me."

"Me too, but I really don't fancy the whole 'meet the parents' thing just yet." I am not joking.

"Probably just as well. How about I stay at yours tonight, before I leave?"

I try to warn him that Sarah is acting strangely, but he says he doesn't mind. To be honest I am glad he comes back with me, as we spend the evening secluded away from everyone else. I am really going to miss him when he goes.

Thursday 20 March

Nick leaves stupidly early in the morning, stealing away before daybreak because that was the cheapest ticket he could find. The bed starts to lose all of its heat the instant he leaves. I feel a sense of dread at facing the long weekend on my own. Later that morning at work, things start to look up. A familiar northern voice calls while I am on the loo. She tells me that she has just had another frazzled interviewee call desperate to change interview slot. Sweetly, she called me the second she got off the phone to check if it was okay.

"Yes!" I gasp.

I must have said it louder than I thought. A voice from the cubicle next door says, "Oh, I am so glad for you dear. I have suffered from constipation all my life, and know exactly how you feel. I am always happy when I am able to squeeze one out."

I send Maddie a Facebook message as soon as I get back to my desk, telling her I can make the wedding after all. She calls me straight away. Excited I can finally come; she says I can bring someone with me.

"Do you want to ask Sarah?"

"How about if I bring someone else?" I counter offer. I am sure Nick won't mind. Besides, he owes me for bailing out on our Bank Holiday plans.

"Would that 'someone else' be male and cute?"
"Possibly."
"Ooh, you are a dark horse," she giggles. "You kept that one quiet".

One thing for sure is that I will definitely not be inviting Sarah.
"She is avoiding you," Scarlett bluntly points out as soon as I get home. "She's going away somewhere with Tom for the weekend. I thought you would be going away yourself, so you wouldn't have noticed."

I tell her that I hope "somewhere" is a damp leaky caravan, surrounded by cowpats, in the middle of torrential rain. Scarlett says that knowing Tom's habits they would probably see that as the height of excitement.

Friday 21 March (Good Friday)

Long lie in. I am feeling lonely, so I call Mum. She interrogates me about what I am wearing to Maddie's wedding. I insist that she doesn't make a drama out of it, and ask her to

252

trust me that I will choose something nice. Mum sounds unconvinced, and asks if I am bringing Sarah. Mum is doing the table arrangements and she stresses it's *vital* that she knows in advance who's coming. I explain that Sarah won't be coming, but I may be bringing someone else.

Who is this "someone" she wonders?

This is an old game. The rules are quite simple. I have to try my best to not let on that a boy might be in the picture. Her objective is to wheedle it out of me that one is. She has first serve.

"Is it a friend from university?"
"No."
"Is it a friend from work?"
"Yes."
"Is it someone who lives in London?"
"Yes."
"Have I met them before?"
"No."
"Have you mentioned them to me before?"
"I don't think so." This is rapidly descending into a real life version of *Guess Who?*
"What is her name?" Ooh, a superb backhand volley.
"Nick," I let slip. It's 15-Love to Mum.
"Oh, it's a him," she replies, moving in for the kill. "Is Nick someone you have known for a long time?"

My objective is now to evade capture and give away as little as possible. Maybe I can get out of this with just giving away his name, and maybe his city of residence. If not, Nick's every last detail will be known by half the village.

"So what does he do?"
"He works with me."

"Oh, a doctor?" I can almost imagine Mum's eyes lighting up

and wondering if she could make it a double-wedding. Well paid, respectable, and free medical advice on tap.

"No, he's in research." Vague but enough to make her shut up. She goes off and calls for Dad, which is going to lead to a bonus round. I decide to pull the ejection handle, and pretend something is burning in the kitchen.

It works. I get away with no further discussion.

"You are prolonging the inevitable," says Scarlett, eavesdropping from the extension line. "You do realise that if you take Nick to the wedding, your parents will find out all they want in about ten minutes. Possibly five. I have seen your mother at work. By the time she is through with him, she will have his dental records and a full credit history."

I tell her to sod off, and mind her own business. I hang up, go downstairs and ask her if she hasn't got better things to do than annoy me all weekend. Scarlett gives me this sob story about how all of her friends have flaked out on her, yet again. As we are both abandoned and at a loose end, she suggests that we should make the most of it and do something together. With nothing better to do, I cautiously agree; my only conditions are that it had better not involve us getting matching tattoos or joining a cult.

Saturday 22 March

We travel into the heart of the night to a gig at possibly the dodgiest venue in the most run-down part of London. Scarlett isn't scared though and seems to know the place well. She is in with the bouncer and the girl at the coat check, who let us in without paying. We then head down the creaky little staircase into the dark death-trap basement. If there's a fire in here, I'm not going to bother trying to escape, as the chances of getting out this place alive are non-existent. Not that there is any danger of a stampede. Apart from a lone person on the mixing deck, there are only four of us in the audience. Our arrival has increased attendance by a third.

The band's music (using the words "band" and "music" loosely here) is terrible. I have a hard time deciding if they haven't tuned their instruments properly, or if they can't play. The singer mumbles, the guitarist misses notes, and the drummer could not keep time if he had Big Ben strapped to his wrist. I try to text Nick to tell him how bad the gig is, but the death-pit walls keep the message from sending. I realise that this place may have been used to film those horror films, where young ladies go missing and end up on meat hooks.

They finish their cacophony, thank all six of the audience, then launch enthusiastically into Oasis's "Wonderwall". Well, I think it is that. The singer gets a good 20% of the words wrong. How can you get the lyrics to one of the most famous songs in the world wrong, and still call yourself as a musician.

I lean closer to Scarlett's ear and whisper, "These guys are terrible!"

"I know," she grins. "But I think the guitarist is quite cute. A bit like Mick Jagger."

Or the tramp that collects change outside Holborn station.

I praise Jesus, Vishnu, Allah, Jehovah, and any other possible deity as the set finally comes to a close. My ears are ringing, and I am trying get over the fact that he sang "..and all the roads we have to walk are sliding."

Scarlett doesn't care. She enthusiastically goes up to the guitarist and tells him that they were amazing. Annoyingly, he doesn't respond, "Oh, no we weren't. We were crap. We are just on the way out to burn our instruments." Instead, the little turd soaks up the undeserved compliments, and sizes up both Scarlett and myself.

The singer comes over. "Groupies. Cool."

I can't think of a more depressing way to be spending my long weekend than being in this chamber of horrors, listening to crap music. The guitarist chances his arm. Despite my blatant lack of interest, he overlooks Scarlett, and instead places his hand on my leg. Scarlett spots this and is livid. She turns vicious, telling him his band is shit and he can stick his guitar up his arse, as that would improve his playing. Happily, she drags me off to a place where there are more people, a better atmosphere, and no danger of either us, or the music, being murdered.

Sunday 23 March

"So what's the situation with you and whatshisname? Why aren't you spending the weekend with him?" asks Scarlett as she munches on a bacon sandwich. We are at a 24-hour greasy spoon cafe in the early hours, and have the kind of hunger you only get after staying out all night.

"He has gone back to see his parents. Things at work have been getting a bit much."

"I don't know about him," she says, mopping up some ketchup with a bit of bread crust. "I have just got this feeling..."

"After last night, you are in no position to be giving advice about men. Besides, wasn't it you who was telling me about all that 'smite thy foe' crap?"

"Forget I said anything," she says, waving her sandwich at me. "Anyway, more importantly, you have to fix things with Sarah."

"She freaked out on me! It's her that should be apologising." I say.

"It's not about who started it. It's about doing the right thing. She is a bit...rough at the moment," she says, putting the sandwich down and trying to fish out something stuck in the back of her teeth. This is typical Scarlett, she is always taking

Sarah's side and blaming things on me. I tell her that I will be mature and grown up, when Sarah decides to behave in a way equally mature and grown up.

"So that's never then."

Monday 24 March (Easter Monday)

A phone call from an unknown number? Telemarketers? No, it's Nick calling from a payphone. He doesn't know where he has left his mobile, which would explain his complete lack of response to my calls and texts. He complains he is slowly dying of boredom at his parent's house, so he decided to cycle to a phone-box, and call where he could have some privacy.

"I swear if I have to play one more round of Pictionary I am going to stick a pencil into my neck and hopefully bleed out."

I try to make him feel better by telling him all about my "lost weekend". It cheers him up. For a second.

"I wish I could be with you." he says, his voice cracking with desperation. "It's so dull here."

"You could always move on to Scrabble. That might help?" I suggest, but his money runs out before he can reply.

Sarah returns home. I am balancing on the back of the sofa trying to find the remote control as she comes in, so the first thing she sees is me bent over and almost losing my balance. I spring up when I hear her, and bearing Scarlett's request in mind, I make a huge effort to be as nice as possible. This works. Sarah becomes friendlier, and tells me that they went down to Devon. They had a lovely time while they were there, but they got stuck in roadworks on the way back.

I tell her that I am pleased she had a good time. With the ice thawing a little, she reminds me about the Assistant's Group tomorrow. I had forgotten completely, and agree to go to it with her. I have something positive to report for once, and don't intend to waste the opportunity.

Tuesday 25 March

The Assistant Group met tonight in a different venue. Spiny is still on leave, so isn't able to host it. Patty has taken the opportunity to arrange a place more convenient for the rest of us. Better still the place she found offers a selection of posh juice and proper coffee.

"They even have those little biscuits," Justine squeals in delight. "By the way, I wanted to tell you about what I read on Facebook..."

"Not now, Justine." I say, just knowing she is building up to mention something Spiny related. Thankful that she is not here, I really don't want to hear about what she is doing elsewhere. In her absence, Cheryl and I decide to co-chair the meeting. The agenda, reading minutes and formal business are carried out in about 5 minutes. We have bigger fish to fry tonight.

Interviews.

Patty gamely steps up and gets the ball rolling. She mentions she has an interview for a London course next week. Melissa and Jane have managed two interviews which is impressive. Meryl is still waiting to hear about a reserve interview. I feed back my news about my single interview. Sarah openly talks about her four rejections, which gains her empathetic noises, and prompts Justine, Cheryl and the others to sympathise that it's not been their year either.

"It was just a practice run; I wasn't expecting to get anything," is said a lot. The recent graduates like Megan, furiously scribble notes. "All it takes is one," people mutter, like a protective spell.

So we went around the room, until we came to bloke-whose-name-I-can-never-remember. Cheryl asks him how it had gone for him. He mumbles something quietly under his breath that none of us can hear. Cheryl asks him to speak up. He mumbles again, equally unclear. Cheryl repeats herself a second time.

"I SAID I HAVEN'T GOT ANYTHING! ARE YOU HAPPY NOW?"

The entire room sits there frozen in shock. No one has any idea what to say. For some reason, at that precise moment, I suddenly remember his name clearly. Robert. I am glad I never asked him to repeat it in the past; I probably would have been floating face-down in a river by now.

"Nothing. Ten years I have been doing this. For nothing," he says, his voice trembling.

I am about say how we all find it brutal, but he starts talking again. "I mean, what is the fucking point? Why am I doing this? It's just ...pointless...to keep jumping through hoop after hoop. Obviously, no one gives a ..." his voice trails off. He slumps back in his chair.

Megan shoots a worried looking glance at me, almost asking me to do something. Drop a curtain, call an ambulance. Anything. Cheryl clears her throat and laughs nervously. She does her best to move the meeting along and regain some normality. Her efforts are in vain. Robert hasn't quite finished yet.

"Why the hell are any of us bothering with this? It's bloody impossible. We just sit here month after month trading our youth away. I have spent my entire twenties practically on minimum wage." He looks around the room at us all. "Face it. None of you have a chance in hell of getting onto a course. Let's all just leave and go do something productive with our lives."

Naturally this leads to several people objecting all at once. Meryl makes the fatal error of saying, "Speak for yourself". Big mistake.

Robert suddenly looks straight at her and snarls, "Of course I am speaking for myself. Do you think I would speak for you, you fat bitch?"

The comment hangs in the air and we are aware that a line has just been crossed. Between sadness and anger. Between acceptable and unacceptable. I know I should do something, but have no idea what to do. Meryl starts sobbing.

"You can't say that..." Cheryl shouts, defending her friend.

Robert turns to face her and sneers back, "Oh be quiet you stupid, vacuous airhead. You haven't had an original thought in your head in your whole life. Don't start getting one now."

Any thought of chairing this meeting and bringing it under control has now gone. Justine is braver than me, and pipes up, "Perhaps if we..."

"And don't you even think about saying anything. With your car-crash-of-a-life, you have no business advising anyone," says Robert, cutting her down before she can finish her sentence. Justine looks crestfallen and Sarah rushes over to comfort her.

"Yeah, yeah, go and play nursemaid to your imbecile friend. That's probably as near to a caring profession you're ever going to get."

The rest of the room starts to shrink back, desperate to avoid Robert's line of fire. I don't. I am now seriously pissed off and aggravated by what he has just told two of my closest friends.

"Okay, that is quite enough Robert." It comes out louder and more forcefully than I intended, "I think it's time for you to leave."

He looks almost surprised by my comment. "You do? You would. You quite like bossing everyone around here don't you?

Queen bee. Little Miss Perfect. Yet, I notice they are hardly banging your door down with interviews, are they?"

I am not rising to this. "Maybe they aren't, but I'm not going around upsetting everyone because of it. The door is over there," I say pointing at the exit.

"Oh, and you would know all about upsetting people," he says, his voice low with menace, "Like fucking another assistant's boyfriend behind her back. Well, that's the rumour. And you have the nerve to say I'm upsetting people?"

I wish that the ground could swallow me up. Hot tears build behind my eyes. I do everything I can to stop myself crying. Everyone else starts looking around at each other. Maybe they are afraid that I am sleeping with all of their boyfriends behind their backs? They must think I am quite the busy girl.

Somehow I recover. "You can believe what you want, but you are going to go now. You won't be coming back." There is only the faintest twinge of shakiness in my voice.

Robert looks like he is about to say something, but thinks better of it. He turns around grabs his bag, and storms out of the room. I take a deep breath and try to bring the meeting to an end. Then I rush off to the loo and collapse into long, heaving sobs.

I look at my face in the mirror and see that my makeup has smudged and run everywhere. I start washing my face in the sink. For some reason, I notice they have the sort of posh liquid soap that my mother always raves about and this makes me laugh loudly. Unstoppably. This is how Justine and Sarah find me; convinced it was all too much for me, and that I am now having a nervous breakdown.

Wednesday 26 March

I am still reeling from yesterday. I was up all of last night, thoughts swirling around my head, wondering what the hell just happened. How did Robert find out? Who else knows? Did Spiny have anything to do with this? What is everyone else thinking about me? I can't even ask about the last point because it was a fairly subdued evening after we got home last night. Sarah has said little, and I think she may have taken Robert's words to heart.

As I can't sleep, I get up stupidly early. I want to call Nick, but remember his phone doesn't work. Mum and Dad are going to be in bed. I can't think of anyone that is going to be up at 4am. I go on Facebook, but after trawling through my feed, I find can't bring myself to care or comment on whether someone has watched a great film, or just come back from holiday.

It's hot and claustrophobic in my room, so I open the window. There is a brief flicker of flame in the garden, and I see a brief glimpse of Scarlett's face as she lights up a cigarette. I creep down and greet her by the wall.

"Jesus! You scared the crap out of me" she says as I startle her.

"Can't sleep," I tell her.

"Yeah?"

"The meeting. That bastard Robert completely humiliated me in front of..." I say, getting more and more worked up.

"Keep your voice down, you're going to wake up half the street." She takes a long drag on her cigarette. I whisper the rest of my story, expecting her to be scandalised. She isn't.

"So?" She stubs out her cigarette and flicks it into the hedge. "He sounds like a tool. I'm surprised you are taking him seriously. Let alone losing sleep over it. I mean, if I did that over every comment some bloke said about me, I would never sleep again." She shivers from the cold, and wraps her jacket tightly around herself.

"But I see the scuzzy guys you hang out with. You have to be kind of expecting it. You don't exactly have the highest standards."

She raises an eyebrow, "Look, I am trying to be nice to you, but you make it hard at times. For once, could you please try and not pass judgement on how I spend my time, or who I sleep with? That's your hang-up, not mine."

I apologise and admit maybe I do need to work on that particular part of my character.

"In any case, why do you care what others think?" she says as we walk up the garden path to the door. "You complain non-stop about that group, and how so-and-so said this or someone else did that, but you go on as if your family has disowned you." She struggles to get her key in the door. I unlock it and open it for her. "If people are going to talk, they are going to talk. Nothing you can do to stop them," she says, dumping her stuff in the hallway.

"Trust me, with my dad 'coming out', I had to put up with my fair share of crap from people at school. Apart from Sarah. Then again, she is the only one whose opinion mattered." she says, as she heads into her room.

Maybe I need to start thinking about whose opinion really matters.

Thursday 27 March

Wanting to keep as low profile as possible, I volunteer to do a little job for Nancy. It's an observation for a case she is working on. Sitting in the dayroom of a supported housing project, I am tasked with looking for aggression triggers for Joe, a long term resident. It takes all of the day and occupies my mind. This is just what I need.

So far, all Joe has done is sit and watch daytime telly. I know this because there is a single line written on my clipboard, which reads *9:00am - Watched daytime TV*. That is all anyone here seems to be doing. As the talk-show nears its end (Title: "Your mum is my dad"), Morris, the activity coordinator, bounces in. His curly hair and perky can-do attitude is at odds with the mood of the grimy, nicotine-stained dayroom.

The activity coordinator is supposed to "provide a wide range of activities and interests to stimulate the physical and mental well-being of the residents". It's a tall order in this place, where there is such a mix of disorders and conditions, ranging from the chaotic and impulsive to the drugged-up and near catatonic. Morris doesn't let any of this get in the way of his mission. There are activities to coordinate and interests to stimulate.

He produces a tape (the ward still has VHS despite it being the Blu-ray era) and feeds it into the clunky top loading video-recorder. The cruel face of the talk show host is replaced with two graceful ballet dancers prancing across the stage.

Yes, Morris has badly misjudged his audience and put *Swan Lake* on.

"I thought you could all do with a bit of a change," he says, oblivious to the groans of the audience. Poor Morris. His heart is in the right place, but his tastes and outlook on life are more suited to Islington-dwelling *Guardian* readers than this place. People start to complain they want to watch *Cash in the Attic*, but Morris is insistent that ballet will be more beneficial to them.

Joe gets up and walks over to the video-recorder. He looks at Morris and then smacks it off the bracket with a swipe of his hand. The video-recorder rips away from its housing and flies across the dayroom, skidding to a halt under the pool table. Two annoyed looking support workers come in, and stride purposefully towards Joe. To their credit, I reckon they look more annoyed at Morris than Joe. I start rapidly writing, trying to note down everything that happens. Perhaps this incident will help shed light on the mystery of Joe's difficult behaviour. If not, at least it will be a good excuse to get them a decent DVD player.

Friday 28 March

By now word has spread about Robert's legendary meltdown. The IAPT crew have come in for a meeting, but the buzz is all about what happened on Tuesday. The accounts flying around have now evolved into something far beyond the actual events. One account is that Robert had stormed into the meeting and, without any warning started having a go at every person there. Another is that he brought a gun into the meeting, and I managed to disarm him, before punching him out.

Where do these stories come from?

So, unlike my normal sleepy Friday, I have an audience of twenty crammed into the Cupboard, all desperate to find out what happened. I explain that it had been a difficult meeting, and that Robert had become upset. He had said some nasty things which meant he had to leave. Someone asks what exactly was said, and I tell them that I didn't want to go into it because the comments were hurtful and untrue.

They speculate on what happened to Robert. Was he going to come back and wreak vengeance on me and the rest of the group? Had I informed the police?

I doubted I would see Robert again. They seem quite disappointed about this and rush off to their meeting looking slightly let down. I should have pretended that the gun disarming story was true. Perhaps it would have scared them into not eating all the biscuits.

Saturday 29 March

All this stress has made me ill. I woke up, throat in pain and with hideous flu-like symptoms. Both Sarah and Scarlett have abandoned me (for work and fun respectively) so I sit alone, bed-bound. I wish Nick was back to take care of me.

I catch up with my emails. There is some big meeting called by the service manager that sounds important. A few emails are floating around about Maddie's wedding. Mum is getting way too involved in all the conversations.

I also notice that several members of the assistant group have now recovered from Tuesday and have started sending tentative group emails. I get several supportive messages about how Robert was out of order and about how well I handled the situation. The most touching one was from Cheryl who is incredibly grateful for me standing up for her (which I can't really remember doing but am happy to take the credit for). Almost all of them talk about how outrageous the accusations that Robert made were, and that people were going to complain to his boss.

Even more touching is the way that Justine comes around as soon as she finds out I am sick, bringing with her a box of supplies and much-needed food. She bustles around making a fuss and plumping up my pillows.

"He said I was stupid. You don't think I am stupid do you?" she asks, referring back to Robert's comments from the other night.

"Well, you may not be the most academic of people, but 'stupid' sums up Robert more than you." I assure her.

She seems happy with this. She pauses for a second and says she has decided not to apply for clinical training again. In the past I would have probably groaned, "Finally!" and then told her what I thought she ought to be doing. I don't. Instead, I tell her to do whatever she feels is best. I will do what I can to help her. This seems to be the right answer, as I am rewarded with more cake and tea.

Sunday 30 March

Justine stayed overnight to look after me. As she fixes breakfast, she asks about the preparation for my interview. I tell her that I have plenty of time and will think about that later. She tells me she has a good feeling about it and reckons that I will get on. I have no idea where she gets that opinion, but unless she has been moonlighting as a member of the interview panel, I am not really sure how valid her opinion is. She hands me my breakfast before saying she has to head home. She tells me she will call later to see how I am doing.

I am feeling a bit perkier by the afternoon. My mood is also helped by a text from Nick saying he has got back, and just before lunch he comes over bringing chocolates and flowers. I am too ill to eat the chocolates, and the flowers make me sneeze all over him. But it's the thought that counts.

"How was your week?" I ask him.

"Same old, same old", he shrugs as he wipes the last drips of snot off his shirt.

"I know the feeling well. Some of the conversations I have with my parents could easily be replaced by a looped tape. Anyway, you are back now."

"You think you will be well enough to come to work tomorrow?" he asks.

"I will probably drag myself in. Sounds important."

"Probably a waste of time." he says, getting up to open the chocolate box.

"Oh, before I forget, are you free on the 25th and 26th of next month? It's Maddie's wedding. I told her that you would be coming as my plus one." I regret saying this as soon as it leaves my mouth. Nick's expression turns to one of pure horror. I shouldn't have sprung it on him like this. Spending a weekend with my friends whilst being introduced to my parents would induce panic in anyone.

"Um, I will check and get back to you," he says quickly.

At least he is thinking about it.

Monday 31 March

The meeting is held at 10am. The entire staff team sit in rows facing two ominously empty chairs. The atmosphere is so tense, I half expect Poirot to come in and start explaining who the murderer is. Nancy and Pamela, the manager, come in last and take the final two seats.

Looking concerned, they let us know that Nick and Olga have both been temporarily suspended this morning, following the investigation of serious misconduct. It's still unclear, but each has incriminated the other as being at fault. We are all asked not to contact either while the matter is being sorted.

I can't believe it.

I try to listen in on the various conversations that break out. Most think it's Olga, mainly because Nick is charming and popular and Olga isn't. I am obviously biased towards my boyfriend, but do my best to stay out of it. As much as Olga and I have clashed in the past, I am still finding it hard to believe that she was negligent or deliberately misleading. Perhaps, all the times she criticised my slacking may have been her way of dealing with her own guilty conscience?

As I leave, Nancy asks me to come to her office. The place is in disarray, with paper everywhere.

"I have had to go through all this over the weekend, she says waving her hand at the piles, "Are you sure you want to do this job in the future?"

"I think I am quite happy being the assistant for now." I say, genuinely glad I am not in her position.

"Listen, I know it's going to be hard, but you can't talk to either Olga or Nick. It's important you don't say or do anything that will get in the way of this investigation."

I start to feel indignant. "If I am being honest, I think it's unfair." I say, choosing my words carefully. "I have got to know them both quite well, and find it hard to believe that either could do such a thing. Now you are asking me to blank them both completely."

Nancy sits back on her chair. "You think you know Nick well? Did he ever tell you about his relationship with the other assistant?"

I tell her that I know all about him and Spiny, and that it's all ancient history.

She shakes her head, "Not her, I meant about him and Rebecca?"

My first reaction is "*Who the hell is Rebecca?*" Then it slowly comes to me. The perfect former occupant of the Cupboard, the girl who had my job before I did.

That Rebecca.

No. I didn't know that.

APRIL

Tuesday 1 April

I keep thinking over what Nancy said yesterday. Don't get me wrong. As a mature woman of the world, I completely understand it is unreasonable of me to judge Nick on his exes, but I can't help feeling outraged. It's like Nick has some kind of pervy fetish for Assistant Psychologists. Christ! Will I have to worry about him lusting after my own assistant when I'm qualified? The whole thing is just a bit too seedy.

Not that I raise the issue with him. Nick is understandably upset about being suspended and under investigation. He was waiting for me when I got home and ranted about how unfair it all was. How Nancy was such a bitch. How Olga has always had it in for him. How no one had any trust for anyone.

This stopped me bringing up the whole Rebecca thing, as it would have been the worst possible time. Tact won over any discomfort I may have had, so I went into supportive girlfriend mode for the rest of the evening.

As we sat having our dinner in front of the telly, I mulled over the idea that life isn't perfect. We don't all automatically fall in love with the boy next door and live happily ever after (which is just as well in my case, as the boy next door is only 5-years old).

I have to accept things may not be perfect. Everyone has baggage. It's practically a requirement in a normal modern relationship. Aren't we all supposed to have long lost children, a gambling addiction, or be secretly into rubber? Maybe I just need to adjust my expectations to the real world and grow up. I am probably over-reacting. I just wish I could talk to someone about it, but I am aware I am avoiding this.

I am worried they are going to think I am a fool. I am even more worried that they might be right.

Wednesday 2 April

I am still in two minds whether to confront Nick or not. He even comments I am acting a bit strange this morning (He has stayed over after getting paralytic on cheap lager last night, so has been pretty strange himself). I also have to lend him another £150 because his suspension means he is now not getting paid at all, and this has left a nasty hole in my budget for this month.

Work is strange as well. Everyone is on edge, and it feels like Nick and Olga are being treated as criminals. Even Eva has been thinking of calling her temp agency and parachuting out of here. All major work is now suspended, and I have done all the remaining tasks I have needed to do.

With all this time, what I should be doing is preparing for my interview, but I can't face it right now. I am not just burying my head in the sand; I am drilling down to the earth's core. Even Nancy suggesting a book that may be helpful for me this morning almost had me sticking my fingers in my ears and pretending she was a hallucination.

Instead, I cope by distracting myself with whatever comes to hand. It's gotten to the point where I have now exhausted the entire internet and Facebook, and am reduced to dredging through my spam mail file looking for interesting things, like fake Gucci handbags or penis enlarging pills...ooh, wait. There is the small matter of finding something to wear for Maddie's hen do this weekend. Now this is something I can constructively use my time for.

Thursday 3 April

Today has probably been the most stable it has been for the longest time. Things at work have started to settle down, and people are a little friendlier. Nick's mood has also improved, and he is slowly getting to know the others. This has gone down particularly well with Scarlett, who again has a fellow layabout to watch *Bargain Hunt* with. Sarah seemed to appreciate him making dinner tonight, not that she was around for long. At the moment she is keeping the most random work pattern; taking odd shifts, and coming home at ungodly hours. As she is leaving tonight, she tells us not to expect to see her around the house much for the next three days. Perhaps she has a second career as a drug courier? We could certainly do with the money.

I haven't told anyone else about the Rebecca issue, and it's now got to the stage where it's in danger of bursting out of me at any second. I nearly raised it with Nick this afternoon, but he seemed happy for the first time in ages, and I couldn't bear to have an argument with him. I have decided to leave it until after Maddie's hen weekend. I will have had a chance to think it over by then.

Friday 4 April

I have had the foresight to book the day as annual leave, so I don't have to wake up stupidly early tomorrow catch the train. Maddie has planned a spa-day tomorrow, followed by a night out in town. Initially, I felt it was a bit of a pain to trek all the way up, but it's far better than her original suggestion to have it in Prague.

My decision to come up early has proven to be a good for two reasons:

1) I witness an encounter on the train between a man trying to use a laptop, and a woman who insists on taking up more than her fair share of the table. I sit transfixed as the man gets slowly wound up as his space is encroached upon. His rising anger is met with complete obliviousness from the woman, who by now has her bag, two magazines, a makeup kit and iPod, all laid out in front of her. Eventually the man explodes in a torrent of abuse, and the entire carriage listens in as he starts incoherently screaming at for her being so inconsiderate and selfish. The temper tantrum goes on for a good fifteen minutes and is followed by another 76 miles of silent, gaze avoiding awkwardness.

They should put this on the adverts for the train company. No one would travel by bus anymore.

2) Away from the house and the Cupboard, I am able to have enough space to think things over. I finally decide to let the whole Rebecca thing go. I never knew her. It shouldn't matter she used to do my job. I can't expect Nick to be as pure as the driven snow (after all he used to date Spiny. Rebecca can't be any worse). I am mature enough to realise it is just my own insecurity bothering me. I feel a sense of relief when I decide to finally let it go.

Not that the calm lasts long. I receive a huffy, whining phone call from Scarlett as I wait for Dad to pick me up from the train platform. She is complaining about Nick spending too much time around the house and doesn't he have his own place to go to. I am surprised; I thought they were getting on well, playing at being layabouts. I ask her to put up with him, as he really needs a bit of space at the moment. Knowing Scarlett, she is probably annoyed about him taking over her favourite comfy chair, or hogging the remote control.

"I still don't see why can't he stay at his own flat?"
"His housemate is a complete control freak and stresses him out," I explain.
"So is mine! I don't go lumbering other people with my problems though." she pouts.

"Stop complaining. I will sort something out when I get back."

"You had better," she says darkly.

She can really be a spoilt cow at times.

Saturday 5 April

The day starts with me, Maddie, her mum Carol, and a few other bridesmaids covering ourselves in mud and then systematically having most of our body hair painfully removed.

Everyone else does this all the time, but as it is my first visit, I have the indignity of having the beautician explain everything in patronising detail, as if to a small child. I let it be known that just because I didn't know the difference between a Fijian hot stone massage and an Indian chakra rebalancing doesn't mean I am a moron. I also get into an argument about how beauty therapy is not really a valid form of evidence based therapy.

I have to be dragged away by Maddie, who mutters that she can't take me anywhere.

"So what's the gossip about this Nick guy? Come on, I want to hear the full story." she demands as we get our massages.

"Well, we sort of work together and..."

"Oh! He is the guy who you were talking about fancying at the Christmas party? The shag/marry/avoid one?"

Cringing, I reluctantly confirm that it is indeed him, and start to fill her in on the colourful saga that has led us to becoming an item. Her expression is hard to read as it's covered in mud, but she says it's great I have finally met someone.

I retreat to the steam room when they decide to go for a colonic irrigation. To me this is the sort of thing the KGB did to

274

political dissidents in the 1960's; it not how I want to spend a Saturday morning. Inexplicably, Maddie's friends seem to think differently and come out raving about how they feel half a stone lighter, and how their skin feels clearer. I can't tell the difference myself, but if I had several litres of water pumped up my jacksy, I would be looking to yell about even the slightest positive change I noticed. Carol talks about how she went for a "herbal and detoxing coffee ground treatment." I really wish she had kept this to herself. I will never receive an offer of a cup of Nescafe from her in quite the same way.

Fleur, Matt's sister, is also with us. She is eighteen and taking a gap year before going to university to study psychology. (What else?) We strike up a conversation and she lets me know her plan to complete her undergraduate degree and "become a psychologist" before she hits twenty-two. I start laughing hysterically. Maddie has to lead me away again, and hisses at me to stop acting weird in front of her future family.

Then it's off to Maddie's house to get ready for the big night out. As I am trying to fit into my outfit for tonight in her bedroom, she goes on about how we are going to be joined by several others this evening and will get a minibus to take us to the wine bar in town.

"...oh and don't forget we have to pick up your mum."

Oh, God no.

Why has she decided to invite Mum, of all people, to her hen night? She defends herself, saying we aren't fourteen anymore and that it's not uncool at our age to have parents around. Mum has always made Maddie feel part of our family and Maddie sees her far more often than she sees me. I can't argue with that.

"Don't worry. Your mum will be totally cool."

Such a lie. As we enter the wine bar, Mum decides she is going to make up for three decades of repression in a single evening. I see her dancing (badly), downing glass after glass of

Pinot Grigio, and screeching, "GET 'EM OFF!" loudly across the dance floor to a lad trying to chat up Fleur.

"Drink up and don't worry," orders Maddie, thrusting a Bacardi Breezer into my hand. I take her suggestion seriously, and before I know it I am up on the table, dancing along with Mum.

Sunday 6 April

I can't really remember how I got home, but judging from the look of tiredness on Dad's face, some severe intervention was necessary. He is such a darling, and has spent all morning nursing a very unwell wife and daughter. He even has to cook lunch, and looks very sweet wearing his little apron trying to stuff a roast into the oven.

I feel so unwell he has to drive me back to London. He puts the back seats down so the Peugeot resembles an ambulance.

"I am glad to see you had a good time," he says, "You looked so much happier than you have been over last few months." He is right. It was just what I needed.

Monday 7 April

I am still feeling a bit fragile in the morning, but fortunately persuade Nancy to let me have a study day to help prepare for my interview. Not that I got much preparation done. Nick proves to be a major distraction.

He constantly keeps talking to me, groping me, and putting the radio on too loudly. All of which doesn't help my concentration or revision. Clearly, I am not the only one who he seems to be distracting because when he nips off to the loo, Scarlett immediately starts moaning at me to get him to leave, like I promised.

I turn it around, and point out her lack of consideration when it comes to other people's property, her own overnight invitations, or that time she obviously had food sex in the kitchen and left me to clear it up.

"What's all this about food sex?" says Nick, coming out of the loo.

"Don't worry. You both deserve each other" she says, shooting us a glare before slamming the door behind her.

"Is it something I said?" he says, looking worried.

"No. It's Scarlett being her usual charming self. Just ignore her."

It's a pity I don't see Sarah all day, as she could probably have helped me prepare. Nick hasn't a clue about clinical interviews and insists on goofing off, or asking me irritating, irrelevant questions like, "Why is psychology considered a real science? Go on, explain that."

ClinPsy would be useful, but every time I go online, I just get anxious, freak out and switch off my computer. Ironically, I probably would have got more preparation done had I gone to work as normal.

Tuesday 8 April

As I arrive home, I am only halfway through the door when I see Scarlett run down the stairs towards me.

"Sarah hasn't been home for ages," she says looking worried.

"So? She is probably at the nursing home. Or at Tom's. You know how she is with her hours at the moment."

"Well, Boring Tom was the one who called me wondering where she is, and I called her work. She was only on the rota until lunchtime." She grabs her leather jacket and slips it on.

"Have you tried calling her?" I ask, starting to get worried.

"Only about a dozen times."

Trying our best to stay calm, we set off. We hunt through the various bars, shops, and cafés that Sarah is known to frequent. Nothing. We call Justine and a few other people who she may have gone to see. No one has heard anything. We aimlessly wander around, trying our best to think about where she may have ended up.

Suddenly, Scarlett has an idea. Grabbing my arm, she drags me off in the direction of the park. She gabbles something about the duck pond. I get panicked and flustered. As we make our way towards the large main entrance gates, I have visions of Sarah drowning herself. Scarlett goes quiet, probably coming to the same conclusion as me. We speed up as we get towards the centre, and can start to see the edge of the pond.

"Look!"

I see the silhouette of Sarah. She is alone on the tiny ornamental bridge that crosses the pond. Scarlett and I glance at each other, before making our way towards her. As we get closer, I can make out she is angrily throwing lumps of bread at the ducks.

"There is a piece for you," she says ripping off a corner of my quite expensive multi-seeded granary loaf, and throwing it to a mallard, "...and one for you, and one for you, but not you!" She directs her gaze at a solitary brown duck, looking forlorn as its friends tear at the chunks of soggy sinking bread. "You don't get to have any. You will never ever, ever get any!" she says venomously.

"Put the bread down and come off the bridge." I realise how ridiculous I must sound.

Sarah turns to us. "She's not getting any bread. She can try again next year."

Scarlett holds out her hands in an encouraging manner. "That's okay, she can do without the bread. She doesn't need it.

Why don't you come off the bridge?" I repeat. (I can tell her another time that I was saving that bread for tomorrow's sandwiches.)

"That's easy for you to say. I am not perfect, and I don't get everything right like you do," she replies angrily. "I am knackered, I am broke and I don't have a dead grandmother's inheritance I can just live off," she says, scowling at Scarlett.

We both stand there, unsure what to say next. A passer-by with a pushchair looks at us, puzzled, wondering if she is watching some pond-based performance art. I cautiously edge my way to Sarah and reach out to her. She suddenly starts crying and drops the bag holding the bread into the pond causing the ranks of ducks underneath to scatter and then start fighting each other for the soggy treasure inside. Sarah turns around to face us, gulping back huge sobs as we huddle her off the bridge and into the snack bar nearby.

It's late, so the place is empty as we walk in. The woman sitting behind the till looks annoyed, as we ruin her plans to close early. I sit Sarah down at a table near the window, as Scarlett goes to the counter to order drinks. "I am sorry for being so silly." she says between sobs, gesturing at the pond.

"You don't need to apologise for anything." I say, wondering if I could have seen this coming.

"I have just worked so hard, you know? No matter what I do, it's like I am running at a brick wall. Nothing's going right." This all sounds horribly familiar. Perhaps we need to give some serious thought to starting a support group.

Scarlett carries three steaming mugs of tea to the table. "Hey you have us. Tom too," she says as she spills half the contents over me, trying to put them down.

"It's just when Robert said that comment about how I would get nowhere, I felt he was right. There is no happy ending." Sarah snuffles and wipes her eyes with her sleeve. And I thought

I was the centre of attention that day. How self-absorbed am I?

Annoyed, Scarlett offers to call some dodgy blokes she knows who will sort Robert out with a quiet word and a cricket bat. She also distracts her by talking about other emotional duck pond moments when they were at school. They get into a lengthy nostalgic discussion about when Sarah's grandma died, or the time that she convinced herself that she had definitely, definitely failed her History A-level but hadn't. (Scarlett did fail it, but in typical style, didn't care.) Eventually we talk Sarah around and manage to calm her down. Good timing too, as the increasingly irate lady at the counter would definitely have chased us out if we hadn't.

Wednesday 9 April

Post-duck pond incident, Sarah is in a better place and feels hugely embarrassed about her mini-breakdown. I told her not to worry; personal experience has shown me that public humiliation is something you simply get used to after a while.

"I owe you this," Sarah says, as she hands me a replacement loaf of posh bread. "I'm really sorry for being so off with you in the last few weeks. You went to the conference, got the interview and everything. I just got jealous, and took it out on you. It wasn't your fault."

"It's just luck..." I start explaining.

"Nah, you worked hard for everything you got. You deserve it. I am glad for you. Really I am," she smiles warmly.

Nick comes into the kitchen and asks where we keep our spare bin liners. I direct him to the cupboard under the stairs. After he leaves, Sarah continues, "Anyway, I know it's no excuse but I have had the week from hell at work. So yesterday I handed in my notice. I should have done it ages ago."

"What about your notice period? Or your reference?"

"It always was a zero-hours contract, so I don't need to work out notice. As for a reference, I dread to think what that cow Debbie would have written. It doesn't matter. Last week I realised some things. I refuse to waste another second of my life in a place like that, and I am definitely going to stop living just for my C.V."

"It's probably for the best," I say, nodding. "Justine seems much happier now she's changed her priorities."

"I don't exactly see myself in the restaurant business, but I'll figure something out. There is one thing I do want to do though. I am going to go back to the Assistant's Group and tell Robert where he can stick his opinion."

I am really not sure if this is the best of ideas, but from the look in Sarah's eyes I don't feel refusing her is an option.

Thursday 10 April

In supervision this morning I tell Nancy about my building fear about my forthcoming interview. Nancy asks me how my preparation is going. I tell her that it isn't.

"Enough is enough," she says, exasperatedly. "You can't put this off any longer. You owe it to yourself to give it the best shot possible. Please don't leave it until the last minute."

"Okay, I'll take it on board." She knows my flaws all too well. "Any other advice or suggestions?"

"Not that you are going to be in the best state to listen to it, but try to keep your answers short and precise. Don't waffle. If you don't know something be honest about it, don't dig your own grave by making something up. Use the anxiety management techniques you have used in the group. Oh, and make sure you cover the basics around your research methods and statistics."

"No waffling, be honest, deep breathing, stats. Got it."

She keeps the bad news right until the end. With a pained expression, she lets me know that my employment contract is not going to be extended. Thanks to the on-going investigation, and the service already having to make cut backs, there isn't enough money in the budget to keep me on. They are going to have to let me go at the end of July. Deep down I knew this was probably coming, but it is still a shock.

"I am really sorry about this. You're doing a brilliant job, and it's not how I would have wanted things to pan out. I will write you a good reference, and keep my eyes open for any posts that might be coming up around here." She looks regretful, the way she always does when she has to deliver bad news.

I am not listening. I am too busy wondering how we are going to be able to keep the house if none of us are working. There is even more pressure on me now to succeed come "judgement day".

Friday 11 April

I am hunting through some old files this afternoon, looking for something from that mad frenzied week of late nights last November. My own stupid fault; a very stressed Nancy mentioned yesterday that some minor detail on the report needs changing, and I volunteer to do it for her if it would save her time.

Toiling away, my eyes get blurry after sorting through dozens of identical looking forms. I find the information in the ninth pile I sort through. Giving myself a little cheer when I find it, I start putting everything back in the filing cabinet. As I do this, I notice the drawer doesn't shut properly. I investigate and find a bunch of files that have fallen into the gap between the drawers, causing the cabinet to jam.

Reaching into the darkness, I fish them out and start to flick through them. I find several with Olga's name printed across the top, along with a date, her signature, and an official looking stamp. They appear to be a section of a much larger dataset of Olga's project. Normally, I would have handed them over to Olga, and grumble resentfully about the lack of thanks I would get for doing this. Without her around, I am not sure who this stuff belongs to.

I spend the rest of the morning going around asking various people. No one in the research office has any clue, and no one seems to be covering for Olga while she is away. After a good hour and half of running around I decide to sod it and just drop it in the service manager's in-tray. Pamela is paid far more than me, so she can deal with it.

Nick is lounging around on the sofa when I get home. He tells me that Sarah and Scarlett are making the most of their freedom and have gone to the cinema. He's broke so couldn't go with them. He asks me how my day had gone, and I moan about how I wasted the morning on a pointless errand that no-one would be grateful for. Nick suddenly sits up and starts paying attention. He asks me about how old the notes were, and what was in them.

He goes from lazy couch potato to Jeremy Paxman. I start feeling uncomfortable, as he probes further, so I try to end the conversation. I shrug it off, saying that I didn't really look at them, I just noticed they were Olga's and as she wasn't around I had handed them over to Pamela.

He broods for the rest of the evening in a passive-aggressive sulk. I tell him he is being childish. He doesn't apologise and insists that I should have told him about the files, as they had something to do with Olga.

"I can't believe how selfish you are being," he grumbles.

"And I don't understand why you are getting upset about this. They are just some boring old files. Come on, I can't call you up about every little thing that happens at work. Even if it does involve Olga."

"Fine," he says, grabbing his coat. "I'm going out for a bit. I don't know when I will be back." Before I can even think about saying anything, I hear his footsteps getting fainter as he walks down the path and past the gate.

Our first proper argument.

I try to text him but he doesn't answer. When the others return, I complain to Scarlett, who seems to be relieved to get control of the remote again. Sarah listens more sympathetically, but is clear she has no desire to get involved.

"Oh, no you don't," she says knowingly. "I am not getting into the situation where I say something, and then you two make it up, and then it becomes all awkward."

It's getting dark outside and he still hasn't come back or answered my texts or calls. Where the hell could he be?

Saturday 12 April

Nick is still not back by morning. He is not answering his phone. I assume he has gone back to his flat to cool off. Even so, I can't stop thinking about his comment about being selfish. Is this true? Should I have told him? Then wouldn't I have to tell Olga as well? What about the official line of not contacting either of them? I hate being caught up in the middle of this and just wish it would all get back to normal.

Happily, Sarah is the most cheerful she has been since we left university. Quitting the home has definitely been the right decision for her. She is even successful in nagging me into starting some interview preparation.

"Just because I crashed and burned doesn't mean you have to," she urges. "I'll even revise with you." I am touched with how generous she is being about all this.

I thank her, and tell her it's good to see her like this. She mentions that her last week at work helped put things into perspective for her. Curious, I wonder what exactly happened and ask what led her to her realisation.

"Enough stalling" she says, "Go upstairs and start preparing. Now"

I reluctantly follow her advice, and spend the afternoon getting up to speed with some of the material I had been avoiding. It is just as well, as I have become quite rusty with much of it.

I work out a timetable of what I need to cover and break it down into about an hour a night of study. Doing it this way isn't going to burn me out, and I will remember it better. Besides, it's good to have something to help me take my mind off of Nick.

Sunday 13 April

Still no sign of Nick.

I do my best not to let it get to me, and throw myself into my preparation. I even surprise myself by going out for a run and doing Yoga in the park. After returning home sweaty and exhausted, I shower, eat, and sit down again to grapple with psychological theory. Evidently, the secret to getting stuff done is to put yourself through hell. That way, boring repetitive tasks, like revision, seem like a treat in comparison.

I am finishing up, when Sarah and Justine drag me downstairs. They ask me to come with them to the Assistant's group tomorrow.

"Why?" I ask, puzzled. "I thought both of you had decided to move on?"

"Just this one last time," Sarah pleads. "We can't leave it like this. Everyone is going to want to see you after what happened last time."

"Yes, because they are going to be gossiping about me." I reply, having no intention of falling into that particular trap.

Justine shakes her head. "That's not true. Everyone has been really sympathetic on Facebook. They all blame Robert. It's like you are Princess Diana and he is the Royal family." It takes a while to get my head around this slightly strange comparison.

"It could be helpful to pick up tips about your interview," says Sarah.

I give in. "Okay. I will go, but it will definitely be the last one."

Monday 14 April

I was only partly right about tonight's meeting being my last one. Technically speaking, we didn't even get as far as holding it.

Spiny was hosting the meeting at her workplace as usual. I had to take three different buses to get there, so I left work early. At the second bus stop, I bump into Megan, who is bursting with excitement. She has managed to snag her first job at a special educational needs school. She is currently waiting for her criminal record bureau check to clear before she can get started. She has a little brother with cerebral palsy and is really interested in getting experience with similar children.

"For what it's worth, I think you will be great at it," I say, congratulating her.

Megan asks me how I have been since the last meeting, and says how vile Robert had been. Apparently, Robert has got into serious trouble after people made complaints to his manager. To be honest, I can't even bring myself to care anymore.

Sarah and Justine are waiting outside the building. We all walk together in a little clump through the long, winding corridors to the meeting room. As soon as we walk in, Patty and Jane tell us that Robert will not be coming today. Jane, in particular, sounds slightly annoyed she is denied a chance for round two.

Spiny is in her usual place right at the front. Cheryl, Meryl and a few others surround her and I can hear her high-pitched voice cut through the general chatter.

"It's a solitaire," she says holding out her hand. The others coo over it.

"I can't believe it. I am SO excited for you!" Meryl breathlessly exclaims, "Well done you. I have had to leave my boyfriend so many hints, and he is still not getting it."

The penny drops first for Sarah who goes over and congratulates her on getting engaged. Spiny flashes the most insincere of smiles as she thanks Sarah. All I can do is wonder which poor sap will be starring in the real-life horror film, *The Bridegroom of Spiny*. To give her credit where it's due, she is certainly a fast worker.

"It was so romantic. He took me to Paris," she trills, "I just thought it was a city break, but he took me to the top of the Eiffel tower and..." My mind starts to wander as I try to think if this could become any more of a cliché. Perhaps he went down on one knee and put the ring in a glass of champagne, while some violinist played Celine Dion songs in the background?

"... We could have done it at home, but Nick wanted to make sure it was special, so we..." Spiny drones on.

"Oh! That's a coincidence," Sarah chips in.

Spiny, annoyed that her monologue has been disturbed, looks at Sarah blankly.

"You know, what with your ex also being called Nick," Sarah prompts, realising that it may not be the most tactful thing to point out only after she has said it.

"Er...my ex isn't called Nick," says Spiny, looking at Sarah as if she is being particularly slow. Meryl giggles, as if to confirm what an idiot Sarah is. I notice that everyone is looking at us now.

"She means the Nick you broke up with in February." I explain. "You know, Nick from the research team?"

Spiny's eyebrow arches upwards. "Duh! We haven't broken up. Not in February. Or ever. Didn't you hear? We just got engaged." She thrusts her ring under my nose to prove her point further. Megan slowly backs away like an animal sensing danger.

"But Nick's been dating me," I murmur, as if on autopilot.

There is a silence as my words hang in the air and the implications sink in. Sarah's expression changes from one of awkwardness to sheer horror. Everyone looks around at each other disbelievingly. A random voice, in the tone of someone finally putting two and two together, says, "Oh, so *that's* who Robert was talking about."

My heart feels like it has just been ripped out of my ribcage. Nick hadn't broken up with Spiny. Hasn't broken up with Spiny. Spiny understands what has happened a split second after I do. Her look goes from mocking pity to outright fury.

"YOU WHORE!" she screams and lunges at me.

I see carefully manicured nails fly towards my face and feel my hair being yanked from the side. Instinctively, I react by raising my arm upwards and punching. My fist connects with Spiny's face. Those old self-defence reflexes coming to my rescue once again, although I am fairly certain Mum never had this particular scenario in mind when she signed me up.

Spiny flies backwards like a rag doll, blood streaming from her nose. Someone starts screaming; it sounds like Jane but I can't be sure. Spiny, still not about to give up, comes rushing back at me. I feel my shirt being ripped, buttons popping off. Her other hand flails at me, and I feel her perfectly manicured nails drag across my cheek and ear.

Unthinkingly, my leg jerks upwards and I knee Spiny in the stomach. This ends everything. Spiny lets out a long high-pitched moan, like a small animal caught in a trap. She lets go of my shirt and slumps over the table next to her. I feel Sarah holding me back from behind, I can only hear the sound of my own heavy breathing, and a trickle of blood trailing down the side of my face. Everyone is looking at me, frightened. As I see my reflection in the window I realise why. I look like I have just stumbled in from a war zone.

Tuesday 15 April

This cannot be happening.

This is all a hideous nightmare. I will wake up any second and will be dragging myself across town to the Cupboard for another day of going through the motions. It's only the stinging swelling on my cheek and dull, throbbing ache of my scalp that drags me back to reality. The painful evidence that yesterday was not just something that happened in my head. I lie in bed, bouncing between crying bitter tears and grinding my teeth in rage.

How could he do it? How much of what he said was true? Did he ever have any genuine feelings for me? How did I not see this coming? What else did he lie about? What does everyone else think of me? Thoughts of betrayal, humiliation and sorrow all compete with each other, but one thought scrambles to the top of the heap. Possibly the most painful of them all:

How much of an idiot am I?

I don't remember much about how I got back last night. I assume that Sarah and Justine guided my near catatonic body back to my bedroom. I haven't left it since. I dimly remember Sarah trying to cajole me into eating something. I turned it down. I don't feel like I could eat anything ever again. All I can do is lie on my bed and look up at the ceiling.

I didn't really sleep last night. Justine texted a few supportive messages, but something had come up for her, so she couldn't come over tomorrow to support me. It's just as well, I am really not up to seeing anyone right now.

Worried, Sarah encouraged me to write something in my diary this morning. I had no intention of doing so, but out of habit I start scribbling. It all pours out.

Sarah takes it on herself to call in sick on my behalf at work. Nancy doesn't sound that surprised, but thanks Sarah for passing on the message. Hearing her reaction makes me feel paranoid. Has Nancy heard about what happened? Who told her? What does she think of me?

I feel dreadful. I look dreadful. I am dreadful.

Wednesday 16 April

Things are not much better today, and Scarlett inadvertently makes me cry by suggesting that I may want to talk to my parents. I can't face Mum's outraged judgement or hearing the disappointment in Dad's voice. Instead, I flail around in my bedclothes and make tantrum noises. This has the effect of making Scarlett back away muttering, "How come I am the only one in the house that hasn't gone mental? If this is what studying psychology does to you, I'm glad I stuck with art."

Sarah has taken the quiet approach of being invisibly supportive, by hovering around in the background. She checks in on me from time to time and makes sure I am eating. She thinks I haven't noticed this, but I have. I am grateful that she is looking out for me.

Around lunchtime there is an angry banging on the front door, followed by raised voices. I peer down from my window, safely hidden behind the net curtain. I see Spiny standing in the garden, angrily jabbing her finger at Sarah. Spiny's face is contorted, red with rage, which brings out the angry bruise that covers the left half of her face.

"Tell me where he is! And while you are at it, I want to talk to that bitch right now!" she shrieks. Mrs Patel from next door, who has been watering her plants all morning, looks on with bemusement. I can see that she's not the only one. From my vantage point of my upstairs window, I notice several other curtains twitching. This may be the most excitement our street has ever seen.

I can't hear what Sarah is saying, but she is calm and makes soothing gestures. Spiny is not listening.

Pointing at her face, she yells, "Look at what she did to me! I will sue her for everything that she has got." (Spiny is welcome to try, but she will be sadly disappointed. All I really have of value is my laptop and my Oyster card).

Scarlett has now come out of the front door and starts squaring up to Spiny. I can see she's relishing her role as house bouncer.

"Okay, Sarah tried to be nice to you," she says loudly. Her straggly, crimson hair is loose and thrashes around as she moves aggressively towards Spiny. "Now I am going to have to spell it out. Stop being ridiculous, and go away. If you don't, I'm going to make sure that the right-side of your face matches the left."

For a second, Spiny looks like she may start something, but she glances up at Scarlett towering over her and thinks twice. Defeated, she stamps down the garden path, angrily kicking at the wheelie bin that has been left by the gate. The bin wobbles for a brief moment, before tipping over. The black bag inside splits, and the contents of it spill out all over Spiny, covering her in bits of egg shells, used tea bags and the scrapings from last night's dinner. This does little to improve Spiny's mood, but I have to admit it helps mine.

Slightly.

After apologising to Mrs Patel, clearing up the spilled rubbish, and assuring the rest of the neighbours that the show is over, Sarah and Scarlett come up to my room. I tell them I caught their latest performance, and thank them both for dealing with Spiny.

"She thought Nick was here," Sarah points out. "That's a bit strange isn't it? I mean why would she think he is here rather than at his own flat?"

"Maybe she has tried there before she came here?" I suggest.

"Nah. It's obvious isn't it?" answers Scarlett. "Think about it. He was always hanging around here. You never saw his place. He was living with her the whole time."

Of course! This explains so many things. The way he always used payphones, never invited me back to his place, the complaints about his "roommate". With a jolt, I realise the whole thing about that week away at Easter with his parents was his Parisian engagement holiday with Spiny. So that's why he was always broke. I laugh out loud at the absurdity of the money I lent him contributing towards Spiny's engagement ring.

Realising this makes everything seem even worse.

I ask the others what they think. Sarah is amazed at how much he lied. Scarlett, on the other hand, is barely surprised at all.

"Been expecting it to happen for ages," she says matter-of-factly. "He was a total nightmare. You dodged a bullet with that one."

"What makes you say that?"

"He was a laugh to begin with, but as soon as you went away for that hen party, he was trying it on with me. I told him to piss off and he got all snarky with me." The fact Scarlett turned him down, indicates that she has higher standards than I previously gave her credit for.

"How come you didn't tell me this before?" I say, slightly annoyed she had held this from me.

"Why do you think I was complaining all the time? The only reason I didn't spell it out, is because I know what you are like. Remember that time you went off on one when you thought I was flirting with your Dad? You went ballistic! If I told you about Nick, you would have taken my head off."

I hate to admit it, but at the time I probably would have. I just saw what I wanted to see. I got swept along with everything. I dread to think what else I didn't know about Nick. It's probably best I don't find out.

Thursday 17 April

I decide to brave it, and go back to work.

For the whole of the journey in, I am dreading the walk between the front door and the Cupboard. I can picture in my head how everyone will stare and smirk at me as I shuffle past them. I can already hear the gossip, "Have you heard about Nick's latest..."; "I can't believe she fell for that one!"; "I always thought she was a bit up herself. Not so perfect now though..." It takes every ounce of strength to push on through the doors and face the humiliation head-on.

Reality is different. It's quiet. Eva at reception asks if I'm feeling better. Everyone else gets on with their own business. No one puts me in the stocks and starts throwing rotten fruit. I go unnoticed.

I find Nancy sitting in the Cupboard, chatting to Olga.

"Hello! I wasn't expecting you," says Nancy, warmly. "I am glad you are here. We were just talking about you."

Oh, I just bet they were.

Olga gives a little smile to me, before nodding to Nancy. She gets up, tells me that she will talk to me later. This leaves Nancy and myself in the Cupboard.

"I need to bring you up to speed with recent developments," says Nancy, offering me my own chair. Unsure of what is happening, I sit down.

"Recent developments?" I dread to think what else could have happened.

"I forgot how cramped it is in here." Nancy says as she glances around the walls. "You know, I started off as an Assistant Psychologist in this very office? Actually, we were in the bit that used to be the gents' urinals before we came here. This place was actually a step-up for us."

This seems highly improbable. First of all, I can't imagine her ever being anyone's assistant. Secondly, the chances of her starting and ending her career in the same building seem extremely remote.

She looks at me, and takes a deep breath. "I'm sorry about the business with you and Nick. I tried to warn you about him. I know he's got, well, a *history* of doing this kind of thing. You have probably gathered that by now. While what he did with you wasn't exactly professional, it wasn't illegal. You were all adults."

"There are many words that I'd use to describe Nick, but 'adult' isn't one of them," I reply. "I'm sorry I ignored you. I should've listened."

"What *is* illegal, is his negligence about the records. That and pinning his mistakes on Olga, which is technically perjury."

Hmm, it looks like I wasn't the only one he screwed over.

"We suspected this from the beginning, but we didn't really have much proof. It was Olga's word against Nick's. It was only when you handed in those missing files we had some hard evidence. The dates and signatures supported Olga's defence and contradicted Nick's story. We showed him these and pointed out the inconsistencies of what he had originally said. It took some time but he finally admitted it."

I struggle to keep up with all of this. "So he's fired?"

Nancy nods. "You look surprised. I thought he would at least have told you that much."

"No. Nick told me very little. About anything when I think about it." I pause and think. "I still don't understand why he did it?"

"I don't think he set out to do it deliberately. He is just irresponsible and thoughtless. That's Nick all over. In the past he's usually got by with talking himself out of trouble. Unfortunately, when it comes to this kind of research, you have to be consistent and keep on top of it, or it all gets out of control."

I look at the floor, slightly ashamed of my first-hand experience of this. I console myself that it was nothing in Nick's league.

Nancy shrugs and continues, "I think it all built up, but instead of doing something about it, he just kept ignoring it and dug himself deeper. Then, when it was all too much, he lied rather than take responsibility. I'm sorry it had to get to this stage. We could have sorted this out much more easily if he had been up front from the start."

Her grand denouement over, Nancy leaves to fetch Olga.

Olga comes back and hugs me, enveloping me in her giant embrace. It was only yesterday she found out that she was in the clear, and is incredibly grateful to be back.

She is especially thankful to me for all of the "investigating" I had done on her behalf. I have no idea what she is talking about, but I get the impression she thought I pulled a *Nancy Drew*, and doggedly hunted down the vital clues that proved her innocence.

I go along with it. Why disappoint her?

Friday 18 April

I make it through another day at work. For my efforts, I find Nick standing on my door step waiting for me.

"I know I messed up, but we need to talk."

"You've got some nerve coming around here. What would you like to talk about? How about your recent engagement and the fiancé you forgot to tell me about? What about fraud and perjury? Or did you want to 'talk' about you trying it on with my housemate?"

I barge past him, rummaging around my bag to find my door key. "I would ask for the money I lent you back, but I know you don't have any. I am going to have to chalk that down to experience."

He comes closer, "Look, I know what you think, but you don't understand. Let me explain." I can feel him put his arm around my shoulders.

I shake it off. "The time for any explanations would have been a long time ago. I don't want to have anything more to do with you, you gutless turd." I shut the door in his face.

I put the kettle on and turn on the telly. I can hear Scarlett and Sarah moving around upstairs. As I bring my cuppa through to the living room, I see Nick has climbed up onto the bay-window ledge. He begins tapping at the glass.

"Piss off or I will call the police," I yell, closing the curtains. It's amazing how small the gap is between nuzzling happily on the sofa, and him being on the other side of the window, threatened with a night in the cells. As I sit down and make myself comfy, my mobile beeps.

I M Sry! Plz tlk 2 me

Even his text speak is starting to irritate me. I don't reply to it. Or the other four or five that follow. Sarah and Scarlett, alarmed by my yelling come down to see what's happening.

"We just have a small vermin problem. He's scratching at the window and making noises. Don't worry about it. If he continues I will call in pest control."

"I don't think you will need to. He's already leaving," Sarah says, as she glances through a gap in the curtains. She got a call from Justine earlier who told her that Spiny had kicked Nick out of their flat. She has also notified everyone on Facebook that they are no longer an item. That is about as official as things get in Spiny's world.

"You know, I almost feel sorry for her," says Sarah. "I know she can be a bit of a pain at times, but even she didn't deserve Nick."

I am not sure. I will have to give that some thought.

Saturday 19 April

I dare to go on Facebook and check my personal email for the first time since the incident. My inbox is bulging with unread messages from the last five days. It's not as bad as I feared. The good thing about modern life is that everyone else is so absorbed in their own lives they barely notice other people messing up theirs.

I find Maddie's registry for wedding presents, a wall-post about a gig that has long since happened, and a chain message from Dad about generating good luck. How dare everyone go about their usual business while my world was falling apart?

I get a touching message from Megan. She writes asking if I am okay, as she was really concerned after the meeting. I email her back telling her that I am fine, but probably won't be coming back to any future meetings. I wish her all the best for the future.

She messages me back saying that she is sorry to hear that. She really enjoyed hanging out with Sarah, Justine and myself ("the veterans" as she calls us), and was hoping to see us some more. I promise to catch up with her soon. After all, I do have more free time on my hands now, and a large hole in my social life.

Sunday 20 April

Phone call from Mum. "How's the interview preparation going, darling?"

Shit.

Monday 21 April
Days till Judgement Day: 3

In addition to being completely off-track with my planned revision schedule, I have now been press-ganged into helping Olga fix the mess that Nick has left behind. If only he could have timed ruining my life more considerately.

I am not really sure what I am supposed to be doing to help Olga. I grasp that Nick has been pretending that a lot of clinical information existed (when it didn't), and saying that things were missing (when they weren't). As I go through it, I come to the conclusion that Nick is really quite stupid. It would have been easier for him to actually do his job properly, rather than go through the elaborate track-covering and lying. It just makes it even more apparent that I barely knew him at all.

Not that I can explain any of this to Olga. She has no awareness of my relationship history with Nick. She probably thinks I am mildly annoyed at having to do some extra work. When I come across evidence of Nick being particularly destructive about his record-keeping, my outbursts of "THAT ARSEHOLE!" startle her. She thinks I am just being loyal, by being so indignant on her behalf.

Tuesday 22 April
Days till Judgement day: 2

Preparation continues and my work helping Olga keeps piling up. As I have taken leave for my interview and Maddie's wedding, I am not going to be in on Thursday and Friday, which gives us even less time to fix everything.

I come in early and plan to leave late, but I keep making errors despite my best efforts. In my defence, this isn't really my job in the first place, and I have had limited time to become familiar with the material I'm supposed to be sorting. It also doesn't help that some of the databases are new to me, and the codes have been labelled in a way to ensure maximum confusion. Is it any wonder that REF/078321/IOP/34323/AB gets mixed up with REF/078312/IOP/34323/AB?

Olga doesn't think so. The tone of her voice reveals her annoyance when she has to help me out converting a missing raw score into a pro-rata scaled score (I have no idea what the difference is and could care even less). Her gratitude is sharply decreasing and she is reverting back to her old self. I don't need this. I am on the verge of walking out the door.

I don't. I carry on.

I end up staying until past 8pm, before rushing home. I jump straight into revision. I get sympathetic looks from Sarah, and even Scarlett brings me up a plate of what is the wateriest lasagne that I have ever tasted. I don't care. I wolf it down before returning to my books. I cannot afford to be fussy. At the moment, food is just fuel, and the less time I take to prepare it, the more time I have to cram more information into my poor, overworked head.

Wednesday 23 April
Days till Judgement day: 1

No! No! No! Time is slipping by too quickly. Despite all my efforts, I still have a massive list of topics I need to revise. Olga isn't giving me a break at work either, and insists on making more and more demands. I complain to Nancy, who manages to get Olga to back off. This is beneficial for both of us. I feel slightly more at ease, and Olga will never know how close she came to being messily beaten to death with a stack of heavy reports.

Despite the situation improving, my anxiety gets the better of me. I rush off to the toilets and start weeping the second the door shuts. As if to underline my distress, the bathroom light bulb picks that moment to blow. Crying in the dark, I ask myself, it can't be like this for everyone, can it?

Somewhere, in the inky blackness of the toilet stall, I find a reserve of determination. It's not about remembering what I have read in the last few days, it's about what I have learned over the last few years. I have fought for every inch of ground without much help. I have overcome obstacles and barriers that would have made most turn back. I have worked *bloody* hard, and I will be damned if I let my anxiety bring me down after having come this far. These feelings will pass, and one day it will all be an amusing story that I entertain random strangers with at social gatherings.

I can do this.

(Will probably still check my statistics textbook one last time though. You never know.)

Thursday 24 April
Judgement day

I arrive early. Stupidly early.

A good luck call from Mum and Dad last night convinced me to take the 7am train to get here in plenty of time. Plenty of time meant that I was *so* early that I had over two hours to spare. Usually, this would be no big deal. Under normal circumstances, I can easily kill two hours deciding which type of coffee to drink, or reading *Heat* magazine. Those rules don't apply today. In my heightened sense of anxiety, I am torn between spending those two hours hiding in the shrubbery or resisting the urge to run away as fast as possible. This urge is not helped by me feeling itchy and uncomfortable in my newly dry-cleaned suit.

Having learned from Sarah's experience, I limit my time at the campus and restrict my coffee intake. I stay in the calm environment of the train station coffee shop until I can put off the inevitable no longer, and gradually make my way up the hill towards the grey forbidding metal gates of the university.

Despite being emailed a detailed map, and checking the internet last night, I still manage to get lost. I wander around the never-ending maze of identical looking department buildings and glass-fronted lecture theatres. Students casually mill around on their way to lectures or perhaps breakfast. Although several are bleary eyed and dishevelled, they all are far more relaxed than I am. I resist the urge to grab them and demand that they enjoy their carefree, blissfully unaware undergraduate lives while they can, because what waits for them outside is a harsh, unforgiving place.

I somehow make it to the relevant departmental building. Sellotaped onto the automatic doors, I see a single sheet of A4 with "Clinical Psychology Interviews" written crudely in green marker pen. A thick arrow is drawn underneath, in the direction of what appears to be a blocked fire escape. I hope it's not an omen about being led to a place where many rush expecting salvation to only cruelly perish.

I enter through the doors and find a harried-looking lady sitting at the desk. She has a peeling sticky label with *Julie* written on it and identifies herself as the course administrator. She asks for my name, which I give, and she welcomes me to the department.

"You are a bit early, but that's alright. Here, take this and go up to room 453 on the second floor." Julie speaks in a soft Northern accent and is friendly, despite being clearly rushed off her feet. She pushes a brown manila envelope at me, which I clutch as I aimlessly start looking around to find out how to get to the next floor. Thankfully, she spots my confusion and guides me towards a stairwell. I feel grateful, and at the same time pray she doesn't report how clueless I am being to the interview panel. I take the stairs up to the second floor, and again get lost looking for room 453. It's just as well I came early; at this rate, I may be in danger of missing my interview.

I eventually manage to find it. Room 453 is a large teaching room that has been cleared to hold the interviewees. All of the desks and tables are stacked at the rear and the chairs have been rearranged in a wide semi-circle. There are already four people inside and the atmosphere is tense. Three blonde women, who look like they are in their late twenties, are reading through the documents in their envelopes. A similarly aged dark-haired man, sits slightly apart from them and seems deeply absorbed in a paperback. I can't help but observe that everyone is wearing matching dark suits, making the room feel even more funereal.

As I walk in, no one is talking, and the only sound audible is the faint hum of the air conditioner. I choose the chair nearest to the door and open my envelope. A printed vignette pops out. I try to read it but the words swim around, and appear as random black marks against a white background. Deep breaths.

The words sharpen into focus. That's better.

The case describes a young woman who is facing significant problems. There are details of mental health issues, homelessness and problems associated with looking after numerous small children unassisted. It's probably not the course's intention, but reading through it· has a calming effect. Going through the details of this poor woman's life, I reflect that no matter how anxious I am this morning, others have it far worse than me. The vignette instructs me to think about how best to help her.

As I start to think the situation over, the man starts talking to two of the other candidates sitting nearest to him. The candidate sitting closest to me takes this as her cue, and strikes up a conversation with me. Before I am even aware of what I am doing we have compared CVs. She talks about her NA, AP, RA posts, her MSc from UCL, and her PGCert from UEL. Listening to this continuous stream of letters it feels a bit like watching *Countdown*. I smile politely and nod, not really sure how best to respond. She seems to have racked up an amazing amount of experience, and from what she is saying she should probably be running the course, rather than being interviewed for a place on it.

Julie comes in and all conversation grinds to a halt. She smiles at me and asks me to come through. I shakily get to my feet and follow her while the others murmur "Good luck". I follow her as she navigates the warren of hallways.

"Don't worry they don't bite," she says, as we arrive at a nondescript looking door. A single plastic chair has been placed outside for candidates to wait on. I feel a weird sense of anti-climax. My fate is to be decided here? I really don't know what I was expecting. Some huge gothic portcullis flanked by golden sculptures, possibly.

She tells me to take a seat and that they will come out and get me shortly. I watch Julie walk off, leaving me alone on the deathchair. In the silence of the corridor, I can feel my heartbeat in my ears. I start doing the deep breathing exercises that I have spent so much time teaching others, and find they work remarkably well. After a few minutes the door opens and a man asks me to come in.

I shuffle to my feet and step into the room.

I would like to record for posterity a blow-by-blow account of what was asked and what I replied. Sadly, I can't really remember too much of what happened. Like a rollercoaster, it was a massive build-up, before being over in ten seconds. I say ten seconds, but my watch reliably informs me that it took forty-five minutes.

I do remember that there was a panel of three: an older bearded man, a matronly woman with a friendly smile, who bore an uncanny resemblance to Maddie's mum, Carol, and a younger, sharp-dressed man wearing steel-rimmed spectacles. The interviewer, who looks like Carol, introduced herself as the course director and thanked me for coming.

The questions were surprisingly straightforward, and the sort of thing I have talked about a million times before with Nancy. The younger male interviewer asked about designing a research study, which I was able to take a shot at, but am aware I stumbled a little on the follow-up questions about how that would work in reality. I was open about what I don't know, and gave some tentative suggestions. The older man asked about the printed vignette, which I felt more confident in answering. The panel also took the trouble to ask me a bit about myself, and the challenge was not to waffle on. Happily, I resisted the temptation to make myself sound like superwoman, and did my best to be thoughtful and open.

Reflective.

And just like that, it was all over. Before I know it I am back out in the corridor.

Someone else is sitting in the deathchair, the dark-haired guy from the waiting room. He is still reading his paperback. He looks up at me, giving a nod of recognition.

"How did it go?"

"Well I survived it." I tell him. "I think I gave it a fair shot."

I notice the cover of his book. *Breakfast at Tiffany's.* I can't stop myself from shaking my head.

He notices. "It helps take my mind off things," he explains. "Have you read it?"

"Oh yes, I quite enjoyed it."

"I am surprised by it. The film has a reputation of being a classic romance, but the novel is actually quite dark. The girl's a bit flaky, only no one in the story seems to see it." I am about to respond, when the door opens. He slowly brings himself to his feet, takes a deep breathe, and moves towards the door.

"Don't worry, they don't bite. Good luck," I whisper, as he goes through.

Friday 25-Saturday 26 April

Maddie's wedding.

I am up at some unholy hour trying to wake Sarah (my guest in lieu of Nick), so we can get the train. The ceremony starts at noon, so we end up standing on a freezing cold station concourse at 6am, carrying a dress, two pairs of shoes, a stupid hat, and an overnight bag. It was a mistake to get back so late from the bar last night, celebrating getting through my interview. It felt like a good idea at the time but less so now, with the pounding in my head increasing as each arriving train is loudly announced.

305

Sarah is holding up a little better than me. However, I try not to think about how we are probably going to have to spend the afternoon drinking more. At this rate, I may as well save myself the time and effort, and just punch myself in the liver, for all the damage I am doing. My delicate state also means I am constantly dropping bits and pieces on the station platform, and even manage to get my head jammed in the train's closing doors. I am just glad that I had no responsibility in coordinating any part of the wedding, as Maddie would certainly not be getting married any time soon.

The train journey is fairly uneventful, but that is probably because I spend most of it drifting off to sleep and inconsiderately slumping onto the people next to me. I wake up two stops before our destination and start making myself look presentable. My attempts to apply makeup in the train toilet don't go down well. The look of horror on Mum's face makes this clear.

"What on earth possessed you to put mascara on your forehead? Why does your lipstick make your mouth look like it's bleeding? Have you gone potty?" she says, as she helps me unload my belongings from the carriage. She clucks over Sarah, complimenting her on her outfit, and the two of them bundle me into the station disabled toilet where they proceed to wash me down with the vigour of an orphanage matron scrubbing a street urchin.

"Sorry, Mum" I say, lamely.

"You smell like a brewery," Mum sniffs, as she aggressively combs my hair. Sarah re-applies my foundation and dabs eye shadow on, delicately. I am too busy being forcibly made acceptable to say anything else.

Dad is waiting in the car and grumbles about how he had just put another pound in the ticket machine. He seems surprised to see Sarah and starts to ask, "I thought you would be bringing..." The sharp glance from me is enough to say that this is a conversation for another time. I am still not fully dressed, so have the indignity of trying to fit into my clothes in the back of the car. I must have mooned half the village on our way to the church.

"Nothing they haven't seen before," says Dad cheerily. "Half the village has probably changed your nappy." They both start cross-examining me about how my interview went.

"It went fine. Stop asking me all these stupid questions. You are so embarrassing!"

We get to the church a few minutes later than expected, so Sarah and I are dropped off out front to tell them we are here while Mum and Dad find parking. Unfortunately, as we burst through the door we realise that everyone else has been seated, and the *Wedding March* has just started playing. For a brief second it looks like we are just about to hold the village's very first lesbian wedding. I see Maddie's nana squint over her bifocals and comment, "Ooh, her makeup is very good. Maddie looks totally different." Carol diplomatically pulls us into an adjacent pew, just as Maddie makes her grand entrance.

Maddie looks lovely in her long, flowing ivory dress. She smiles at me as she walks up the aisle. I can see Matt waiting at the front and I have to concede he scrubs up well. I can barely recognise him without his *Black Sabbath* T shirt and ginger facial fuzz. In a Moss Bros suit and a shave, he could pass as any normal bloke. Matt's sister, Fleur, gives me a little nod as she follows Maddie up the aisle, holding a bunch of flowers. My hangover is not helping things, and the church organ feels like a sledgehammer to my brain every time it hits high C. I scan the wedding programme, and wonder how I am going to get through "Jerusalem".

The vicar welcomes us all and bids us to be seated. His voice is quite low so I can hardly hear him. My mind starts to wander and unthinkingly I take my mobile out to check Facebook, which Sarah has to snatch off me and hiss, "Put that away. Have some respect." I apologise, looking shamefacedly around me to see who else may have witnessed my rudeness.

Thankfully the congregation's attention are diverted. Just as the vicar announces, "Does anyone know of any lawful impediment why these two should not be joined in holy matrimony?" the door slowly creaks open, and my parents pop their heads through.

"Sorry, couldn't find parking. Had to go up by Parson's field." explains Dad apologetically. There is a moment of shock, before the entire church bursts out laughing. Mum is mortified.

After the ceremony, and while we pose for photos, Maddie tells me that their entrance was the definite high point of their wedding. She is glad I was able to make it in time, and thanks me for making the effort. "I can't talk now, but I will come find you once I've said hello to everyone," she promises.

The reception is being held at the Fox and Hounds, which is only a few streets away. Sarah and I follow Mum and Dad as they make their way down the narrow road. We find several of the wedding party occupying a large table in the middle. They all sit down, as I go up to the bar to fetch drinks.

I am standing at the bar, when someone taps me on the shoulder and a male voice says, "You were right. They didn't bite. Great entrance by the way." For a terrifying moment I think it is Aled of Pizza Hut fame. I feel a flood of relief when I recognise the speaker. It's the other applicant I met at the interview yesterday.

"What are *you* doing *here*?" I ask, shoving up to make space for him at the bar.

"I am an old friend of Matt. We used to work as security guards together when we were both living in Bristol." I have a dim memory of Matt going away for about a year or so after we all left school, to start a band, or something equally ill-advised. "And you?" he asks.

"I used to be Maddie's best friend"
"Used to be? Did you two have a falling out?"
"Nothing so dramatic. We were inseparable growing up, but

308

then I left for university and...Well you know how it goes."

"Only too well I'm afraid. Can I ask just one favour?" he says.

"That depends."

"Can we not compare notes or exchange CVs'?"

"Deal!" I agree. Before I can say anything else, Matt comes barrelling over and grabs him.

"Nappies! You made it. Excellent! Come over and meet the boys." He is dragged over to the crowd of disreputable young men that have colonised the area by the cigarette machine.

Nappies?

I wander around for a bit, saying hello to a few familiar faces. I stop to speak to Carol who greets me with a hug, and tells me how pretty I look. We talk about Maddie's honeymoon plans, until the bride herself comes over, takes my arm, and drags me off to the ladies.

"So what happened with this hunk, Nick, then?" she asks. I sadly shake my head and start to recount the entire humiliating story.

"Cor. He was shagging his ex the whole time. Dirty bugger!" She commiserates and then talks about her own ups and downs before the wedding. She had second thoughts then changed her mind. Then Matt had second thoughts and changed his mind.

"It's all turned out okay in the end. It always does," she says brightly.

The happy couple are going to move in with Matt's family when they get back from their honeymoon in Majorca. They are happy to stay there until he finds a steady job and then they will look for a place on their own. "We can't all be high flying independent city types like you," she sighs.

After a few hours of catching up on the recent village gossip, I go outside for some fresh air. Matt's friend is already there, holding a small bag.

"Nappies?" I say teasingly.

"It's a long story, but it involves Matt and a misunderstanding with a pushchair. Most people call me Sam." He extends a hand, which I shake. A taxi pulls up, and he picks up his bag "That's my ride. Anyway it was really nice to meet you. I hope we meet again. As trainees."

"I hope so too." I wave, as his taxi screeches away.

The party goes on until the early hours of Saturday morning. We all enjoy it, and end up coming home around the time the milkman is making his deliveries. I sleep through most of the following day, but wake up about tea-time. Mum brings in a cuppa to me while I am still in bed.

"I am not sure what has happened with you in the last few weeks. I know you think I am an old fogey and don't notice things, but your father and I have been worried." She looks tired and concerned, and for once I don't see her as prying. I see her for what she is. A greying, middle-aged woman who is worried about her daughter.

"You're right Mum. Things weren't good for a while, but I am getting through it now."

"What if you don't get an offer?" she says anxiously.

"I will think of something." I reply. Sarah has coped fine. Justine is doing okay. I am pretty sure I will be too.

Sunday 27 April

The train journey back is long, filled with delays and impromptu stops. Sarah doesn't seem to mind, having enjoyed the weekend; both at the wedding and being with my parents afterwards.

"They are really nice your Mum and Dad. As was that bloke you were talking to," she says, cheekily.

"Nah, he's just someone I met at the interviews on Thursday. Seems nice though."

"Ooh, the competition. I hope you were able to remain civil. Or is that why he suddenly disappeared?" Sarah is trying to wind me up.

"Don't start. I seem to have an unfortunate habit of punching people that annoy me. Anyway, who knows what will happen. I am happy I got this far. If it's bad news we can go job hunting together in the summer."

Sarah looks out of the window. "Ah, about that. I am not really going to be looking for work in the near future."

"You win the lottery?"

"Not exactly." She looks uncomfortable. "I'm moving out. Tom's accountancy firm is opening up an office in Manchester. They are promoting him and moving him up there. He asked me to go with him, and I sort of agreed." I am not really sure what to think about that, it just seems vaguely anti-feminist and old-fashioned.

"Wow. That seems really sudden. I mean what about your plans for training?" I do my best to hide the dismay from my voice.

"I have been thinking about other options." she says "Maybe training to be a psychotherapist or a counsellor. I will still get to do face-to-face work with patients, and I was never really that keen on research or management."

"You will have to pay for your own training though, won't

311

you?" I ask, not too sure about how other therapists fund their education.

"Probably. Tom has said he will help me out and support me if he needs to. It's better than just waiting around and hoping. At least I will finally be moving in the right direction," she reasons.

The scenery whips past the train window as I take in what she has said. I can't blame her. If I was given a similar offer, I would probably jump at it. All things considered, it's a good move for her, even though I will miss her like crazy. I try not to think about how I will manage without her. Or what will happen if I am left alone to the tender mercies of Scarlett.

Monday 28 April

I am not expecting a call quite so soon. So when my mobile goes off in the middle of a large meeting, my first thought is that it's Mum. I have already had to take three calls earlier this morning about leaving things behind at their house, including my Oyster card, mobile phone adapter, and my best pair of shoes.

"What could it possibly be now?" I hiss, trying to keep my voice as low as possible.

"Oh, I am sorry is this a bad time?" Instead of hearing Mum, I hear Julie on the other end.

I leap out of my chair, mouth my apologies to the others at the meeting, and scramble to the hallway. "No! No! Wait! No, it's fine. I can talk." I scan the corridor for somewhere that balances phone reception and privacy, and move into the nook near the double doors out front. It's cold, but it's private.

I can tell from the tone of her voice that it's not good news. Julie starts off by thanking me for coming, and that I did really well. The panel liked me *but* there were lots of really good applicants. I expect the inevitable rejection, but she tells me that

I am placed on the reserve list. If enough people turn down their offered place, I may still have a chance.

Although it is better than an outright rejection, it looks like I am back in limbo. Julie is also unable to tell me where I am on the reserve list. This irked me initially, but the more I think about it I realise it's for the best. If I got to number one on the reserve, and term started without me, there would not be enough alcohol in the world to drown my sorrows. However, in the meantime I'm now resigned to being on a constant state of red alert.

I just want it to be over now. This is getting beyond a joke.

Tuesday 29 April
No call.

I am now officially sick of everyone saying, "Oooh" or making a face as if they have witnessed a nasty accident when I tell them I am on the reserve list. That is almost as annoying as when people say, "How exciting. Still in with a chance."

Sarah says, I need to forget it, and move on. Olga is even blunter, stating, "You were not chosen. Deal with it. Now get on with your work." I really hope she doesn't decide to make a jump to any kind of caring role in the future. I don't think Samaritans could handle the increased workload.

Every incoming phone call is now accompanied by held breath and an unbearable spike in tension. I nearly tore the head off a woman wondering if I would be interested in double glazing this afternoon. I am also spending far too much time on ClinPsy speculating about how quickly and how far the reserve list moves. Infuriatingly, there is no way to make any strong prediction. One year, it went down ten places; another, it hardly moved at all. However, being in this position, I now truly understand why people believe in astrology, tarot cards, and reading tea leaves. If you put anyone under enough pressure, they will start making to make predictions based on the flimsiest of evidence.

It gets so bad at one point I think, "If I hold my breath for two minutes that will be a sign I will definitely get a place." I make it to eighty three seconds before my lungs started burning and I started to gasp in pain, making Olga spin around and bark, "If you are having an asthma attack, can you do it outside please?" I had better stop this nonsense before I lose it completely.

Wednesday 30 April
No call.

Last night was absolutely horrid. I managed to snatch about two hours sleep. I kept having dreams of being in my seventies and still renting a room in this house, while applying for the fourtieth time.

I also dreamt I was starring in a Channel 5 documentary "The World's Oldest Assistant Psychologist". The interviewer kept asking patronising questions about why my life had turned out so badly, and what it was like to be three times the age of my next oldest peer. Sarah was being interviewed and was talking into the camera, "Her parents paid for tennis lessons and everything. They were so let down by her. In the end they just died. Of disappointment really."

Then I woke up.

It's 5am. I can't sleep anymore, so go online. Bad move. Facebook confronts me with several photos of Nick at a party. Although he never kept his own profile (or possibly he did, but lied about it), the photos have been put up there by one of the people at work. In one of the photos, Nick had the audacity to wear a look of smug self-satisfaction, posing with one hand jauntily holding up a beer, with the other entwined around a slender blonde. My blood pressure soars as I hastily block the offending contact with an angry stamp of my finger.

The insomnia makes doing anything at work ten times harder than normal. I wander around the building with a gauzy, grey filter covering everything. I take just a second too long to answer questions. My movements only start after a brief delay. Even basic things like making a cup of tea require twice as much effort. At one point, I even find myself photocopying material that I should have been shredding.

Adding to the fun is the screaming match Scarlett has with Sarah, when she finds out about her move to Manchester. This ends in Scarlett accusing Sarah of selling-out and that the move was a one-way ticket "to a boring marriage, snot-faced children and the slow death of bourgeois, middle-class life". I am impressed. Scarlett can be very articulate when she wants to be.

Sarah calmly defends herself, but eventually has enough of it. Her final words are, "Tough. I have made up my mind. I am going." She doesn't say this in anger, it's a simple statement of fact.

Scarlett sulkily asks me, "I suppose you are going to be moving out as well."

"Do you want me to?" I assume she will jump at the chance. She is always pointing out how sarcastic and condescending I am. She will now be free to listen to her music as loud as possible, shag noisily, and have all her friends round whenever she wants.

"Please don't go. I've got used to you. You are quite likable. In your own way," she says almost tearful. It's at that point I start to appreciate what it might be like for her. For all of Scarlett's bluster and bravado, her life is even more inconstant than mine is. Her entire life has always been up in the air. For the first time in her life, she has had two stable, consistent(ish) people in her life, who aren't always flaking out on her. Now, she is in danger of losing what little she has. Looking at it from this perspective, I feel sorry for her.

"I am not sure what is going to happen with me, but I will let you know as soon as I do. I will think of something, and you can move in with me if you want." Maybe not a wise move, but a compassionate one.

"Yeah, well. I will think about it," she says, not yet willing to give up her tough-girl image entirely.

MAY

Thursday 1 May
No call.

My attempt to play it cool, and let fate take its own course, officially comes to an end at 11:43am. I finally crack and call up Julie at the university. I try to sound as nonchalant as possible.

"Hello, Julie. I had a missed call on my phone, and the number seemed to be similar to yours, so I thought I would check to make sure. It wasn't you? Never mind. Anyway, since you are there I may as well ask if there has been any movement on the reserve list". Shameless, I know.

Julie is sympathetic. They have some confirmations, but some candidates are still making up their mind, or considering multiple offers. (Those lucky bastards. Oh, if only...). She acknowledges it is a difficult time for me, and again promises she will let me know as soon as she hears any news.

I feel reassured for a good thirty minutes. Then have the burning urge to call back at 1pm, just to check if there haven't been any developments since we last spoke. I mean someone could have been hit by a bus, or an entire building of celebrating offer holders may have been tragically electrocuted by faulty wiring. It's only the thought of an irate Julie quietly striking my name off the reserve list that holds me back from doing this.

With the self-discipline of a samurai, I concentrate on getting back to my work. It pays off. I feel a tremendous sense of accomplishment I complete the last item from my in-tray, including the last bit of Nick's mess that Olga and I have had to clear up. As I file away that final scrap of paper, I feel as if I have just shovelled the last sod of earth onto his grave. The second I finish, I physically feel so much better, as if a giant hand has swept away the last of my baggage about Nick. Perhaps Olga has done me a favour; the whole exercise was more therapeutic than I thought.

Friday 2 May
No call.

It has been my first peaceful, lazy Friday for ages. With the backlog of work now completed, and only the most cursory amount of admin to cover, I am back to checking Facebook, surfing the net, and generally trying to find something to do. While I am not exactly sure I enjoy the feast/famine pace of assistant life, I definitely appreciate the perk of having quiet time.

As it approaches lunchtime, Justine knocks at the cupboard door. It's a pleasant surprise, as I haven't seen her in ages. At first glance, I think that she has a job as a nursing assistant, but on closer examination I realise that she is wearing chef's whites.

Excited, she explains that she has enrolled on an apprenticeship in catering college. It has been a bit of a rush getting it all sorted, but with Dave's help (and a few predictable mishaps on the way), she managed to get it all sorted. It's why she hasn't been around as much recently. It's the end of her first week and the class has been let off for a few hours. She has already been praised quite a bit and has been singled out as a natural. I am considerably less surprised than she is.

"Congratulations, by the way. I read about your reserve list place on Facebook. Cor, you must have done well," she says, as

318

she spins on Olga's chair.

"I am not getting my hopes up, but I have been fortunate to get this far. Fingers crossed. Anyway, I am starving. Coming out for lunch?" We head to the coffee shop. As we tuck into our sandwiches, she turns to me with a guilty look.

"I have something to tell you. I did know that Nick had got engaged to you-know-who. She had been dropping hints for months about diamond rings and where he would 'pop the question'. Then there were all the photos from Paris. I even thought she was talking about a different Nick at first, until I saw those. I tried to tell you, but you did keep telling me not to mention what she was posting."

I laugh. I assure her that none of it was her fault, and I am not blaming her for anything. Even if she had told me it probably wouldn't have made much of a difference. I would have probably passed it off as Justine getting the wrong end of the stick, yet again. As she leaves for a pastry class this afternoon, we plan to meet up in a week or so.

She promises she will bring me a celebration/commiseration cake. I can't wait.

Saturday 3 May

Tragic as it is, I find myself checking my voicemail on a Saturday morning on the off-chance that Julie may have left a message. Sadly, my voicemail inbox stubbornly remains empty. I mooch around the house feeling restless, and unable to concentrate on anything in particular. Eventually, this gets tiring for Sarah and Scarlett, who decide to drag me out to get some much needed fresh air. So, I find myself sitting in a pub beer garden, eating lunch and getting slightly merry on cider, as they both talk at me.

"Cheer up," Scarlett says, "whatever the outcome, you will

drag yourself to work the following morning, go through the motions, come home, put off making dinner as long as possible, and spend the rest of the evening slumped in front of the telly. That is basically your life for the next forty years."

"Well, she might go on holiday once in a while..." says Sarah, doing her best to sweeten Scarlett's prediction. Although this should be depressing, it is oddly comforting to think that some things will probably never change.

After lunch Sarah and Scarlett decide to head off to the West End to go window shopping. They ask me to come along, but I turn them down. Instead, I find myself wandering off alone, Before I know it, I am sitting by the bank of the Thames, not exactly sure how I got here.

A little tired by now, I feel like sitting down and reading something. Mentally cursing the fact that anything readable is probably on my bookcase in my room, I rummage about my bag to see if there is something else I could read. The only thing I find is my reflective journal. Force of habit has me turning to a new page to start to write, but am unable to as my pen is in my work jacket.

Frustrated, I flick through the pages, and am impressed by how I have been able to keep this thing going on a daily basis for the last six months. It is only then I realise I haven't actually read any of it yet. So, I flick to the front and start going through it from the beginning. I wince as I read the first page. It's like listening to a tape of your voice, only much, much worse.

Sitting here reading in the patchy spring sunshine, listening to the river, I start to think over the last few months. My first thought is "Did I do all that?" quickly followed by "Why did I do that?"

Then it dawns on me that there is one thing I still need to write.

Sunday 4 May

Dear seven-months-ago me.

It's been a while. I know what you are going to say. You are stressed out and snowed under with all that application form-filling and that you don't have time to be reading messages from your future self. Please hear me out. Besides, we both know that you are really just procrastinating and putting it off until later. You are probably thinking by now you will have had several interviews, maybe even secretly hoping for an offer.

I hate to tell you this, but the next few months aren't going to be so straightforward. A lot of things will happen, not all of it good. That's not to say it's all negative. The good news is that you will have a lovely Christmas break, Maddie will get married (I know, that was my reaction too), and you have the inestimable pleasure of punching out Spiny to look forward to.

However, I would really appreciate it if you will take a few seconds to consider the following:

- You may want to listen to what others have to say a bit more often. What they actually say, not what you think they are saying.

- An offer of alcohol is an option, not a gauntlet being thrown down. Consider saying "no" once in a while. Especially at conferences.

- Your suspicions were right all along; half the stuff people write on Facebook is total rubbish. Feel free to treat 90% of what you read with the contempt it duly deserves.

- Scarlett likes you more than she shows. Justine is smarter than you think. Sarah is sadder than she seems. Try to be kinder to all of them.

- That idea about getting with Nick from work. Forget it. He is a complete arse. The only thing you will get from him is a broken heart, misery, and a reputation among the Assistant's Group that will define you for eternity. Avoid.

So we come to the main reason for me writing to you, my ulterior motive. In the near future you are going to doubt yourself a lot. My advice to you is not to do this. Although I can't guarantee to you that things will be great in the future, you are mostly doing okay. I think we are going to be fine.

Lots of love

Your future self

PS: If someone mentions "Pizza Hut" just run. Don't look back.

Monday 5 May

In the way these things tend to happen, I am trying to grab my keys which have managed to fall underneath my desk. Trying hard not to inhale and suffocate from the dust that has never been vacuumed, or to think just how undignified I would look if someone came in at this precise moment, I am just about grab them when I hear my ringtone start to chirp. I bang my head on the underside of the desk and scrabble around trying to grab my mobile. I eventually find it, just as it's about to ring off. I press answer as I inhale a lungful of dust. I start coughing.

"Hello, Natalie speaking," I croak, trying my best not to splutter down the phone.

"Hi, Natalie. It's Julie. I really hope I didn't disturb you, but I promised that I would call as soon as I heard any news. We would like to offer you a place on our clinical training course, and I was wondering if you would be interested in accepting it. You don't have to answer straight away, but if you would like to join us..."

ABOUT THE AUTHOR

Spatch Logan is the pseudonym of a clinical psychologist working in the south east of England. He has a clinical role within the NHS and currently holds an academic post at a university. Starting out in the wild and heady world of forensics, his further tours of duty have included: eating disorders, older adult community mental health, and general adult mental health.

He hopes he never has cause to meet you in a professional capacity but you can find him, and more of his writing at: http://spatchlogan.wordpress.com

Or you can e-mail him at: Spatchlogan@gmail.com

CPSIA information can be obtained at www.ICGtesting.com
Printed in the USA
LVOW05s1353141014

408702LV00001B/172/P